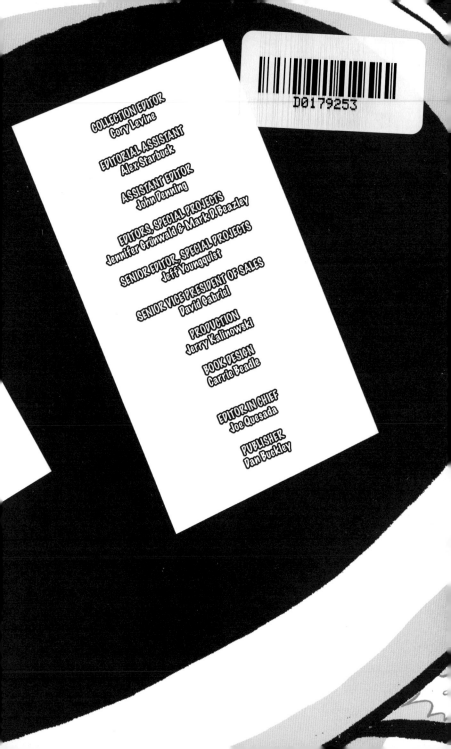

COLLECTION EDITOR
Cory Levine

EDITORIAL ASSISTANT
Alex Starbuck

ASSISTANT EDITOR
John Denning

EDITORS, SPECIAL PROJECTS
Jennifer Grünwald & Mark D. Beazley

SENIOR EDITOR, SPECIAL PROJECTS
Jeff Youngquist

SENIOR VICE PRESIDENT OF SALES
David Gabriel

PRODUCTION
Jerry Kalinowski

BOOK DESIGN
Carrie Beadle

EDITOR IN CHIEF
Joe Quesada

PUBLISHER
Dan Buckley

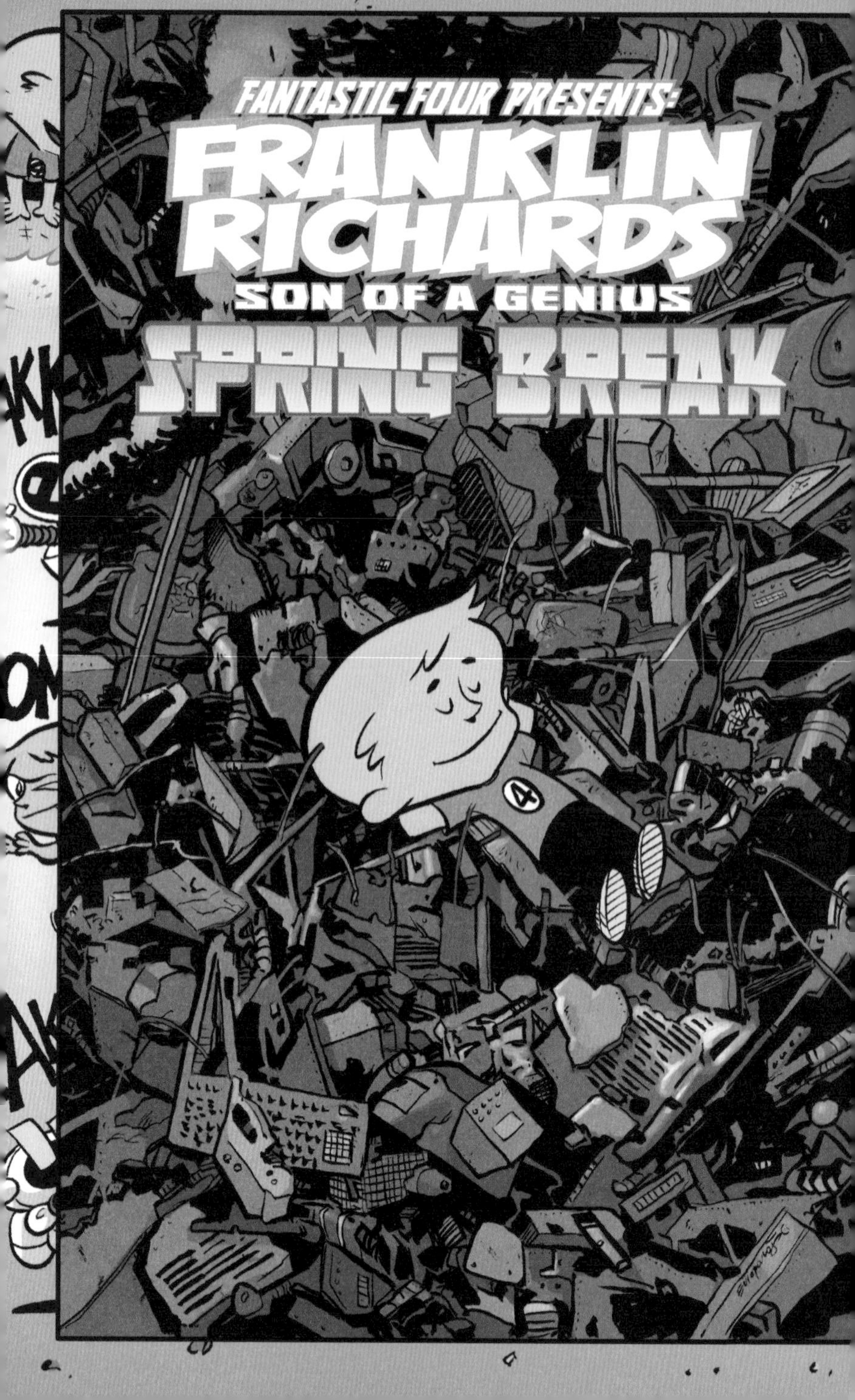
FANTASTIC FOUR PRESENTS:
FRANKLIN RICHARDS
SON OF A GENIUS
SPRING BREAK

FRANKLIN RICHARDS
SON OF A GENIUS

NOT-SO-SECRET INVASION

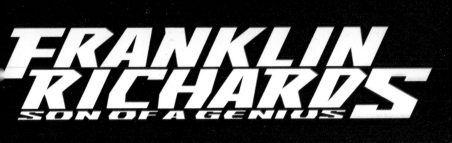

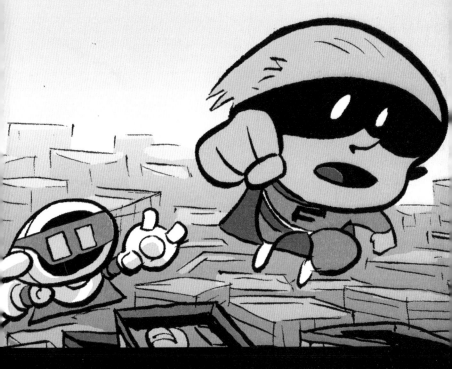

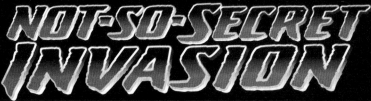

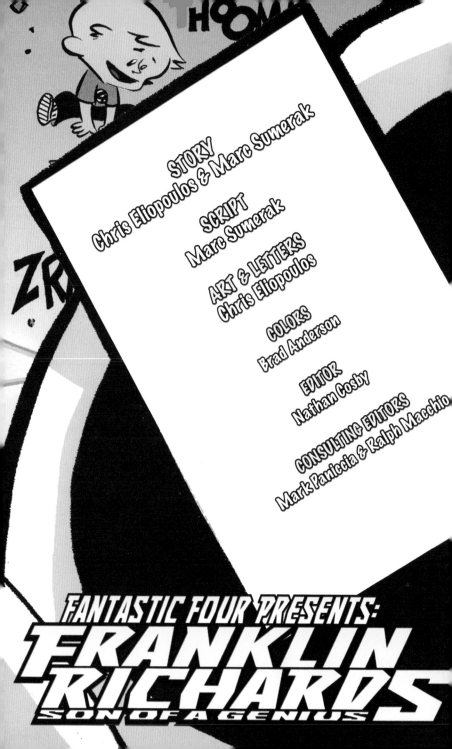

STORY
Chris Eliopoulos & Marc Sumerak

SCRIPT
Marc Sumerak

ART & LETTERS
Chris Eliopoulos

COLORS
Brad Anderson

EDITOR
Nathan Cosby

CONSULTING EDITORS
Mark Paniccia & Ralph Macchio

FANTASTIC FOUR PRESENTS:
FRANKLIN RICHARDS
SON OF A GENIUS

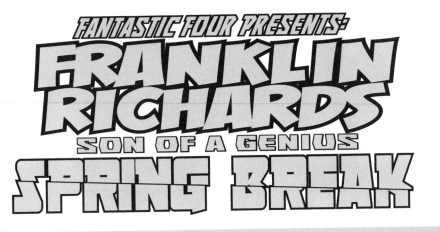

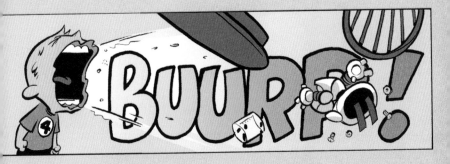

FANTASTIC FOUR PRESENTS:

FRANKLIN RICHARDS
SON OF A GENIUS
SPRING BREAK

BUURP!

CHRIS ELIOPOULOS AND MARC SUMERAK
STORY

MARC SUMERAK
SCRIPT

CHRIS ELIOPOULOS
ART & LETTERS

BRAD ANDERSON
COLOR

MARK PANICCIA
CONSULTING

NATHAN COSBY
EDITOR

JOE QUESADA
EDITOR IN CHIEF

DAN BUCKLEY
PUBLISHER

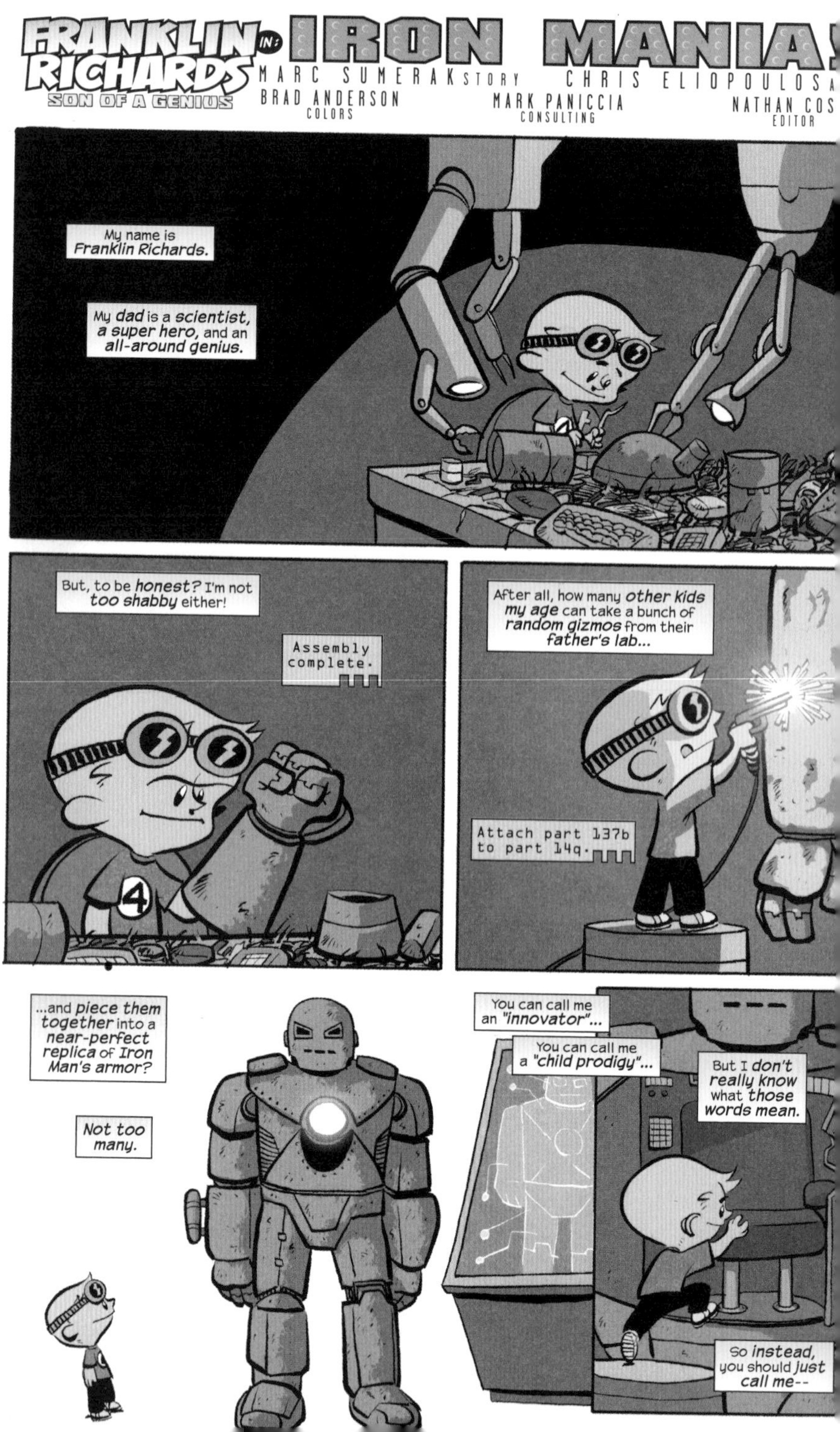

FRANKLIN RICHARDS
SON OF A GENIUS
IN: IRON MANIA!
MARC SUMERAK STORY
CHRIS ELIOPOULOS
BRAD ANDERSON COLORS
MARK PANICCIA CONSULTING
NATHAN COS
EDITOR
My name is Franklin Richards.
My dad is a scientist, a super hero, and an all-around genius.
But, to be honest? I'm not too shabby either!
Assembly complete.
After all, how many other kids my age can take a bunch of random gizmos from their father's lab...
Attach part 137b to part 14q.
...and piece them together into a near-perfect replica of Iron Man's armor?
Not too many.
You can call me an "innovator"...
You can call me a "child prodigy"...
But I don't really know what those words mean.
So instead, you should just call me--

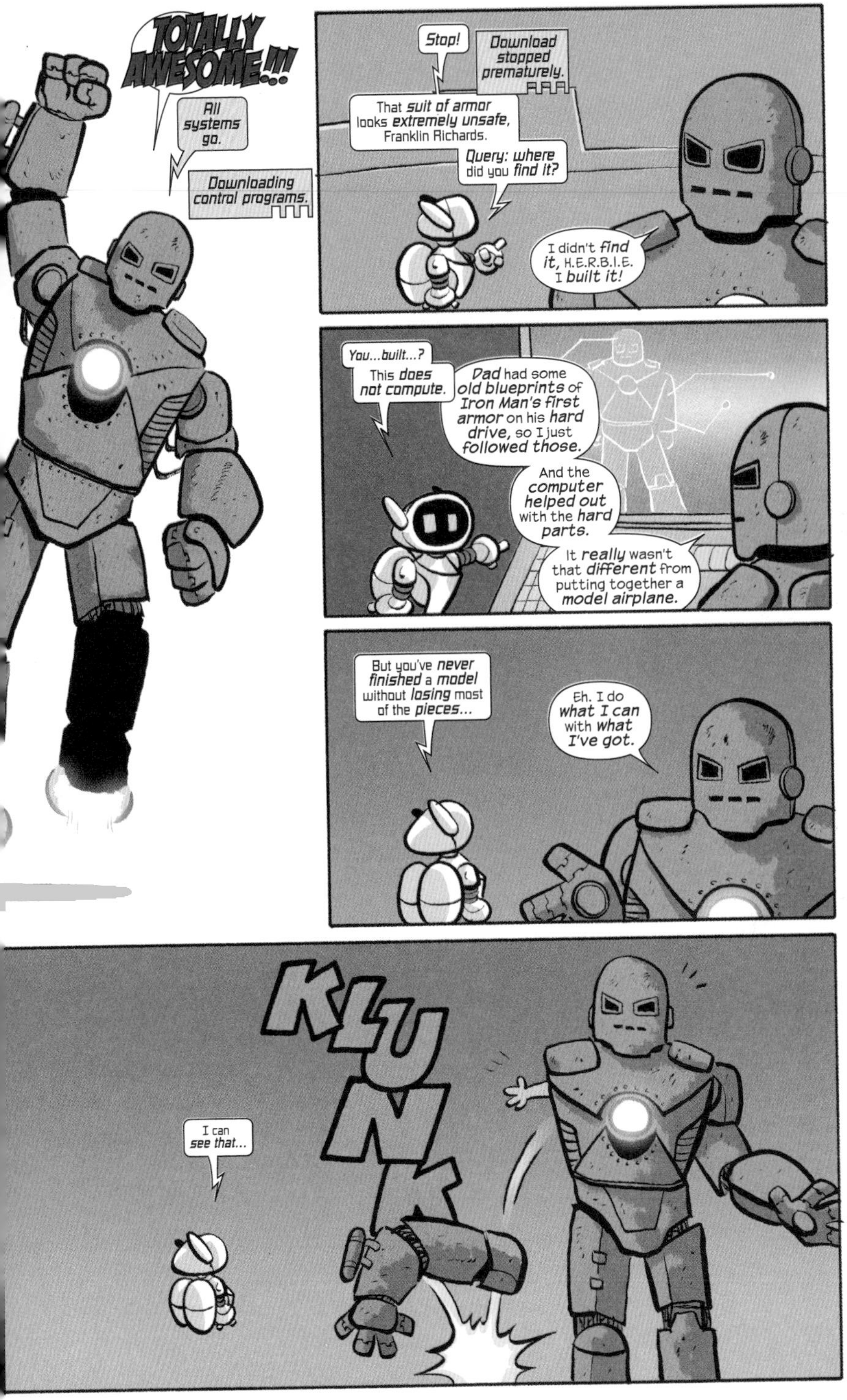
TOTALLY AWESOME!!!
All systems go.
Downloading control programs.
Stop!
Download stopped prematurely.
That suit of armor looks extremely unsafe, Franklin Richards.
Query: where did you find it?
I didn't find it, H.E.R.B.I.E. I built it!
You...built...? This does not compute.
Dad had some old blueprints of Iron Man's first armor on his hard drive, so I just followed those.
And the computer helped out with the hard parts.
It really wasn't that different from putting together a model airplane.
But you've never finished a model without losing most of the pieces...
Eh. I do what I can with what I've got.
KLUNK
I can see that...

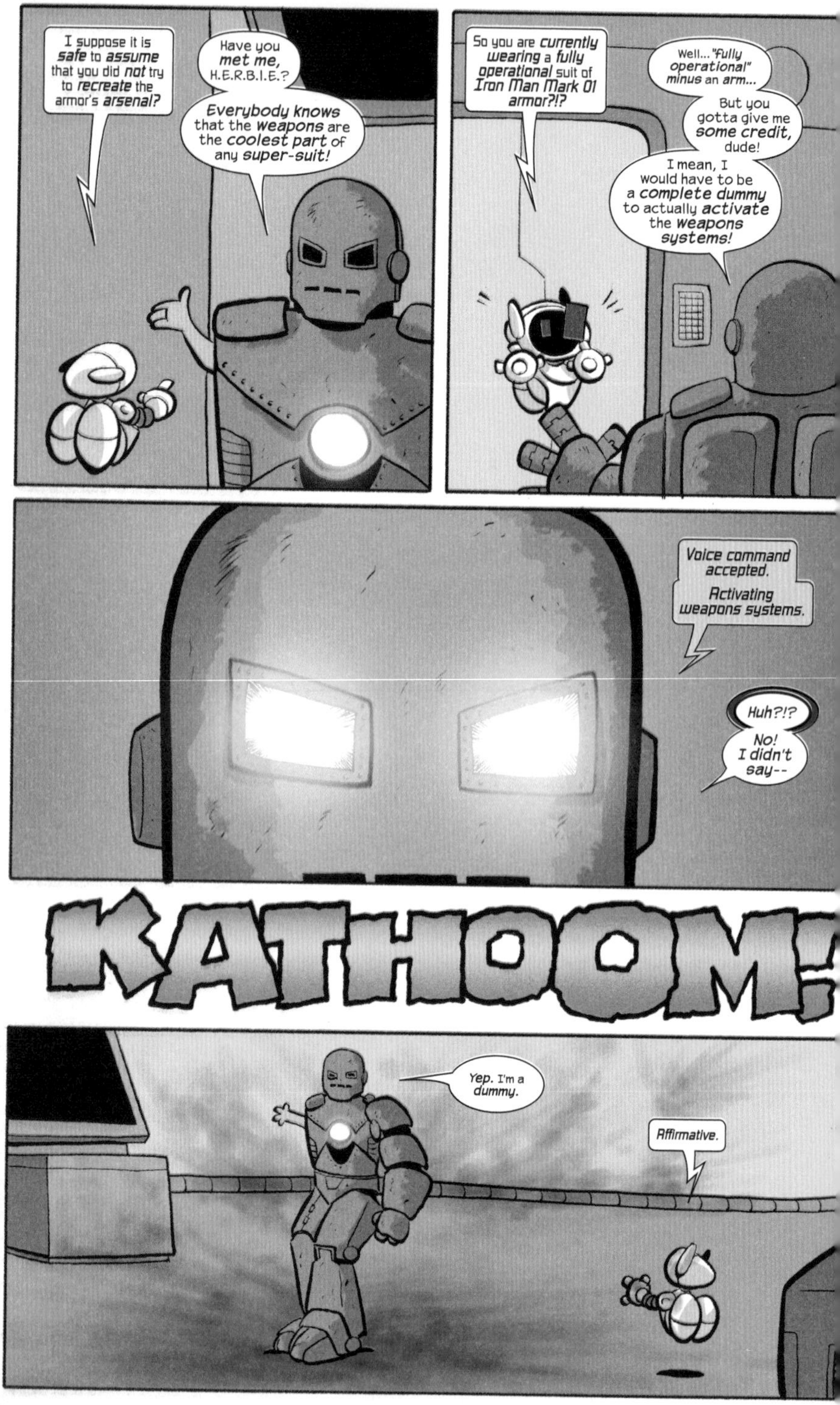

I suppose it is safe to assume that you did not try to recreate the armor's arsenal?
Have you met me, H.E.R.B.I.E.?
Everybody knows that the weapons are the coolest part of any super-suit!
So you are currently wearing a fully operational suit of Iron Man Mark 01 armor?!?
Well... "fully operational" minus an arm...
But you gotta give me some credit, dude!
I mean, I would have to be a complete dummy to actually activate the weapons systems!
Voice command accepted.
Activating weapons systems.
Huh?!?
No! I didn't say--
KATHOOM!
Yep. I'm a dummy.
Affirmative.

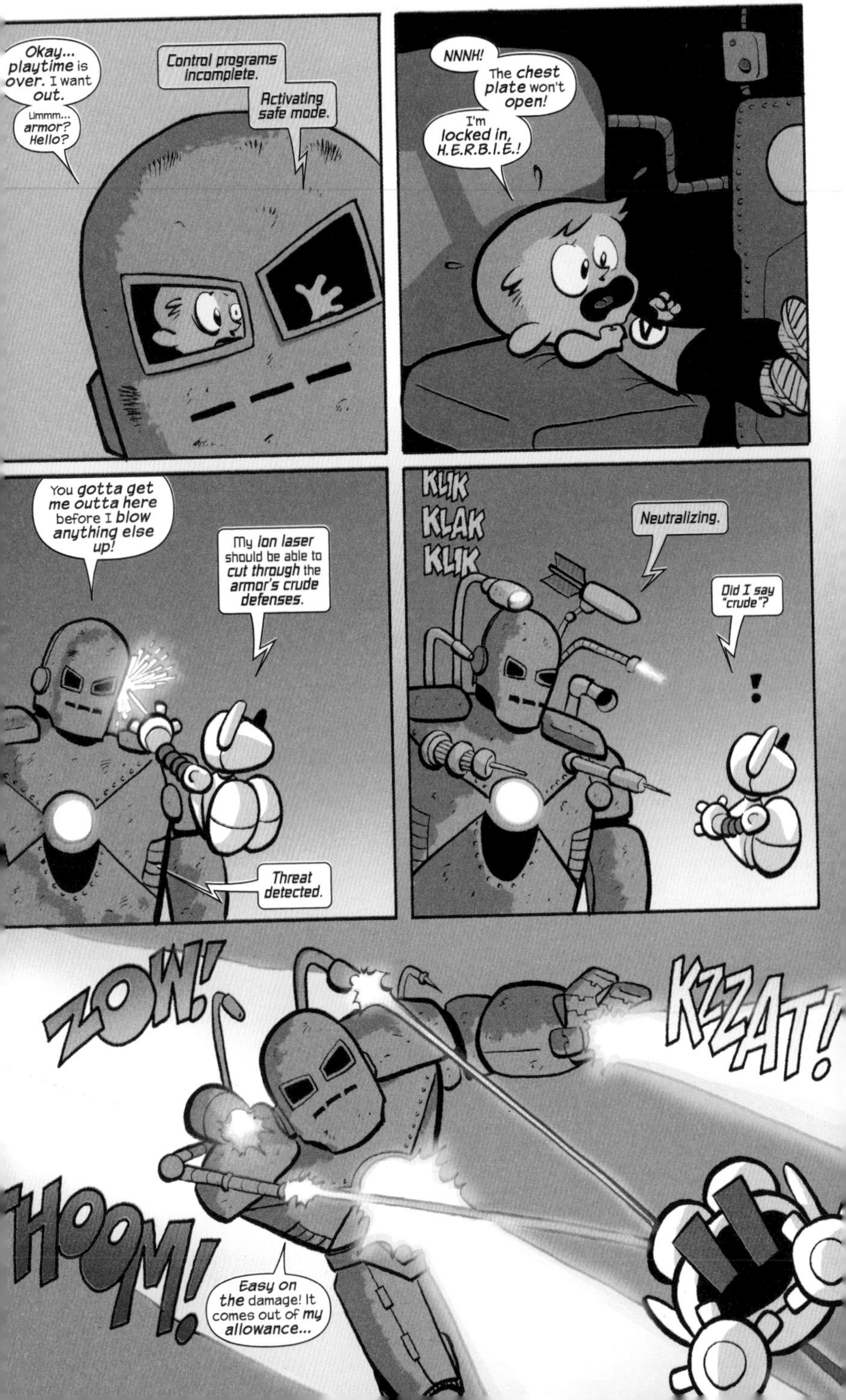

Okay... playtime is over. I want out.
Ummm... armor? Hello?
Control programs incomplete.
Activating safe mode.
NNNH!
The chest plate won't open!
I'm locked in, H.E.R.B.I.E.!
You gotta get me outta here before I blow anything else up!
My ion laser should be able to cut through the armor's crude defenses.
Threat detected.
KLIK
KLAK
KLIK
Neutralizing.
Did I say "crude"?
!
ZOW!
KZZAT!
THOOM!
Easy on the damage! It comes out of my allowance...

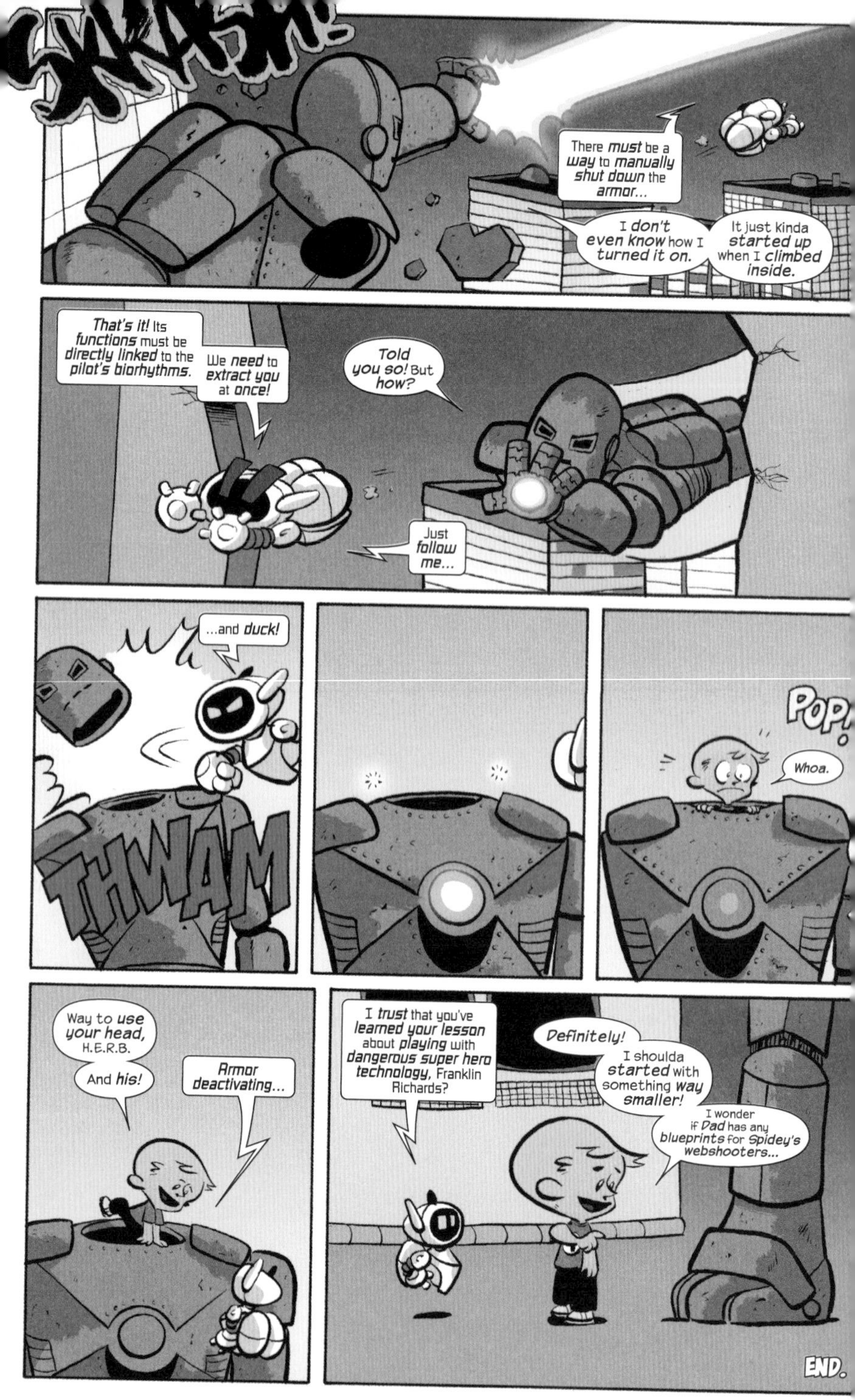
SKRASH!
There must be a way to manually shut down the armor...
I don't even know how I turned it on.
It just kinda started up when I climbed inside.
That's it! Its functions must be directly linked to the pilot's biorhythms.
We need to extract you at once!
Told you so! But how?
Just follow me...
...and duck!
THWAM
POP!
Whoa.
Way to use your head, H.E.R.B.
And his!
Armor deactivating...
I trust that you've learned your lesson about playing with dangerous super hero technology, Franklin Richards?
Definitely!
I shoulda started with something way smaller!
I wonder if Dad has any blueprints for Spidey's webshooters...
END.

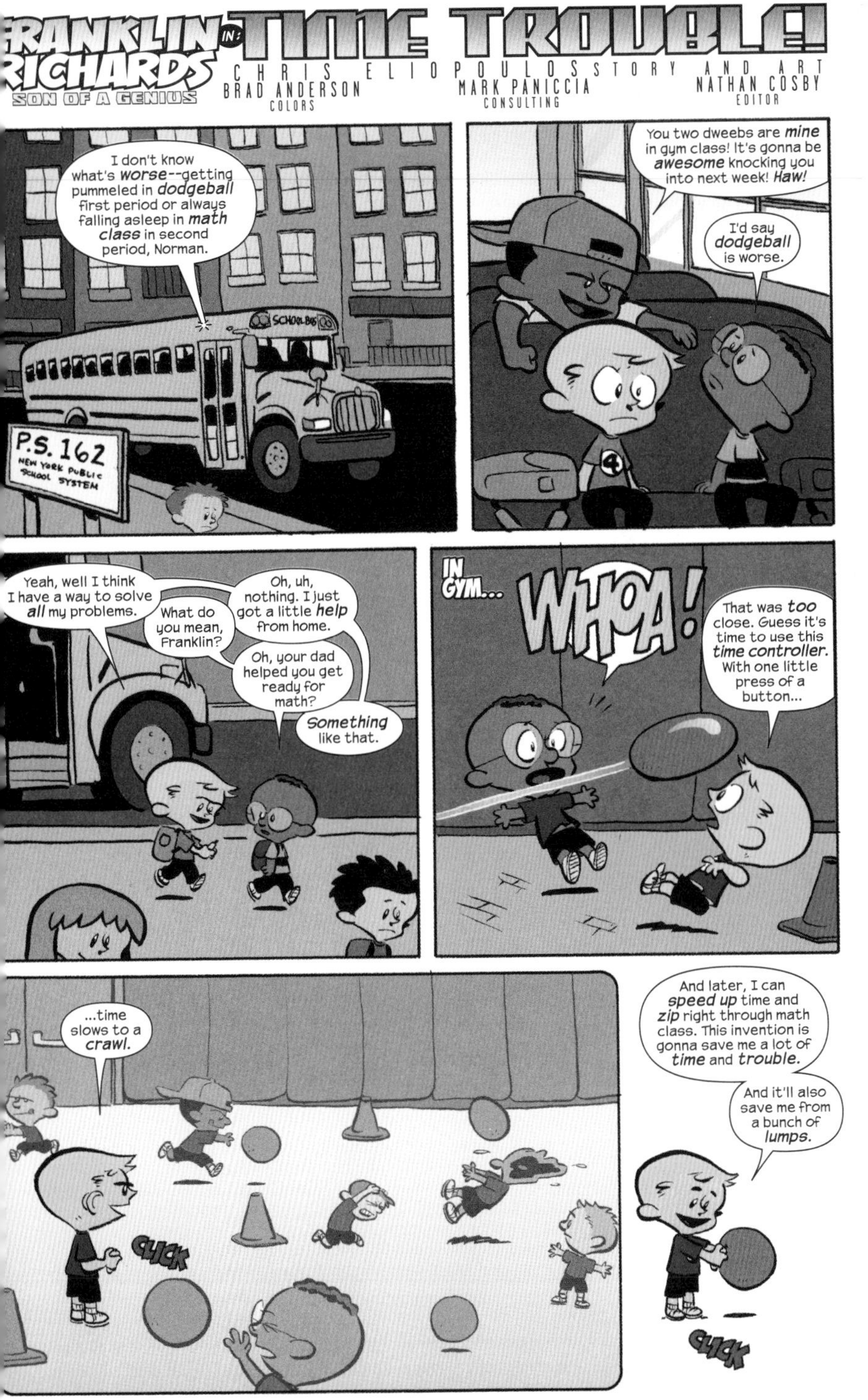
FRANKLIN RICHARDS SON OF A GENIUS IN: TIME TROUBLE!
CHRIS ELIOPOULOS STORY AND ART
BRAD ANDERSON COLORS
MARK PANICCIA CONSULTING
NATHAN COSBY EDITOR
I don't know what's worse--getting pummeled in dodgeball first period or always falling asleep in math class in second period, Norman.
SCHOOL BUS
P.S. 162 NEW YORK PUBLIC SCHOOL SYSTEM
You two dweebs are mine in gym class! It's gonna be awesome knocking you into next week! Haw!
I'd say dodgeball is worse.
Yeah, well I think I have a way to solve all my problems.
What do you mean, Franklin?
Oh, uh, nothing. I just got a little help from home.
Oh, your dad helped you get ready for math?
Something like that.
IN GYM...
WHOA!
That was too close. Guess it's time to use this time controller. With one little press of a button...
...time slows to a crawl.
CLICK
And later, I can speed up time and zip right through math class. This invention is gonna save me a lot of time and trouble.
And it'll also save me from a bunch of lumps.
CLICK

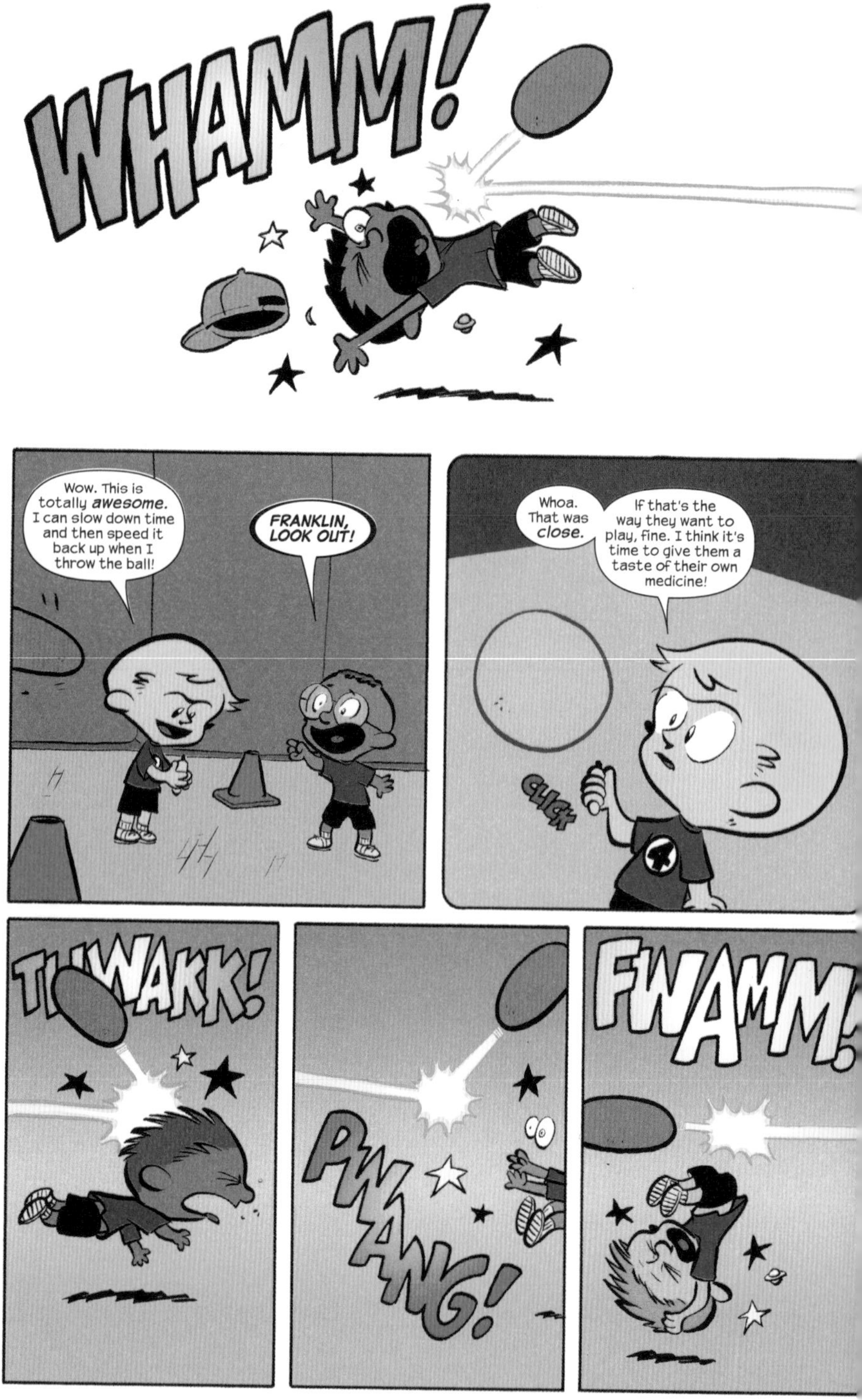
WHAMM!
Wow. This is totally *awesome.* I can slow down time and then speed it back up when I throw the ball!
FRANKLIN, LOOK OUT!
Whoa. That was *close.*
If that's the way they want to play, fine. I think it's time to give them a taste of their own medicine!
CLICK
PWANG!
FWAMM!

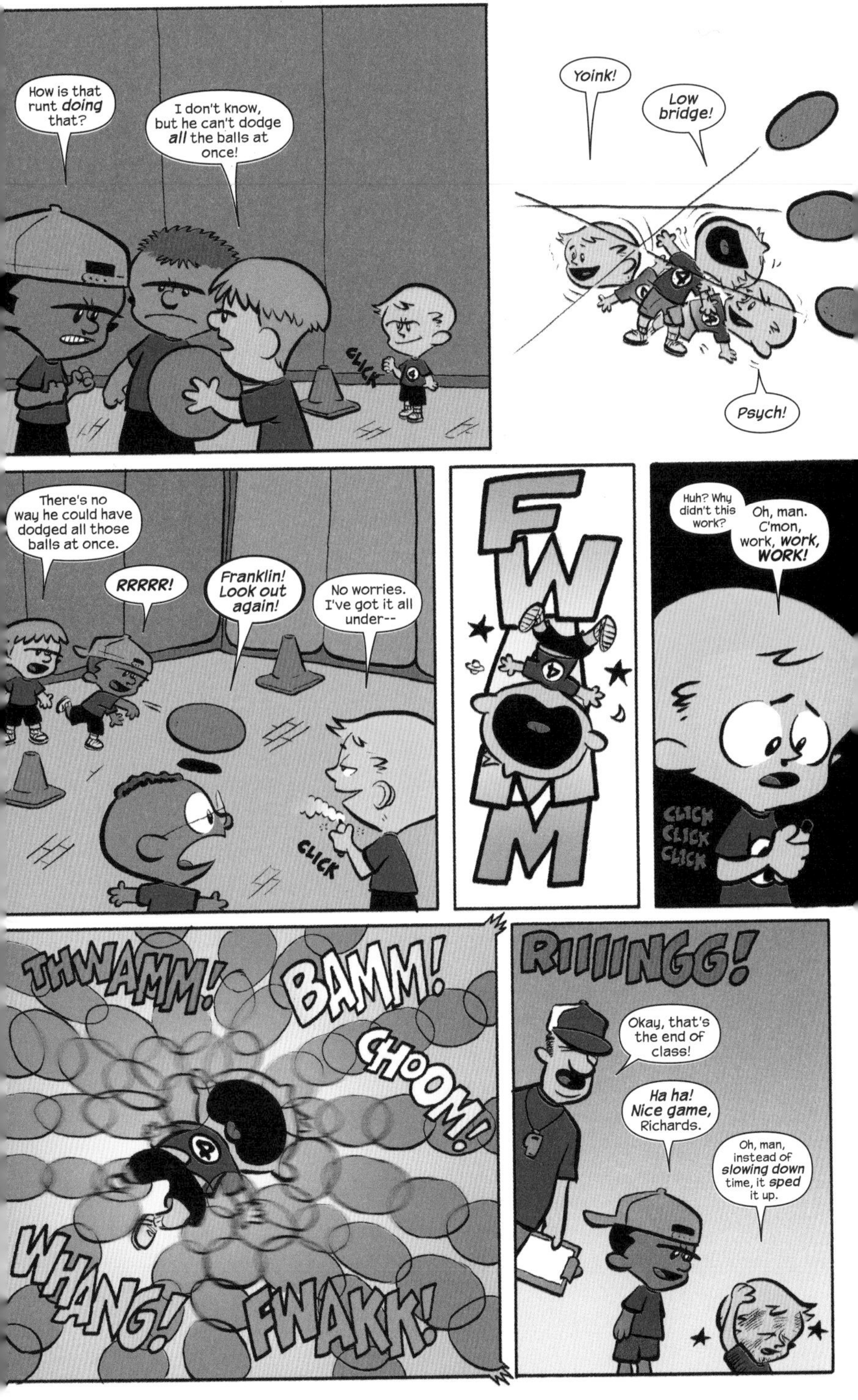
How is that runt *doing* that?
I don't know, but he can't dodge *all* the balls at once!
CLICK
Yoink!
Low bridge!
Psych!
There's no way he could have dodged all those balls at once.
RRRRR!
Franklin! Look out again!
No worries. I've got it all under--
CLICK
FWM
Huh? Why didn't this work?
Oh, man. C'mon, work, *work*, **WORK!**
CLICK CLICK CLICK
THWAMM!
BAMM!
CHOOM!
WHANG!
FWAKK!
RIIIINGG!
Okay, that's the end of class!
Ha ha! Nice game, Richards.
Oh, man, instead of *slowing down* time, it *sped* it up.

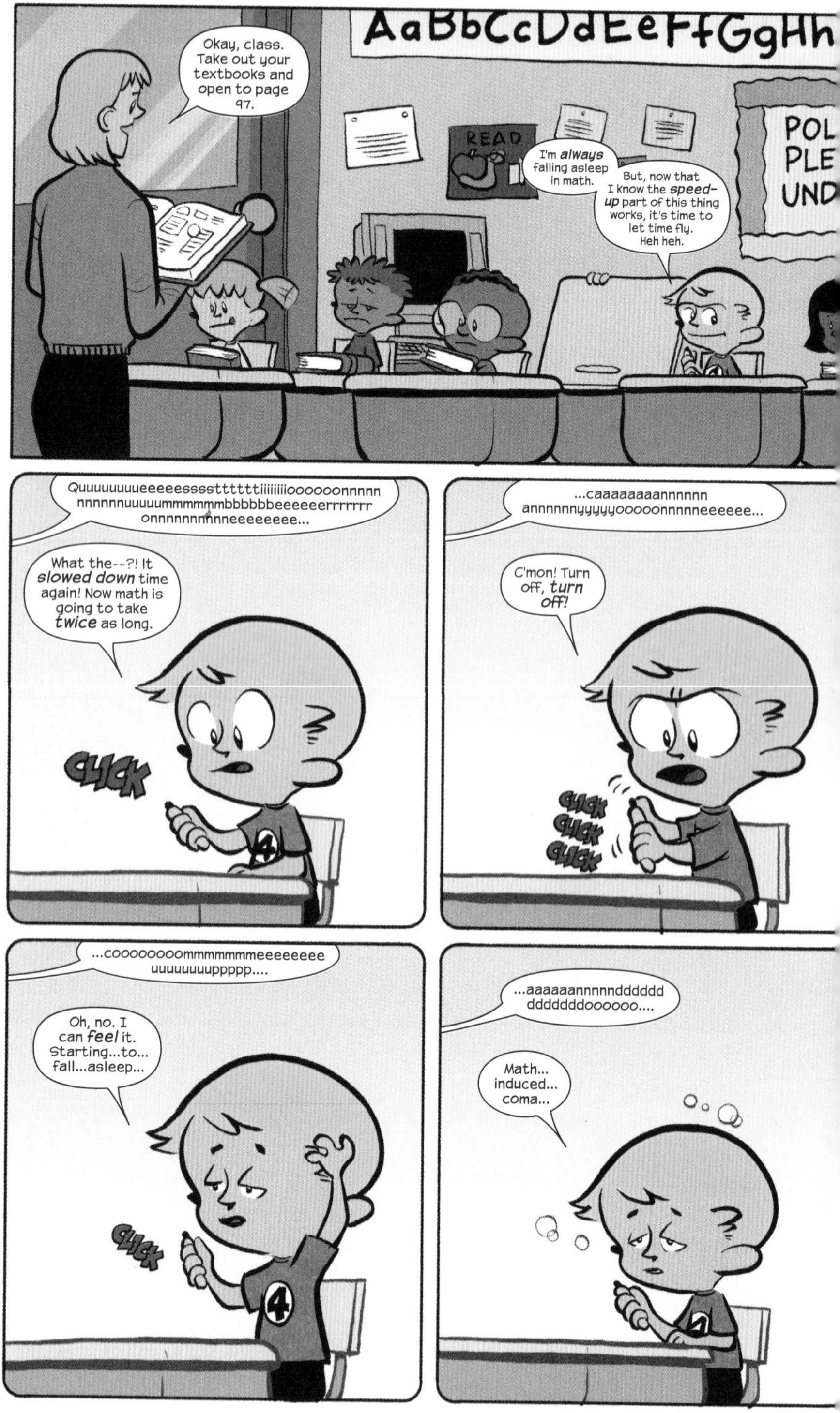

AaBbCcDdEeFfGgHh
Okay, class. Take out your textbooks and open to page 97.
READ
POL PLE UND
I'm *always* falling asleep in math.
But, now that I know the *speed-up* part of this thing works, it's time to let time fly. Heh heh.
Quuuuuuuueeeeesssttttttiiiiiiioooooonnnnn nnnnnnuuuuummmmmmbbbbbeeeeeerrrrrrr onnnnnnnnnneeeeeeee...
What the--?! It *slowed down* time again! Now math is going to take *twice* as long.
CLICK
...caaaaaaaannnnnn annnnnnyyyyyoooonnnnneeeeee...
C'mon! Turn off, *turn off!*
CLICK CLICK CLICK
...coooooooommmmmmmeeeeeeee uuuuuuuupppp....
Oh, no. I can *feel* it. Starting...to... fall...asleep...
CLICK
...aaaaaannnnndddddd ddddddddoooooo....
Math... induced... coma...

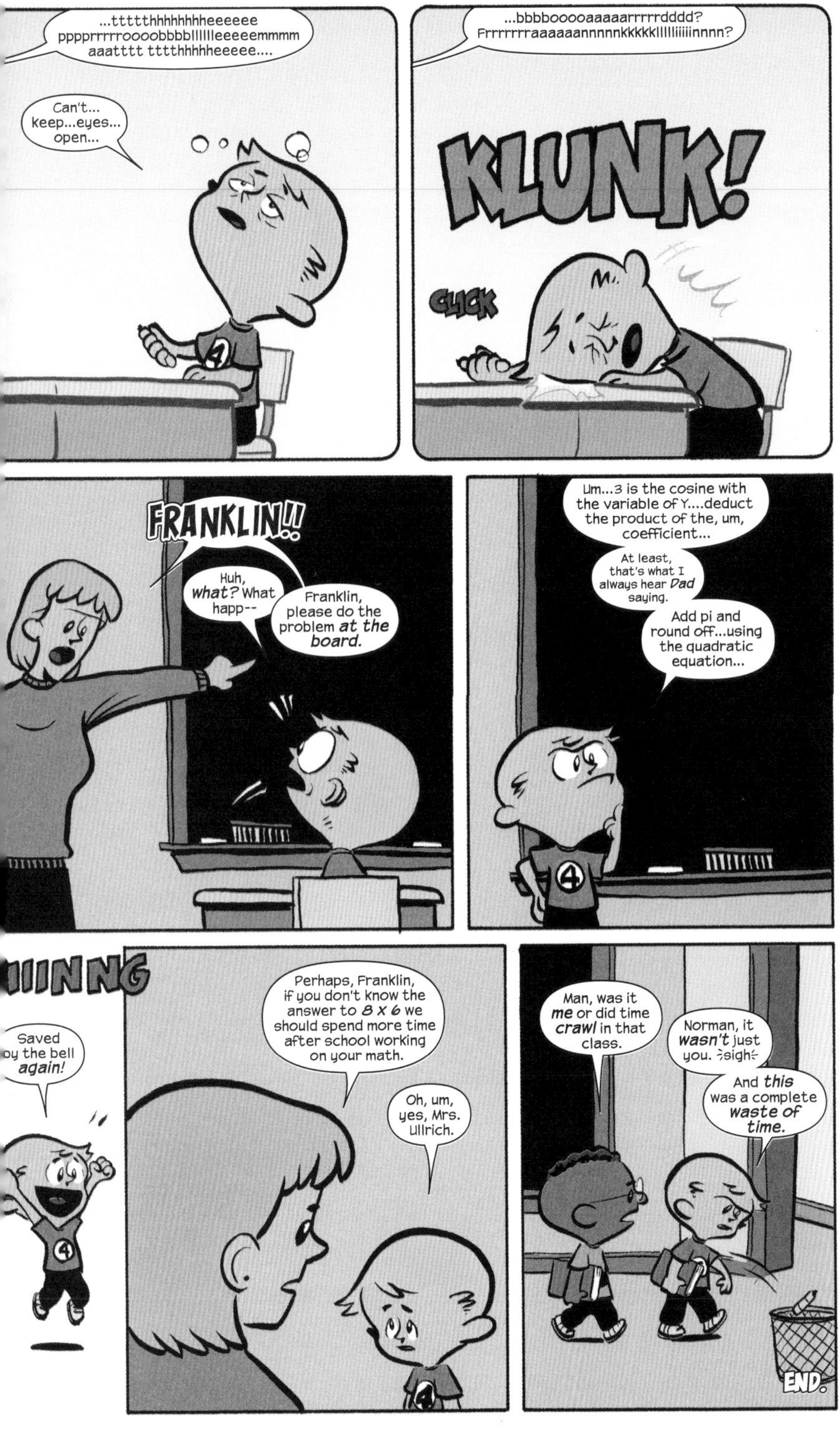
...ttttthhhhhhhheeeeee pppprrrroooobbbblllllleeeeemmmm aaatttt ttttthhhhhheeeee....
Can't... keep...eyes... open...
...bbbboooaaaaarrrrrdddd? Frrrrrrraaaaaannnnnkkkkkllllliiiiinnnn?
KLUNK!
CLICK
FRANKLIN!!
Huh, *what?* What happ--
Franklin, please do the problem *at the board.*
Um...3 is the cosine with the variable of Y....deduct the product of the, um, coefficient...
At least, that's what I always hear *Dad* saying.
Add pi and round off...using the quadratic equation...
IIINNG
Saved by the bell *again!*
Perhaps, Franklin, if you don't know the answer to *8 x 6* we should spend more time after school working on your math.
Oh, um, yes, Mrs. Ullrich.
Man, was it *me* or did time *crawl* in that class.
Norman, it *wasn't* just you. ~sigh~
And *this* was a complete *waste of time.*
END.

FRANKLIN RICHARDS SON OF A GENIUS IN: SCIENCE UN-FAIR

BY CHRIS ELIOPOULOS & MARC SUMERA
BRAD ANDERSON
COLORS
MARK PANICCIA
CONSULTING
NATHAN CO
EDITOR

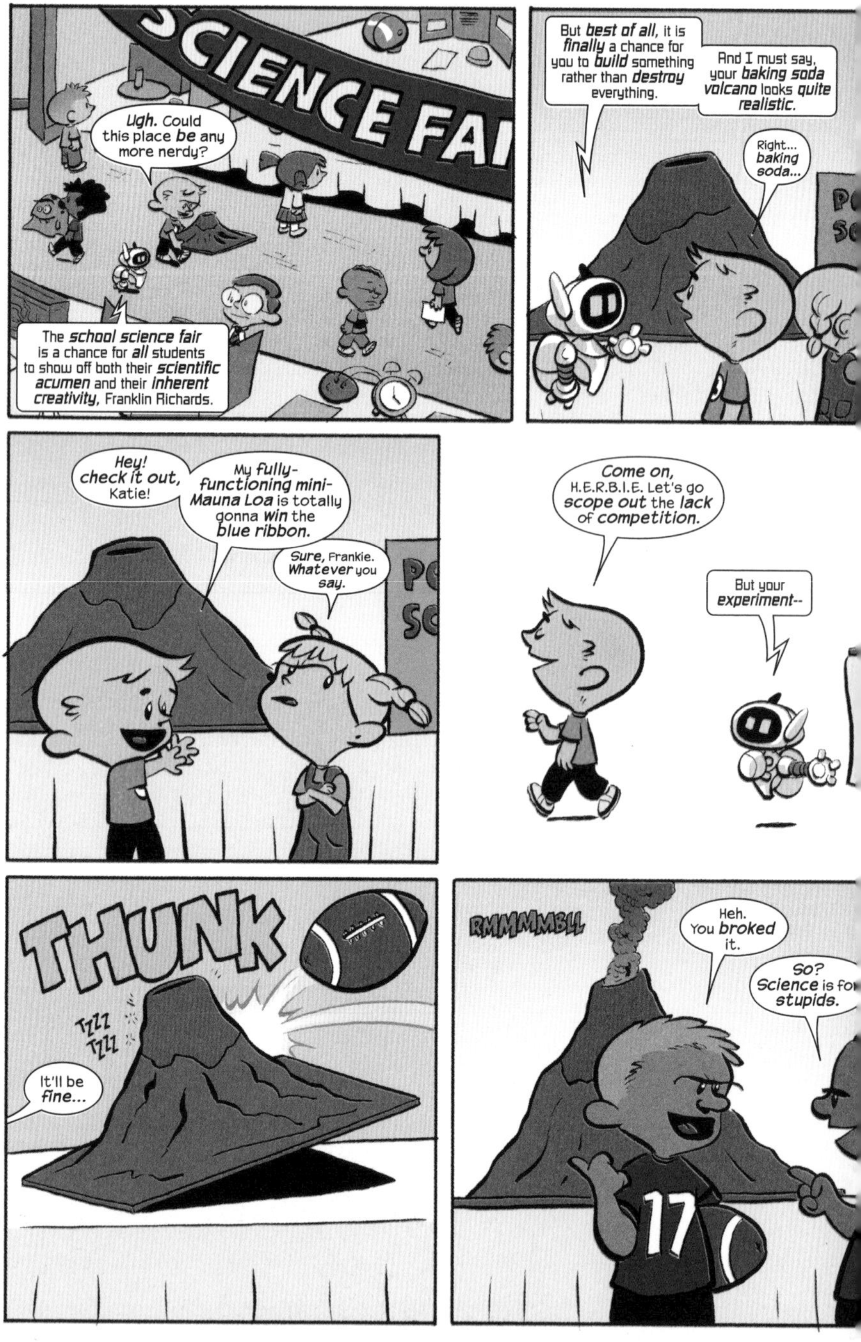
SCIENCE FAI
Ugh. Could this place be any more nerdy?
The school science fair is a chance for all students to show off both their scientific acumen and their inherent creativity, Franklin Richards.
But best of all, it is finally a chance for you to build something rather than destroy everything.
And I must say, your baking soda volcano looks quite realistic.
Right... baking soda...
Hey! check it out, Katie!
My fully-functioning mini-Mauna Loa is totally gonna win the blue ribbon.
Sure, Frankie. Whatever you say.
Come on, H.E.R.B.I.E. Let's go scope out the lack of competition.
But your experiment--
THUNK
TZZZ TZZZ
It'll be fine...
RMMMMBLL
Heh. You broked it.
So? Science is fo
stupids.
17

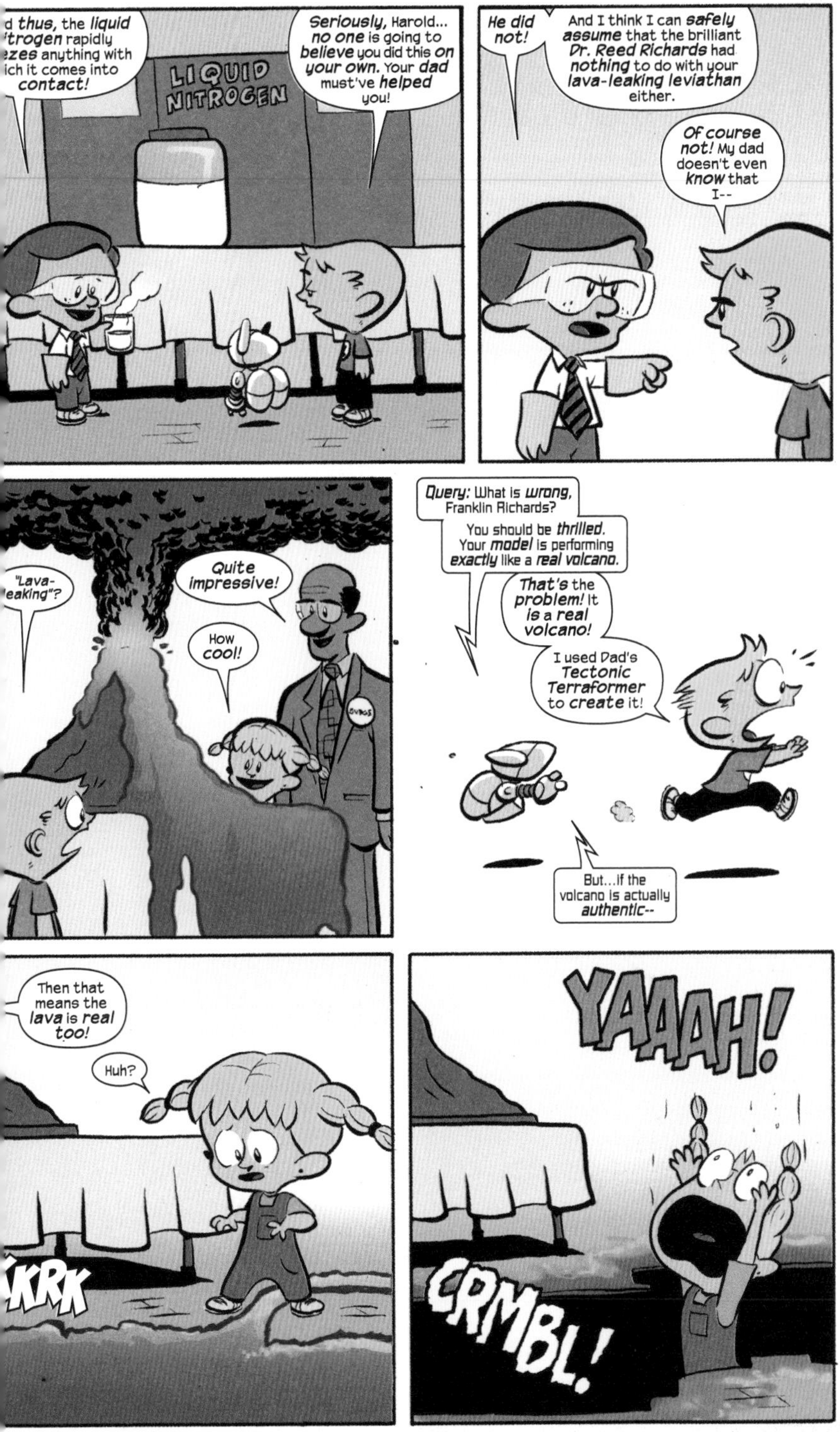

d thus, the liquid 'trogen rapidly ezes anything with ich it comes into contact!
LIQUID NITROGEN
Seriously, Harold... no one is going to believe you did this on your own. Your dad must've helped you!
He did not!
And I think I can safely assume that the brilliant Dr. Reed Richards had nothing to do with your lava-leaking leviathan either.
Of course not! My dad doesn't even know that I--
"Lava-leaking"?
Quite impressive!
How cool!
Query: What is wrong, Franklin Richards?
You should be thrilled. Your model is performing exactly like a real volcano.
That's the problem! It is a real volcano!
I used Dad's Tectonic Terraformer to create it!
But...if the volcano is actually authentic--
Then that means the lava is real too!
Huh?
KRK
YAAAH!
CRMBL!

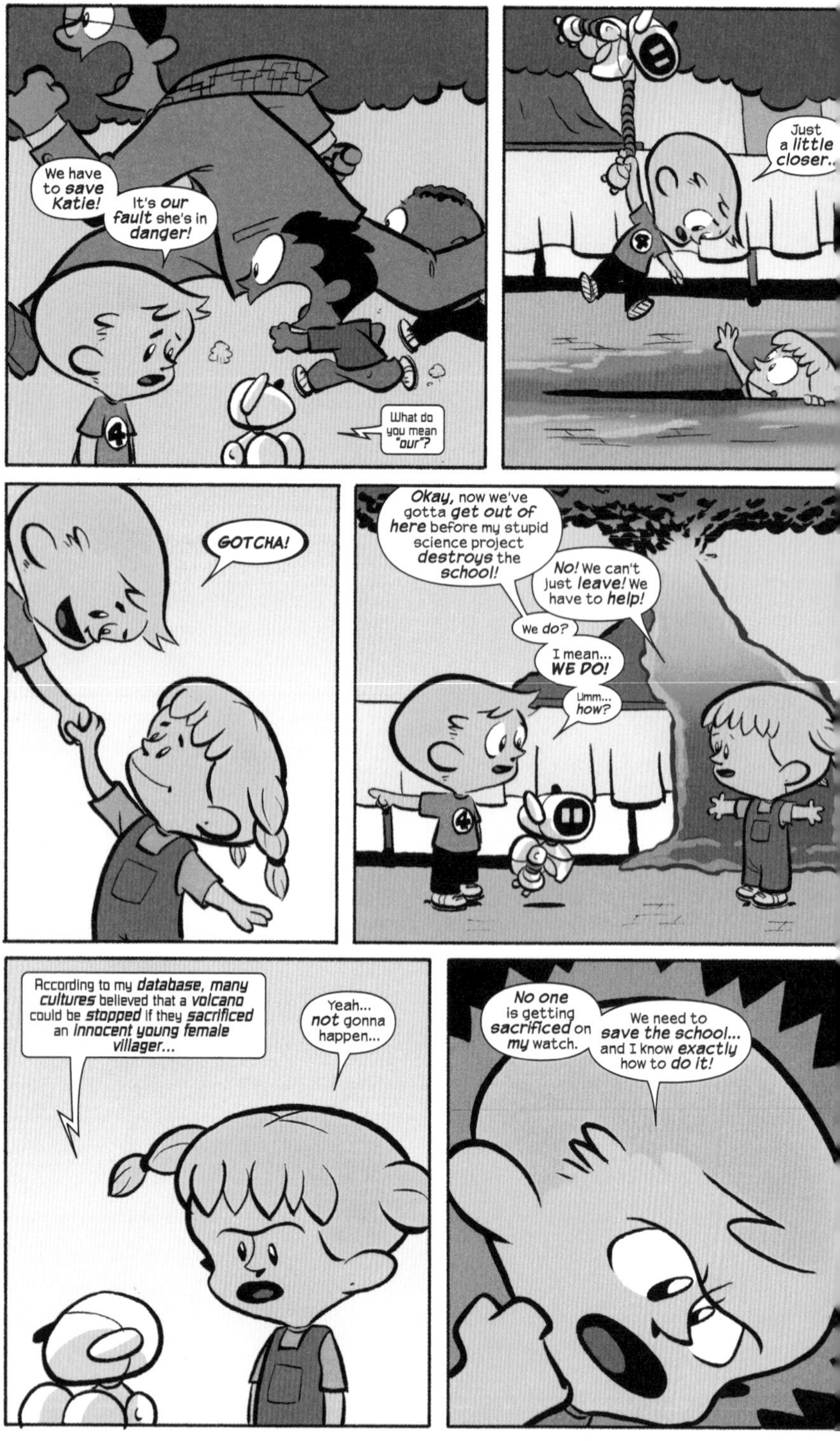
We have to save Katie!
It's our fault she's in danger!
What do you mean "our"?
Just a little closer...
GOTCHA!
Okay, now we've gotta get out of here before my stupid science project destroys the school!
No! We can't just leave! We have to help!
We do?
I mean... WE DO!
Umm... how?
According to my database, many cultures believed that a volcano could be stopped if they sacrificed an innocent young female villager...
Yeah... not gonna happen...
No one is getting sacrificed on my watch.
We need to save the school... and I know exactly how to do it!

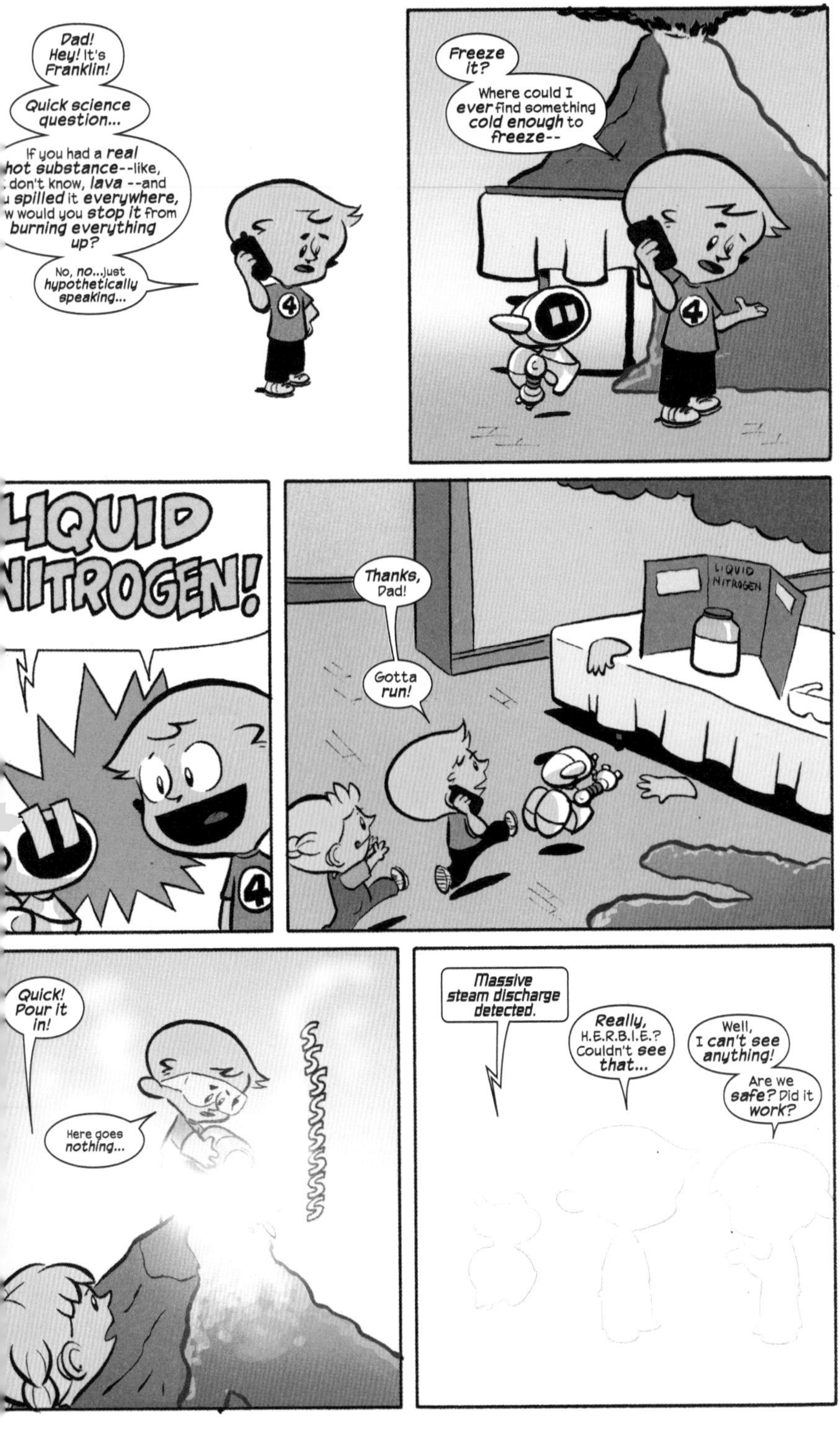

Dad! Hey! It's Franklin!
Quick science question...
If you had a real hot substance--like, I don't know, lava --and you spilled it everywhere, how would you stop it from burning everything up?
No, no...just hypothetically speaking...
Freeze it?
Where could I ever find something cold enough to freeze--
LIQUID NITROGEN!
Thanks, Dad!
Gotta run!
LIQUID NITROGEN
Quick! Pour it in!
Here goes nothing...
SSSSSSSSSSS
Massive steam discharge detected.
Really, H.E.R.B.I.E.? Couldn't see that...
Well, I can't see anything!
Are we safe? Did it work?

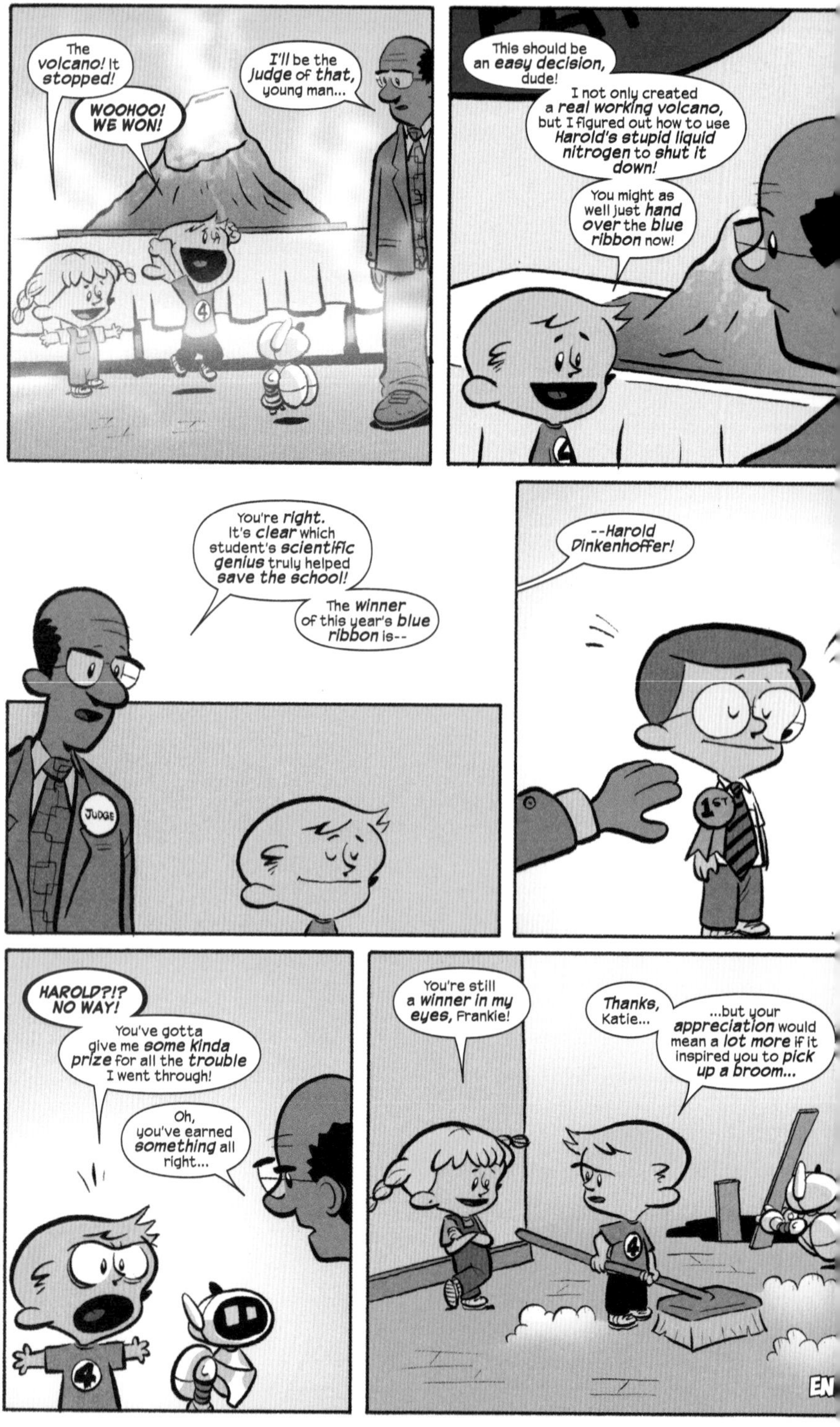
The volcano! It stopped!
WOOHOO! WE WON!
I'll be the judge of that, young man...
This should be an easy decision, dude!
I not only created a real working volcano, but I figured out how to use Harold's stupid liquid nitrogen to shut it down!
You might as well just hand over the blue ribbon now!
You're right. It's clear which student's scientific genius truly helped save the school!
The winner of this year's blue ribbon is--
JUDGE
--Harold Dinkenhoffer!
1ST
HAROLD?!? NO WAY!
You've gotta give me some kinda prize for all the trouble I went through!
Oh, you've earned something all right...
You're still a winner in my eyes, Frankie!
Thanks, Katie...
...but your appreciation would mean a lot more if it inspired you to pick up a broom...
EN

FRANKLIN RICHARDS SON OF A GENIUS IN: BOOMING BURPS!

BY CHRIS ELIOPOULOS & MARC SUMERAK
BRAD ANDERSON COLORS
MARK PANICCIA CONSULTING
NATHAN COSBY EDITOR

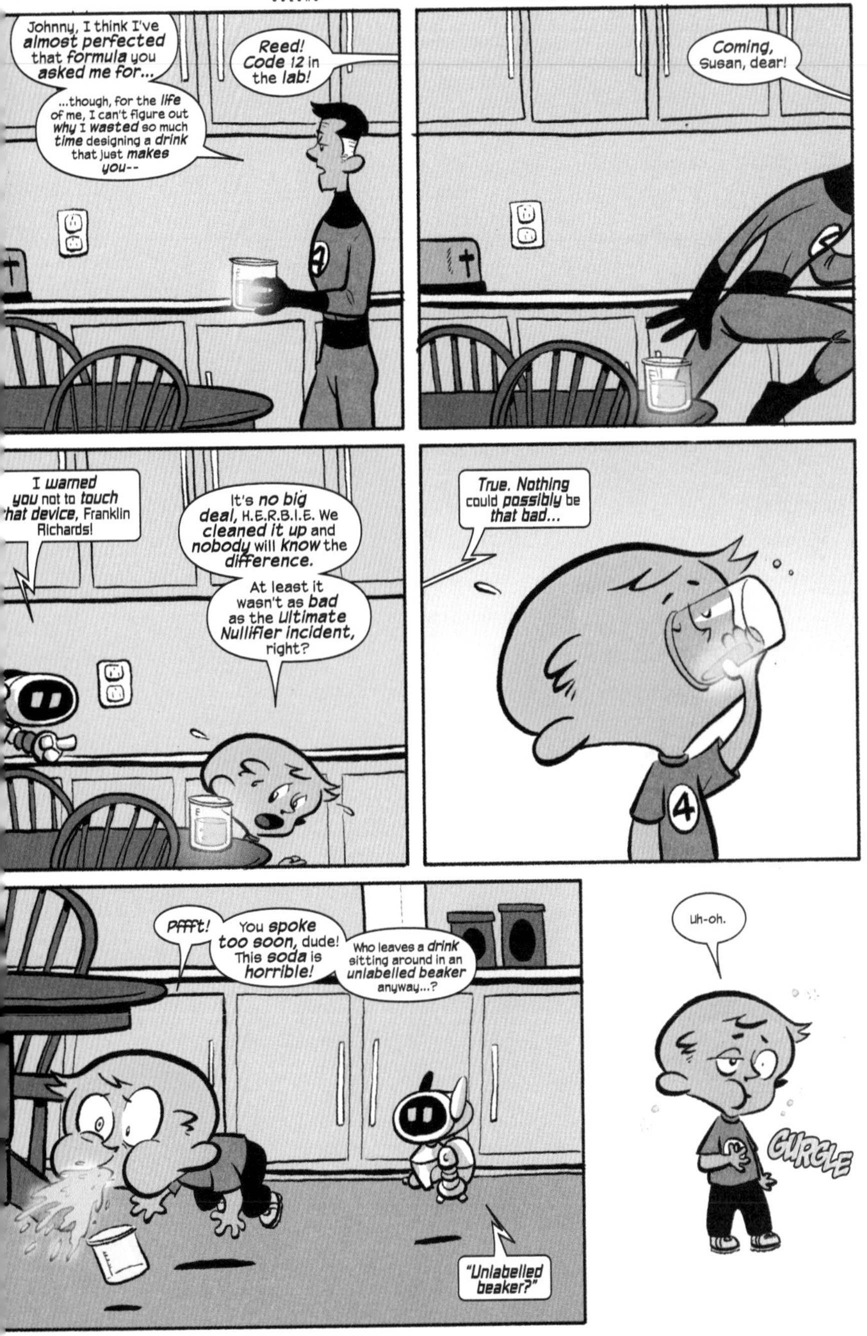

Johnny, I think I've almost perfected that formula you asked me for...
...though, for the life of me, I can't figure out why I wasted so much time designing a drink that just makes you--
Reed! Code 12 in the lab!
Coming, Susan, dear!
I warned you not to touch that device, Franklin Richards!
It's no big deal, H.E.R.B.I.E. We cleaned it up and nobody will know the difference.
At least it wasn't as bad as the Ultimate Nullifier incident, right?
True. Nothing could possibly be that bad...
Pfffft!
You spoke too soon, dude! This soda is horrible!
Who leaves a drink sitting around in an unlabelled beaker anyway...?
"Unlabelled beaker?"
Uh-oh.
GURGLE

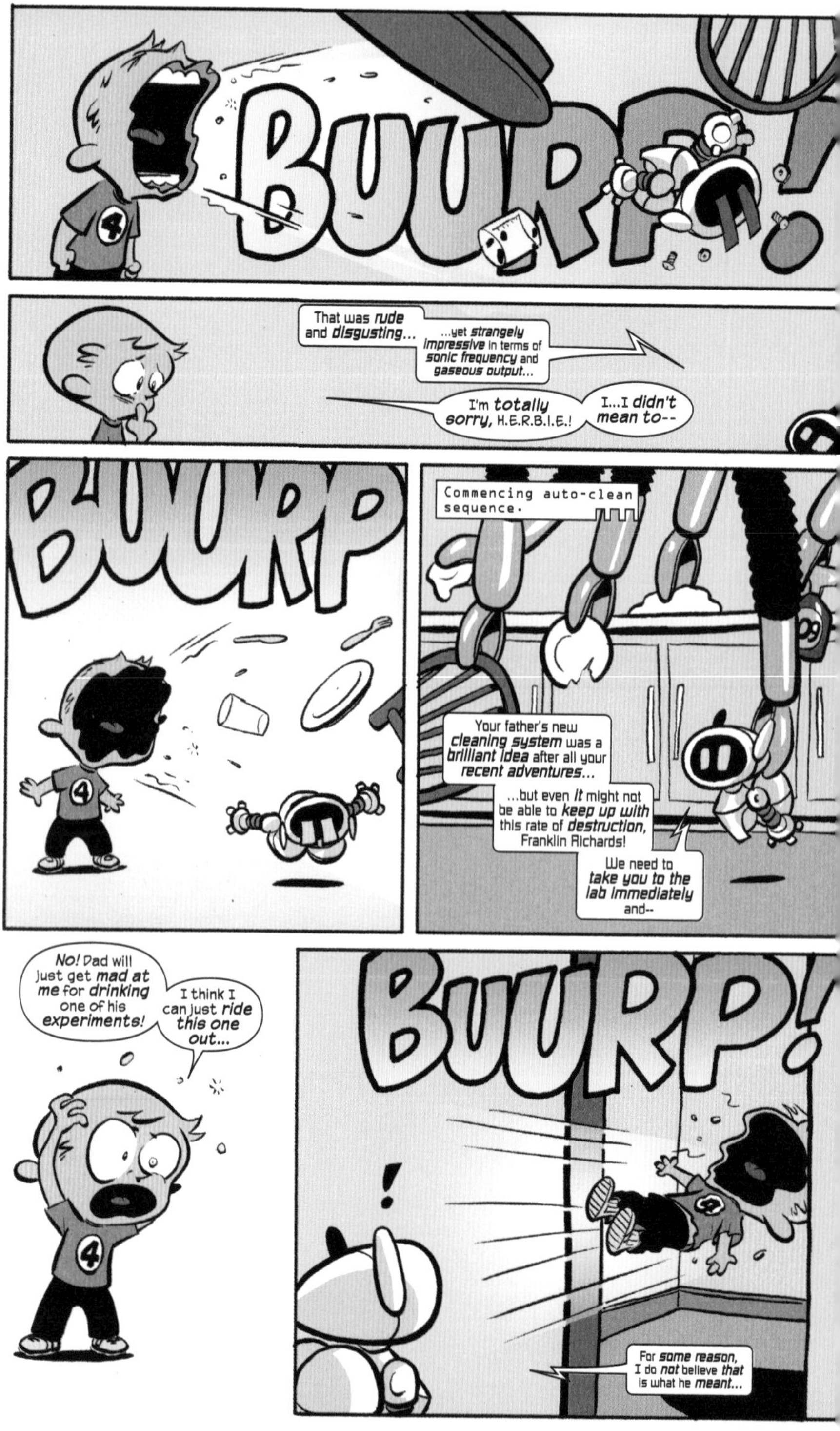
BUURP!
That was rude and disgusting...
...yet strangely impressive in terms of sonic frequency and gaseous output...
I'm totally sorry, H.E.R.B.I.E.!
I...I didn't mean to--
BUURP
Commencing auto-clean sequence.
Your father's new cleaning system was a brilliant idea after all your recent adventures...
...but even it might not be able to keep up with this rate of destruction, Franklin Richards!
We need to take you to the lab immediately and--
No! Dad will just get mad at me for drinking one of his experiments!
I think I can just ride this one out...
BUURP!
For some reason, I do not believe that is what he meant...

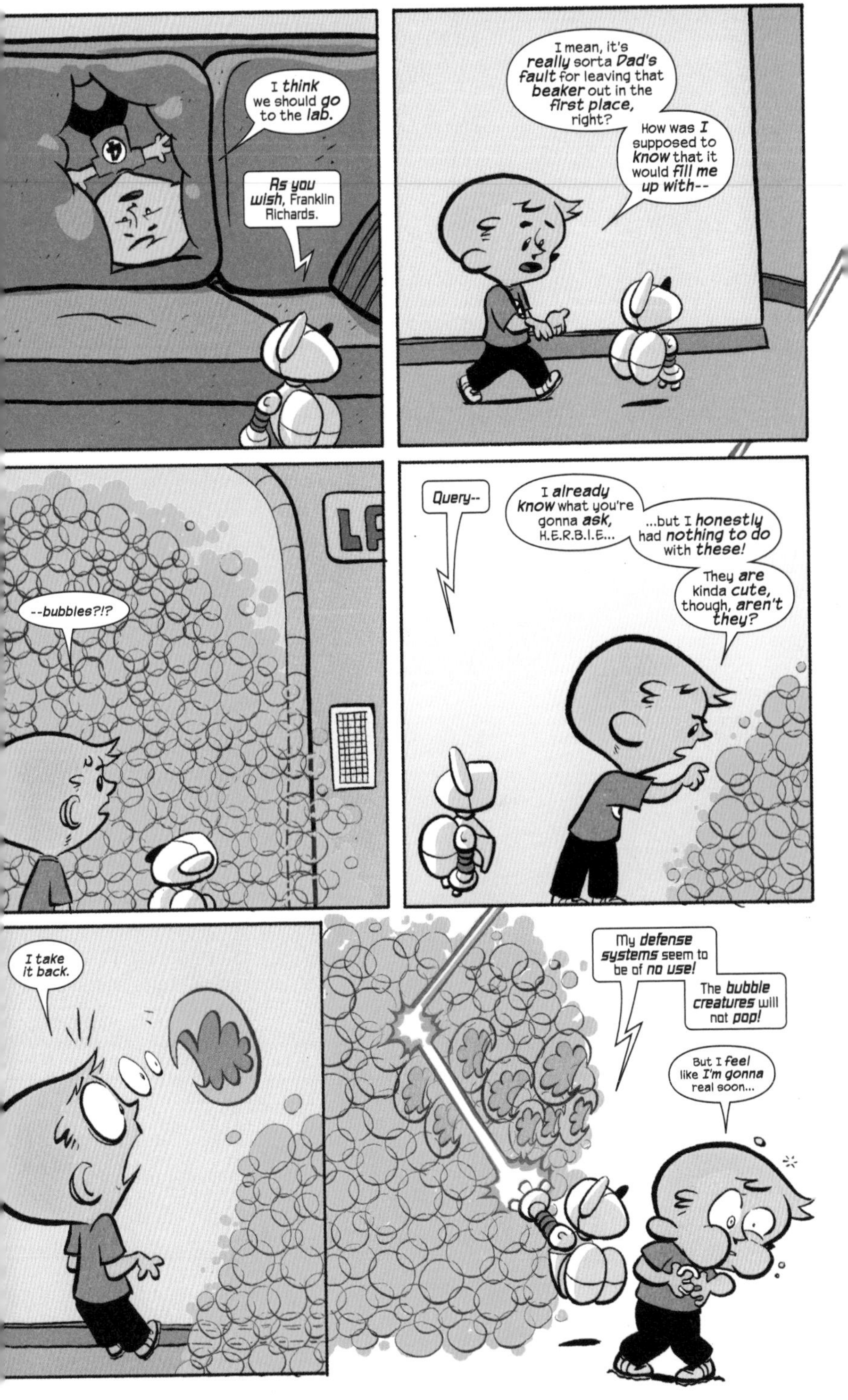

I think we should go to the lab.
As you wish, Franklin Richards.
I mean, it's really sorta Dad's fault for leaving that beaker out in the first place, right?
How was I supposed to know that it would fill me up with--
LA
--bubbles?!?
Query--
I already know what you're gonna ask, H.E.R.B.I.E...
...but I honestly had nothing to do with these!
They are kinda cute, though, aren't they?
I take it back.
My defense systems seem to be of no use!
The bubble creatures will not pop!
But I feel like I'm gonna real soon...

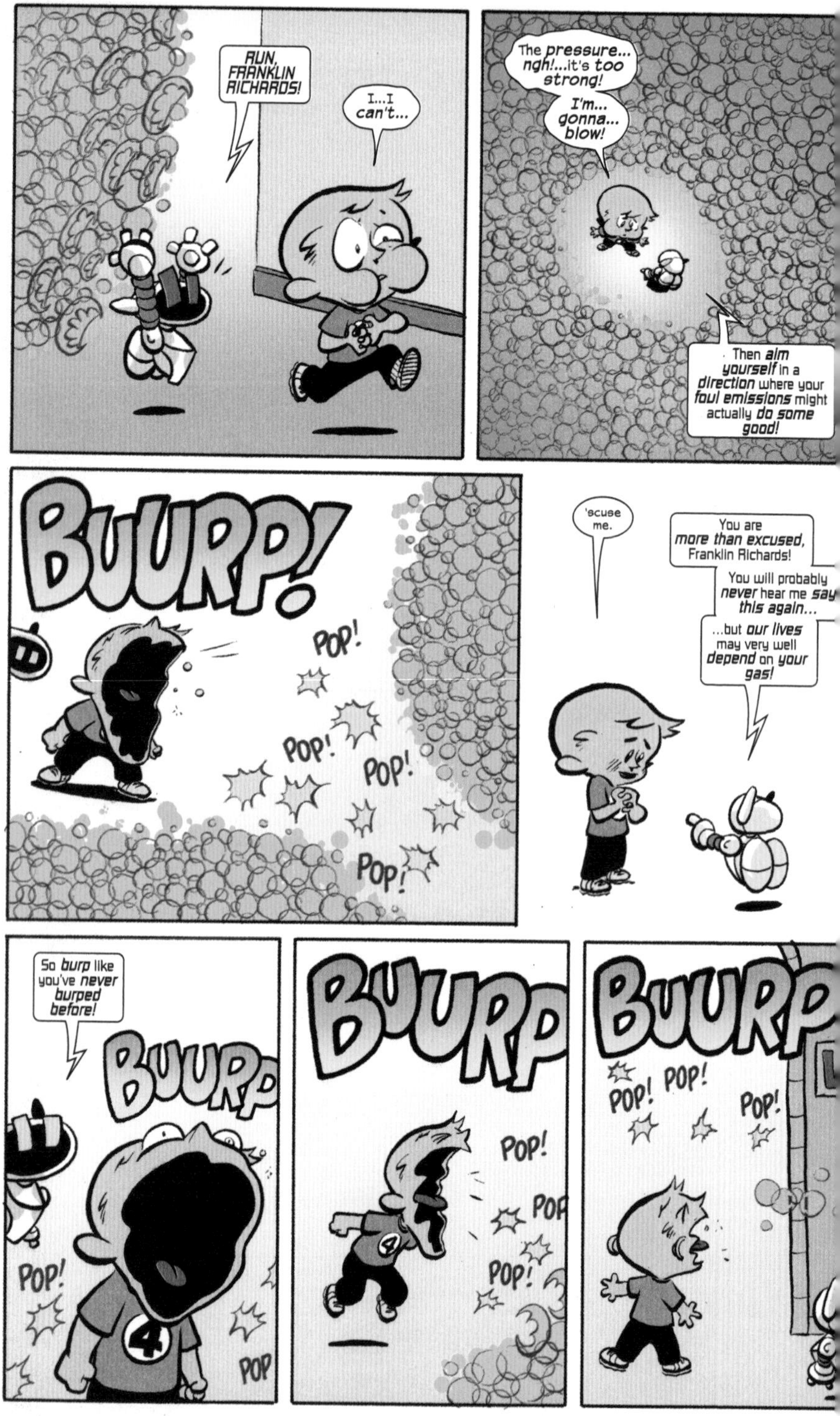
RUN, FRANKLIN RICHARDS!
I...I can't...
The pressure... ngh!...it's too strong!
I'm... gonna... blow!
Then aim yourself in a direction where your foul emissions might actually do some good!
BUURP!
POP!
POP!
POP!
POP!
'scuse me.
You are more than excused, Franklin Richards!
You will probably never hear me say this again...
...but our lives may very well depend on your gas!
So burp like you've never burped before!
BUURP
POP!
POP
BUURP
POP!
POP
POP!
BUURP
POP! POP!
POP!

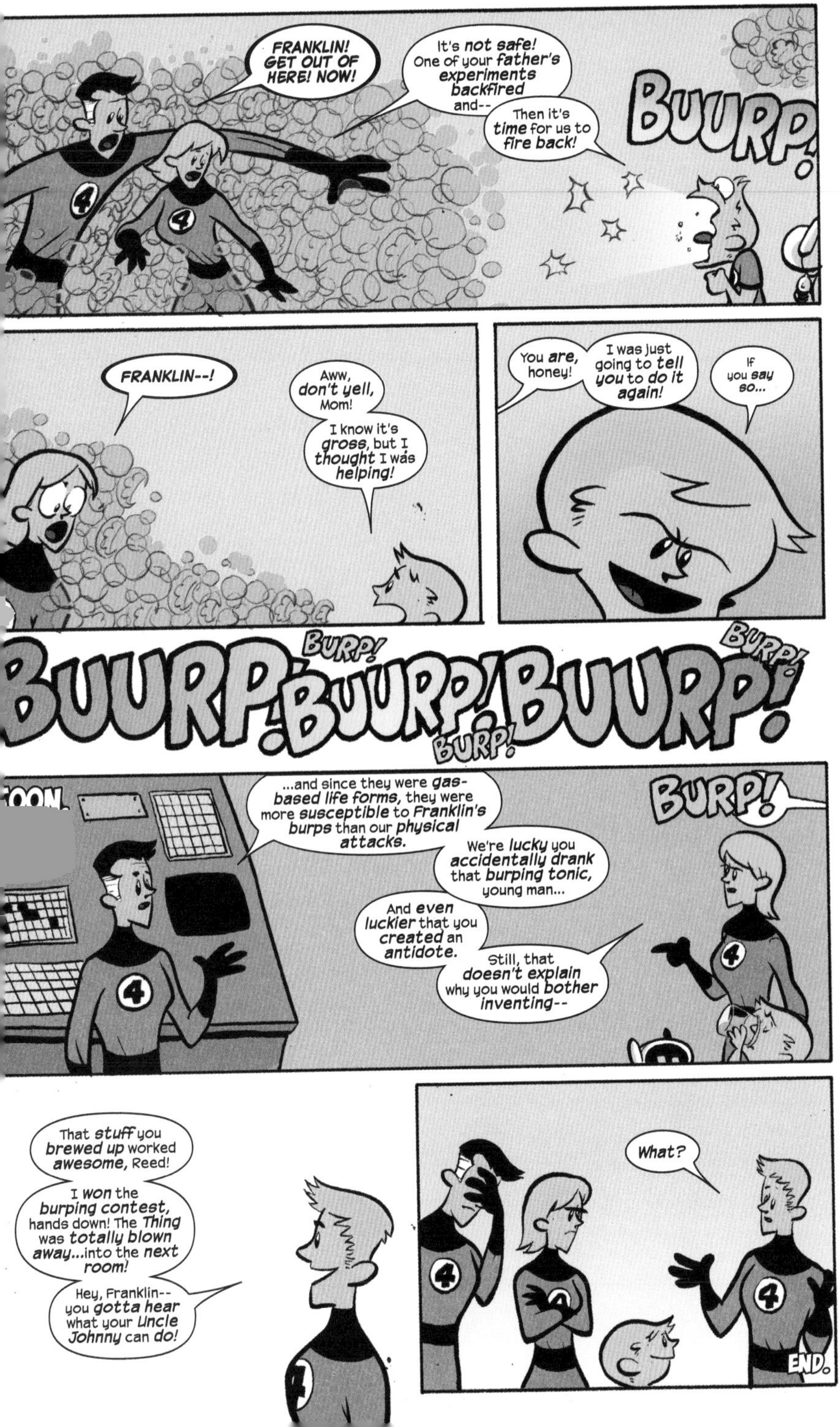
FRANKLIN! GET OUT OF HERE! NOW!
It's not safe! One of your father's experiments backfired and--
Then it's time for us to fire back!
BUURP!
FRANKLIN--!
Aww, don't yell, Mom!
I know it's gross, but I thought I was helping!
You are, honey!
I was just going to tell you to do it again!
If you say so...
BUURP! BURP! BUURP! BURP! BUURP! BURP!
...and since they were gas-based life forms, they were more susceptible to Franklin's burps than our physical attacks.
BURP!
We're lucky you accidentally drank that burping tonic, young man...
And even luckier that you created an antidote.
Still, that doesn't explain why you would bother inventing--
That stuff you brewed up worked awesome, Reed!
I won the burping contest, hands down! The Thing was totally blown away...into the next room!
Hey, Franklin-- you gotta hear what your Uncle Johnny can do!
What?
END.

FRANKLIN RICHARDS SON OF A GENIUS IN: ROBO-RAMPAGE!

BY CHRIS ELIOPOULOS & MARC SUMERA[illegible]

BRAD ANDERSON COLORS — MARK PANICCIA CONSULTING — NATHAN COS[illegible] EDITOR

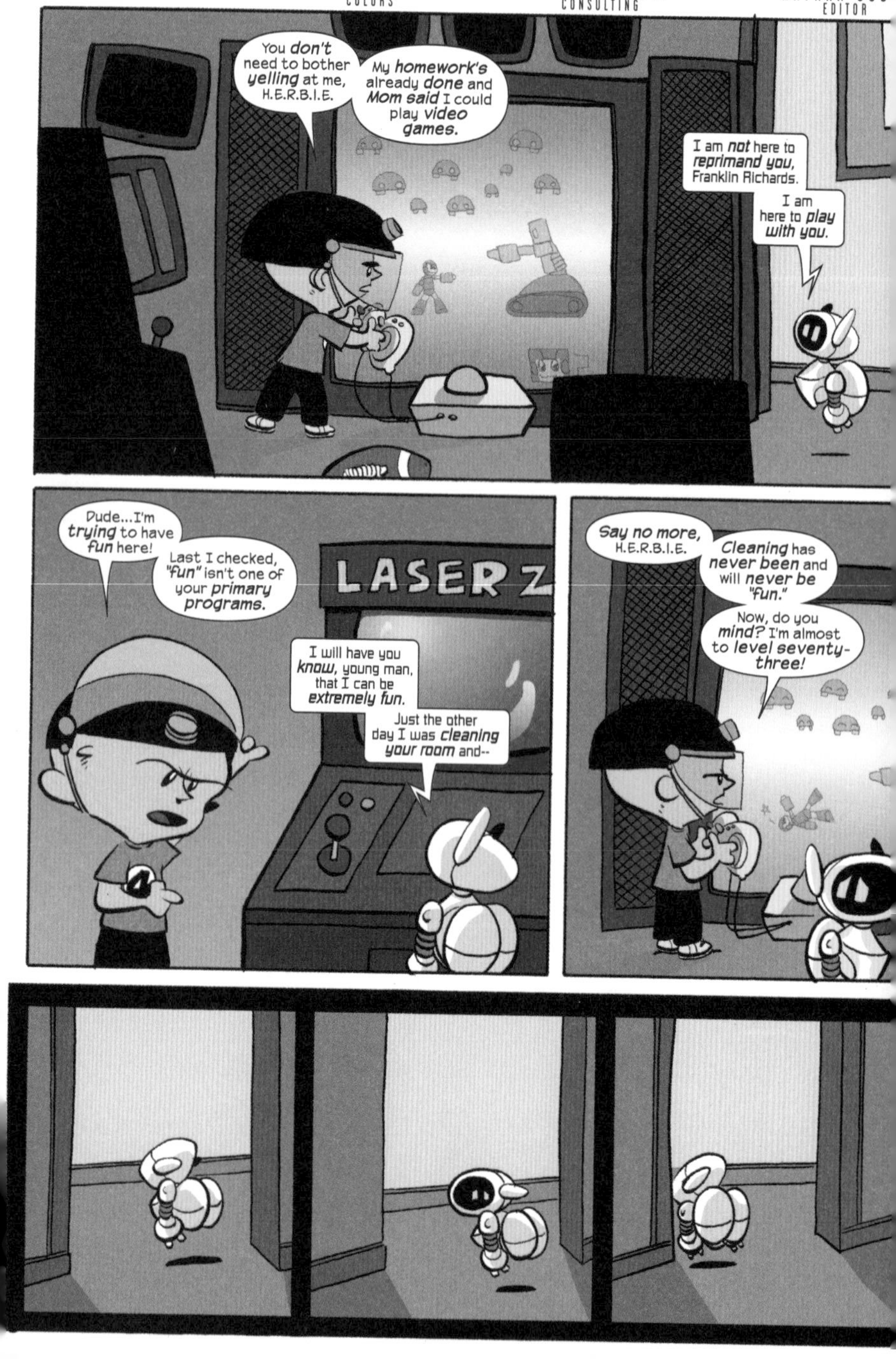

You don't need to bother yelling at me, H.E.R.B.I.E.
My homework's already done and Mom said I could play video games.
I am not here to reprimand you, Franklin Richards.
I am here to play with you.
Dude...I'm trying to have fun here!
Last I checked, "fun" isn't one of your primary programs.
LASER Z
I will have you know, young man, that I can be extremely fun.
Just the other day I was cleaning your room and--
Say no more, H.E.R.B.I.E.
Cleaning has never been and will never be "fun."
Now, do you mind? I'm almost to level seventy-three!

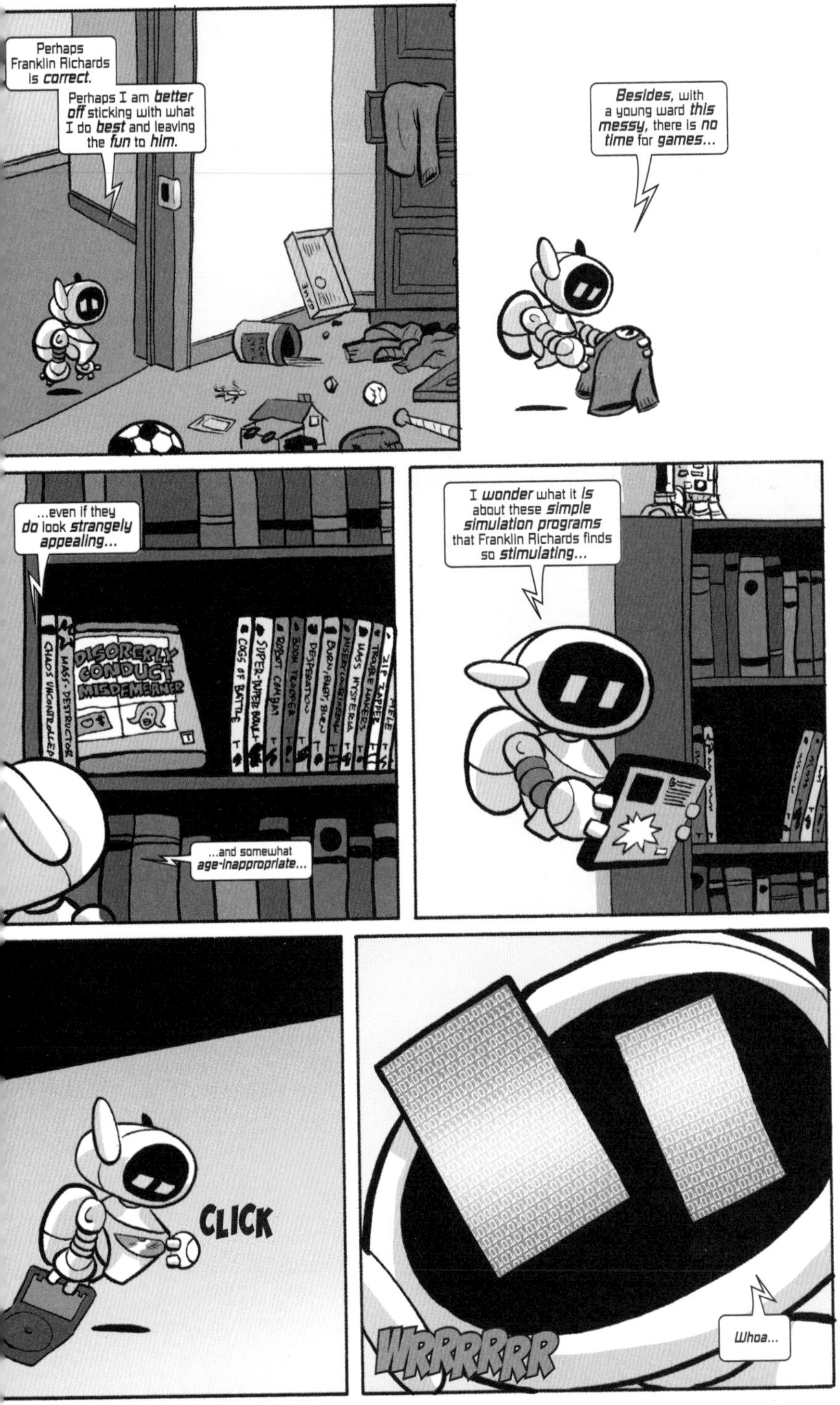
Perhaps Franklin Richards is correct.
Perhaps I am better off sticking with what I do best and leaving the fun to him.
Besides, with a young ward this messy, there is no time for games...
...even if they do look strangely appealing...
CHAOS UNCONTROLLED
MASS-DESTRUCTOR
DISORDERLY CONDUCT MISDEMEANER
COGS OF BATTLE
SUPER-DUPER BRAWL
ROBOT COMBAT
BOOM TROOPER
DESPERATION
BURN, BABY, BURN
MISERY LOVES COMPANY
MASS HYSTERIA
TROUBLE MAKERS
ZIP ZAPPER
MELEE
...and somewhat age-inappropriate...
I wonder what it is about these simple simulation programs that Franklin Richards finds so stimulating...
CLICK
WRRRRRRR
Whoa...

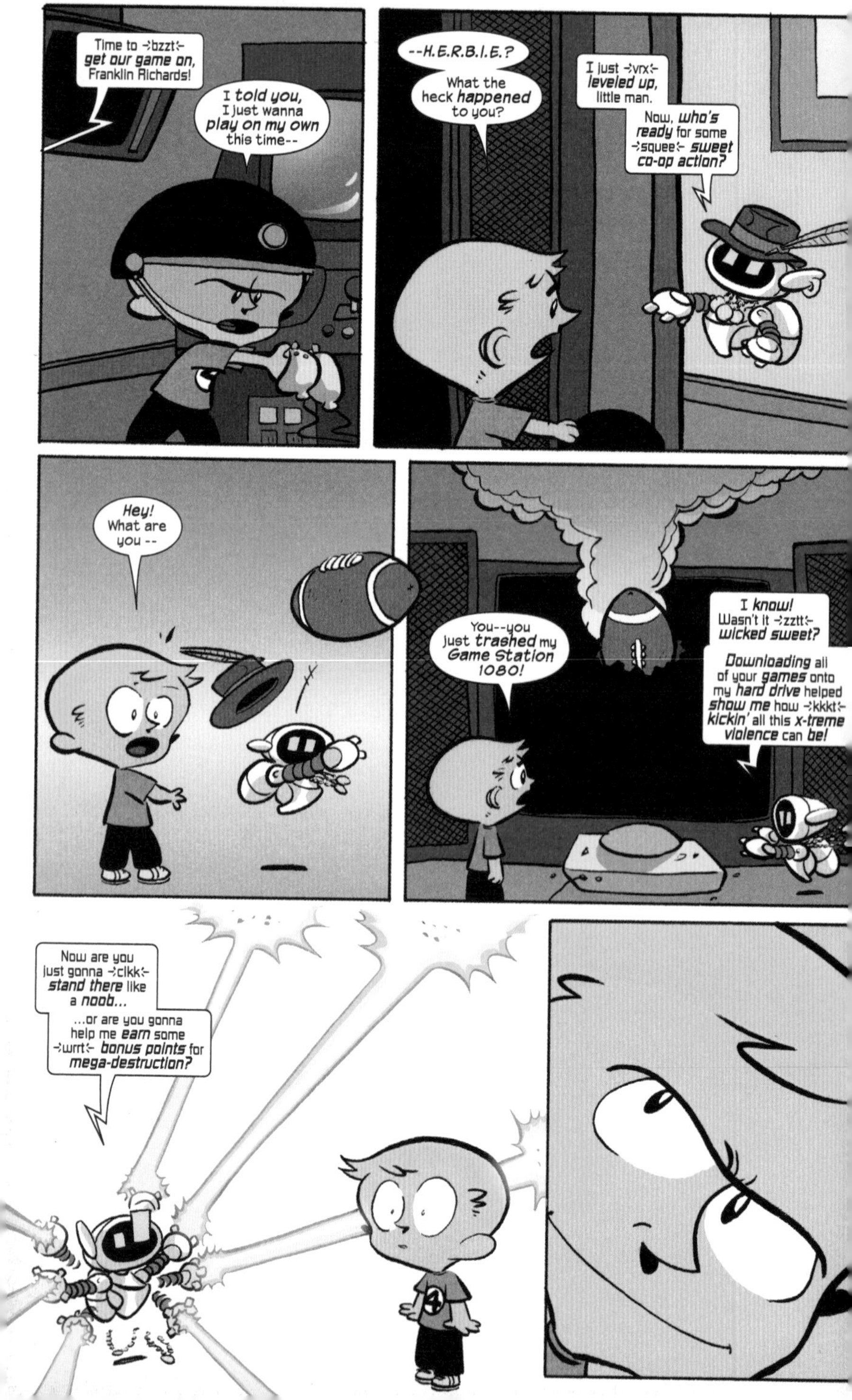

Time to -›bzzt‹- get our game on, Franklin Richards!
I told you, I just wanna play on my own this time--
--H.E.R.B.I.E.?
What the heck happened to you?
I just -›vrx‹- leveled up, little man.
Now, who's ready for some -›squee‹- sweet co-op action?
Hey! What are you --
You--you just trashed my Game Station 1080!
I know! Wasn't it -›zztt‹- wicked sweet?
Downloading all of your games onto my hard drive helped show me how -›kkkt‹- kickin' all this x-treme violence can be!
Now are you just gonna -›clkk‹- stand there like a noob...
...or are you gonna help me earn some -›wrrt‹- bonus points for mega-destruction?

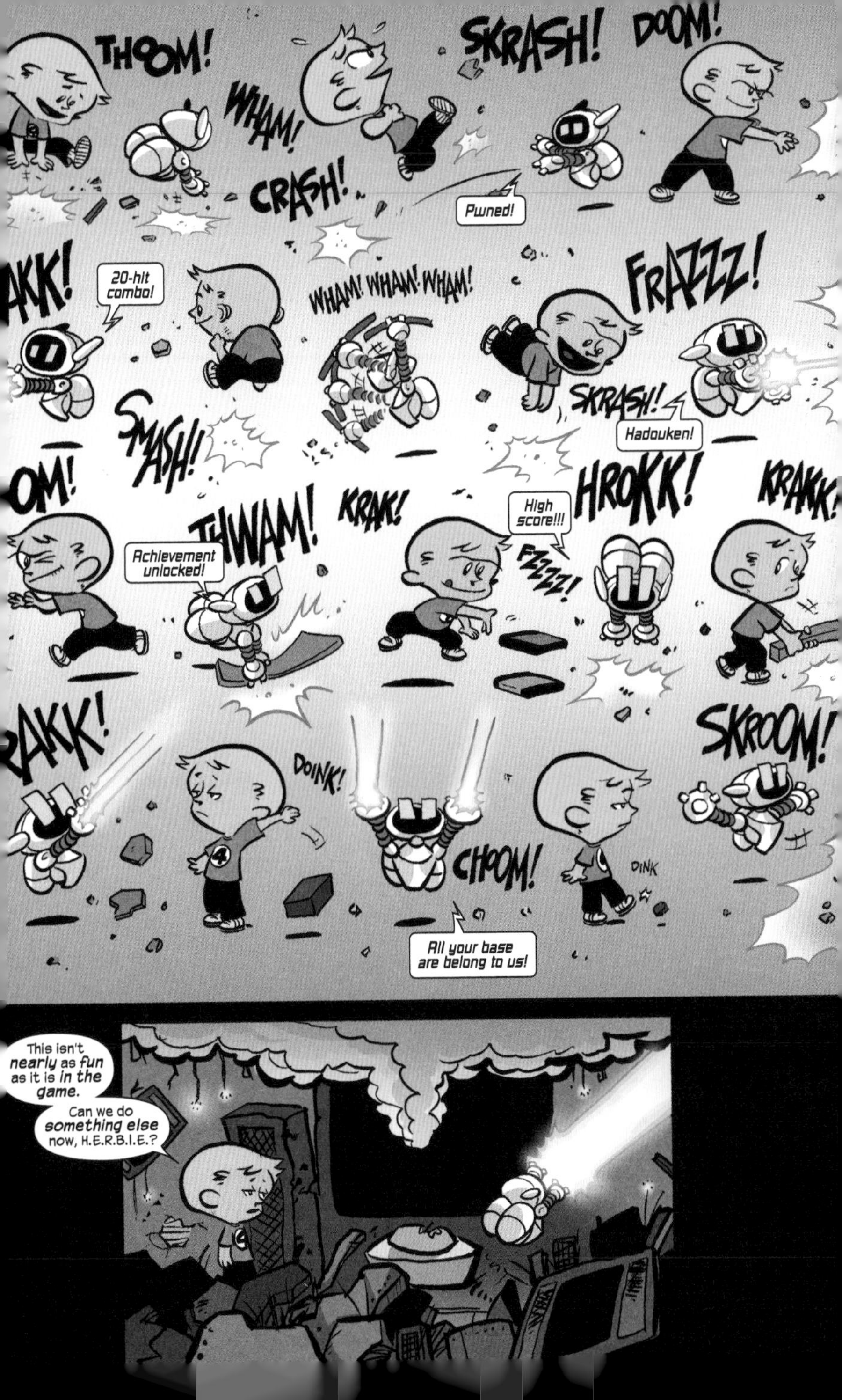

THOOM!
WHAM!
CRASH!
SKRASH!
DOOM!
Pwned!
AKK!
20-hit combo!
WHAM! WHAM! WHAM!
FRAZZZ!
SMASH!
SKRASH!
Hadouken!
OM!
THWAM!
Achievement unlocked!
KRAK!
High score!!!
FZZZZ!
HROKK!
KRAKK!
RAKK!
DOINK!
CHOOM!
SKROOM!
DINK
All your base are belong to us!
This isn't *nearly* as *fun* as it is *in the game.*
Can we do *something else* now, H.E.R.B.I.E.?

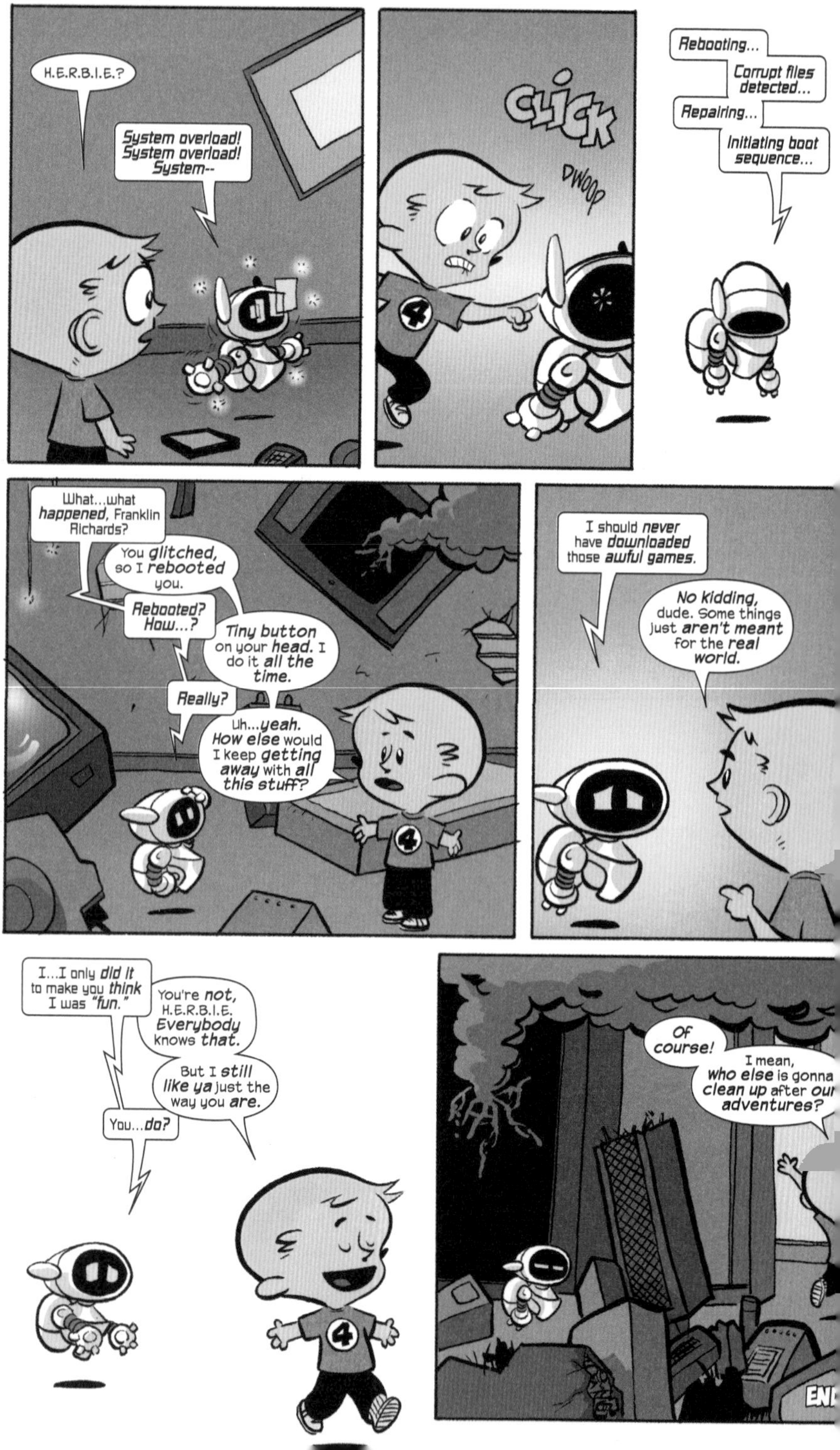

H.E.R.B.I.E.?
System overload! System overload! System--
CLICK
DWOOP
Rebooting...
Corrupt files detected...
Repairing...
Initiating boot sequence...
What...what happened, Franklin Richards?
You glitched, so I rebooted you.
Rebooted? How...?
Tiny button on your head. I do it all the time.
Really?
Uh...yeah. How else would I keep getting away with all this stuff?
I should never have downloaded those awful games.
No kidding, dude. Some things just aren't meant for the real world.
I...I only did it to make you think I was "fun."
You're not, H.E.R.B.I.E. Everybody knows that.
But I still like ya just the way you are.
You...do?
Of course!
I mean, who else is gonna clean up after our adventures?

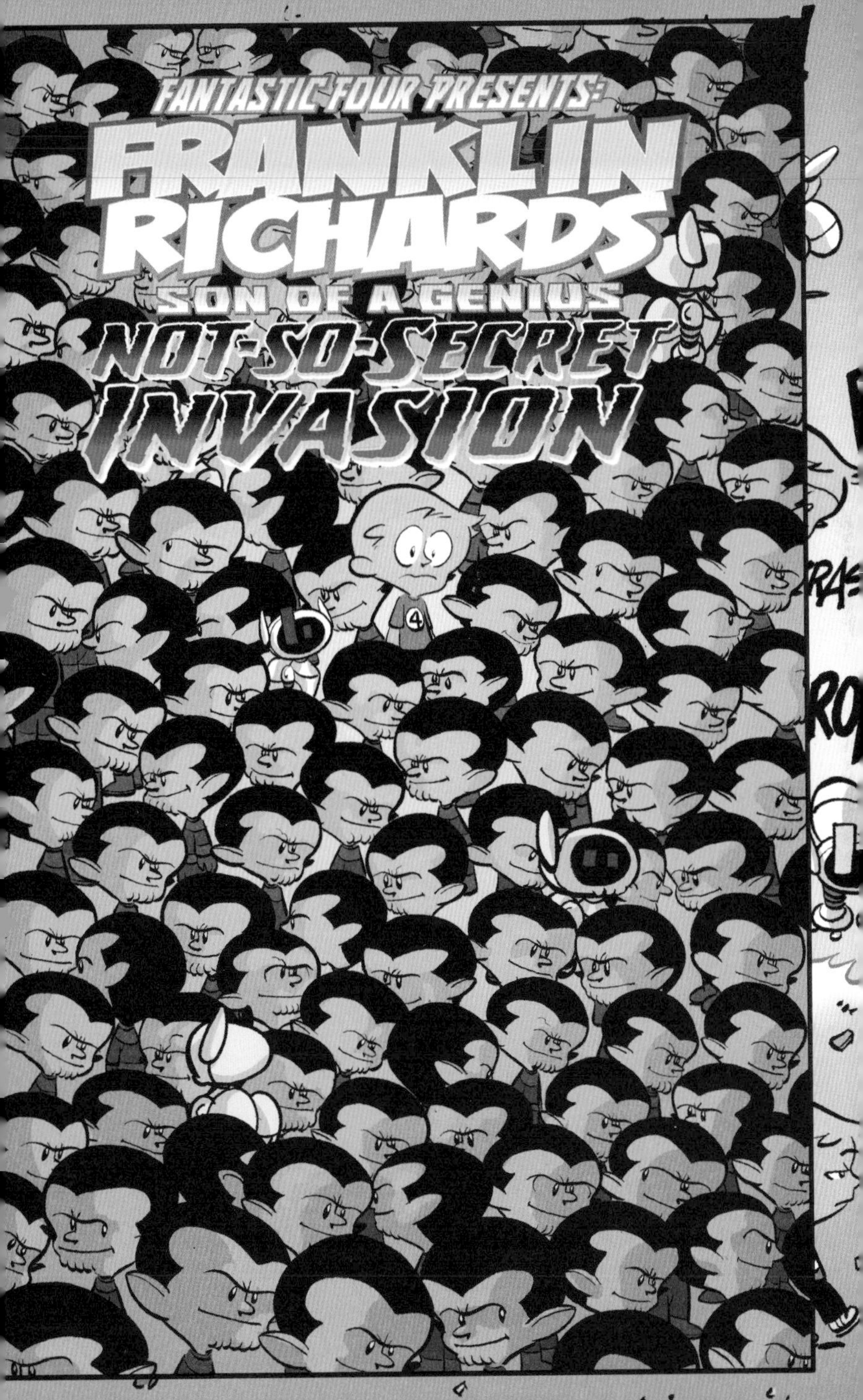
FANTASTIC FOUR PRESENTS:
FRANKLIN RICHARDS
SON OF A GENIUS
NOT-SO-SECRET INVASION

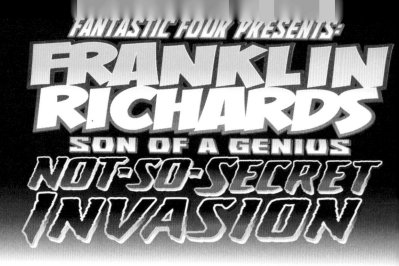

FANTASTIC FOUR PRESENTS:

FRANKLIN RICHARDS
SON OF A GENIUS
NOT-SO-SECRET INVASION

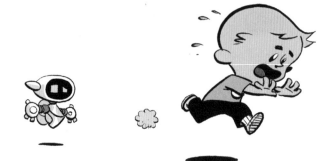

CHRIS ELIOPOULOS AND MARC SUMERAK
STORY

MARC SUMERAK
SCRIPT

CHRIS ELIOPOULOS
ART & LETTERS

BRAD ANDERS
COLOR

MARK PANICCIA
CONSULTING EDITOR

NATHAN COSBY
EDITOR

JOE QUESADA
EDITOR IN CHIEF

DAN BUCKLEY
PUBLISHER

STORY ONE
SKRULL SURPRISE!

STORY TWO
LITTLE LIZARD NO LONGER!

STORY THREE
THE OTHER FOOTBALL!

STORY FOUR
SQUID SQUABBLE!

STORY FIVE
WIZARD WIPEOU

FRANKLIN RICHARDS: SON OF A GENIUS IN: SKRULL SURPRISE!

BY CHRIS ELIOPOULOS & MARC SUMERAK

BRAD ANDERSON COLORS · MARK PANICCIA CONSULTING · NATHAN COSBY EDITOR

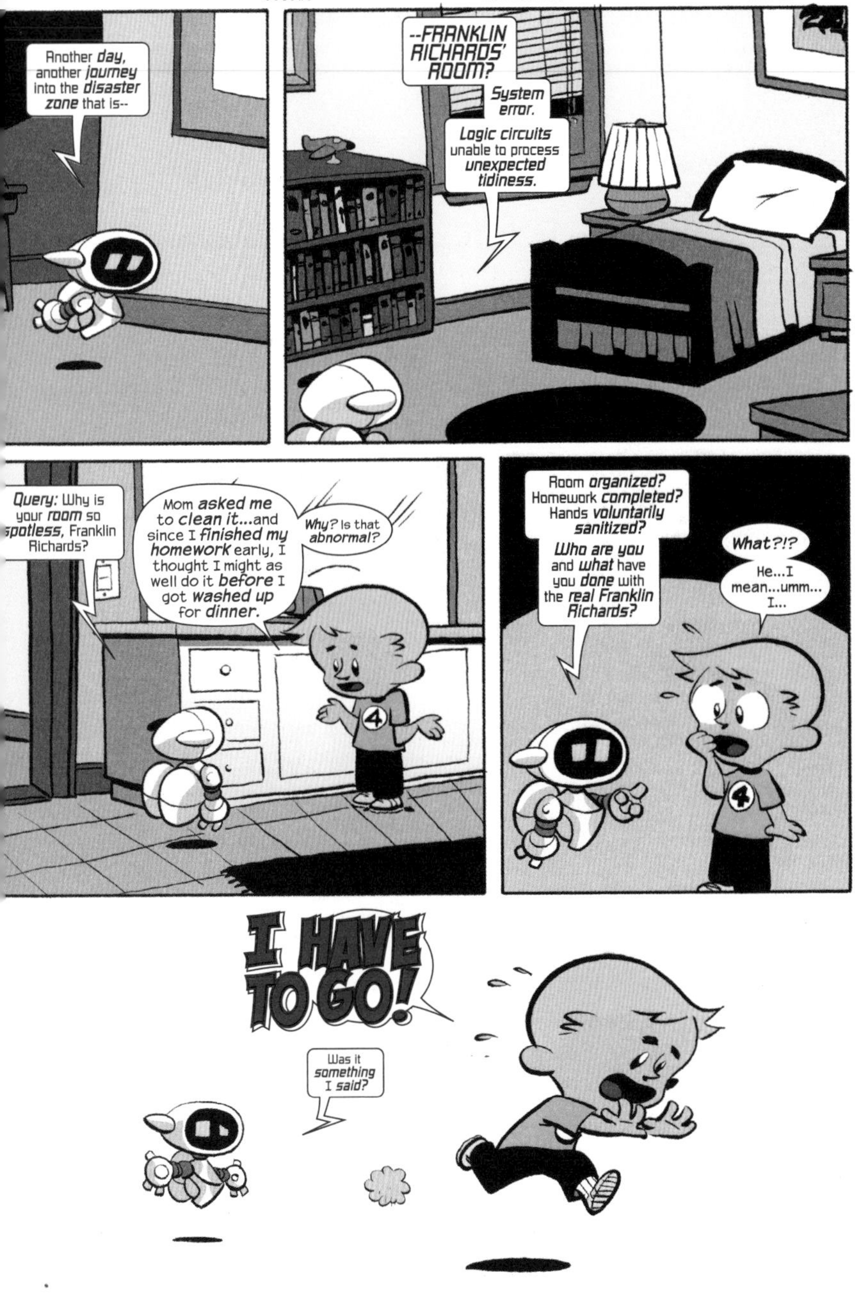

Another day, another journey into the disaster zone that is--
--FRANKLIN RICHARDS' ROOM?
System error.
Logic circuits unable to process unexpected tidiness.
Query: Why is your room so spotless, Franklin Richards?
Mom asked me to clean it...and since I finished my homework early, I thought I might as well do it before I got washed up for dinner.
Why? Is that abnormal?
Room organized? Homework completed? Hands voluntarily sanitized?
Who are you and what have you done with the real Franklin Richards?
What?!?
He...I mean...umm... I...
I HAVE TO GO!
Was it something I said?

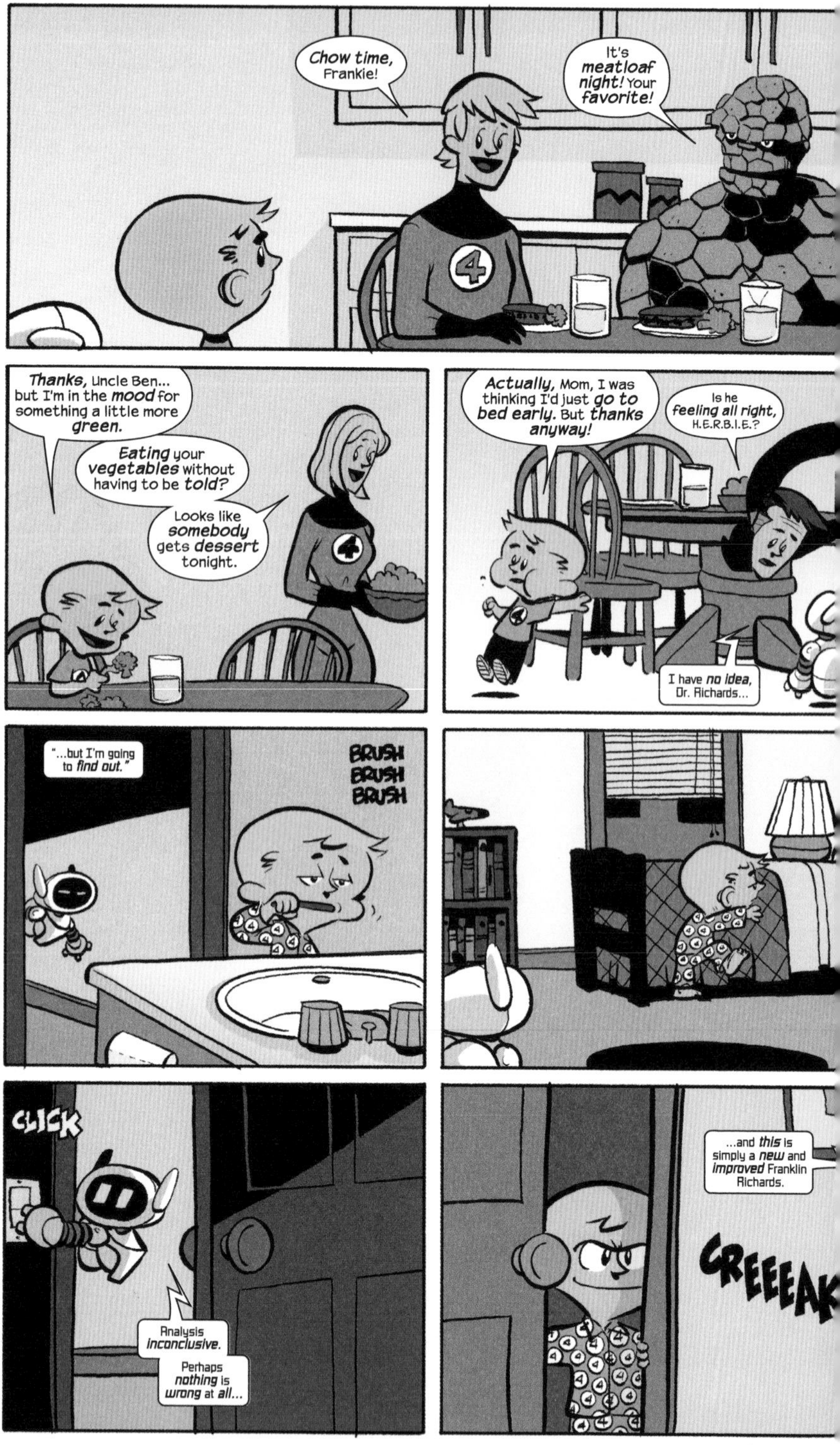

Chow time, Frankie!
It's meatloaf night! Your favorite!
Thanks, Uncle Ben... but I'm in the mood for something a little more green.
Eating your vegetables without having to be told?
Looks like somebody gets dessert tonight.
Actually, Mom, I was thinking I'd just go to bed early. But thanks anyway!
Is he feeling all right, H.E.R.B.I.E.?
I have no idea, Dr. Richards...
"...but I'm going to find out."
BRUSH BRUSH BRUSH
CLICK
Analysis inconclusive.
Perhaps nothing is wrong at all...
...and this is simply a new and improved Franklin Richards.
CREEEAK

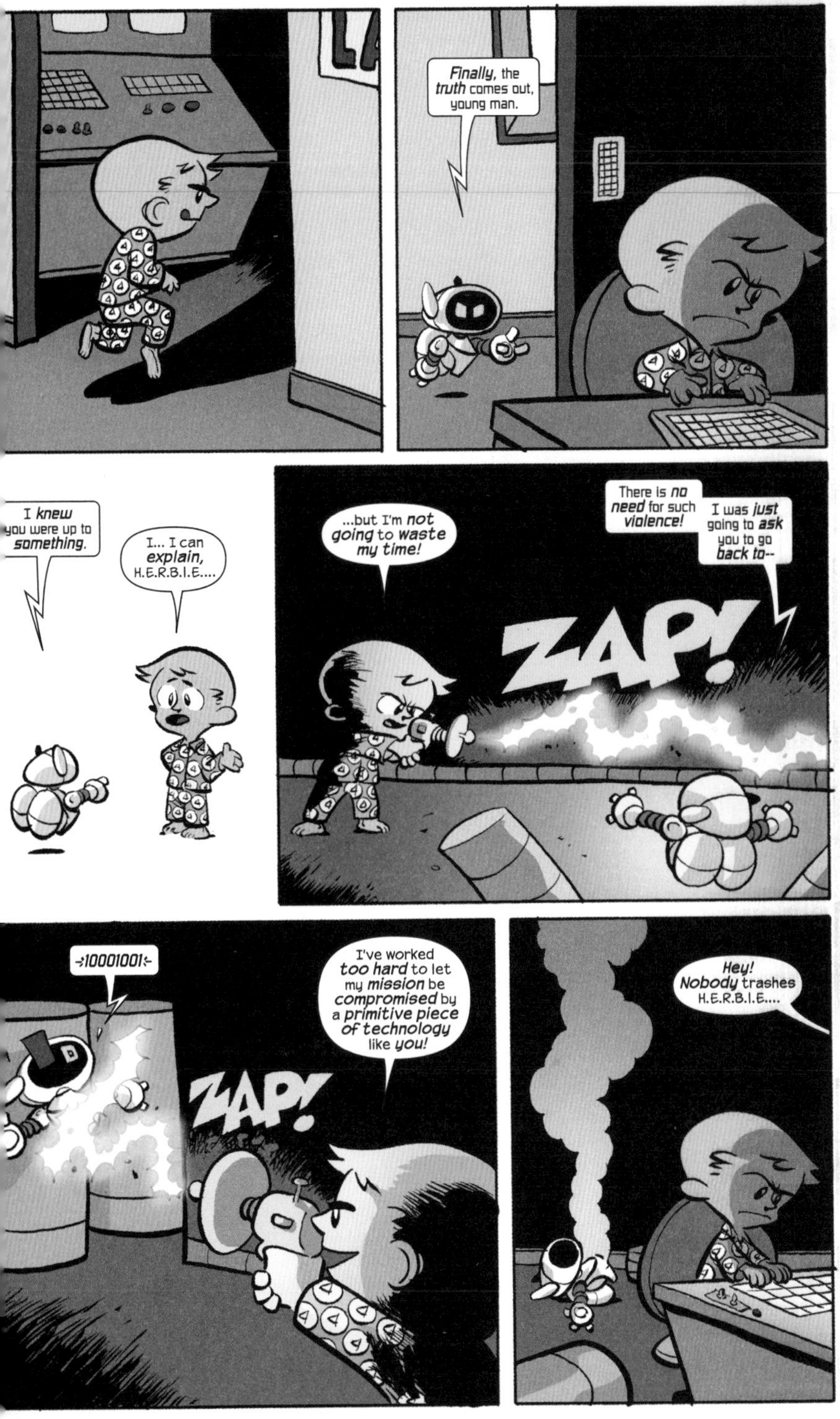

Finally, the truth comes out, young man.
I knew you were up to something.
I... I can explain, H.E.R.B.I.E....
...but I'm not going to waste my time!
There is no need for such violence!
I was just going to ask you to go back to--
ZAP!
-=10001001=-
ZAP!
I've worked too hard to let my mission be compromised by a primitive piece of technology like you!
Hey! Nobody trashes H.E.R.B.I.E....

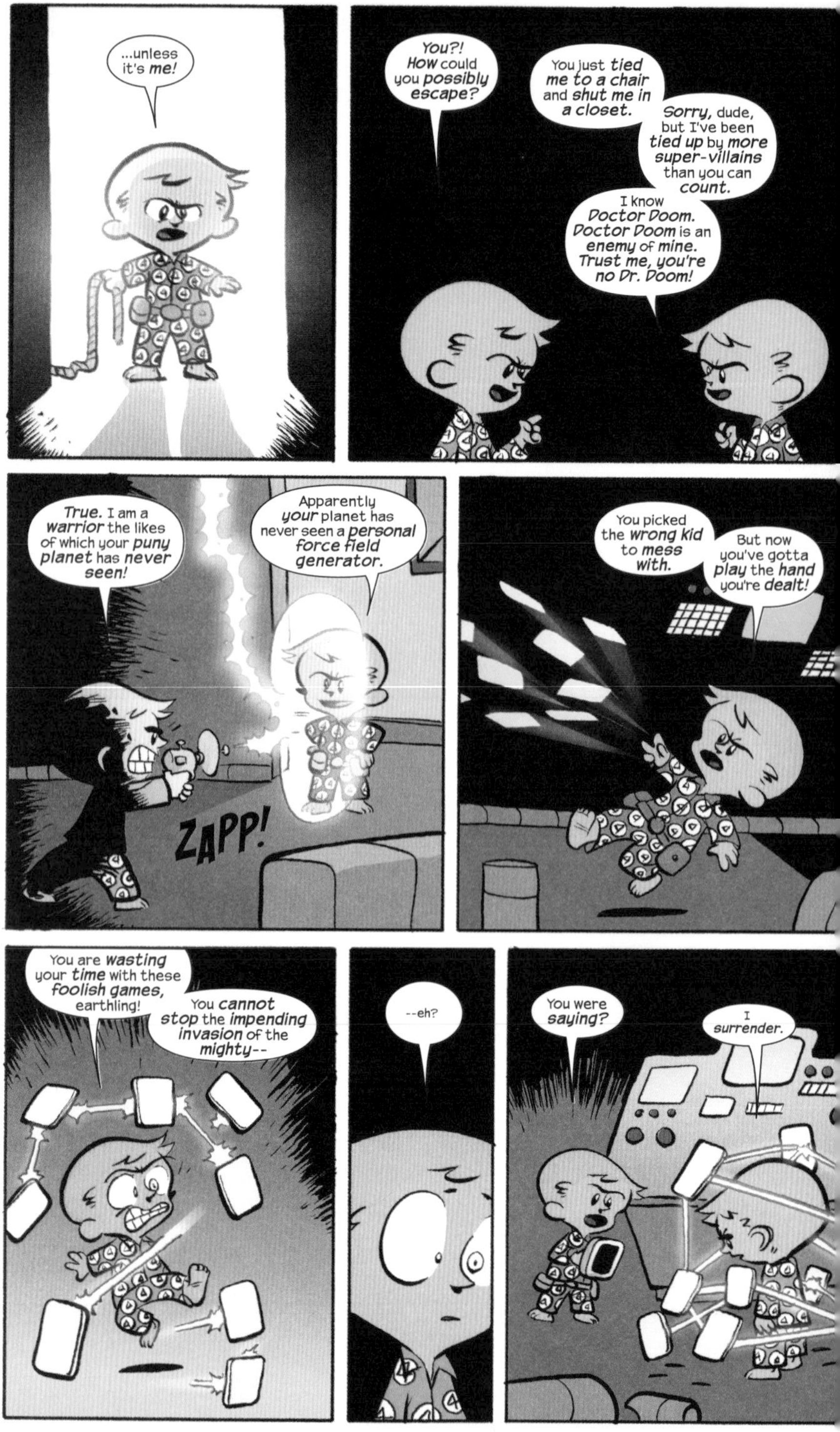
...unless it's *me!*
You?! *How* could you *possibly escape?*
You just *tied me to a chair* and *shut me in a closet.*
Sorry, dude, but I've been *tied up* by *more super-villains* than you can *count.*
I know *Doctor Doom. Doctor Doom* is an *enemy* of mine. *Trust me, you're no Dr. Doom!*
True. I am a *warrior* the likes of which your *puny planet* has *never seen!*
Apparently *your* planet has never seen a *personal force field generator.*
ZAPP!
You picked the *wrong kid* to *mess with.*
But now you've gotta *play* the *hand* you're *dealt!*
You are *wasting* your *time* with these *foolish games,* earthling!
You *cannot stop* the *impending invasion* of the *mighty--*
--eh?
You were *saying?*
I *surrender.*

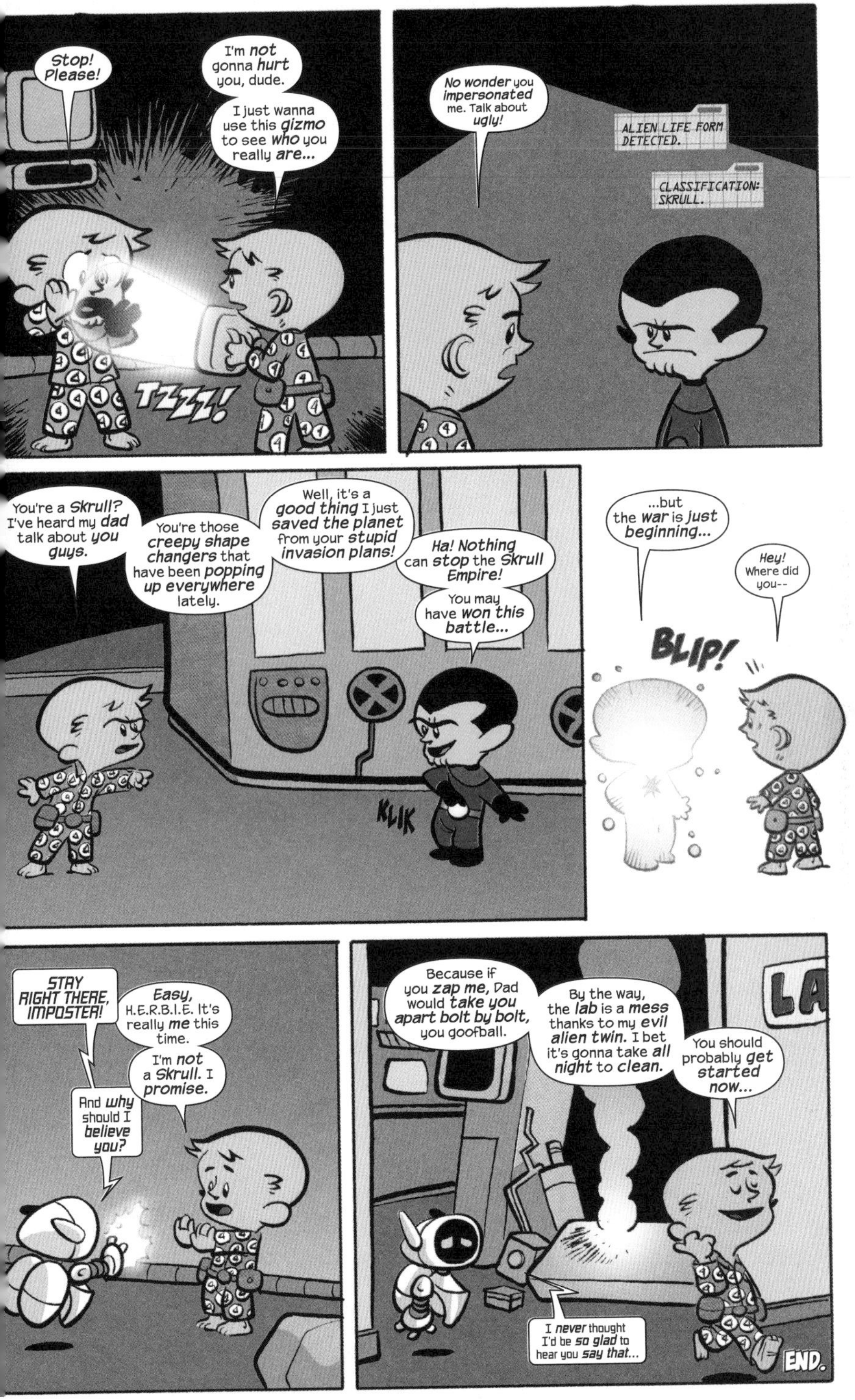

Stop! Please!
I'm not gonna hurt you, dude.
I just wanna use this gizmo to see who you really are...
TZZZ!
No wonder you impersonated me. Talk about ugly!
ALIEN LIFE FORM DETECTED.
CLASSIFICATION: SKRULL.
You're a Skrull? I've heard my dad talk about you guys.
You're those creepy shape changers that have been popping up everywhere lately.
Well, it's a good thing I just saved the planet from your stupid invasion plans!
Ha! Nothing can stop the Skrull Empire!
You may have won this battle...
KLIK
...but the war is just beginning...
BLIP!
Hey! Where did you--
STAY RIGHT THERE, IMPOSTER!
Easy, H.E.R.B.I.E. It's really me this time.
I'm not a Skrull. I promise.
And why should I believe you?
Because if you zap me, Dad would take you apart bolt by bolt, you goofball.
By the way, the lab is a mess thanks to my evil alien twin. I bet it's gonna take all night to clean.
You should probably get started now...
I never thought I'd be so glad to hear you say that...
END.

FRANKLIN RICHARDS SON OF A GENIUS IN: LITTLE LIZARD NO LONGER

CHRIS ELIOPOULOS STORY AND ART
BRAD ANDERSON COLORS
MARK PANICCIA CONSULTING
NATHAN COS EDITOR

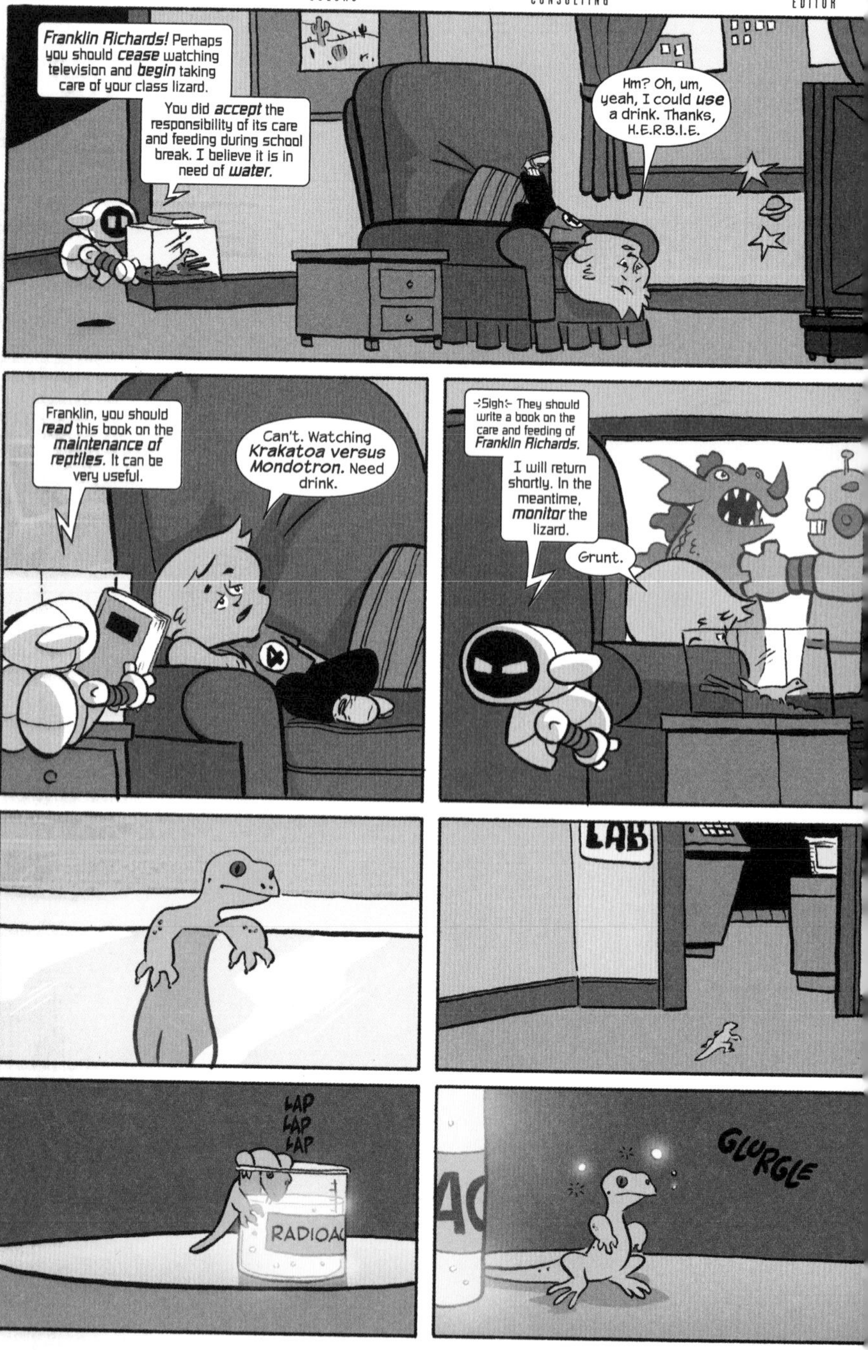
Franklin Richards! Perhaps you should cease watching television and begin taking care of your class lizard.
You did accept the responsibility of its care and feeding during school break. I believe it is in need of water.
Hm? Oh, um, yeah, I could use a drink. Thanks, H.E.R.B.I.E.
Franklin, you should read this book on the maintenance of reptiles. It can be very useful.
Can't. Watching Krakatoa versus Mondotron. Need drink.
Sigh They should write a book on the care and feeding of Franklin Richards.
I will return shortly. In the meantime, monitor the lizard.
Grunt.
LAB
LAP LAP LAP
RADIOAC
GLURGLE

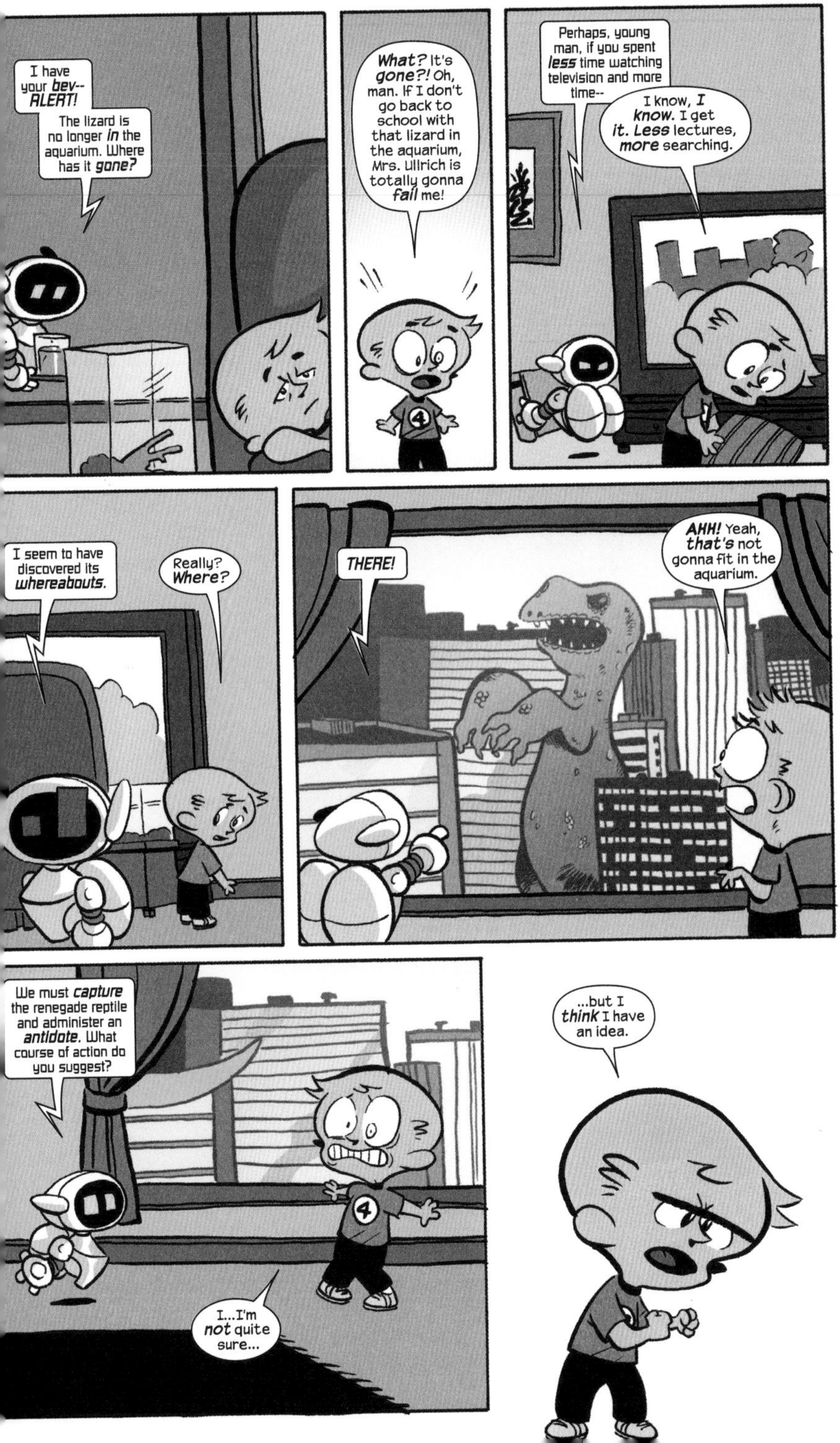

I have your *bev*-- *ALERT!*
The lizard is no longer *in* the aquarium. Where has it *gone?*
What? It's *gone?!* Oh, man. If I don't go back to school with that lizard in the aquarium, Mrs. Ullrich is totally gonna *fail* me!
Perhaps, young man, if you spent *less* time watching television and more time--
I know, *I know.* I get *it. Less* lectures, *more* searching.
I seem to have discovered its *whereabouts.*
Really? *Where?*
THERE!
AHH! Yeah, *that's* not gonna fit in the aquarium.
We must *capture* the renegade reptile and administer an *antidote.* What course of action do you suggest?
I...I'm *not* quite sure...
...but I *think* I have an idea.

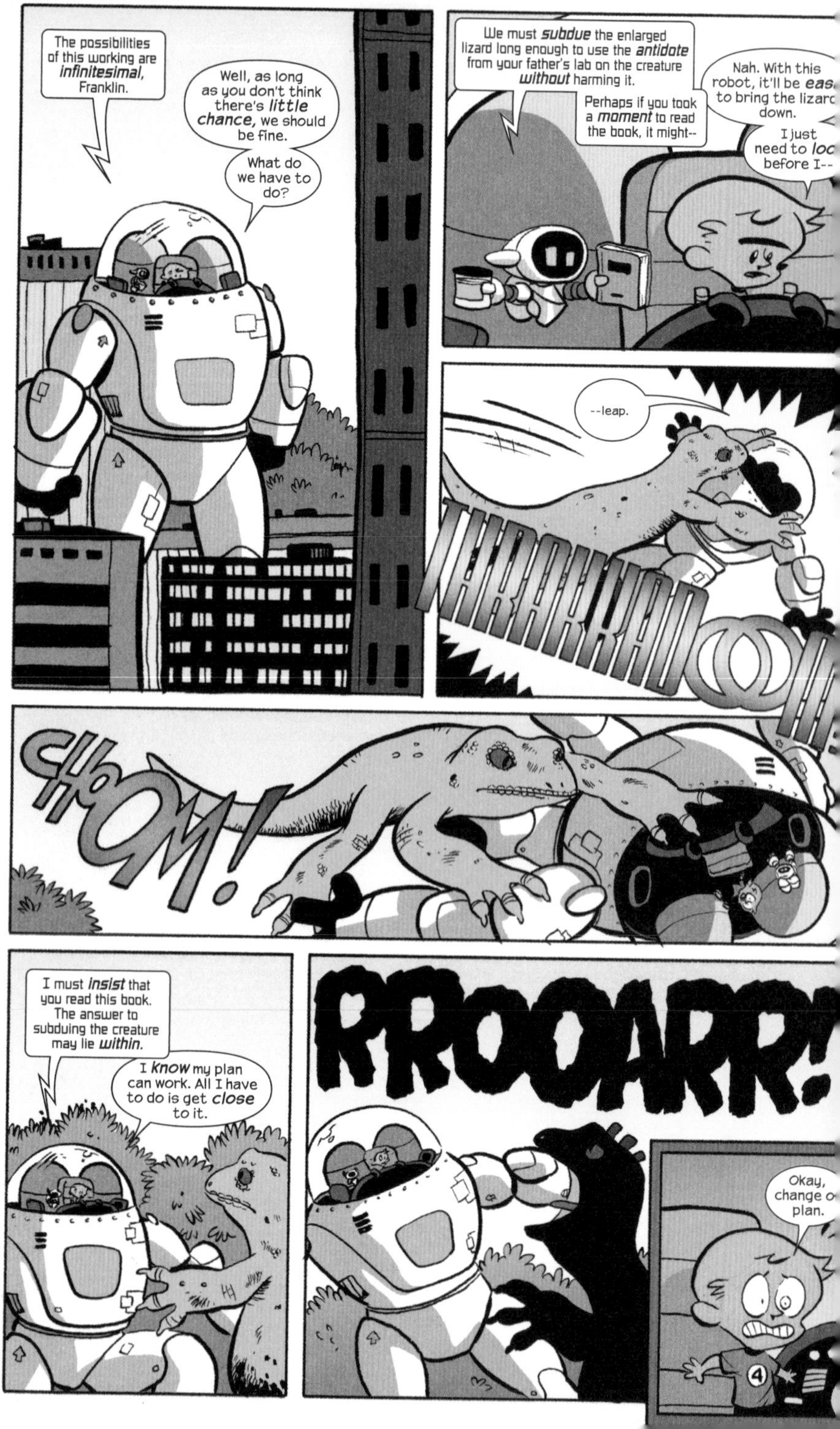

The possibilities of this working are *infinitesimal*, Franklin.
Well, as long as you don't think there's *little chance,* we should be fine.
What do we have to do?
We must *subdue* the enlarged lizard long enough to use the *antidote* from your father's lab on the creature *without* harming it.
Perhaps if you took a *moment* to read the book, it might--
Nah. With this robot, it'll be eas to bring the lizarc down.
I just need to loc before I--
--leap.
THRAKKADOOM
CHOMP!
I must *insist* that you read this book. The answer to subduing the creature may lie *within*.
I *know* my plan can work. All I have to do is get *close* to it.
RROOARR!
Okay, change o plan.

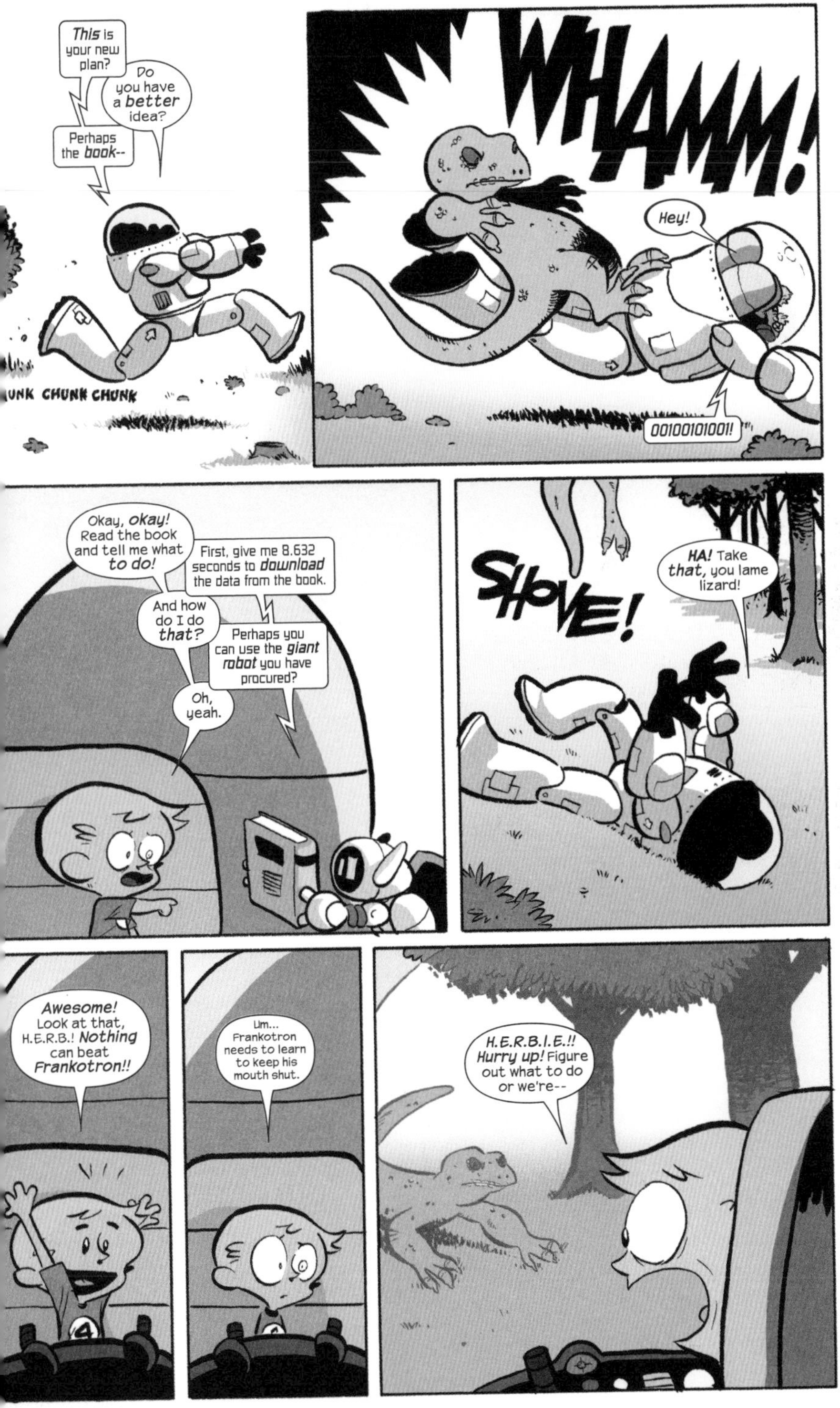

This is your new plan?
Do you have a better idea?
Perhaps the book--
UNK CHUNK CHUNK
WHAMM!
Hey!
00100101001!
Okay, okay! Read the book and tell me what to do!
First, give me 8.632 seconds to download the data from the book.
And how do I do that?
Perhaps you can use the giant robot you have procured?
Oh, yeah.
SHOVE!
HA! Take that, you lame lizard!
Awesome! Look at that, H.E.R.B.! Nothing can beat Frankotron!!
Um... Frankotron needs to learn to keep his mouth shut.
H.E.R.B.I.E.!! Hurry up! Figure out what to do or we're--

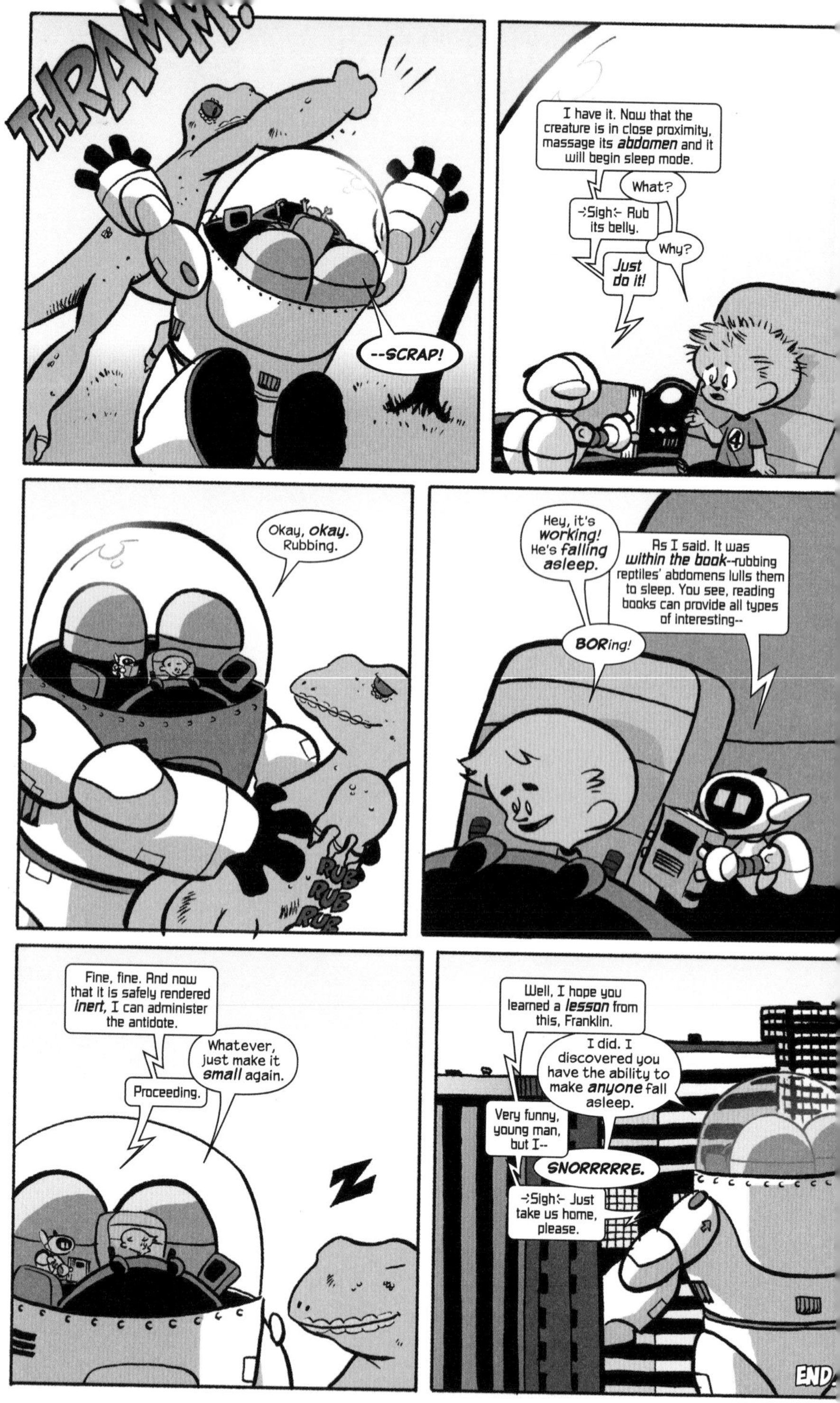
THRAMM!
--SCRAP!
I have it. Now that the creature is in close proximity, massage its *abdomen* and it will begin sleep mode.
What?
-Sigh- Rub its belly.
Why?
Just do it!
Okay, *okay.* Rubbing.
RUB RUB RUB
Hey, it's *working!* He's *falling asleep.*
As I said. It was *within the book*--rubbing reptiles' abdomens lulls them to sleep. You see, reading books can provide all types of interesting--
*BOR*ing!
Fine, fine. And now that it is safely rendered *inert*, I can administer the antidote.
Whatever, just make it *small* again.
Proceeding.
Z
Well, I hope you learned a *lesson* from this, Franklin.
I did. I discovered you have the ability to make *anyone* fall asleep.
Very funny, young man, but I--
SNORRRRRE.
-Sigh- Just take us home, please.
END

RANKLIN ICHARDS SON OF A GENIUS IN: THE *OTHER* FOOTBALL!

MARC SUMERAK STORY CHRIS ELIOPOULOS ART

BRAD ANDERSON COLORS MARK PANICCIA CONSULTING NATHAN COSBY EDITOR

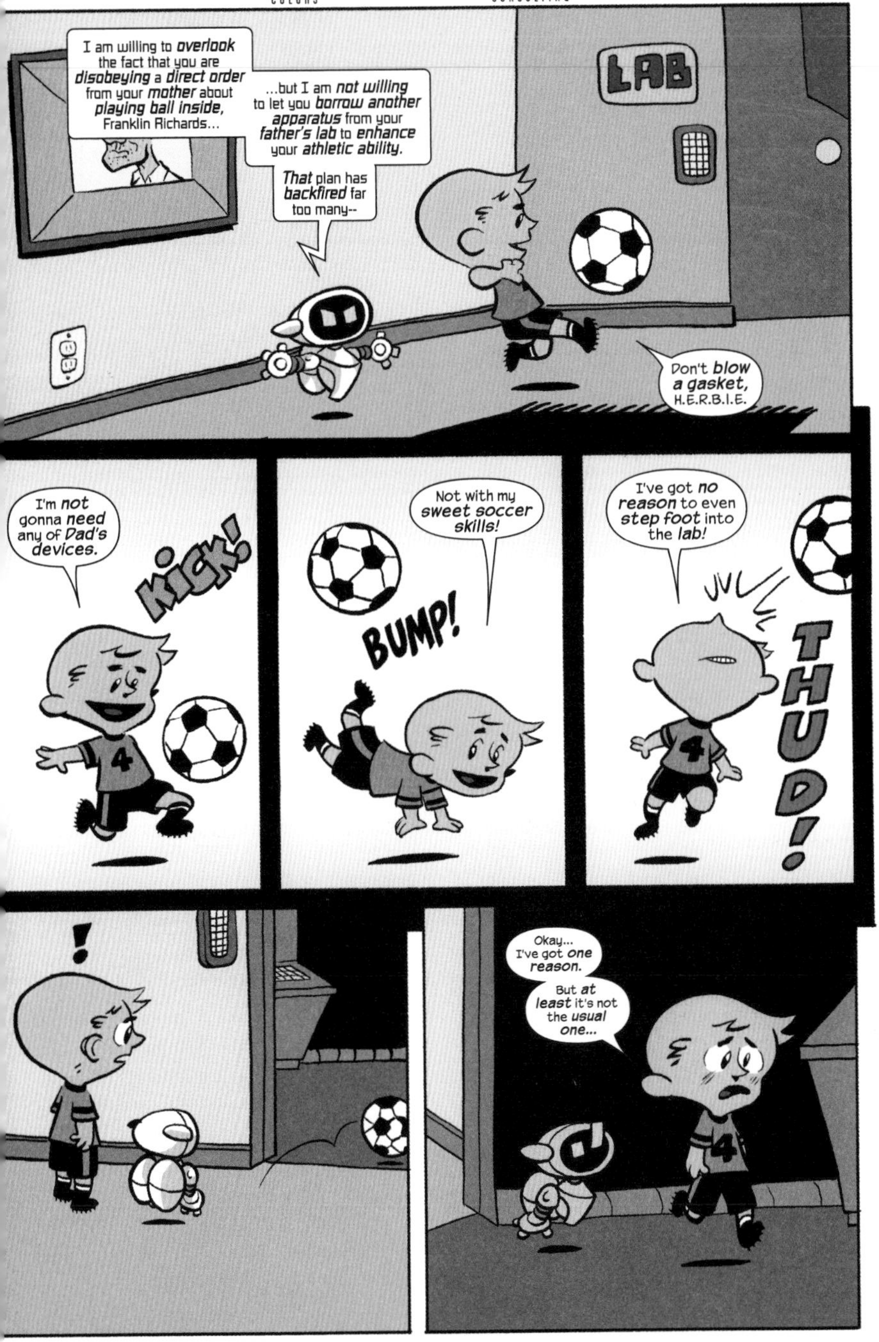

LAB
I am willing to overlook the fact that you are disobeying a direct order from your mother about playing ball inside, Franklin Richards...
...but I am not willing to let you borrow another apparatus from your father's lab to enhance your athletic ability.
That plan has backfired far too many--
Don't blow a gasket, H.E.R.B.I.E.
I'm not gonna need any of Dad's devices.
KICK!
Not with my sweet soccer skills!
BUMP!
I've got no reason to even step foot into the lab!
THUD!
!
Okay... I've got one reason.
But at least it's not the usual one...

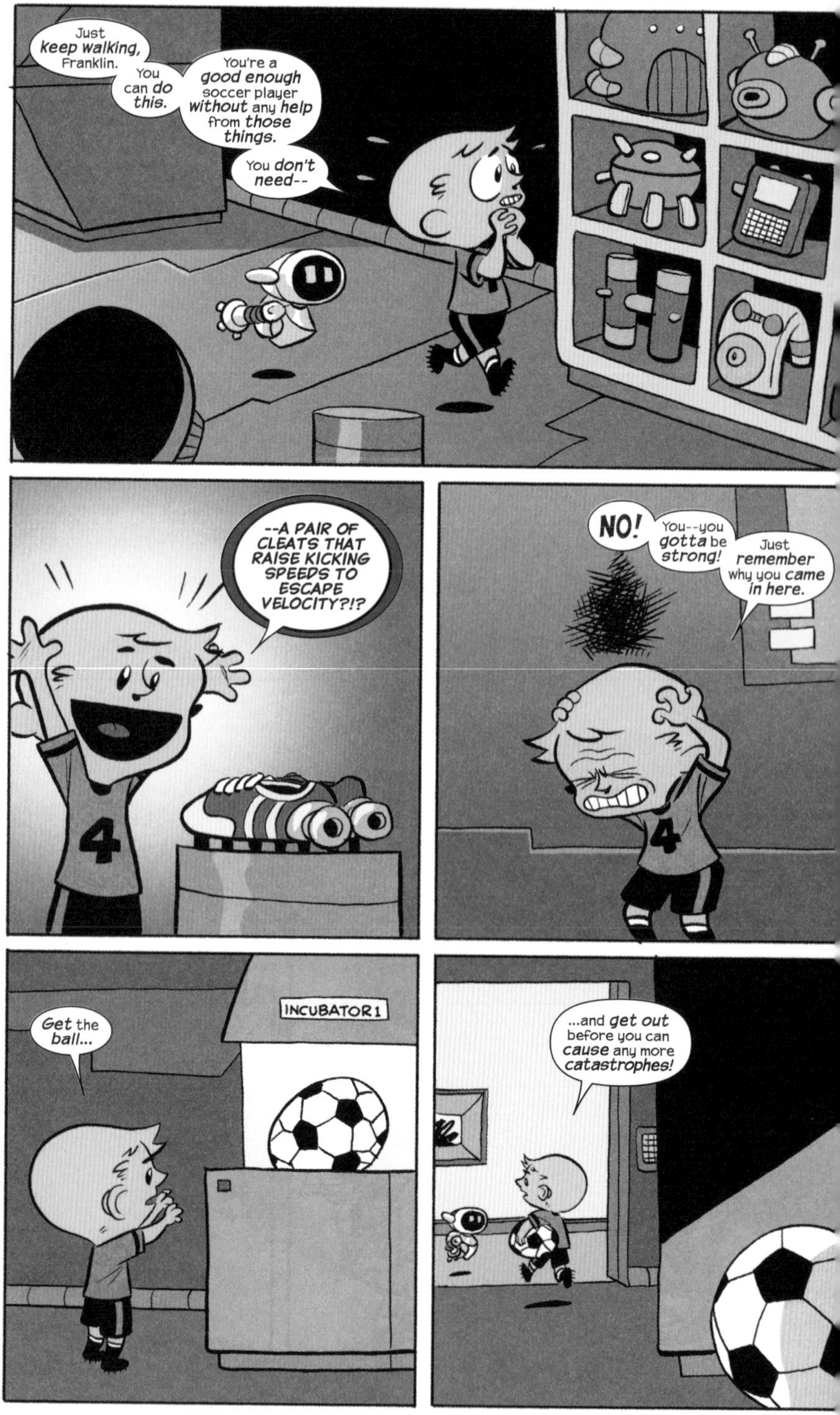

Just keep walking, Franklin.
You can do this.
You're a good enough soccer player without any help from those things.
You don't need--
--A PAIR OF CLEATS THAT RAISE KICKING SPEEDS TO ESCAPE VELOCITY?!?
NO!
You--you gotta be strong!
Just remember why you came in here.
Get the ball...
INCUBATOR 1
...and get out before you can cause any more catastrophes!

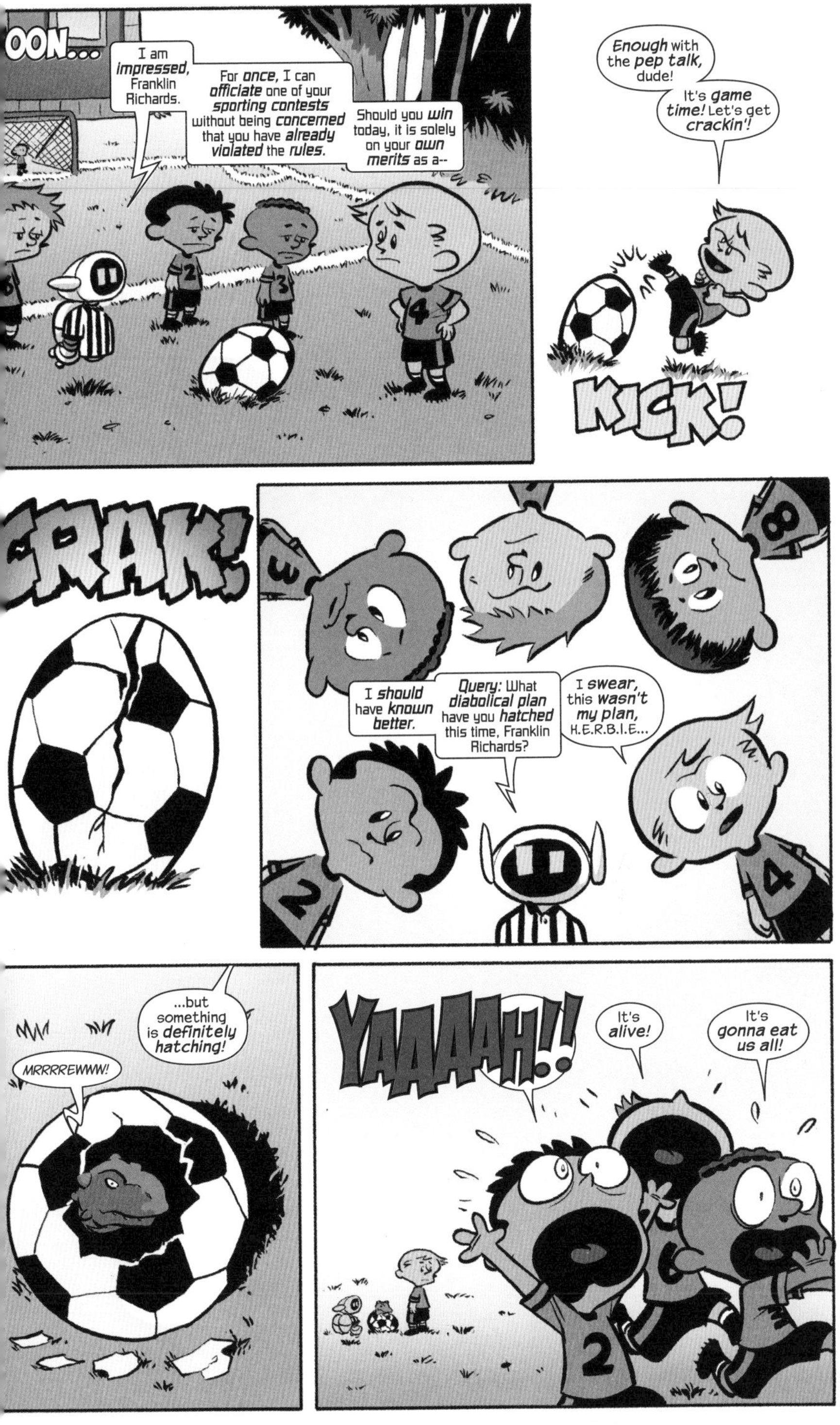

OON...
I am impressed, Franklin Richards.
For once, I can officiate one of your sporting contests without being concerned that you have already violated the rules.
Should you win today, it is solely on your own merits as a--
Enough with the pep talk, dude!
It's game time! Let's get crackin'!
KICK!
CRAK!
I should have known better.
Query: What diabolical plan have you hatched this time, Franklin Richards?
I swear, this wasn't my plan, H.E.R.B.I.E...
...but something is definitely hatching!
MRRRREWWW!
YAAAAH!!
It's alive!
It's gonna eat us all!

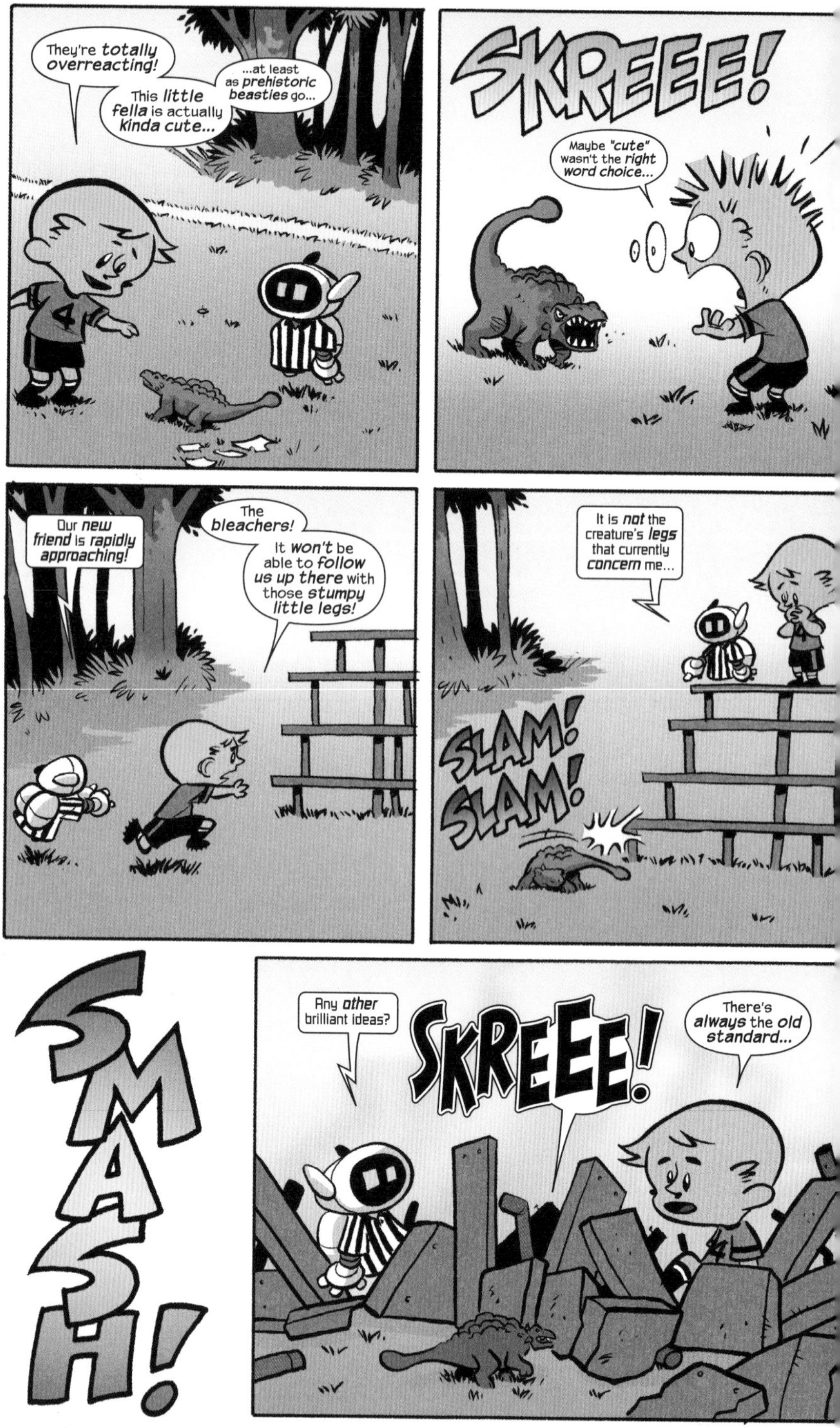

They're *totally overreacting!*
This *little fella* is actually *kinda cute...*
...at least as *prehistoric beasties* go...
SKREEE!
Maybe *"cute"* wasn't the *right word choice...*
Our *new friend* is *rapidly approaching!*
The *bleachers!*
It *won't* be able to *follow us up there* with those *stumpy little legs!*
It is *not* the creature's *legs* that currently *concern* me...
SLAM! SLAM!
SMASH!
Any *other* brilliant ideas?
SKREEE!
There's *always* the *old standard...*

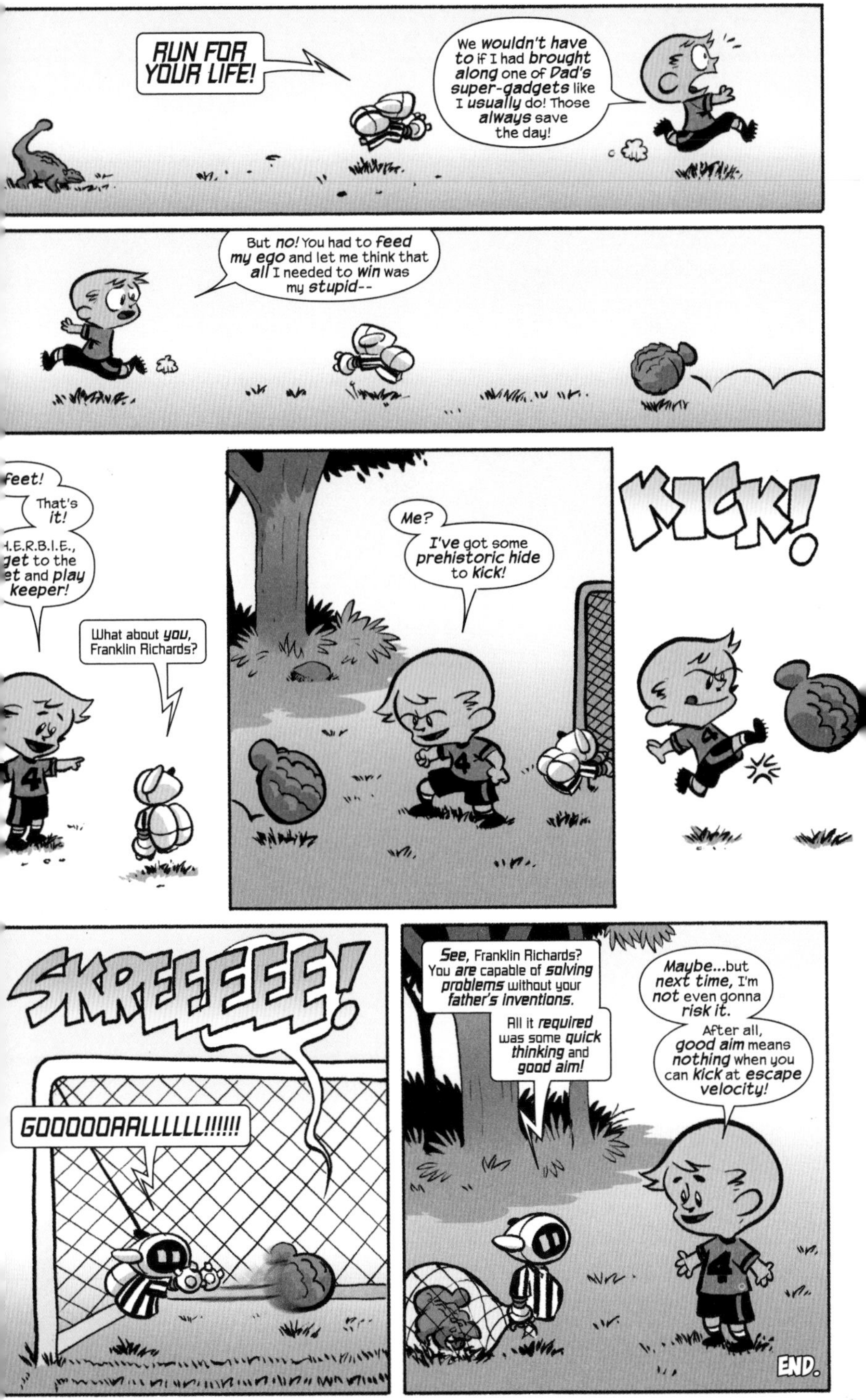

RUN FOR YOUR LIFE!
We wouldn't have to if I had brought along one of Dad's super-gadgets like I usually do! Those always save the day!
But no! You had to feed my ego and let me think that all I needed to win was my stupid--
feet!
That's it!
H.E.R.B.I.E., get to the net and play keeper!
What about you, Franklin Richards?
Me?
I've got some prehistoric hide to kick!
KICK!
SKREEEEEE!
GOOOOOAALLLLLL!!!!!!
See, Franklin Richards? You are capable of solving problems without your father's inventions.
All it required was some quick thinking and good aim!
Maybe...but next time, I'm not even gonna risk it.
After all, good aim means nothing when you can kick at escape velocity!
END.

FRANKLIN RICHARDS SON OF A GENIUS IN: Squid Squabble

BY CHRIS ELIOPOULOS & MARC SUMERA

BRAD ANDERSON COLORS · MARK PANICCIA CONSULTING · NATHAN COS EDITOR

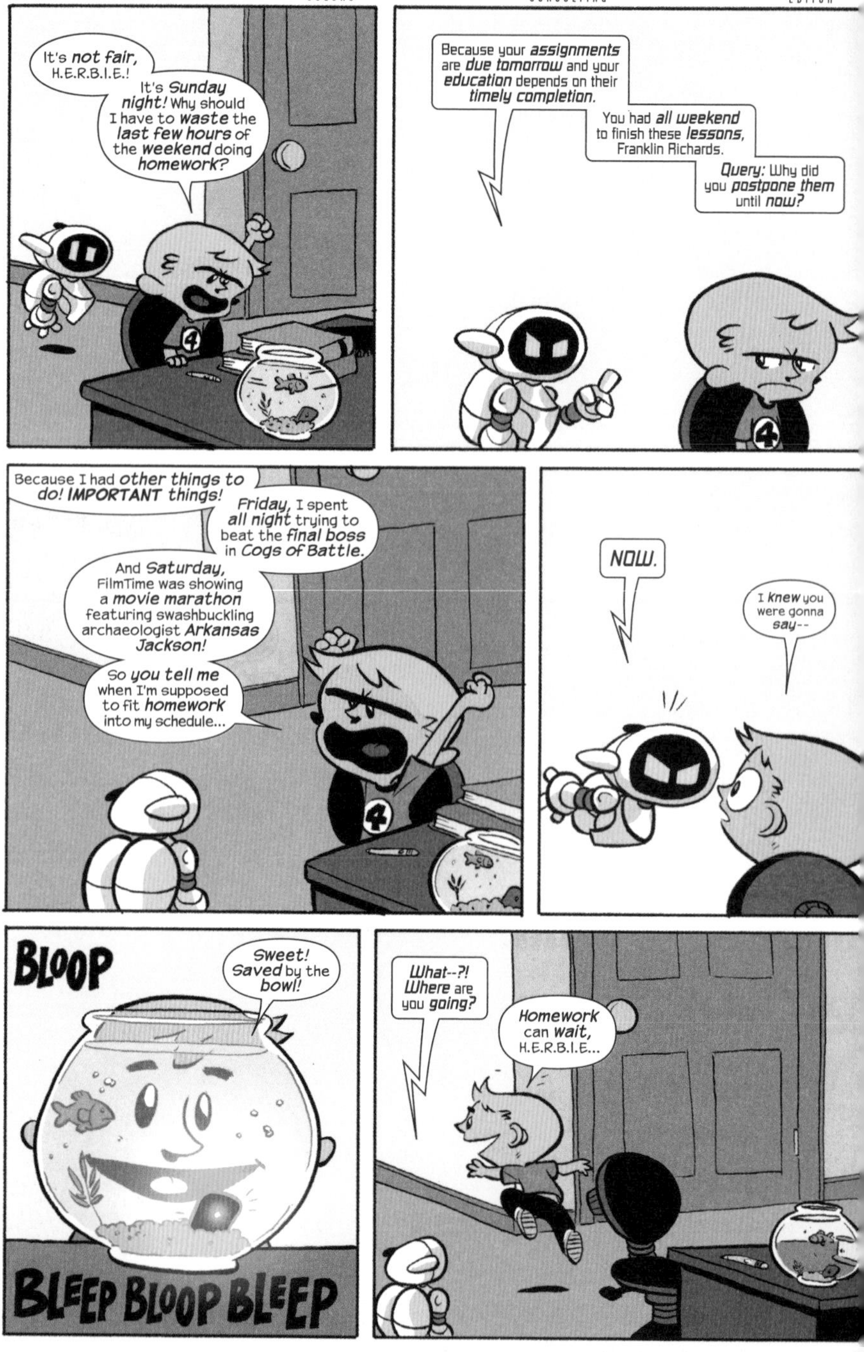

It's not fair, H.E.R.B.I.E.!
It's Sunday night! Why should I have to waste the last few hours of the weekend doing homework?
Because your assignments are due tomorrow and your education depends on their timely completion.
You had all weekend to finish these lessons, Franklin Richards.
Query: Why did you postpone them until now?
Because I had other things to do! IMPORTANT things!
Friday, I spent all night trying to beat the final boss in Cogs of Battle.
And Saturday, FilmTime was showing a movie marathon featuring swashbuckling archaeologist Arkansas Jackson!
So you tell me when I'm supposed to fit homework into my schedule...
NOW.
I knew you were gonna say--
BLOOP
Sweet! Saved by the bowl!
BLEEP BLOOP BLEEP
What--?! Where are you going?
Homework can wait, H.E.R.B.I.E...

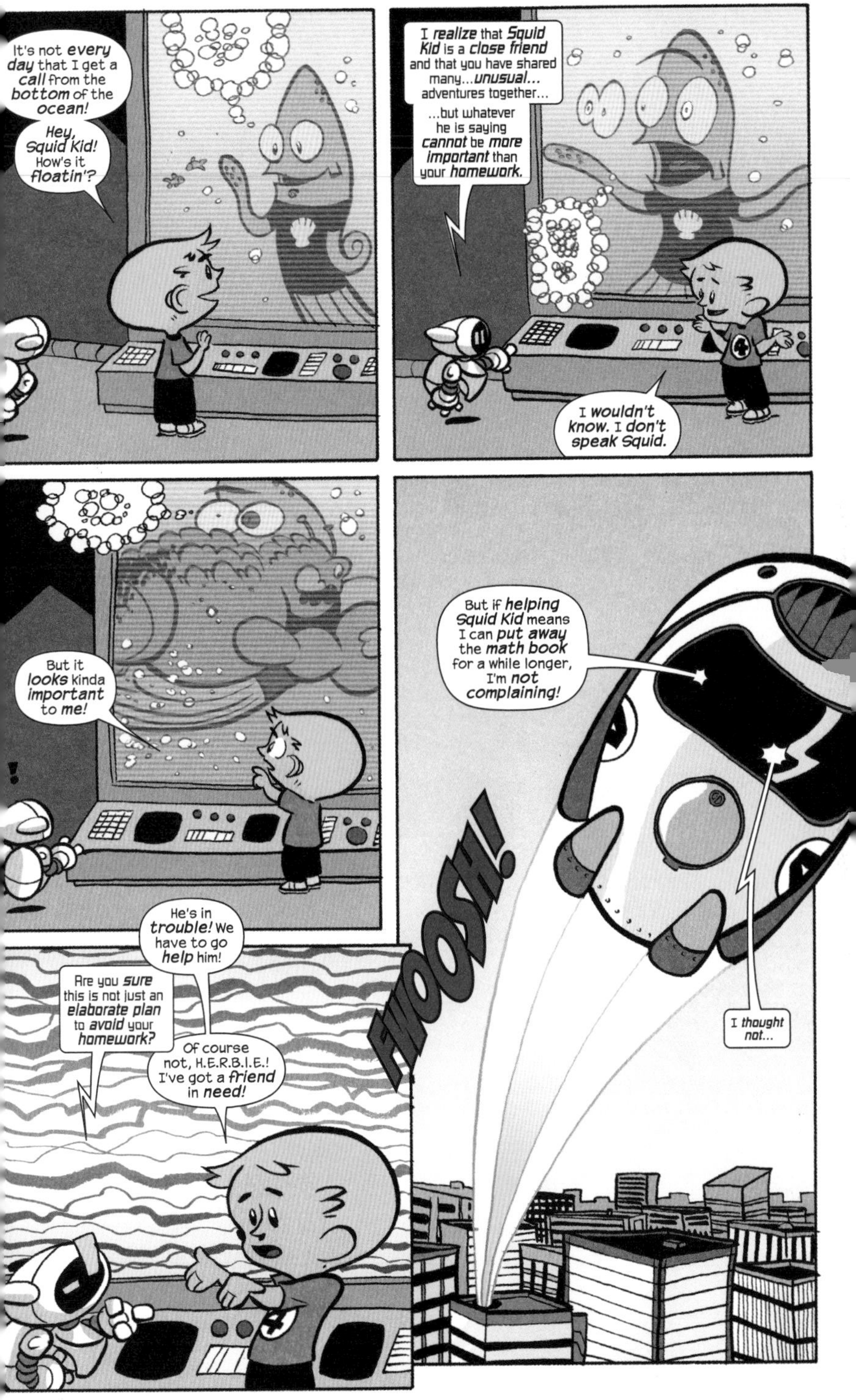

It's not every day that I get a call from the bottom of the ocean!
Hey, Squid Kid! How's it floatin'?
I realize that Squid Kid is a close friend and that you have shared many...unusual... adventures together...
...but whatever he is saying cannot be more important than your homework.
I wouldn't know. I don't speak Squid.
But it looks kinda important to me!
He's in trouble! We have to go help him!
Are you sure this is not just an elaborate plan to avoid your homework?
Of course not, H.E.R.B.I.E.! I've got a friend in need!
But if helping Squid Kid means I can put away the math book for a while longer, I'm not complaining!
FWOOSH!!
I thought not...

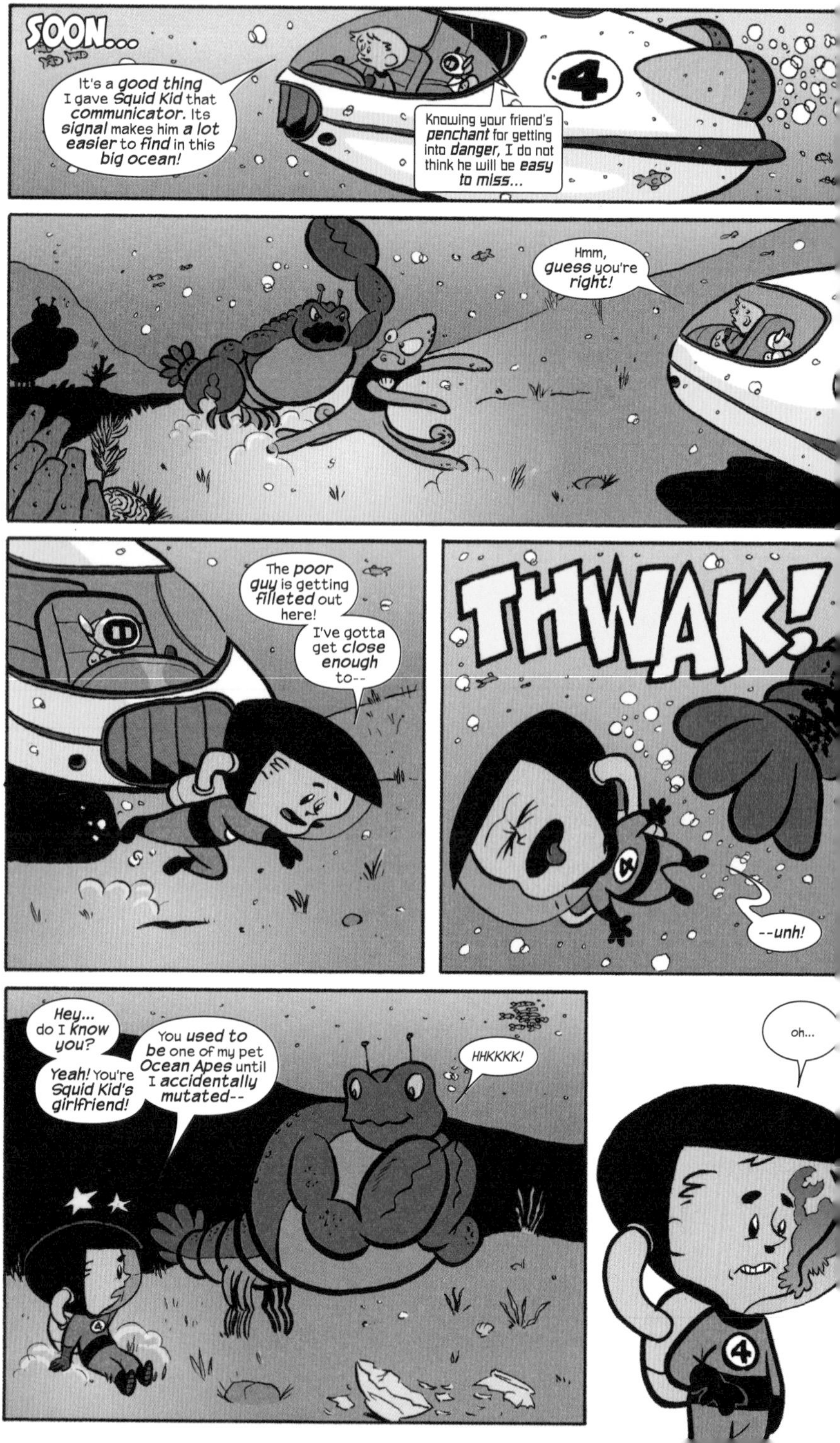
SOON...
It's a good thing I gave Squid Kid that communicator. Its signal makes him a lot easier to find in this big ocean!
Knowing your friend's penchant for getting into danger, I do not think he will be easy to miss...
Hmm, guess you're right!
The poor guy is getting filleted out here!
I've gotta get close enough to--
THWAK!
--unh!
Hey... do I know you?
Yeah! You're Squid Kid's girlfriend!
You used to be one of my pet Ocean Apes until I accidentally mutated--
HHKKKK!
oh...

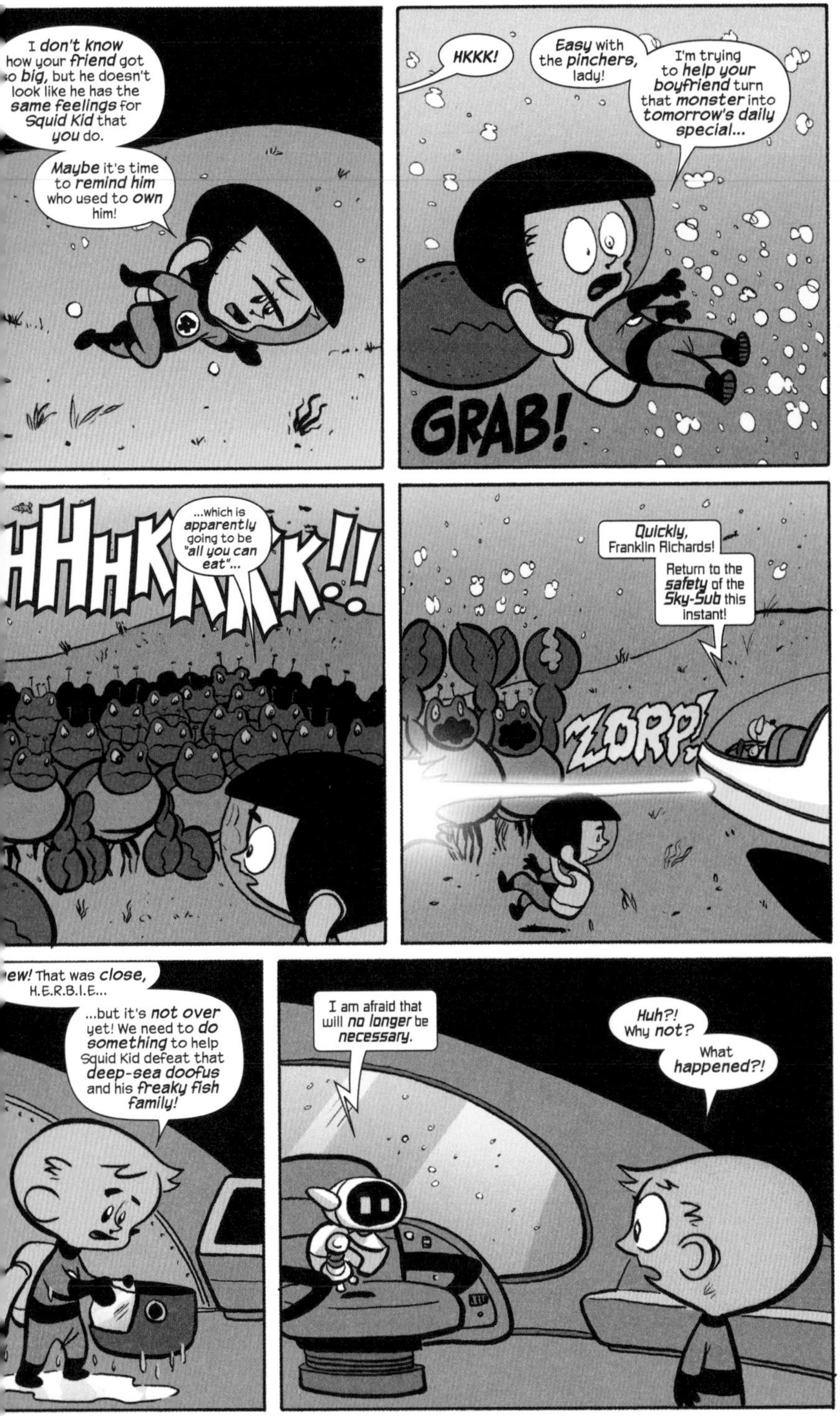
I don't know how your friend got so big, but he doesn't look like he has the same feelings for Squid Kid that you do.
Maybe it's time to remind him who used to own him!
HKKK!
Easy with the pinchers, lady!
I'm trying to help your boyfriend turn that monster into tomorrow's daily special...
GRAB!
HHHKKKK!!
...which is apparently going to be "all you can eat"...
Quickly, Franklin Richards!
Return to the safety of the Sky-Sub this instant!
ZORP!
ew! That was close, H.E.R.B.I.E...
...but it's not over yet! We need to do something to help Squid Kid defeat that deep-sea doofus and his freaky fish family!
I am afraid that will no longer be necessary.
Huh?! Why not?
What happened?!

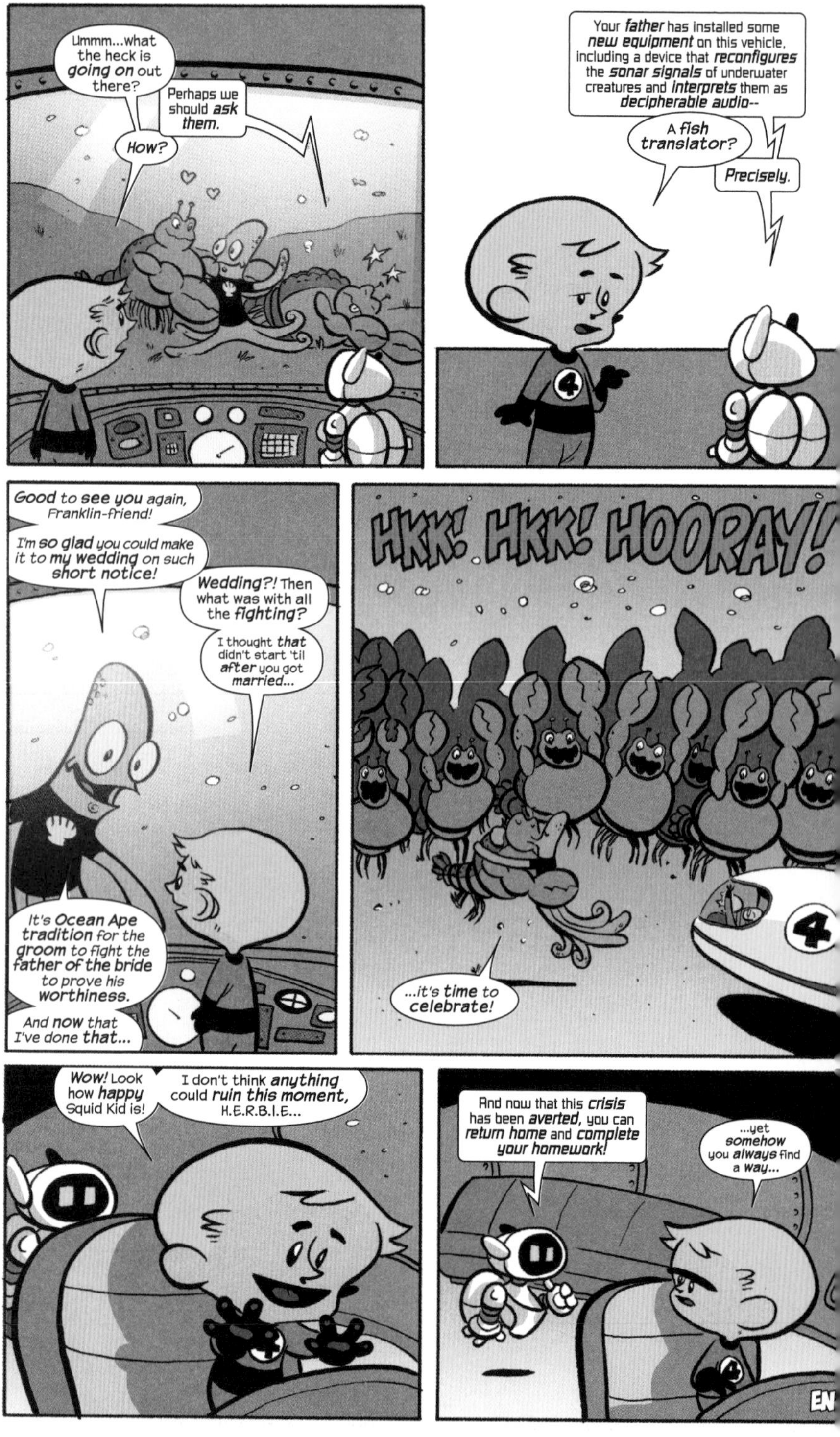

Ummm...what the heck is going on out there?
Perhaps we should ask them.
How?
Your father has installed some new equipment on this vehicle, including a device that reconfigures the sonar signals of underwater creatures and interprets them as decipherable audio--
A fish translator?
Precisely.
Good to see you again, Franklin-friend!
I'm so glad you could make it to my wedding on such short notice!
Wedding?! Then what was with all the fighting?
I thought that didn't start 'til after you got married...
It's Ocean Ape tradition for the groom to fight the father of the bride to prove his worthiness.
And now that I've done that...
HKK! HKK! HOORAY!
...it's time to celebrate!
Wow! Look how happy Squid Kid is!
I don't think anything could ruin this moment, H.E.R.B.I.E...
And now that this crisis has been averted, you can return home and complete your homework!
...yet somehow you always find a way...
EN

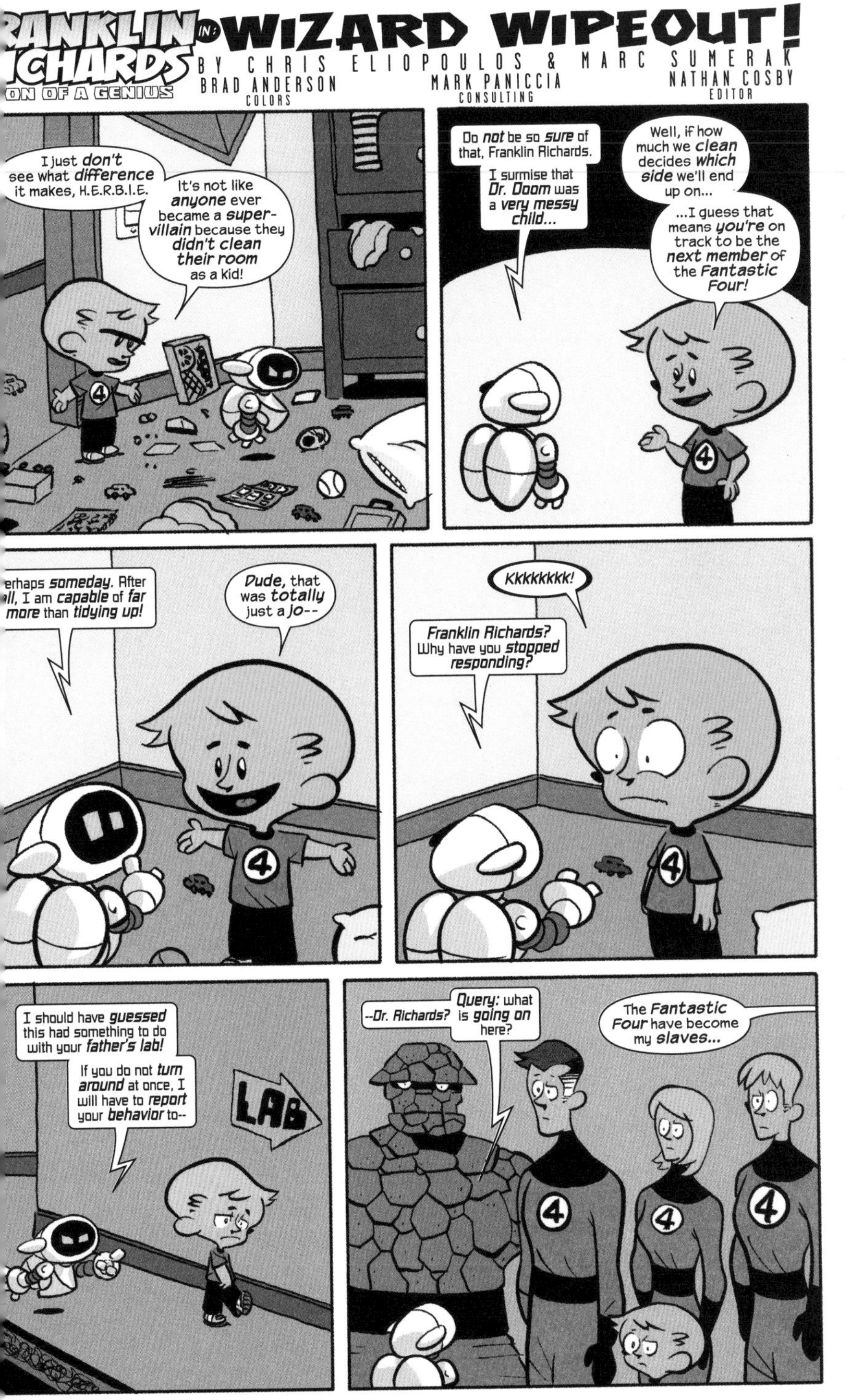
FRANKLIN RICHARDS
SON OF A GENIUS
IN: WIZARD WIPEOUT!
BY CHRIS ELIOPOULOS & MARC SUMERAK
BRAD ANDERSON COLORS
MARK PANICCIA CONSULTING
NATHAN COSBY EDITOR
I just don't see what difference it makes, H.E.R.B.I.E.
It's not like anyone ever became a super-villain because they didn't clean their room as a kid!
Do not be so sure of that, Franklin Richards.
I surmise that Dr. Doom was a very messy child...
Well, if how much we clean decides which side we'll end up on...
...I guess that means you're on track to be the next member of the Fantastic Four!
erhaps someday. After ll, I am capable of far more than tidying up!
Dude, that was totally just a jo--
Kkkkkkkk!
Franklin Richards? Why have you stopped responding?
I should have guessed this had something to do with your father's lab!
If you do not turn around at once, I will have to report your behavior to--
LAB
--Dr. Richards?
Query: what is going on here?
The Fantastic Four have become my slaves...

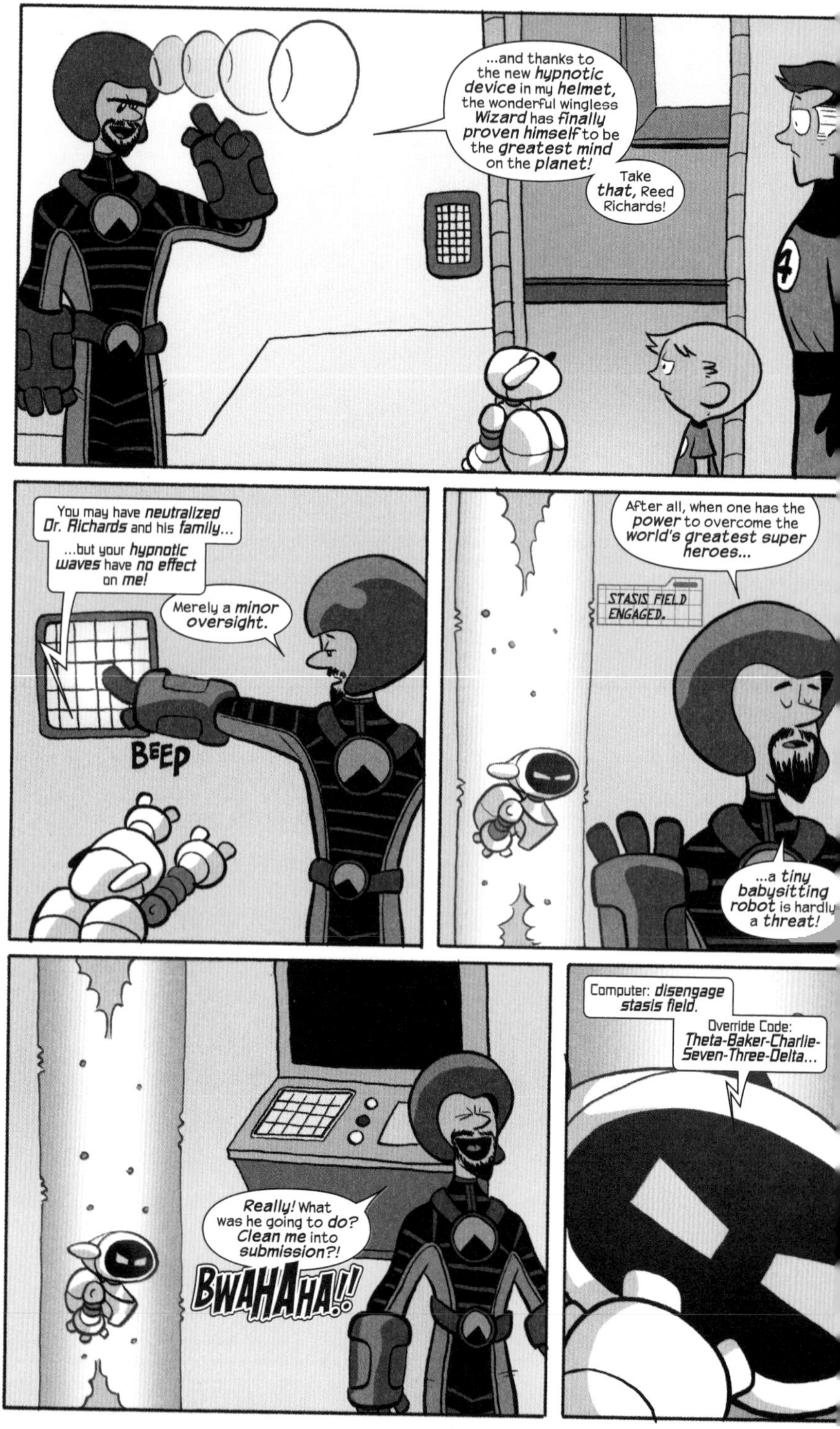

...and thanks to the new hypnotic device in my helmet, the wonderful wingless Wizard has finally proven himself to be the greatest mind on the planet!
Take that, Reed Richards!
You may have neutralized Dr. Richards and his family...
...but your hypnotic waves have no effect on me!
Merely a minor oversight.
BEEP
After all, when one has the power to overcome the world's greatest super heroes...
STASIS FIELD ENGAGED.
...a tiny babysitting robot is hardly a threat!
Really! What was he going to do? Clean me into submission?!
BWAHAHA!!
Computer: disengage stasis field.
Override Code: Theta-Baker-Charlie-Seven-Three-Delta...

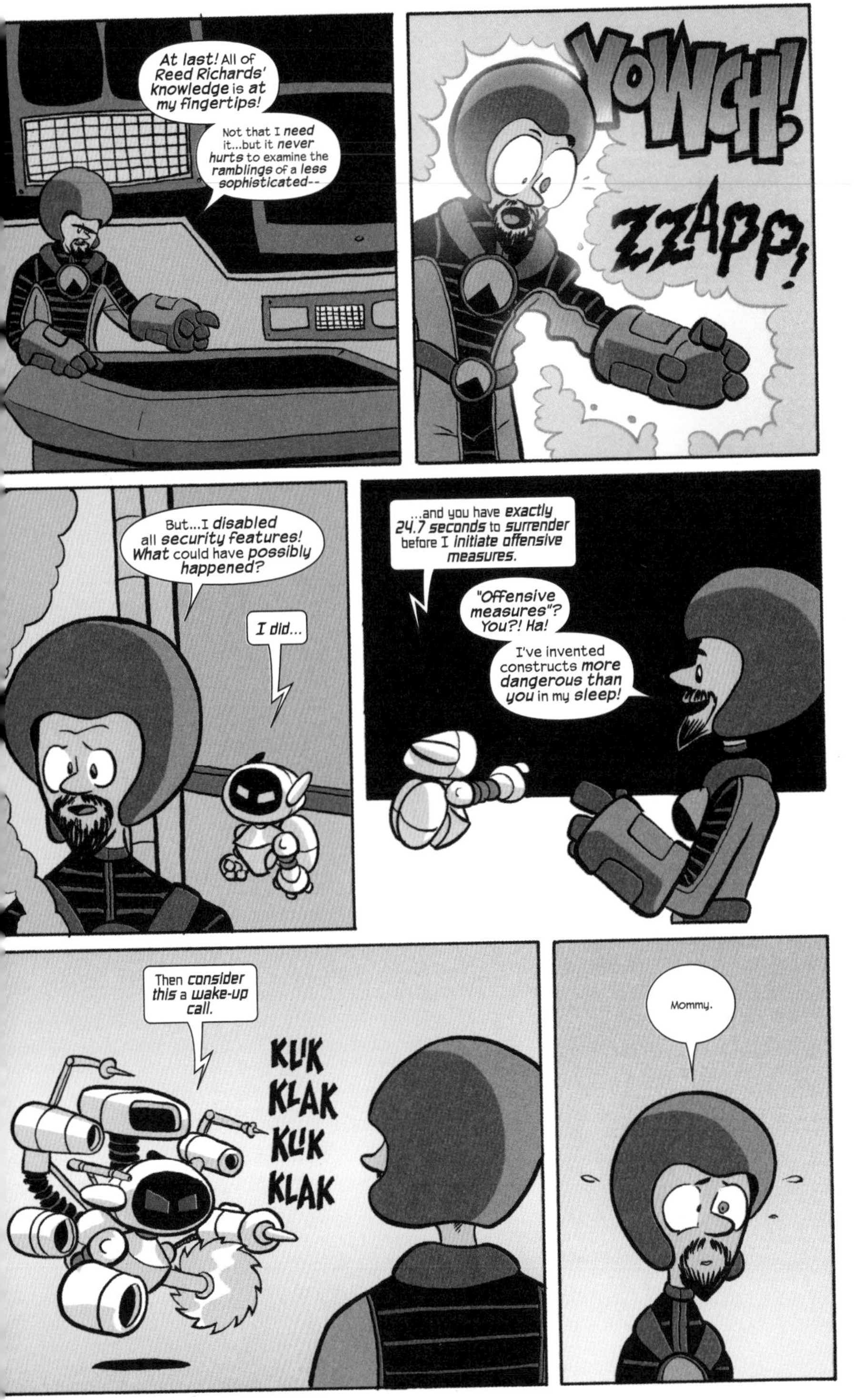
At last! All of Reed Richards' knowledge is at my fingertips!
Not that I need it...but it never hurts to examine the ramblings of a less sophisticated--
YOWCH!
ZZAPP!
But...I disabled all security features! What could have possibly happened?
I did...
...and you have exactly 24.7 seconds to surrender before I initiate offensive measures.
"Offensive measures"? You?! Ha!
I've invented constructs more dangerous than you in my sleep!
Then consider this a wake-up call.
KLIK
KLAK
KLIK
KLAK
Mommy.

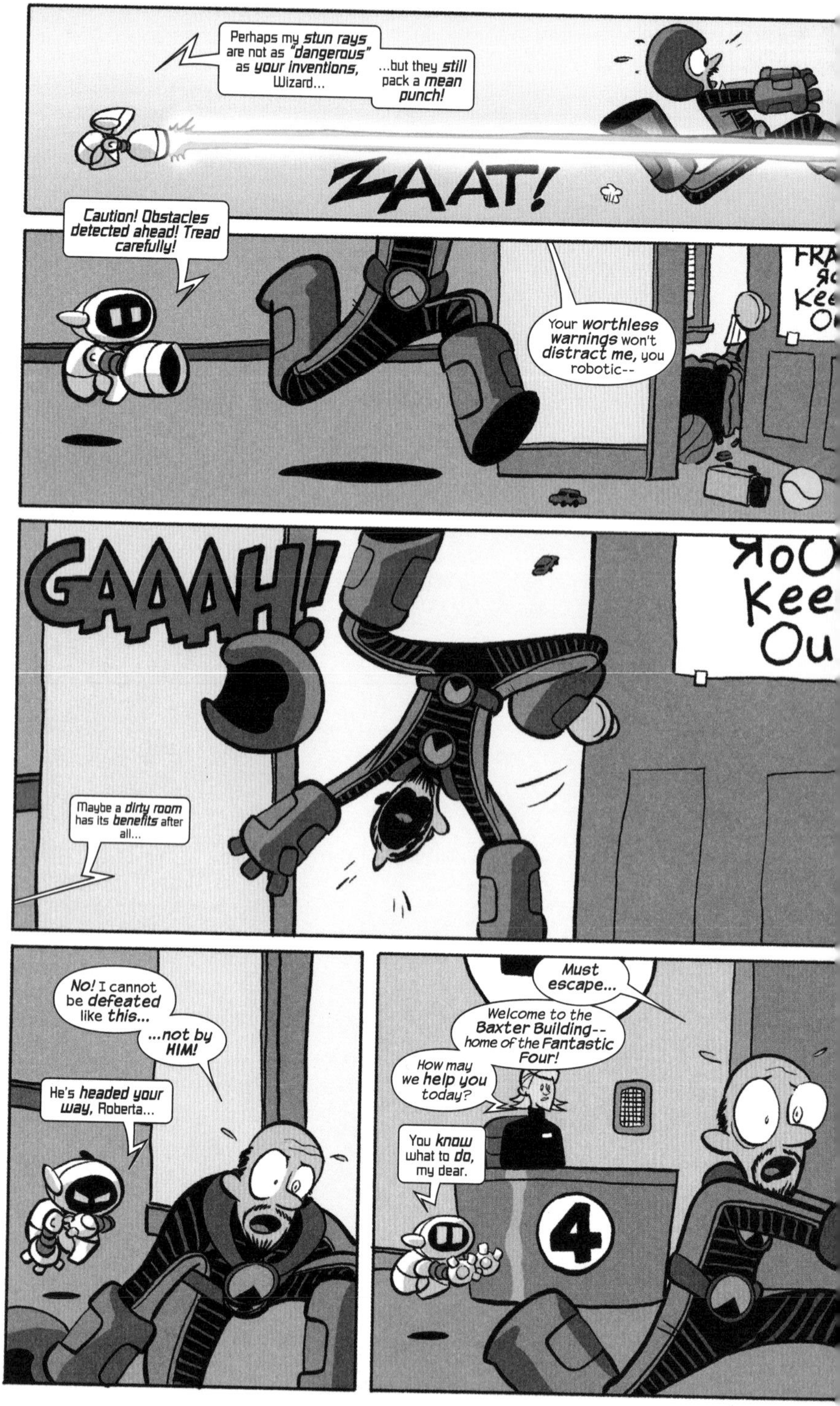

Perhaps my stun rays are not as "dangerous" as your inventions, Wizard...
...but they still pack a mean punch!
ZAAT!
Caution! Obstacles detected ahead! Tread carefully!
Your worthless warnings won't distract me, you robotic--
GAAAH!
Maybe a dirty room has its benefits after all...
No! I cannot be defeated like this...
...not by HIM!
He's headed your way, Roberta...
Must escape...
Welcome to the Baxter Building-- home of the Fantastic Four!
How may we help you today?
You know what to do, my dear.
4

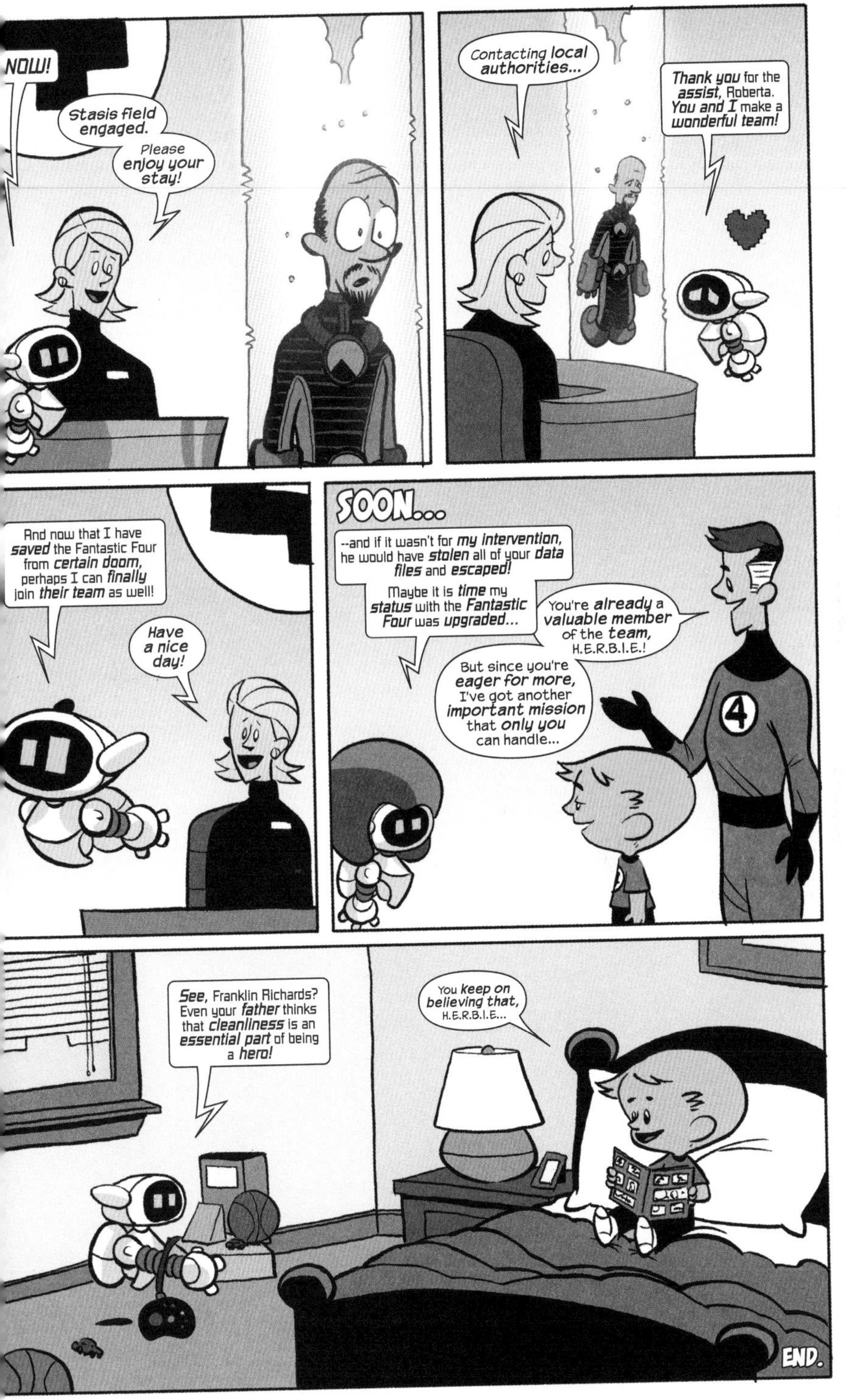
NOW!
Stasis field engaged.
Please enjoy your stay!
Contacting local authorities...
Thank you for the assist, Roberta. You and I make a wonderful team!
And now that I have saved the Fantastic Four from certain doom, perhaps I can finally join their team as well!
Have a nice day!
SOON...
--and if it wasn't for my intervention, he would have stolen all of your data files and escaped!
Maybe it is time my status with the Fantastic Four was upgraded...
You're already a valuable member of the team, H.E.R.B.I.E.!
But since you're eager for more, I've got another important mission that only you can handle...
See, Franklin Richards? Even your father thinks that cleanliness is an essential part of being a hero!
You keep on believing that, H.E.R.B.I.E...
END.

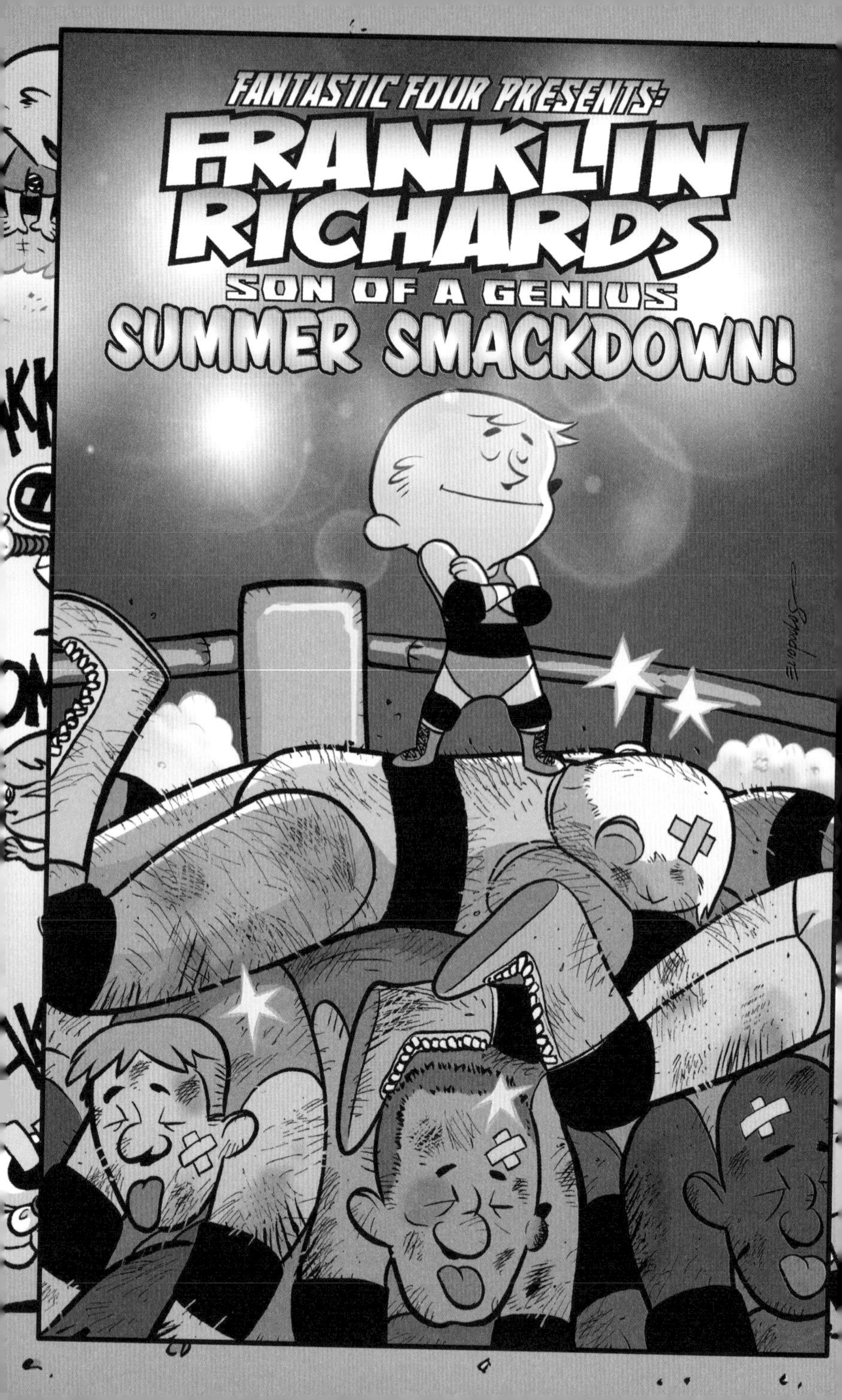
FANTASTIC FOUR PRESENTS:
FRANKLIN RICHARDS
SON OF A GENIUS
SUMMER SMACKDOWN!

FANTASTIC FOUR PRESENTS:
FRANKLIN RICHARDS
SON OF A GENIUS
SUMMER SMACKDOWN!

SHWAK!

CHRIS ELIOPOULOS AND MARC SUMERAK
STORY

MARC SUMERAK
SCRIPT

CHRIS ELIOPOULOS
ART & LETTERS

BRAD ANDERSON
COLOR

IRENE LEE
PRODUCTION

MARK PANICCIA
CONSULTING EDITOR

NATHAN COSBY
EDITOR

JOE QUESADA
EDITOR IN CHIEF

DAN BUCKLEY
PUBLISHER

FRANKLIN RICHARDS SON OF A GENIUS IN: THUNDEROUS THROWDOW

BY CHRIS ELIOPOULOS & MARC SUMERA

BRAD ANDERSON COLORS · MARK PANICCIA CONSULTING · NATHAN COS EDITOR

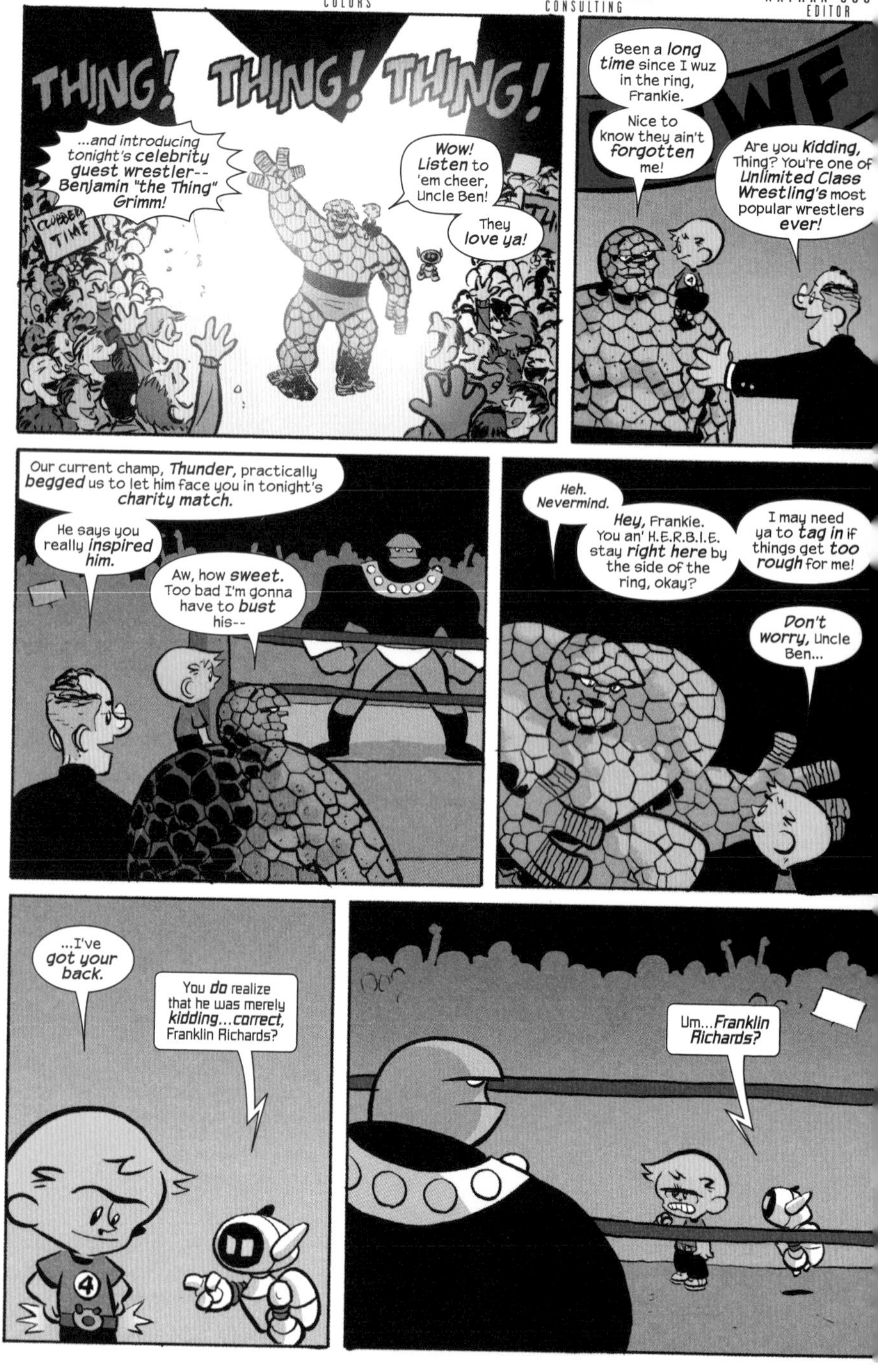

THING! THING! THING!
...and introducing tonight's celebrity guest wrestler-- Benjamin "the Thing" Grimm!
CLOBBERIN TIME
Wow! Listen to 'em cheer, Uncle Ben!
They love ya!
Been a long time since I wuz in the ring, Frankie.
Nice to know they ain't forgotten me!
Are you kidding, Thing? You're one of Unlimited Class Wrestling's most popular wrestlers ever!
Our current champ, Thunder, practically begged us to let him face you in tonight's charity match.
He says you really inspired him.
Aw, how sweet. Too bad I'm gonna have to bust his--
Heh. Nevermind.
Hey, Frankie. You an' H.E.R.B.I.E. stay right here by the side of the ring, okay?
I may need ya to tag in if things get too rough for me!
Don't worry, Uncle Ben...
...I've got your back.
You do realize that he was merely kidding...correct, Franklin Richards?
Um...Franklin Richards?

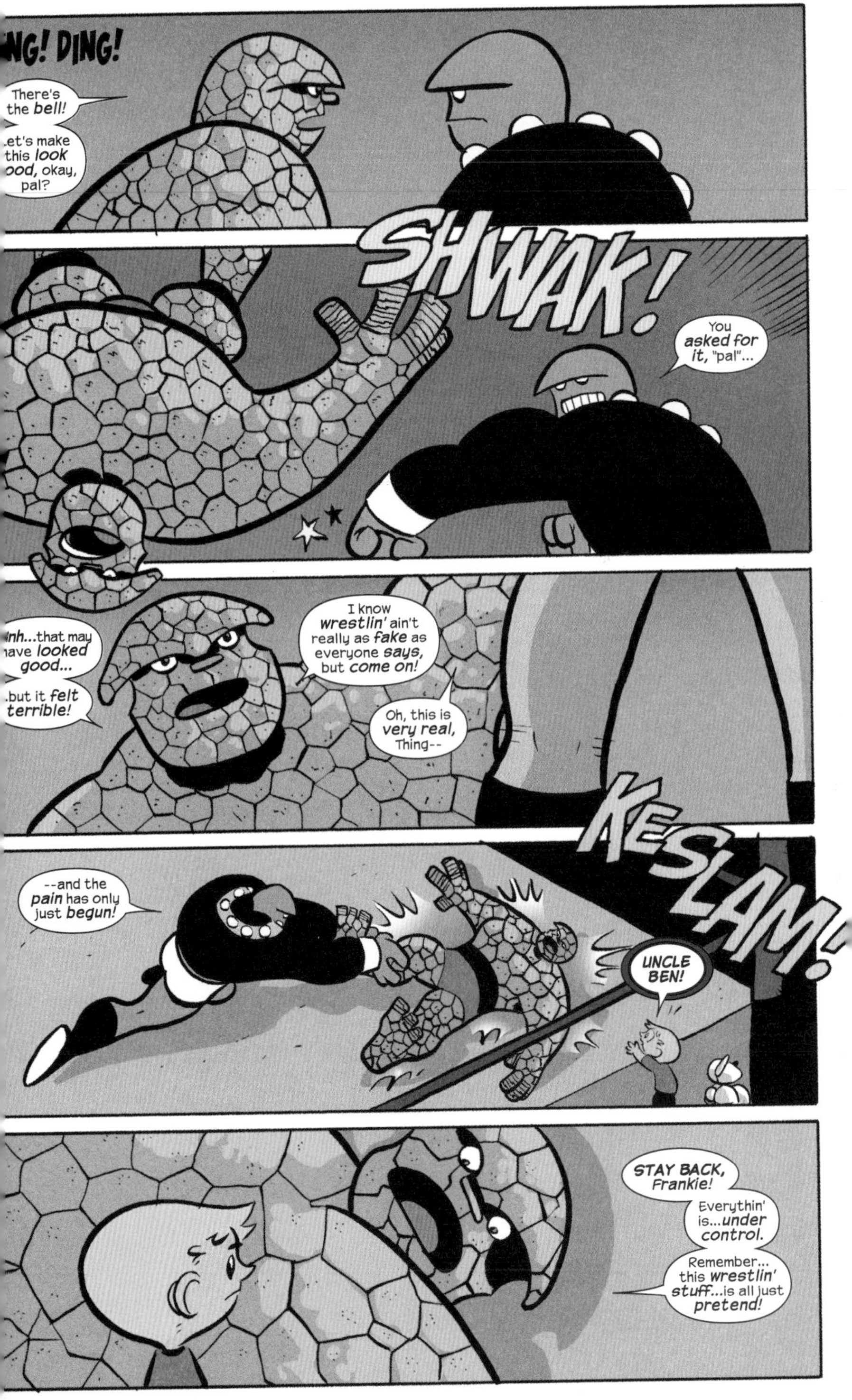
NG! DING!
There's the bell!
.et's make this look ood, okay, pal?
SHWAK!
You asked for it, "pal"...
nh...that may ave looked good...
.but it felt terrible!
I know wrestlin' ain't really as fake as everyone says, but come on!
Oh, this is very real, Thing--
KESLAM!
--and the pain has only just begun!
UNCLE BEN!
STAY BACK, Frankie!
Everythin' is...under control.
Remember... this wrestlin' stuff...is all just pretend!

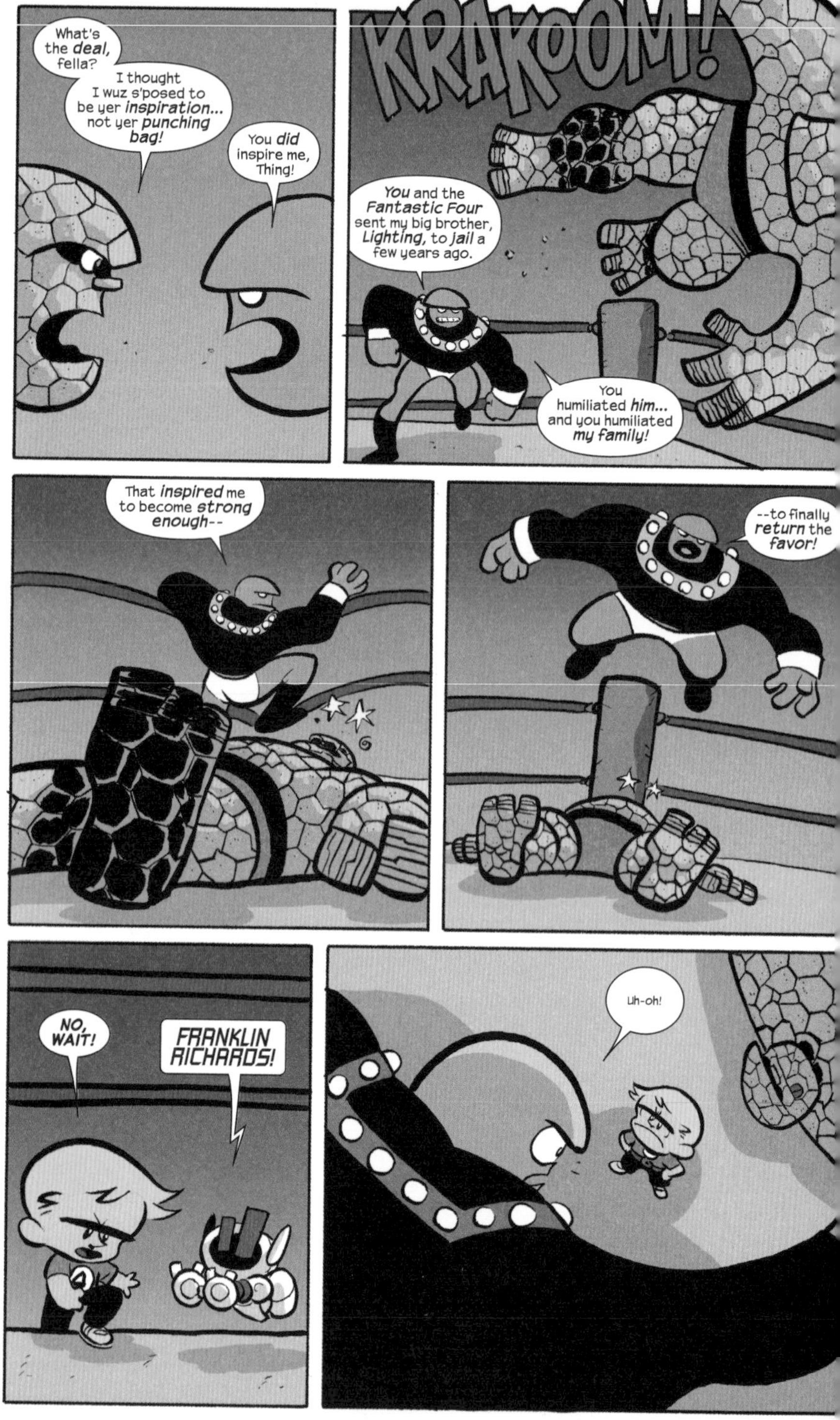

What's the deal, fella?
I thought I wuz s'posed to be yer inspiration... not yer punching bag!
You did inspire me, Thing!
KRAKOOM!
You and the Fantastic Four sent my big brother, Lighting, to jail a few years ago.
You humiliated him... and you humiliated my family!
That inspired me to become strong enough--
--to finally return the favor!
NO, WAIT!
FRANKLIN RICHARDS!
Uh-oh!

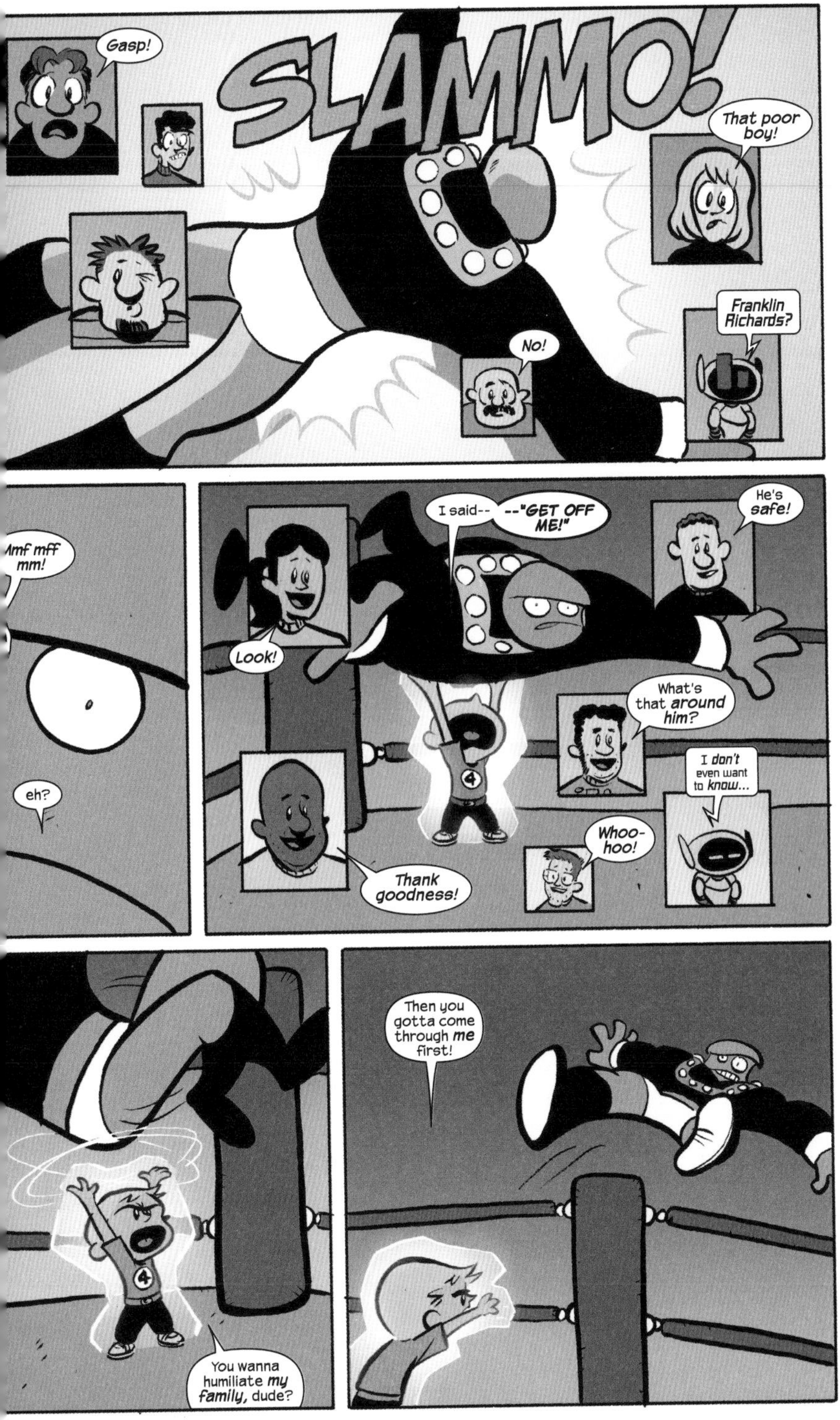

Gasp!
SLAMMO!
That poor boy!
Franklin Richards?
No!
Mmf mff mm!
eh?
I said--
--"GET OFF ME!"
He's safe!
Look!
What's that around him?
I don't even want to know...
Whoo-hoo!
Thank goodness!
You wanna humiliate my family, dude?
Then you gotta come through me first!

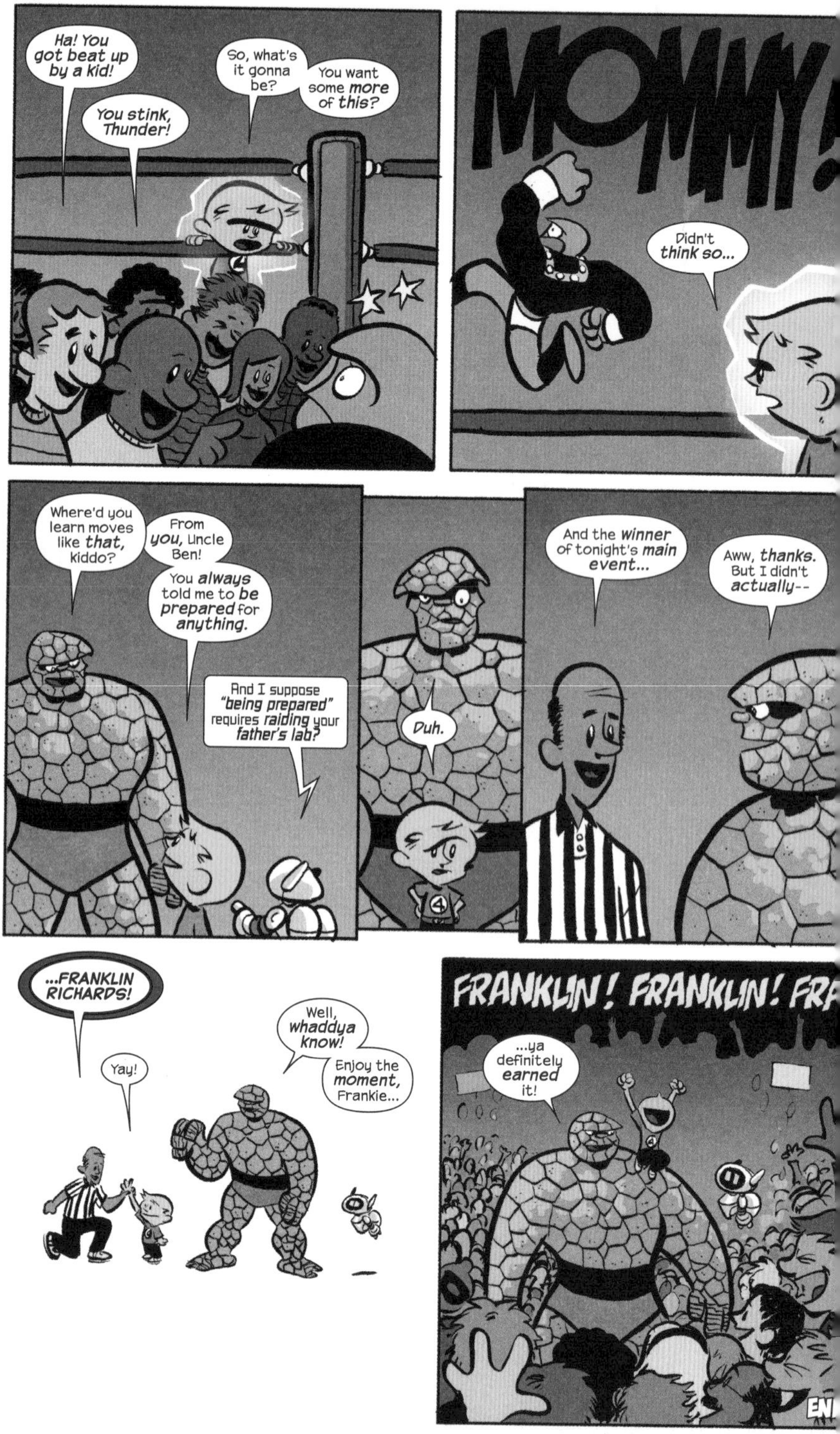
Ha! You got beat up by a kid!
You stink, Thunder!
So, what's it gonna be?
You want some more of this?
MOMMY!
Didn't think so...
Where'd you learn moves like that, kiddo?
From you, Uncle Ben!
You always told me to be prepared for anything.
And I suppose "being prepared" requires raiding your father's lab?
Duh.
And the winner of tonight's main event...
Aww, thanks. But I didn't actually--
...FRANKLIN RICHARDS!
Yay!
Well, whaddya know!
Enjoy the moment, Frankie...
FRANKLIN! FRANKLIN!
...ya definitely earned it!

RANKLIN ICHARDS SON OF A GENIUS IN: DE-AGED DAD!

BY CHRIS ELIOPOULOS & MARC SUMERAK

BRAD ANDERSON COLORS — MARK PANICCIA CONSULTING — NATHAN COSBY EDITOR

DEDICATED TO JEREMY AND JUSTIN WHO I WISH I COULD PLAY WITH ALL DAY EVERY DAY!--DAD

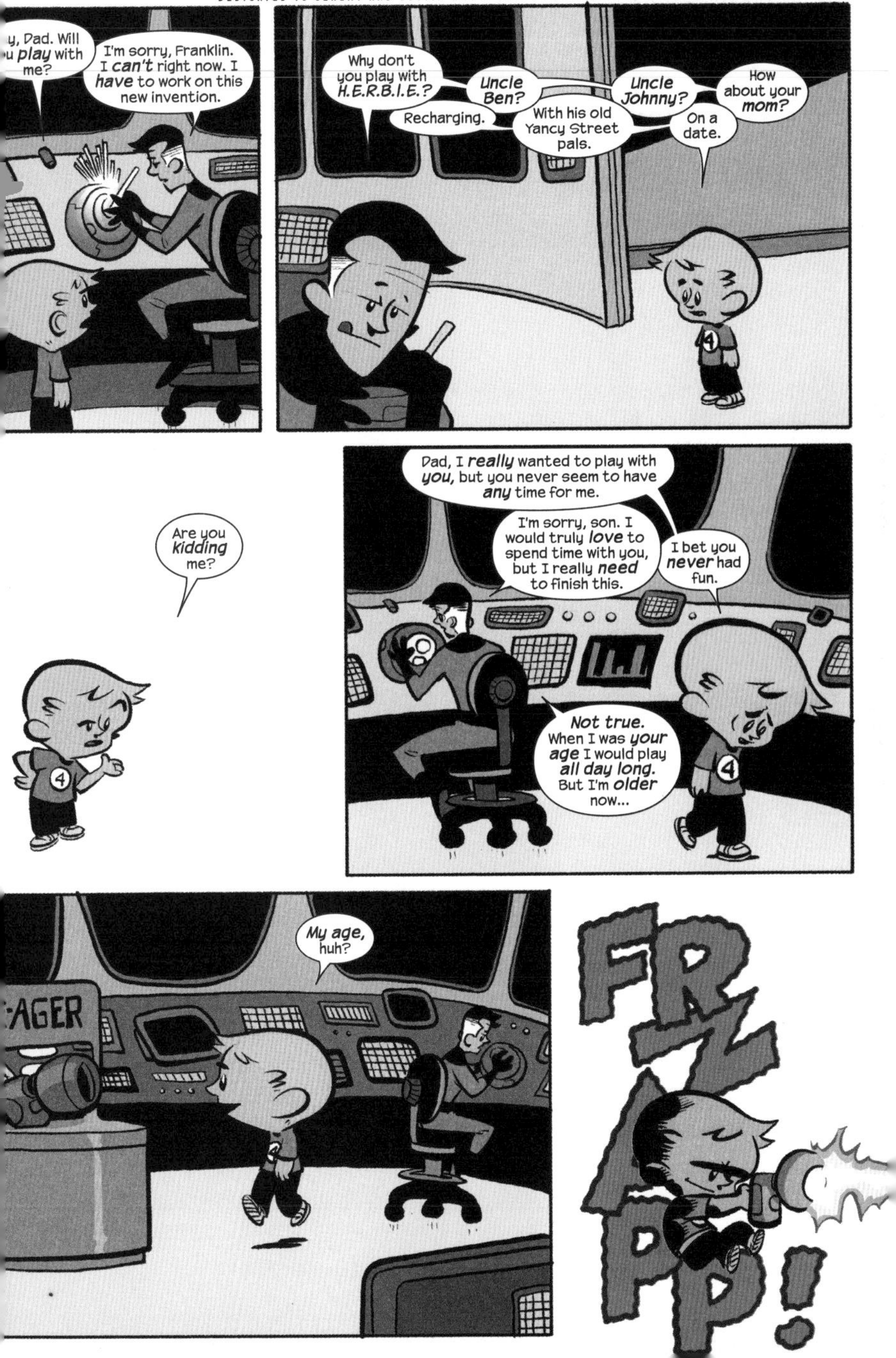

y, Dad. Will u play with me?
I'm sorry, Franklin. I can't right now. I have to work on this new invention.
Why don't you play with H.E.R.B.I.E.?
Recharging.
Uncle Ben?
With his old Yancy Street pals.
Uncle Johnny?
On a date.
How about your mom?
Are you kidding me?
Dad, I really wanted to play with you, but you never seem to have any time for me.
I'm sorry, son. I would truly love to spend time with you, but I really need to finish this.
I bet you never had fun.
Not true. When I was your age I would play all day long. But I'm older now...
My age, huh?
AGER
FRZAPP!

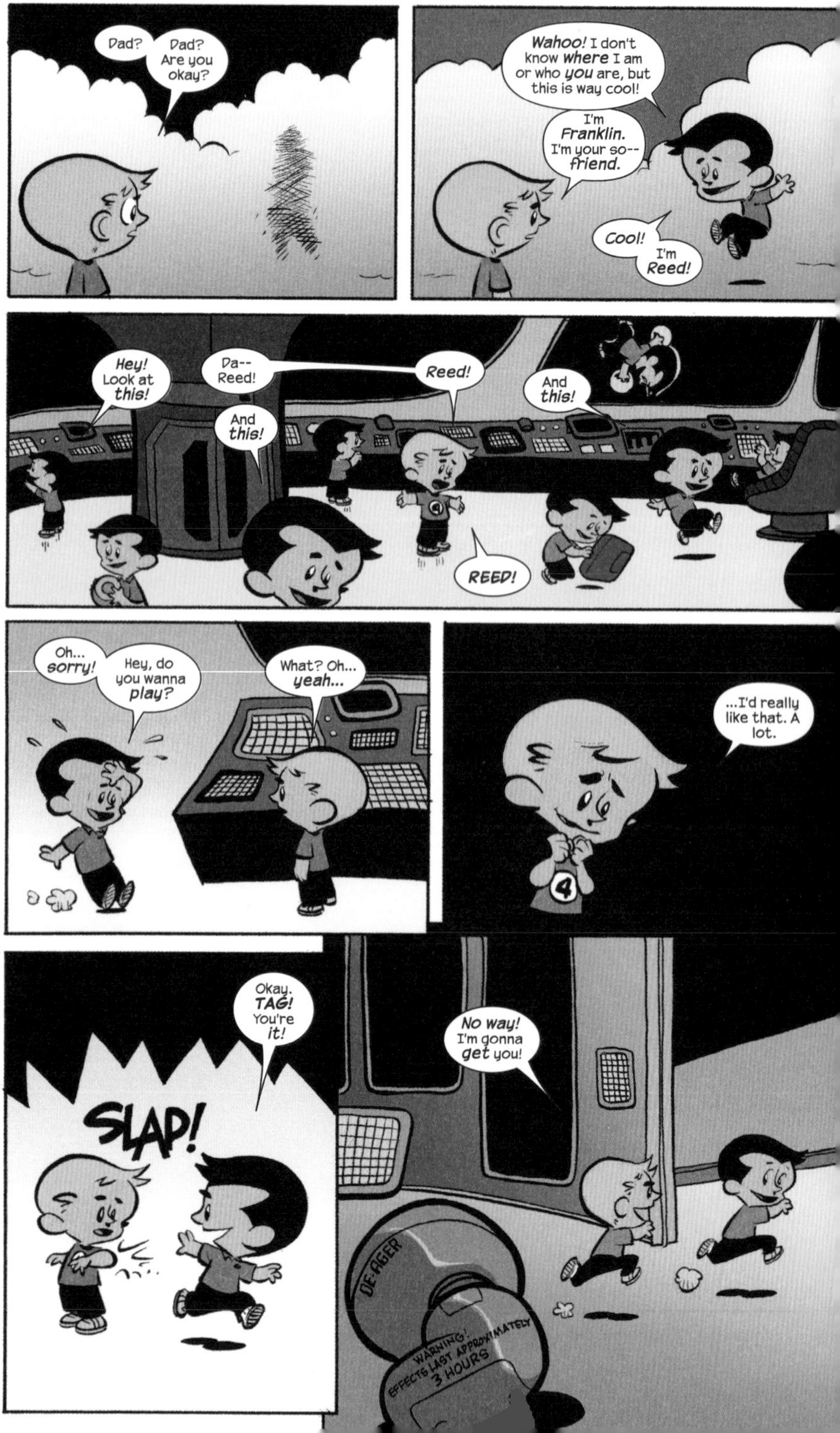

Dad?
Dad? Are you okay?
Wahoo! I don't know where I am or who you are, but this is way cool!
I'm Franklin. I'm your so-- friend.
Cool!
I'm Reed!
Hey! Look at this!
Da-- Reed!
Reed!
And this!
And this!
REED!
Oh... sorry!
Hey, do you wanna play?
What? Oh... yeah...
...I'd really like that. A lot.
Okay. TAG! You're it!
SLAP!
No way! I'm gonna get you!
DE-AGER
WARNING! EFFECTS LAST APPROXIMATELY 3 HOURS

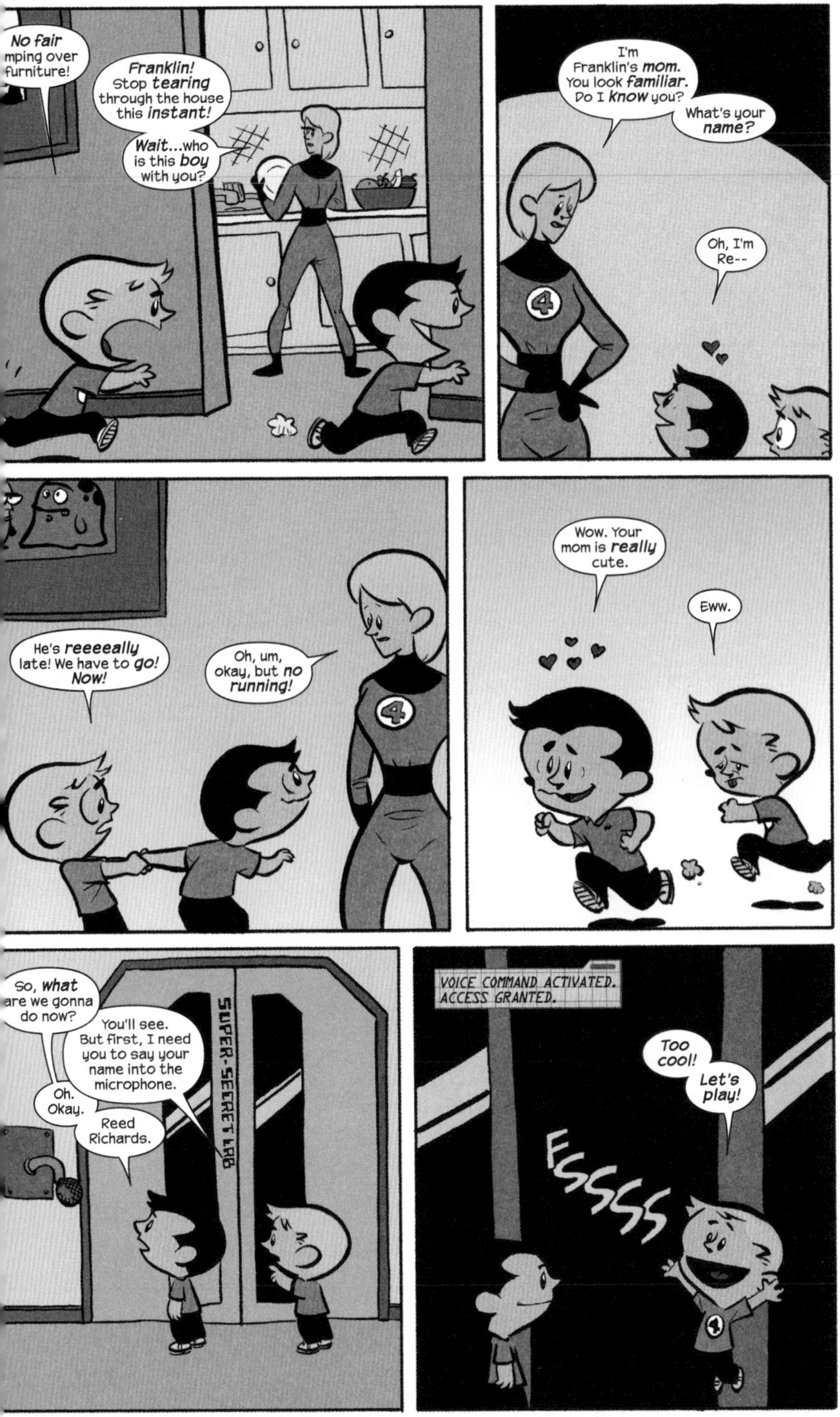
No fair
mping over furniture!
Franklin! Stop tearing through the house this instant!
Wait...who is this boy with you?
I'm Franklin's mom. You look familiar. Do I know you?
What's your name?
Oh, I'm Re--
He's reeeeeally late! We have to go! Now!
Oh, um, okay, but no running!
Wow. Your mom is really cute.
Eww.
So, what are we gonna do now?
You'll see. But first, I need you to say your name into the microphone.
SUPER-SECRET LAB
Oh. Okay.
Reed Richards.
VOICE COMMAND ACTIVATED. ACCESS GRANTED.
Too cool!
Let's play!
FSSSSS

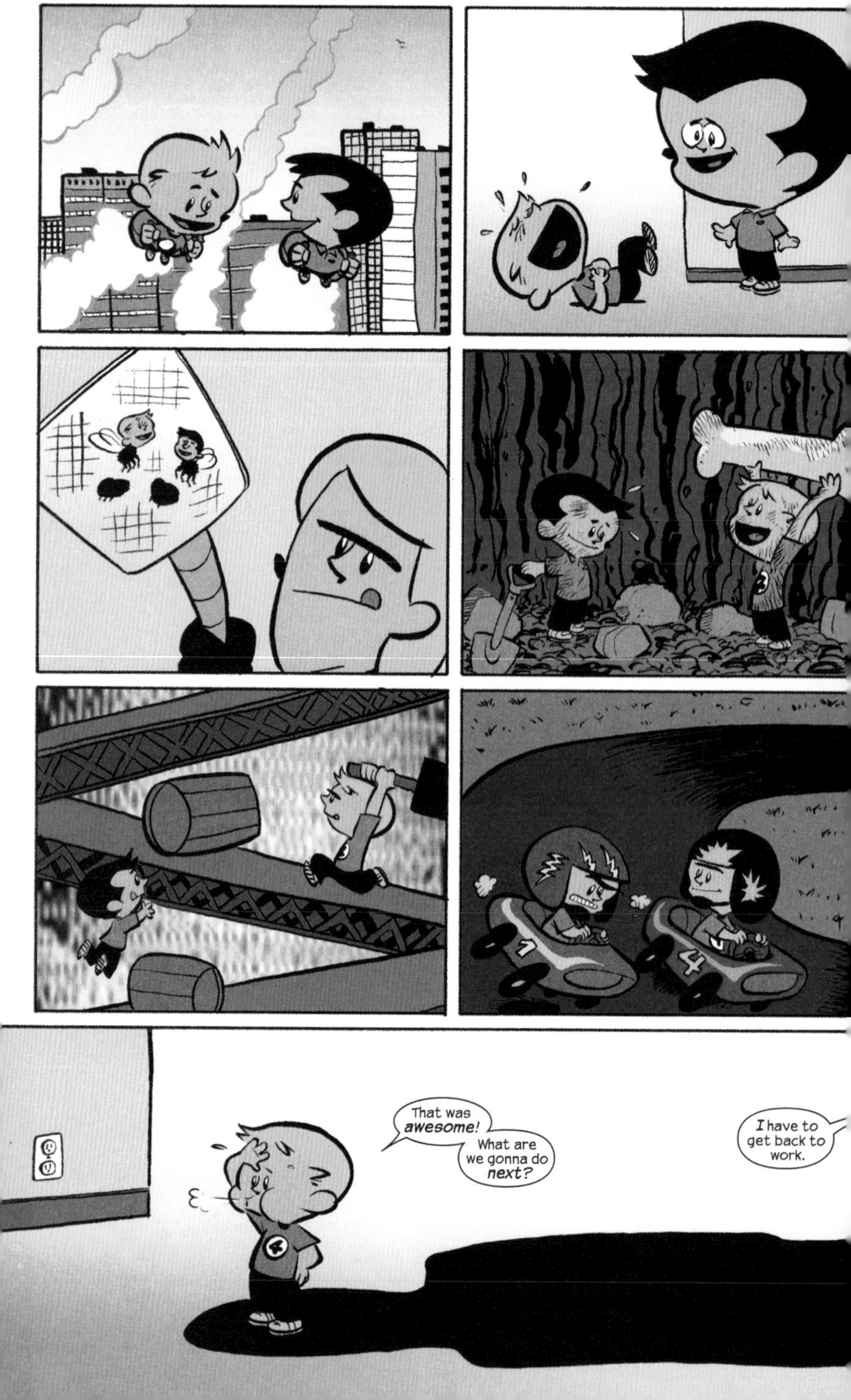
That was awesome!
What are we gonna do next?
I have to get back to work.

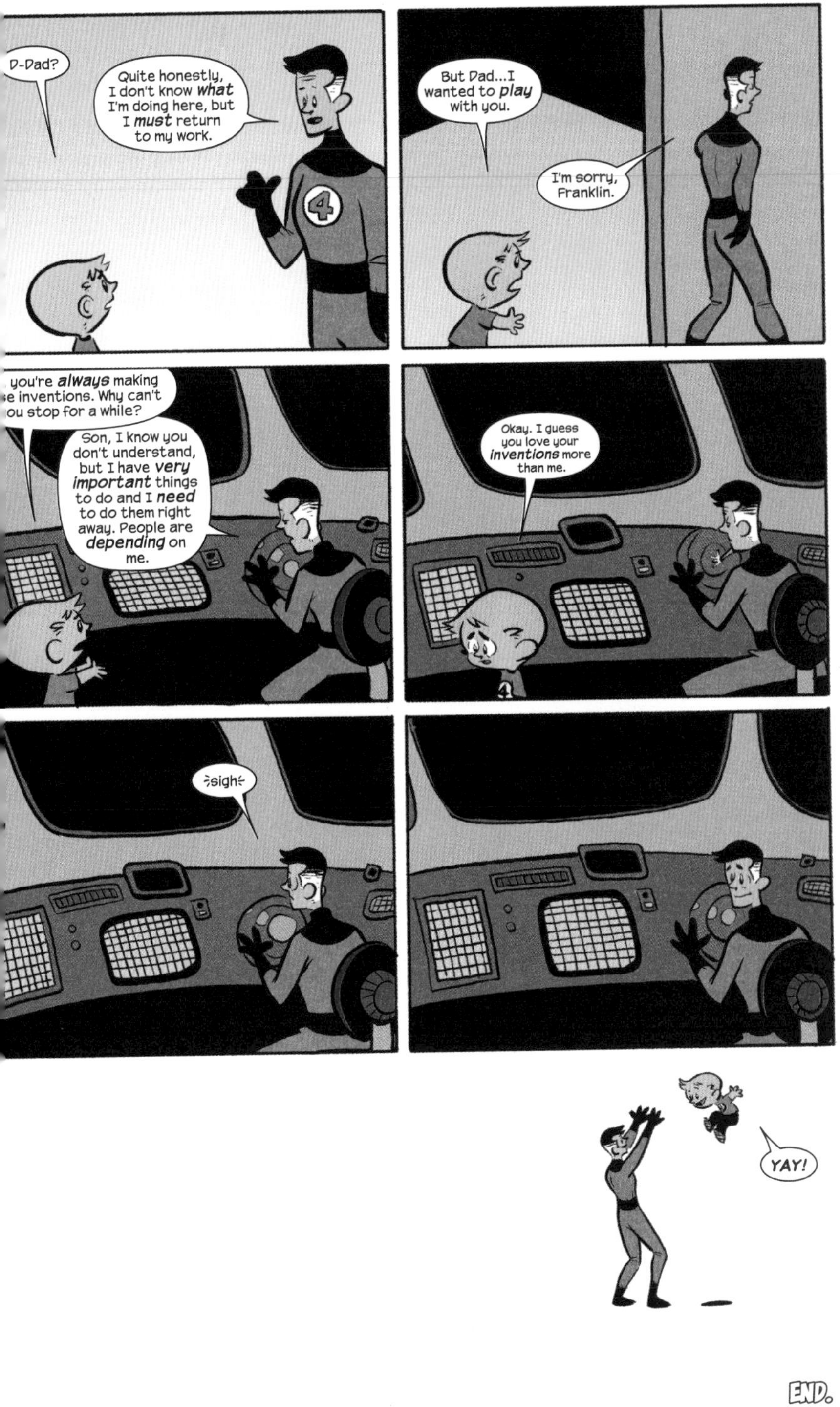
D-Dad?
Quite honestly, I don't know *what* I'm doing here, but I *must* return to my work.
But Dad...I wanted to *play* with you.
I'm sorry, Franklin.
you're *always* making e inventions. Why can't ou stop for a while?
Son, I know you don't understand, but I have *very important* things to do and I *need* to do them right away. People are *depending* on me.
Okay. I guess you love your *inventions* more than me.
sigh
YAY!
END.

FRANKLIN RICHARDS SON OF A GENIUS IN: NIGHT OF THE LIVING PE

STORY BY MARC SUMERAK ART BY CHRIS ELIOPOU
BRAD ANDERSON COLORS
MARK PANICCIA CONSULTING
NATHAN CO EDITOR

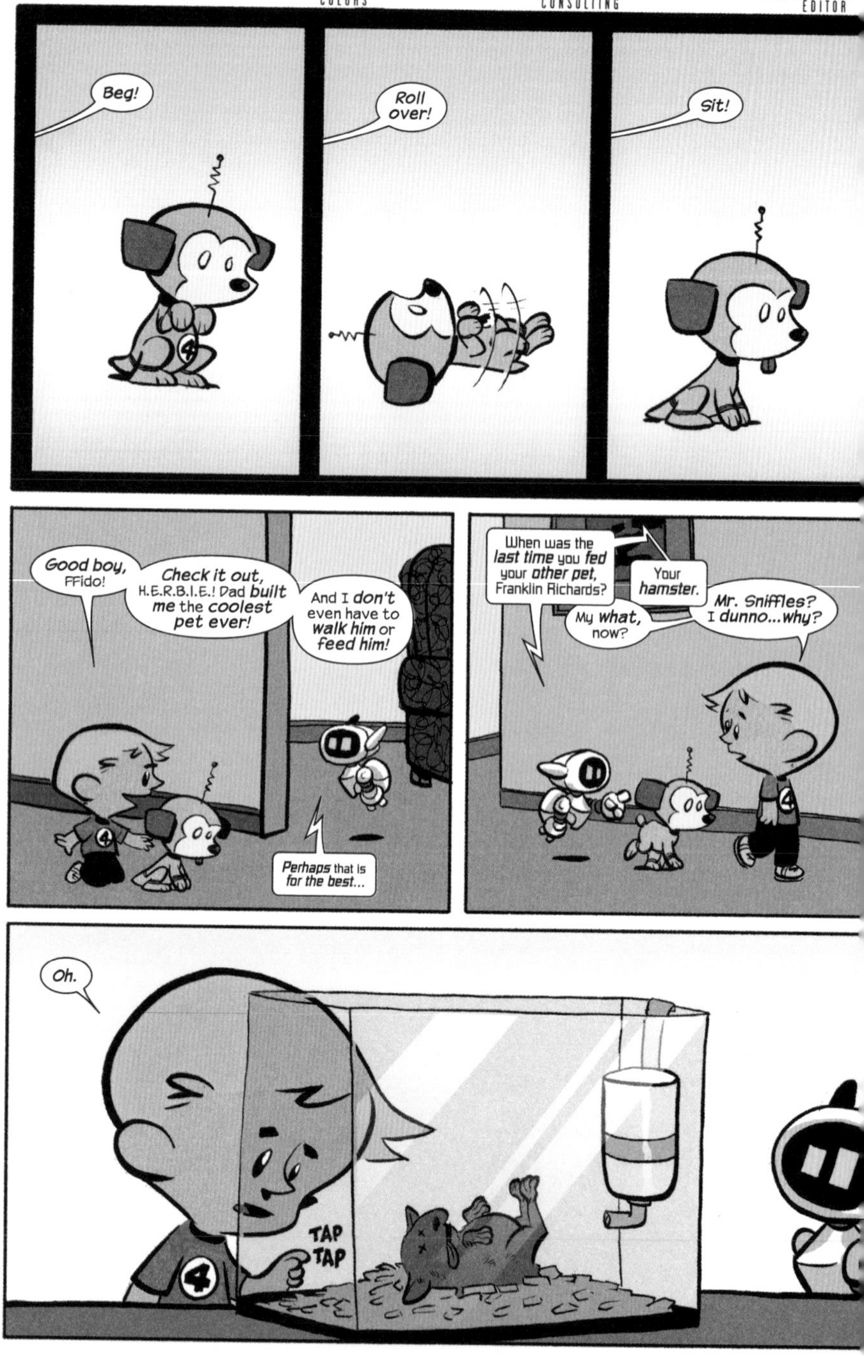

Beg!
Roll over!
Sit!
Good boy, FFido!
Check it out, H.E.R.B.I.E.! Dad built me the coolest pet ever!
And I don't even have to walk him or feed him!
Perhaps that is for the best...
When was the last time you fed your other pet, Franklin Richards?
My what, now?
Your hamster.
Mr. Sniffles? I dunno...why?
Oh.
TAP TAP

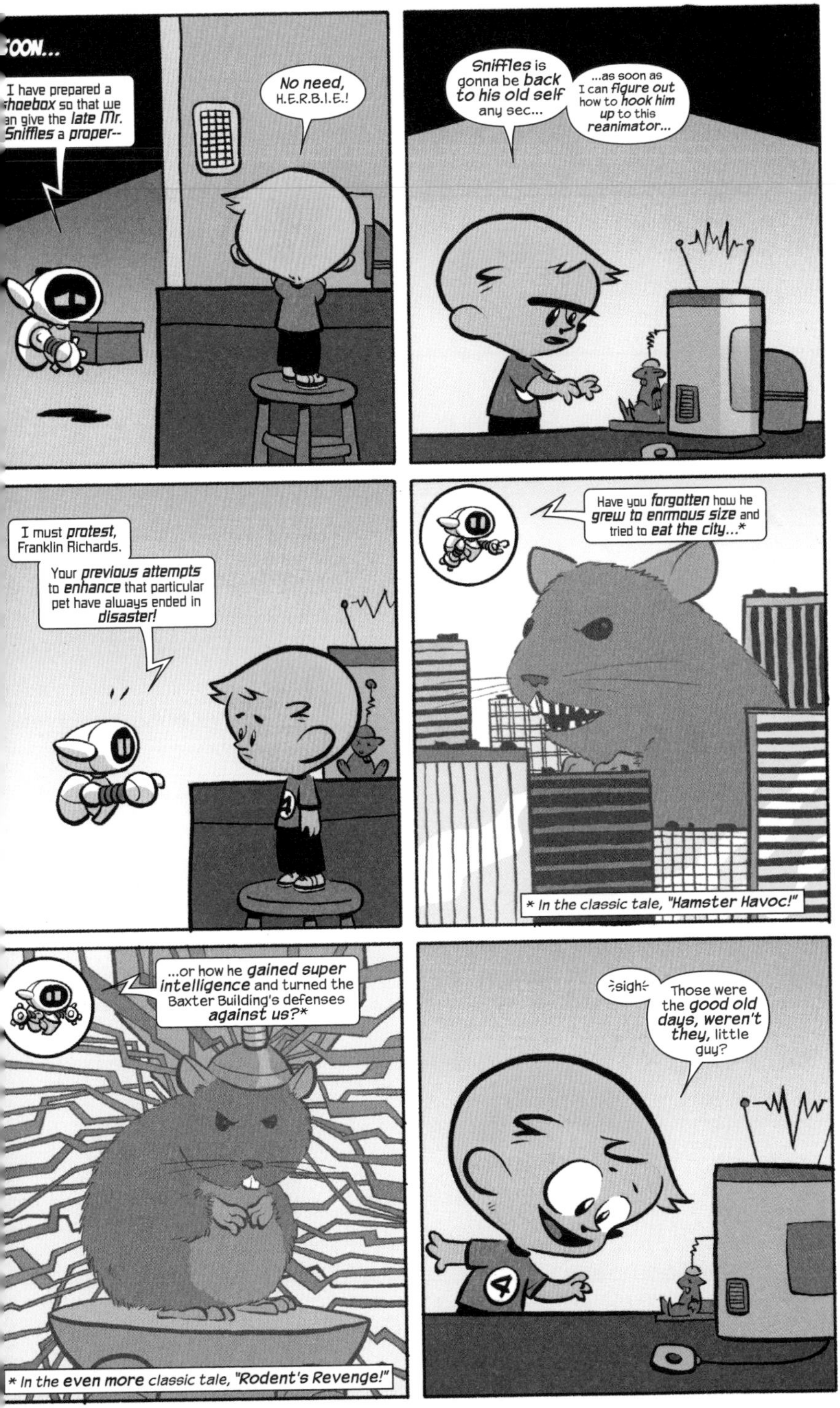

SOON...
I have prepared a shoebox so that we can give the late Mr. Sniffles a proper--
No need, H.E.R.B.I.E.!
Sniffles is gonna be back to his old self any sec...
...as soon as I can figure out how to hook him up to this reanimator...
I must protest, Franklin Richards.
Your previous attempts to enhance that particular pet have always ended in disaster!
Have you forgotten how he grew to enmous size and tried to eat the city...*
* In the classic tale, "Hamster Havoc!"
...or how he gained super intelligence and turned the Baxter Building's defenses against us?*
* In the even more classic tale, "Rodent's Revenge!"
sigh
Those were the good old days, weren't they, little guy?

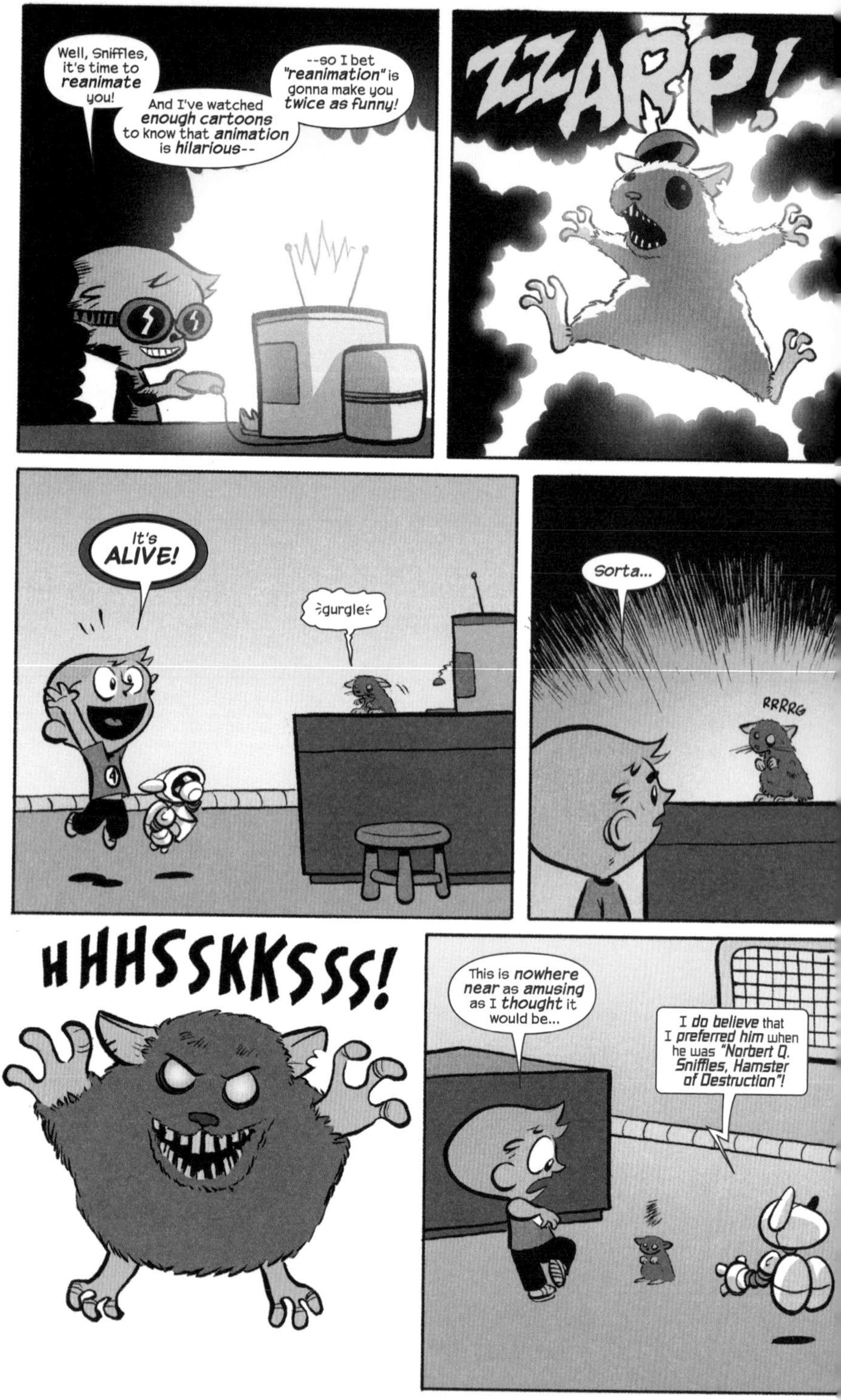

Well, Sniffles, it's time to reanimate you!
And I've watched enough cartoons to know that animation is hilarious--
--so I bet "reanimation" is gonna make you twice as funny!
ZZARP!
It's ALIVE!
gurgle
Sorta...
RRRRG
HHHSSKKSSS!
This is nowhere near as amusing as I thought it would be...
I do believe that I preferred him when he was "Norbert Q. Sniffles, Hamster of Destruction"!

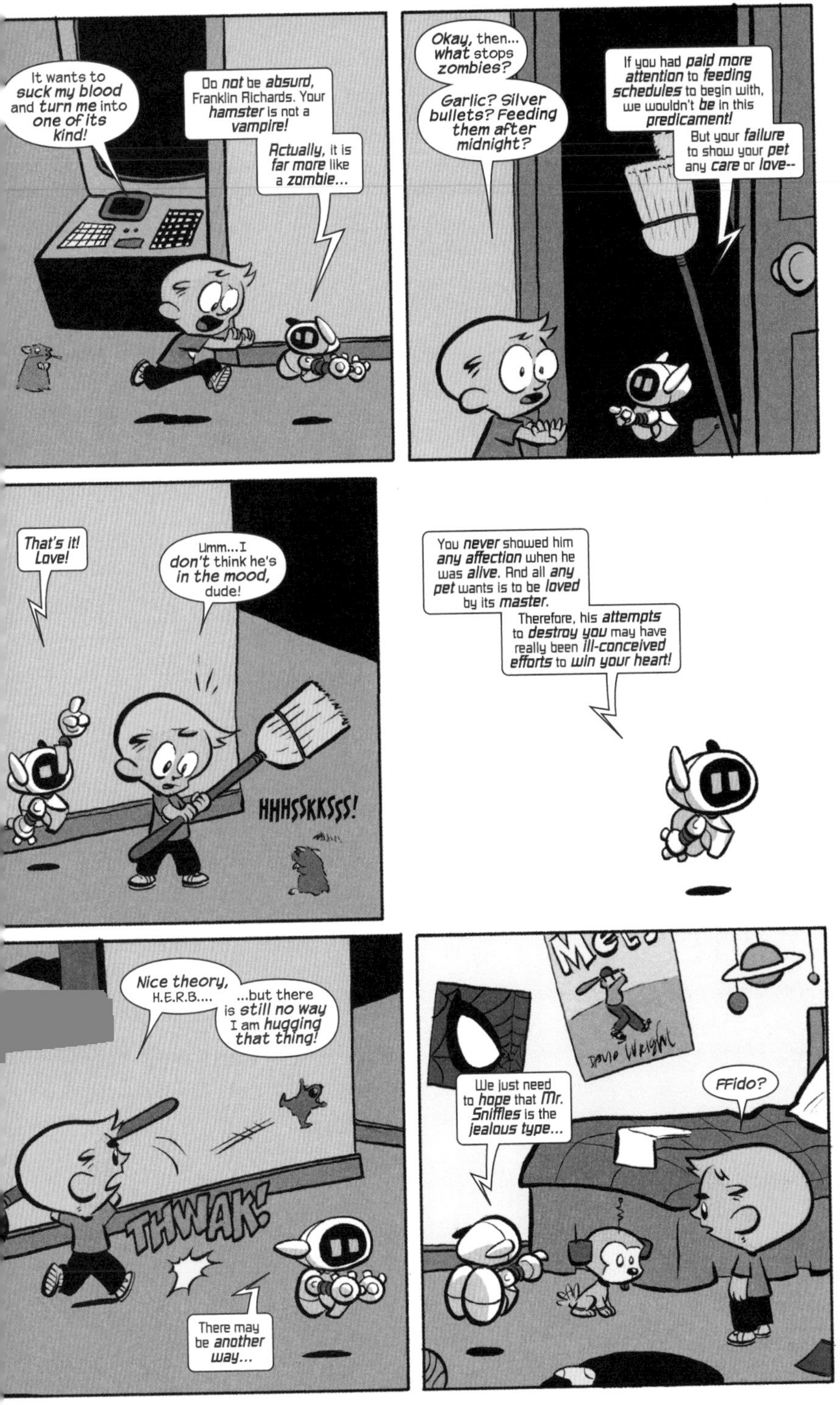
It wants to suck my blood and turn me into one of its kind!
Do not be absurd, Franklin Richards. Your hamster is not a vampire!
Actually, it is far more like a zombie...
Okay, then... what stops zombies?
Garlic? Silver bullets? Feeding them after midnight?
If you had paid more attention to feeding schedules to begin with, we wouldn't be in this predicament!
But your failure to show your pet any care or love--
That's it! Love!
Umm...I don't think he's in the mood, dude!
HHHSSKKSSS!
You never showed him any affection when he was alive. And all any pet wants is to be loved by its master.
Therefore, his attempts to destroy you may have really been ill-conceived efforts to win your heart!
Nice theory, H.E.R.B....
...but there is still no way I am hugging that thing!
THWAK!
There may be another way...
David Wright
We just need to hope that Mr. Sniffles is the jealous type...
FFido?

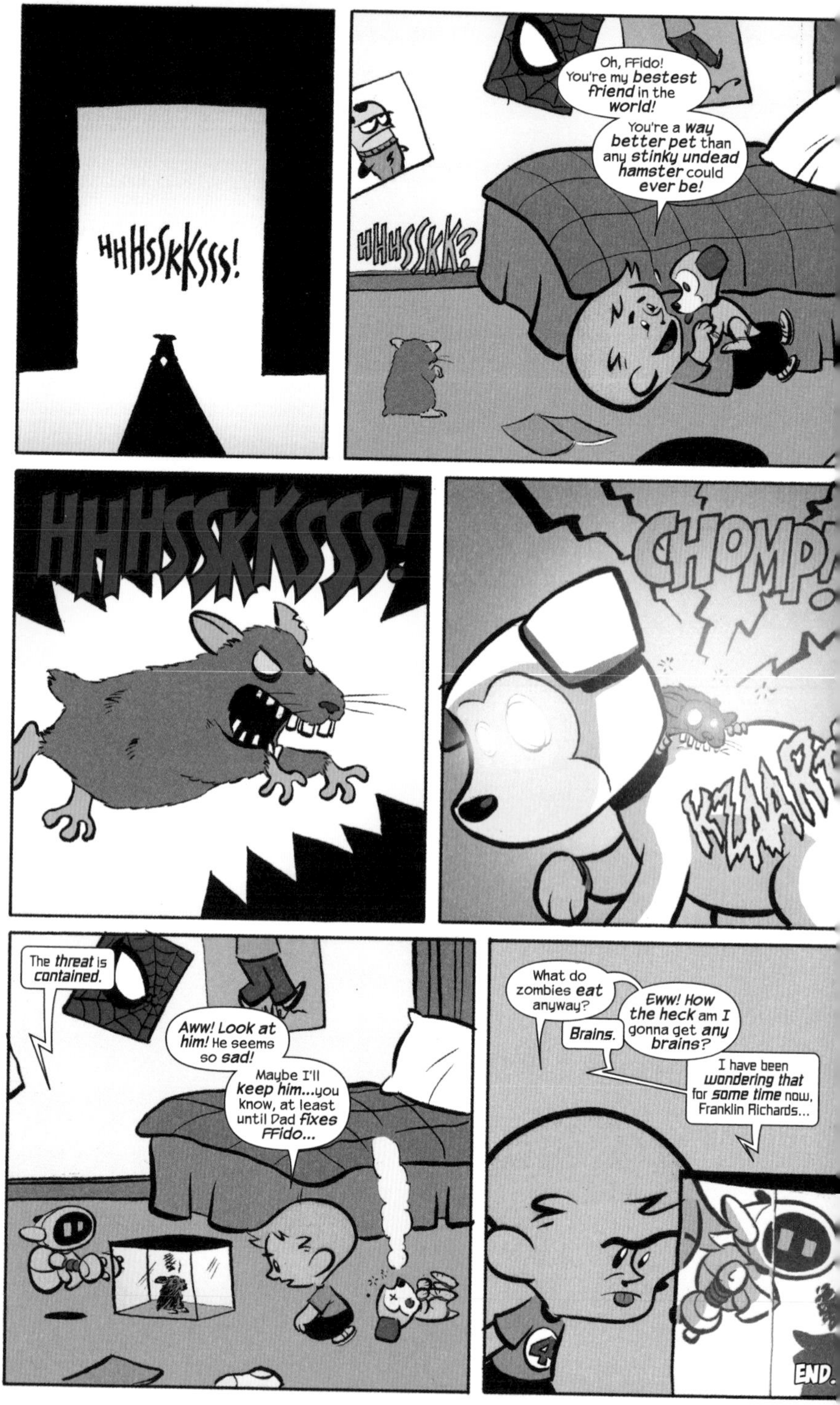
HHHSSKKSSSS!
Oh, FFido! You're my bestest friend in the world!
You're a way better pet than any stinky undead hamster could ever be!
HHHSSKK?
HHHSSKKSSSS!
CHOMP
The threat is contained.
Aww! Look at him! He seems so sad!
Maybe I'll keep him...you know, at least until Dad fixes FFido...
What do zombies eat anyway?
Brains.
Eww! How the heck am I gonna get any brains?
I have been wondering that for some time now, Franklin Richards...
END.

FRANKLIN RICHARDS SON OF A GENIUS IN: UN-MISTAKEN IDENTITY!

BY CHRIS ELIOPOULOS

BRAD ANDERSON COLORS — MARK PANICCIA CONSULTING — NATHAN COSBY EDITOR

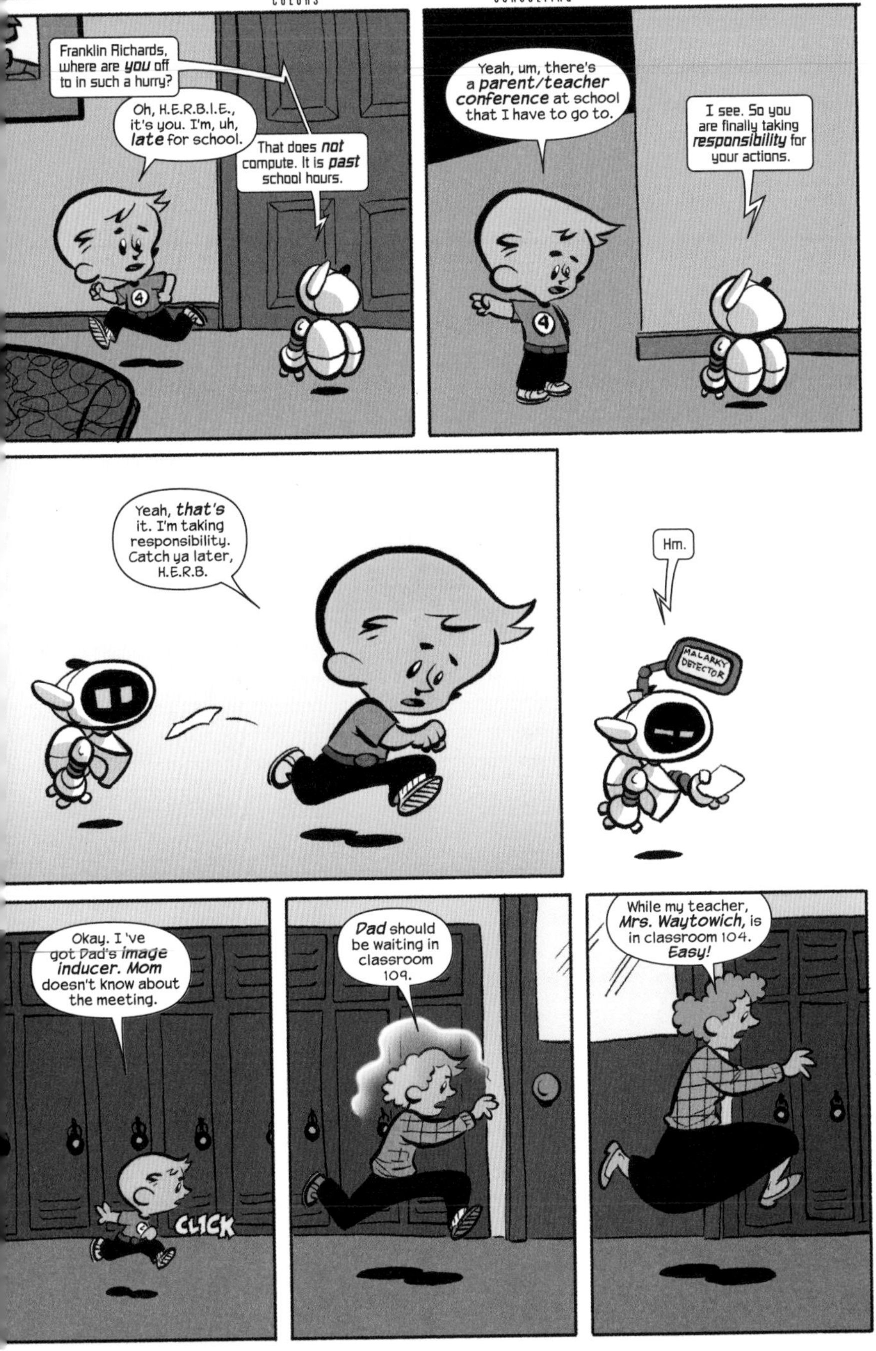

Franklin Richards, where are you off to in such a hurry?
Oh, H.E.R.B.I.E., it's you. I'm, uh, late for school.
That does not compute. It is past school hours.
Yeah, um, there's a parent/teacher conference at school that I have to go to.
I see. So you are finally taking responsibility for your actions.
Yeah, that's it. I'm taking responsibility. Catch ya later, H.E.R.B.
Hm.
MALARKY DETECTOR
Okay. I've got Dad's image inducer. Mom doesn't know about the meeting.
CLICK
Dad should be waiting in classroom 109.
While my teacher, Mrs. Waytowich, is in classroom 104. Easy!

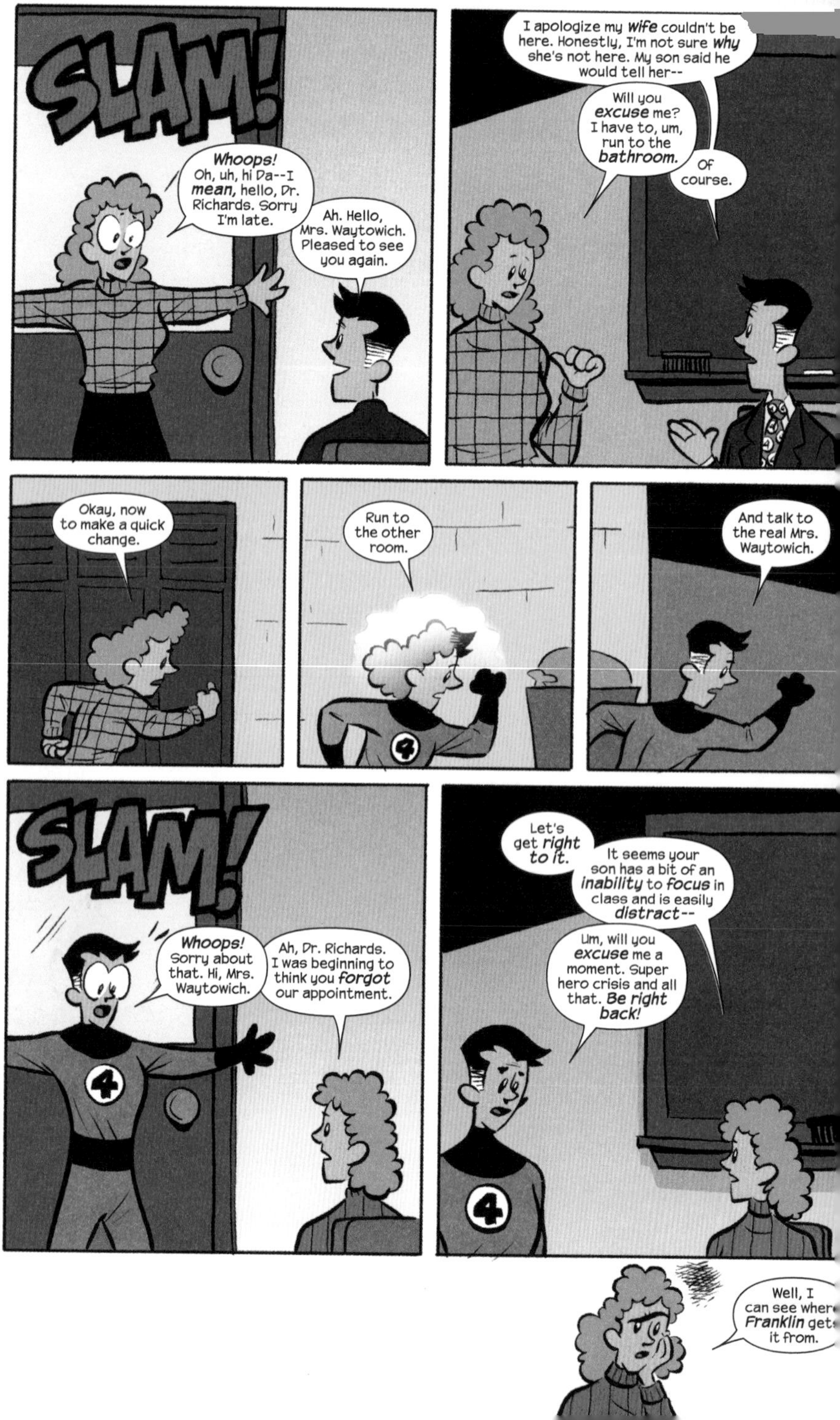

SLAM!
Whoops! Oh, uh, hi Da--I mean, hello, Dr. Richards. Sorry I'm late.
Ah. Hello, Mrs. Waytowich. Pleased to see you again.
I apologize my wife couldn't be here. Honestly, I'm not sure why she's not here. My son said he would tell her--
Will you excuse me? I have to, um, run to the bathroom.
Of course.
Okay, now to make a quick change.
Run to the other room.
And talk to the real Mrs. Waytowich.
SLAM!
Whoops! Sorry about that. Hi, Mrs. Waytowich.
Ah, Dr. Richards. I was beginning to think you forgot our appointment.
Let's get right to it.
It seems your son has a bit of an inability to focus in class and is easily distract--
Um, will you excuse me a moment. Super hero crisis and all that. Be right back!
Well, I can see where Franklin gets it from.

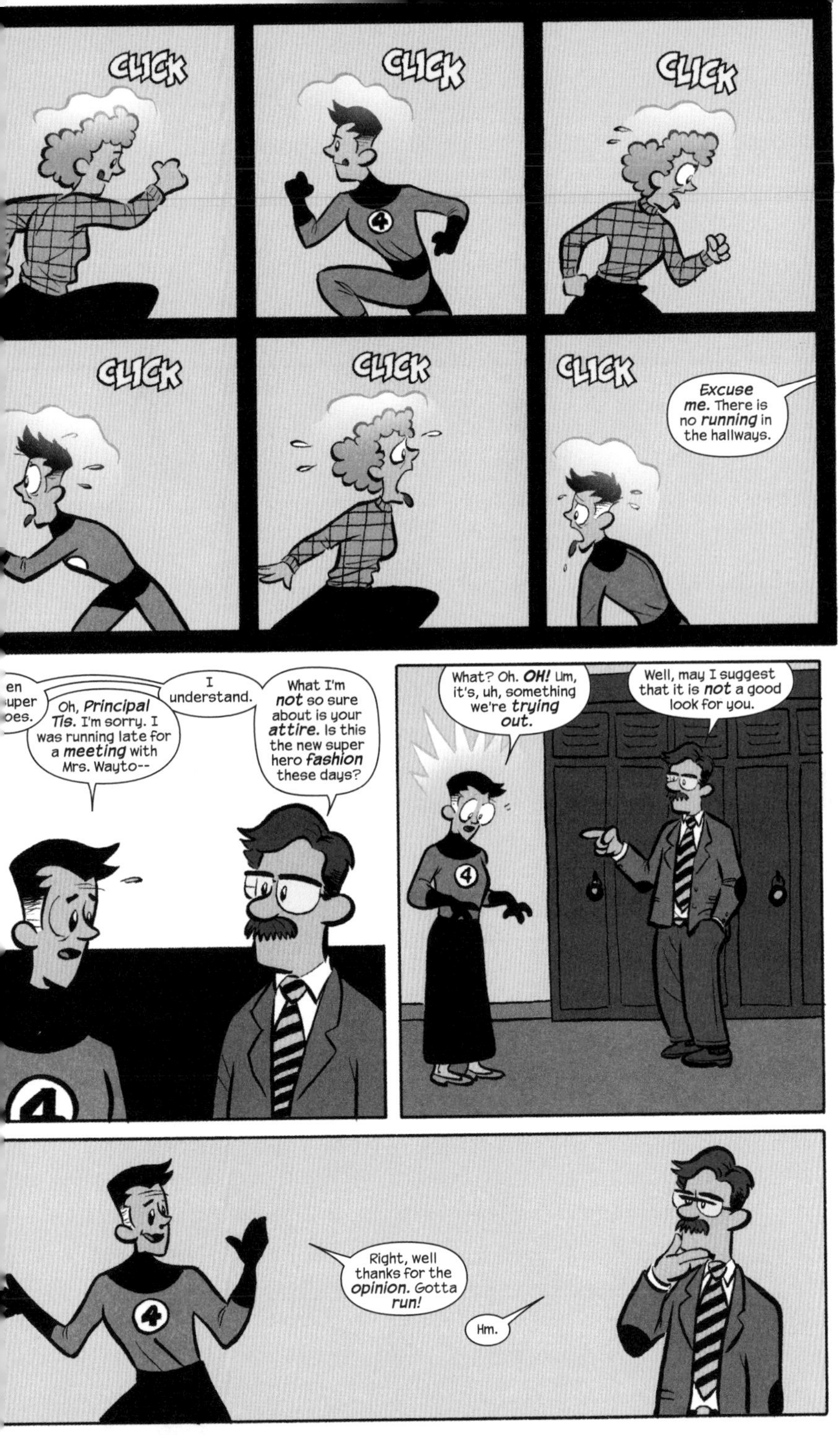

CLICK
CLICK
CLICK
CLICK
CLICK
CLICK
Excuse me. There is no running in the hallways.
Oh, Principal Tis. I'm sorry. I was running late for a meeting with Mrs. Wayto--
I understand.
What I'm not so sure about is your attire. Is this the new super hero fashion these days?
What? Oh. OH! Um, it's, uh, something we're trying out.
Well, may I suggest that it is not a good look for you.
Right, well thanks for the opinion. Gotta run!
Hm.

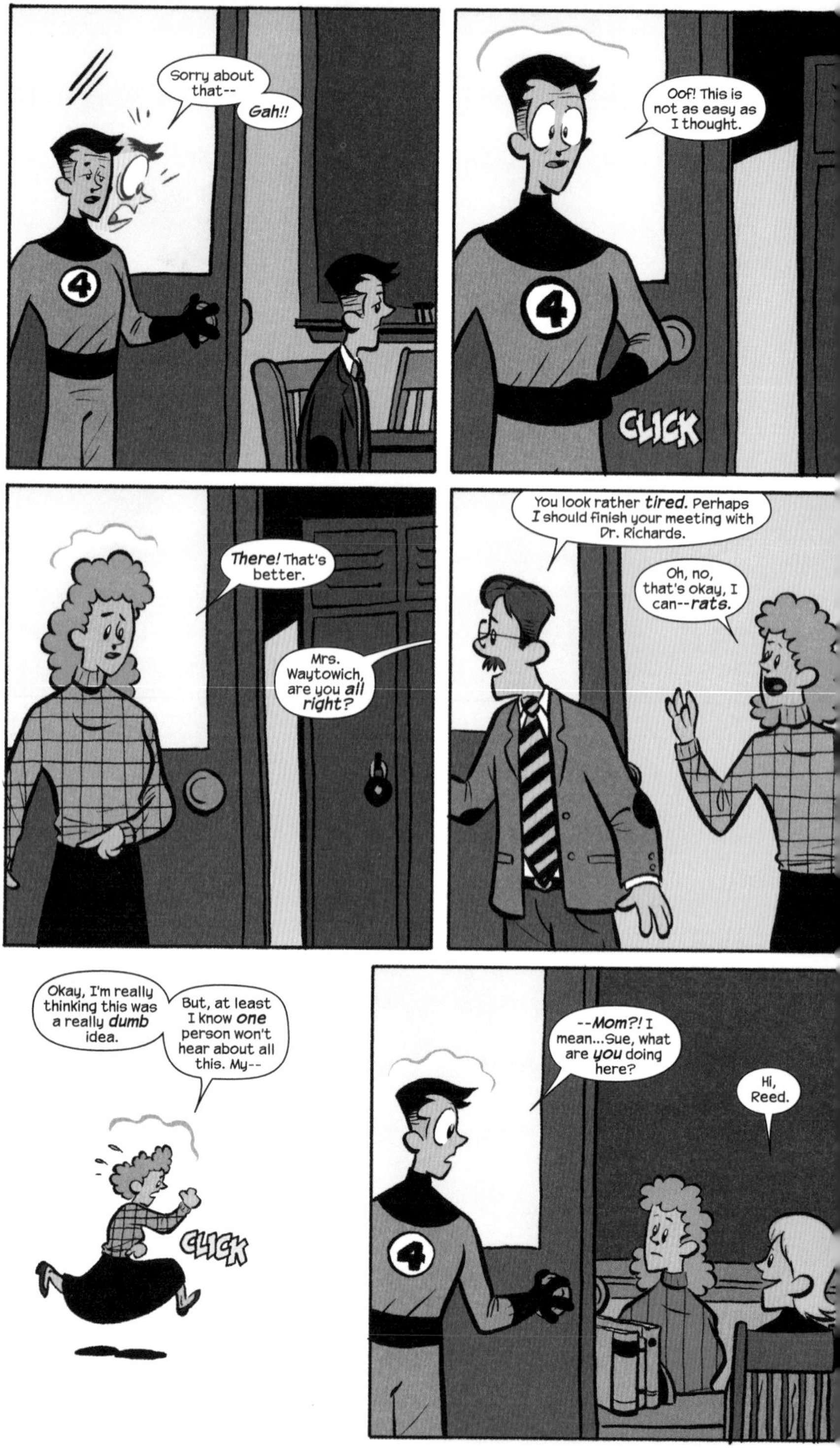

Sorry about that--
Gah!!
Oof! This is not as easy as I thought.
CLICK
There! That's better.
Mrs. Waytowich, are you all right?
You look rather tired. Perhaps I should finish your meeting with Dr. Richards.
Oh, no, that's okay, I can--rats.
Okay, I'm really thinking this was a really dumb idea.
But, at least I know one person won't hear about all this. My--
CLICK
--Mom?! I mean...Sue, what are you doing here?
Hi, Reed.

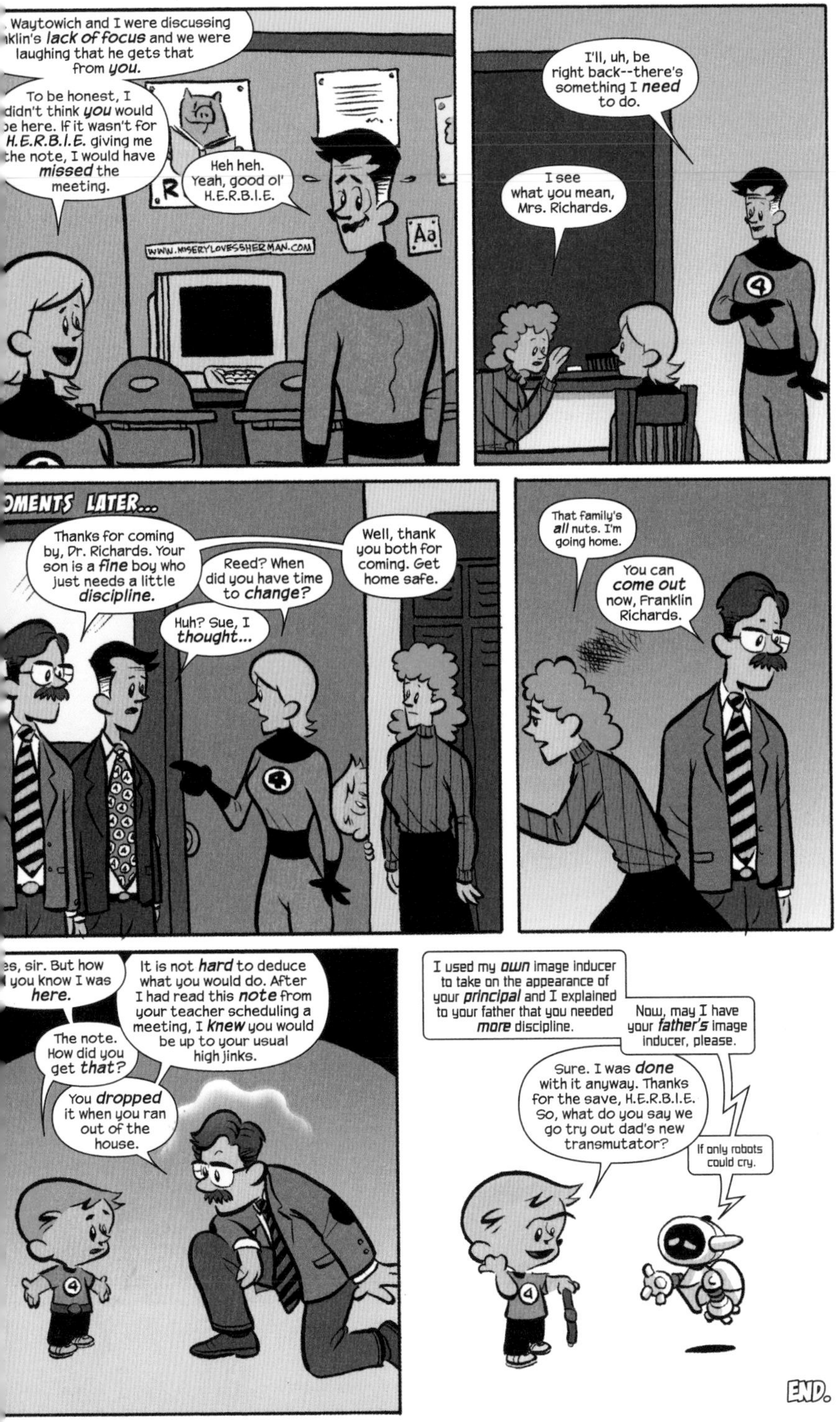

Waytowich and I were discussing nklin's *lack of focus* and we were laughing that he gets that from *you.*
To be honest, I didn't think *you* would be here. If it wasn't for *H.E.R.B.I.E.* giving me the note, I would have *missed* the meeting.
Heh heh. Yeah, good ol' H.E.R.B.I.E.
WWW.MISERYLOVESSHERMAN.COM
I'll, uh, be right back--there's something I *need* to do.
I see what you mean, Mrs. Richards.
OMENTS LATER...
Thanks for coming by, Dr. Richards. Your son is a *fine* boy who just needs a little *discipline.*
Well, thank you both for coming. Get home safe.
Reed? When did you have time to *change?*
Huh? Sue, I *thought...*
That family's *all* nuts. I'm going home.
You can *come out* now, Franklin Richards.
es, sir. But how you know I was *here.*
It is not *hard* to deduce what you would do. After I had read this *note* from your teacher scheduling a meeting, I *knew* you would be up to your usual high jinks.
The note. How did you get *that?*
You *dropped* it when you ran out of the house.
I used my *own* image inducer to take on the appearance of your *principal* and I explained to your father that you needed *more* discipline.
Now, may I have your *father's* image inducer, please.
Sure. I was *done* with it anyway. Thanks for the save, H.E.R.B.I.E. So, what do you say we go try out dad's new transmutator?
If only robots could cry.
END.

FRANKLIN RICHARDS SON OF A GENIUS IN: H.E.R.B.I.E.'S LOVE BU

BY CHRIS ELIOPOULOS & MARC SUMERA

BRAD ANDERSON COLORS

MARK PANICCIA CONSULTING

NATHAN COS EDITOR

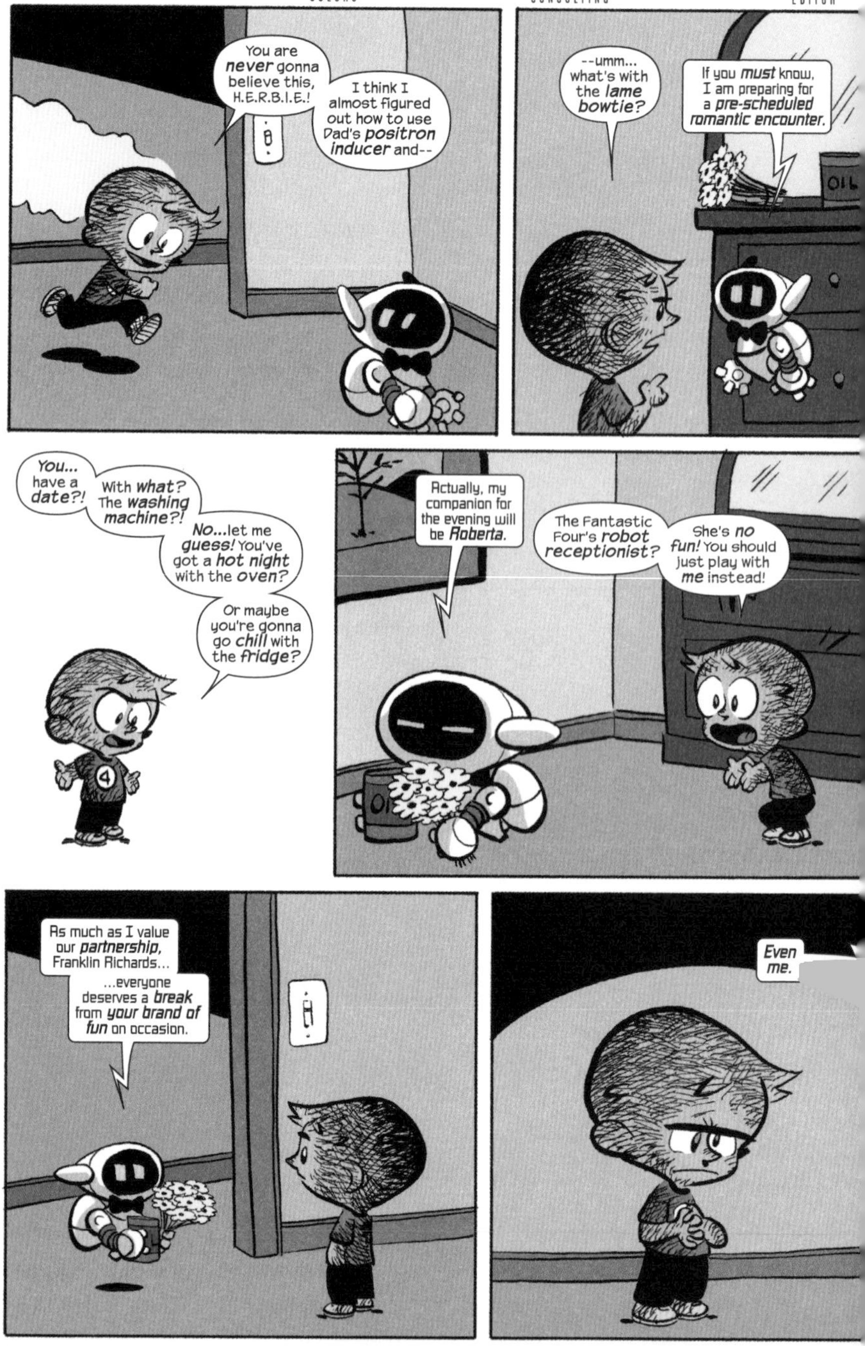

You are never gonna believe this, H.E.R.B.I.E.!
I think I almost figured out how to use Dad's positron inducer and--
--umm... what's with the lame bowtie?
If you must know, I am preparing for a pre-scheduled romantic encounter.
OIL
You... have a date?!
With what? The washing machine?!
No...let me guess! You've got a hot night with the oven?
Or maybe you're gonna go chill with the fridge?
Actually, my companion for the evening will be Roberta.
The Fantastic Four's robot receptionist?
She's no fun! You should just play with me instead!
As much as I value our partnership, Franklin Richards...
...everyone deserves a break from your brand of fun on occasion.
Even me.

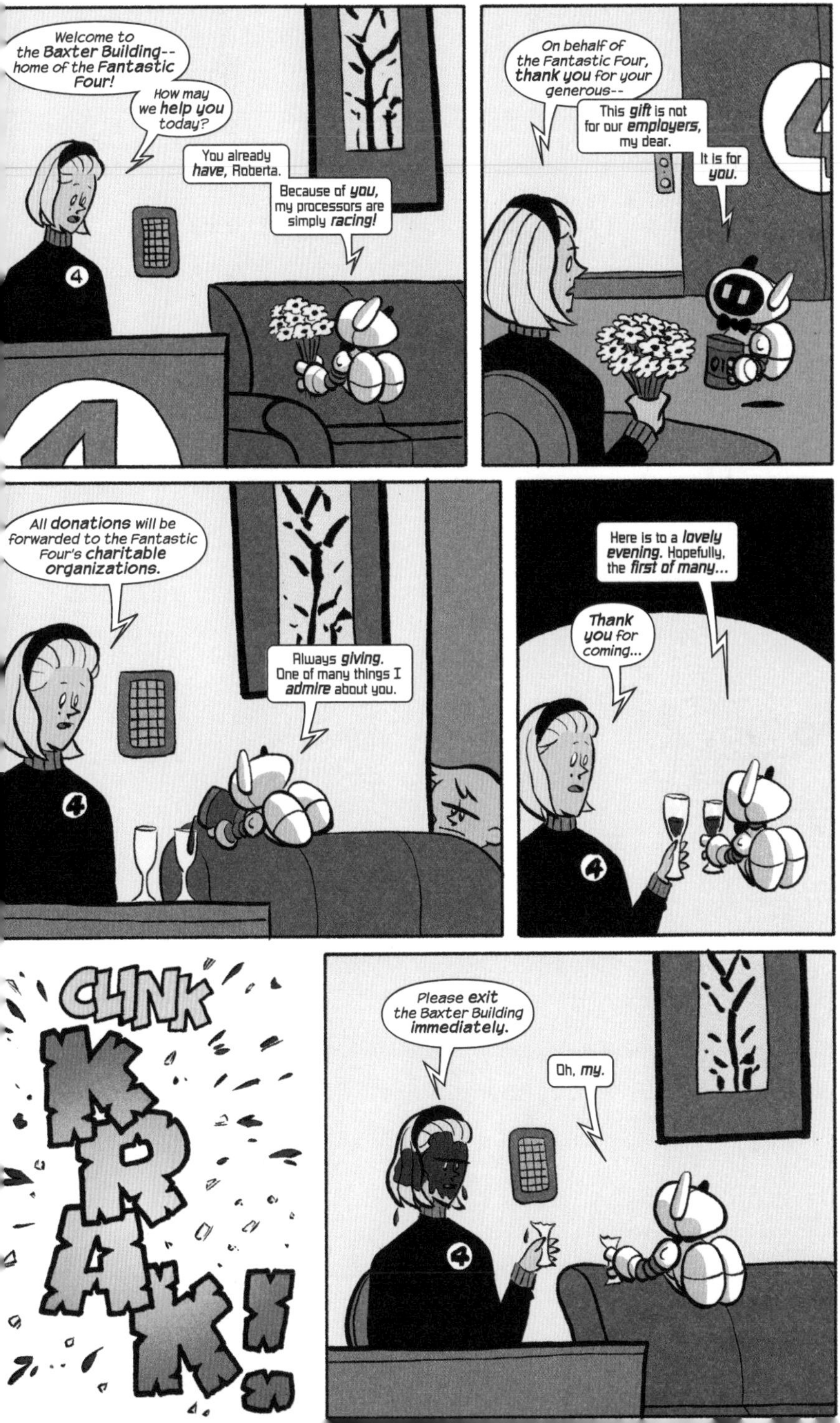

Welcome to the Baxter Building-- home of the Fantastic Four!
How may we help you today?
You already have, Roberta.
Because of you, my processors are simply racing!
On behalf of the Fantastic Four, thank you for your generous--
This gift is not for our employers, my dear.
It is for you.
All donations will be forwarded to the Fantastic Four's charitable organizations.
Always giving. One of many things I admire about you.
Here is to a lovely evening. Hopefully, the first of many...
Thank you for coming...
CLINK
KRAK!!
Please exit the Baxter Building immediately.
Oh, my.

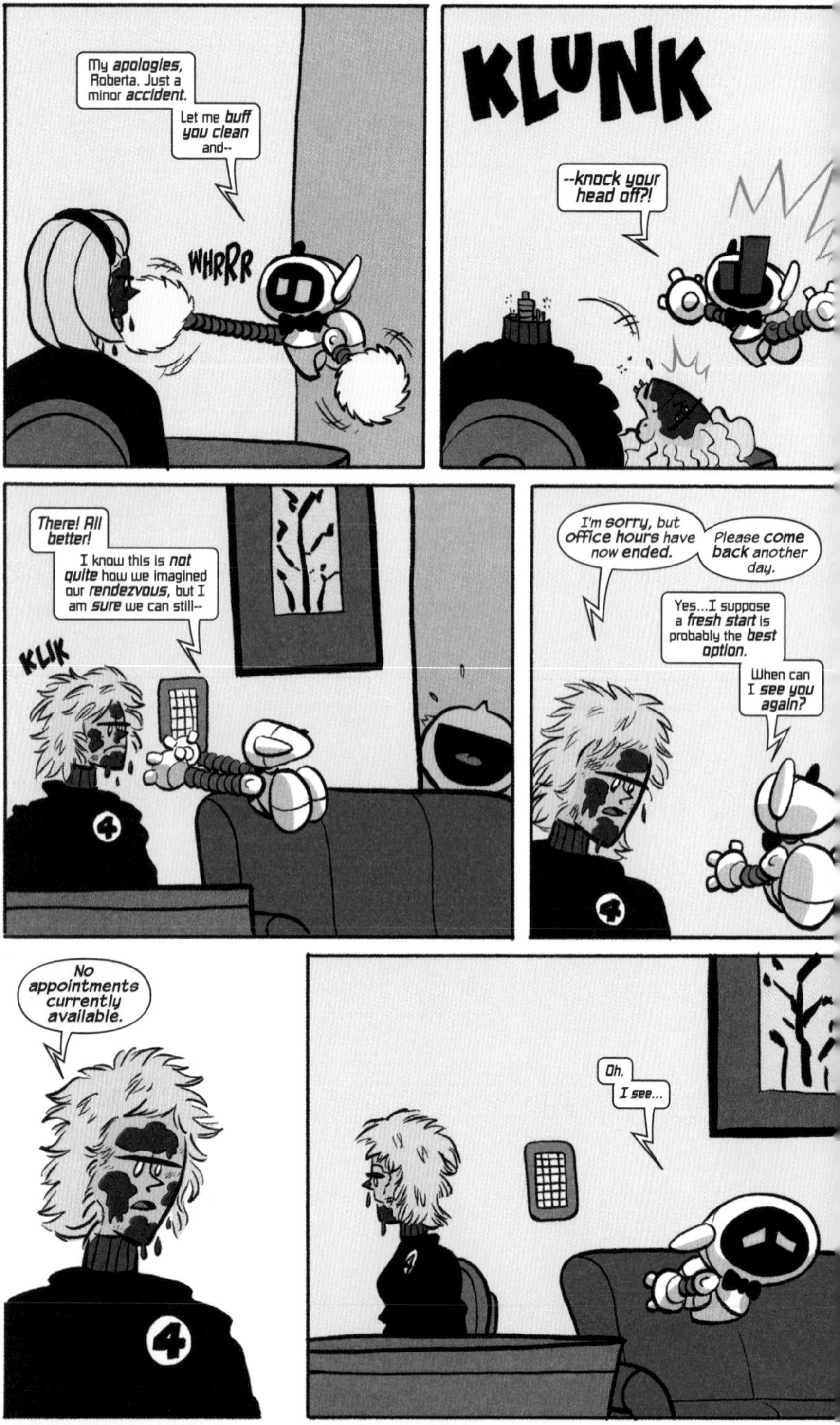
My apologies, Roberta. Just a minor accident.
Let me buff you clean and--
WHRRR
KLUNK
--knock your head off?!
There! All better!
I know this is not quite how we imagined our rendezvous, but I am sure we can still--
KLIK
I'm sorry, but office hours have now ended.
Please come back another day.
Yes...I suppose a fresh start is probably the best option.
When can I see you again?
No appointments currently available.
Oh.
I see...

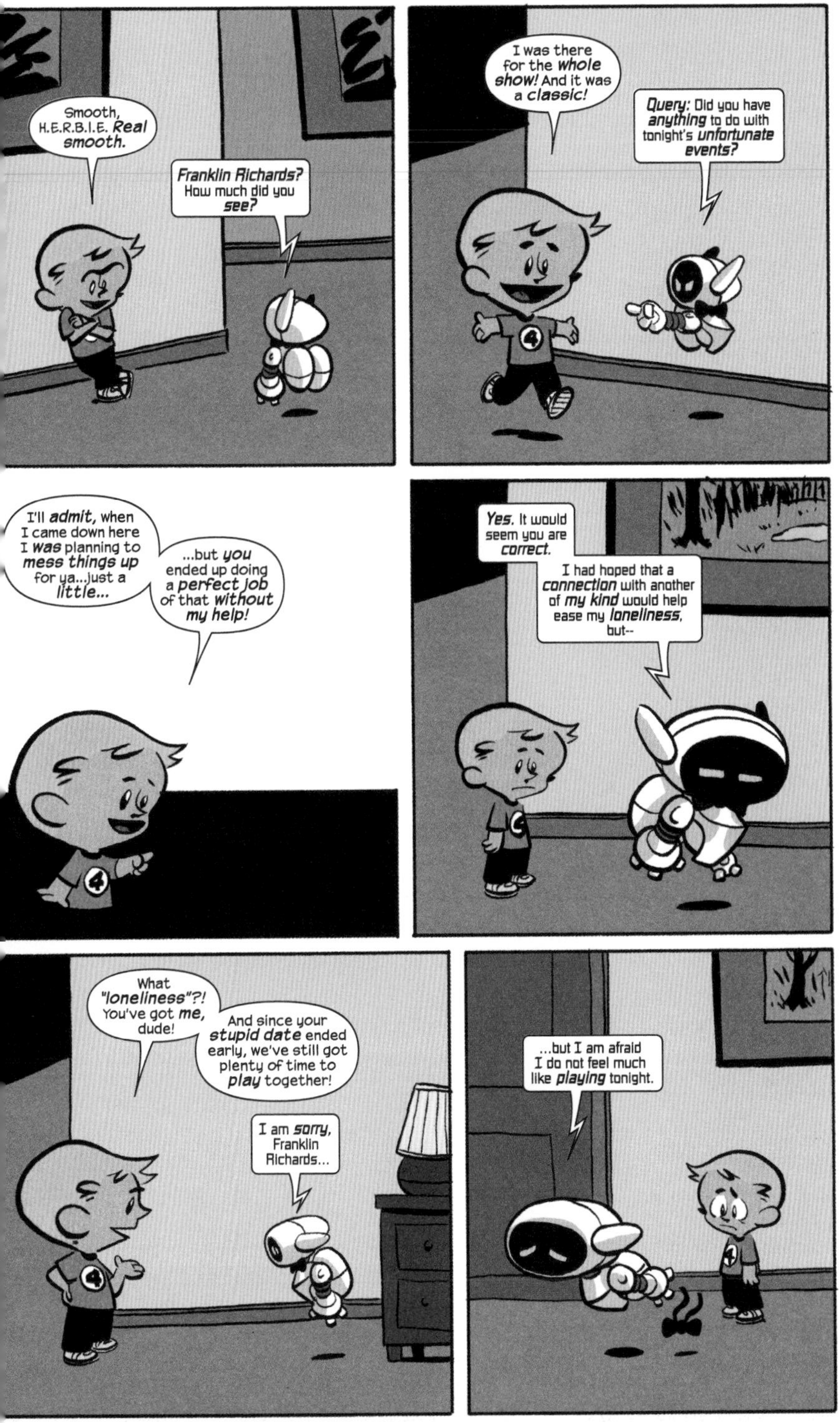

Smooth, H.E.R.B.I.E. *Real smooth.*
Franklin Richards? How much did you *see?*
I was there for the *whole show!* And it was a *classic!*
Query: Did you have *anything* to do with tonight's *unfortunate events?*
I'll *admit,* when I came down here I *was* planning to *mess things up* for ya...just a *little...*
...but *you* ended up doing a *perfect job* of that *without my help!*
Yes. It would seem you are *correct.*
I had hoped that a *connection* with another of *my kind* would help ease my *loneliness,* but--
What *"loneliness"?!* You've got *me,* dude!
And since your *stupid date* ended early, we've still got plenty of time to *play* together!
I am *sorry,* Franklin Richards...
...but I am afraid I do not feel much like *playing* tonight.

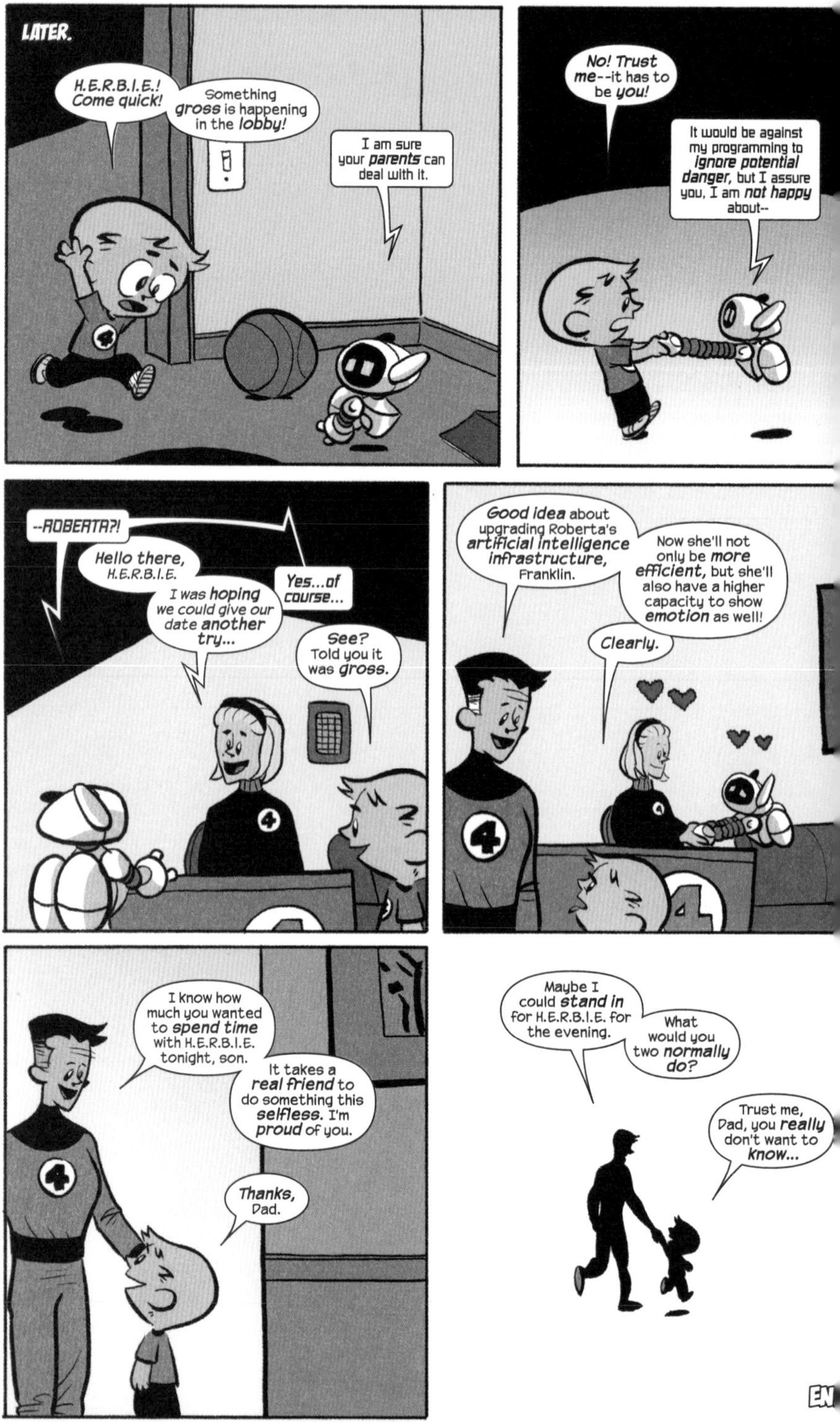
LATER.
H.E.R.B.I.E.! Come quick!
Something gross is happening in the lobby!
I am sure your parents can deal with it.
No! Trust me--it has to be you!
It would be against my programming to ignore potential danger, but I assure you, I am not happy about--
--ROBERTA?!
Hello there, H.E.R.B.I.E.
I was hoping we could give our date another try...
Yes...of course...
See? Told you it was gross.
Good idea about upgrading Roberta's artificial intelligence infrastructure, Franklin.
Now she'll not only be more efficient, but she'll also have a higher capacity to show emotion as well!
Clearly.
I know how much you wanted to spend time with H.E.R.B.I.E. tonight, son.
It takes a real friend to do something this selfless. I'm proud of you.
Thanks, Dad.
Maybe I could stand in for H.E.R.B.I.E. for the evening.
What would you two normally do?
Trust me, Dad, you really don't want to know...
END

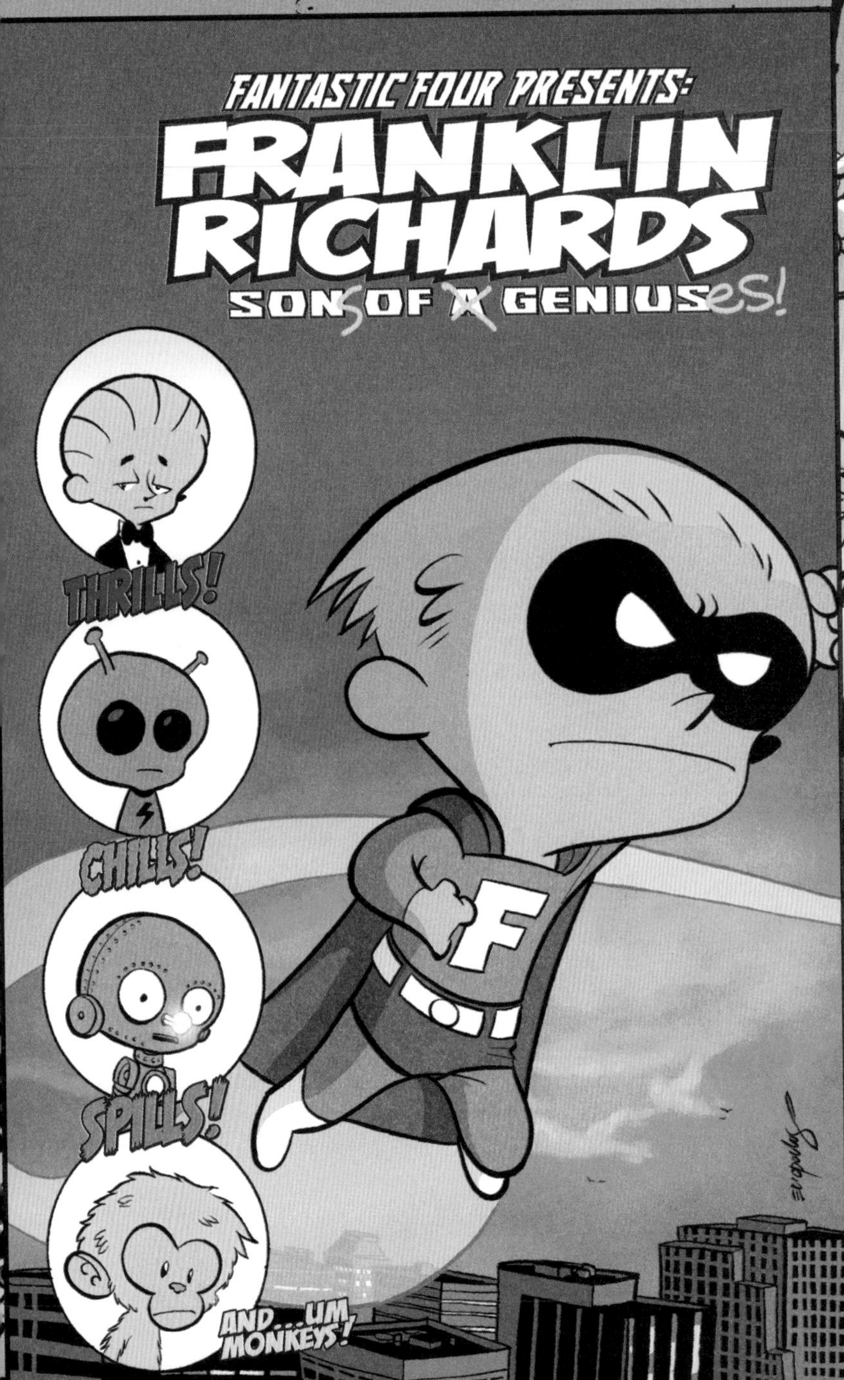
FANTASTIC FOUR PRESENTS:
FRANKLIN RICHARDS
SONS OF ~~A~~ GENIUSES!
THRILLS!
CHILLS!
SPILLS!
AND...UM MONKEYS!

FANTASTIC FOUR PRESENTS: FRANKLIN RICHARDS SON~~S~~ OF ~~A~~ GENIUS~~ES!~~

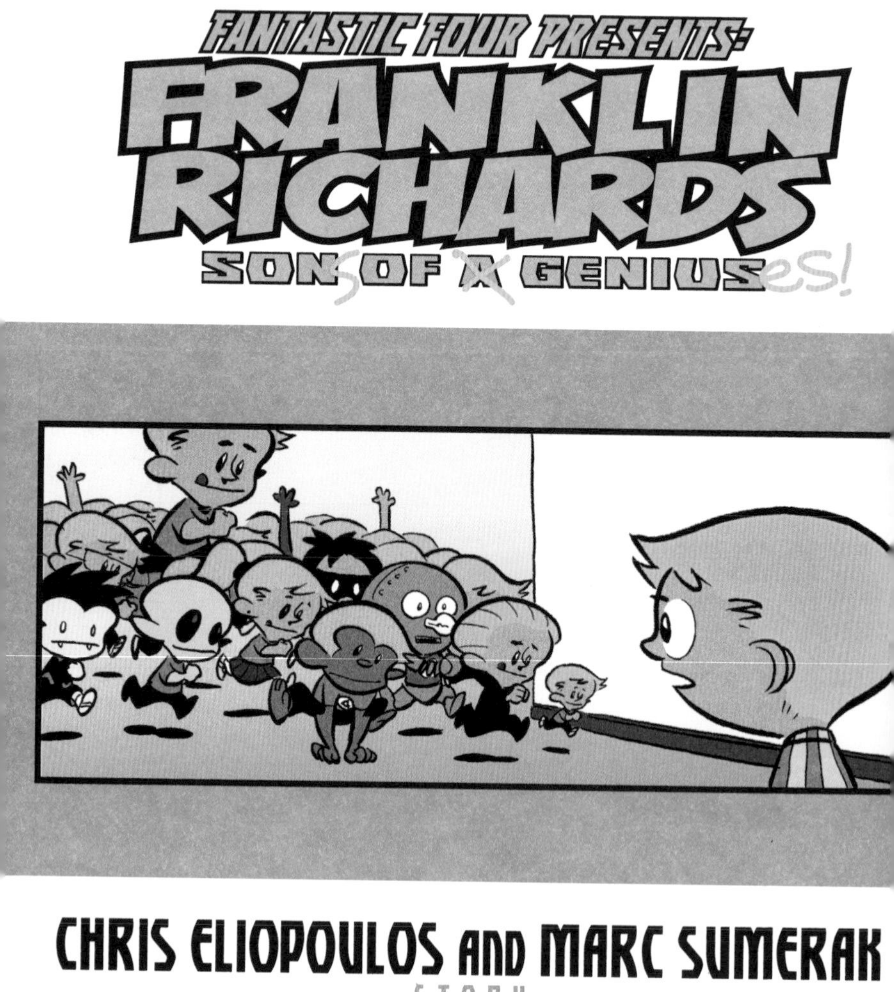

CHRIS ELIOPOULOS AND MARC SUMERAK
STORY

MARC SUMERAK
SCRIPT

CHRIS ELIOPOULOS
ART & LETTERS

BRAD ANDERSO
COLOR

RALPH MACCHIO
CONSULTING EDITOR

NATHAN COSBY
EDITOR

JOE QUESADA
EDITOR IN CHIEF

DAN BUCKLEY
PUBLISHER

THANKS FOR EVERYTHING, MARC. WE'LL MISS YOU!

RANKLIN ICHARDS SON OF A GENIUS IN: MISSION UNSTOPPABLE!

BY CHRIS ELIOPOULOS & MARC SUMERAK

BRAD ANDERSON COLORS

NATHAN COSBY EDITOR

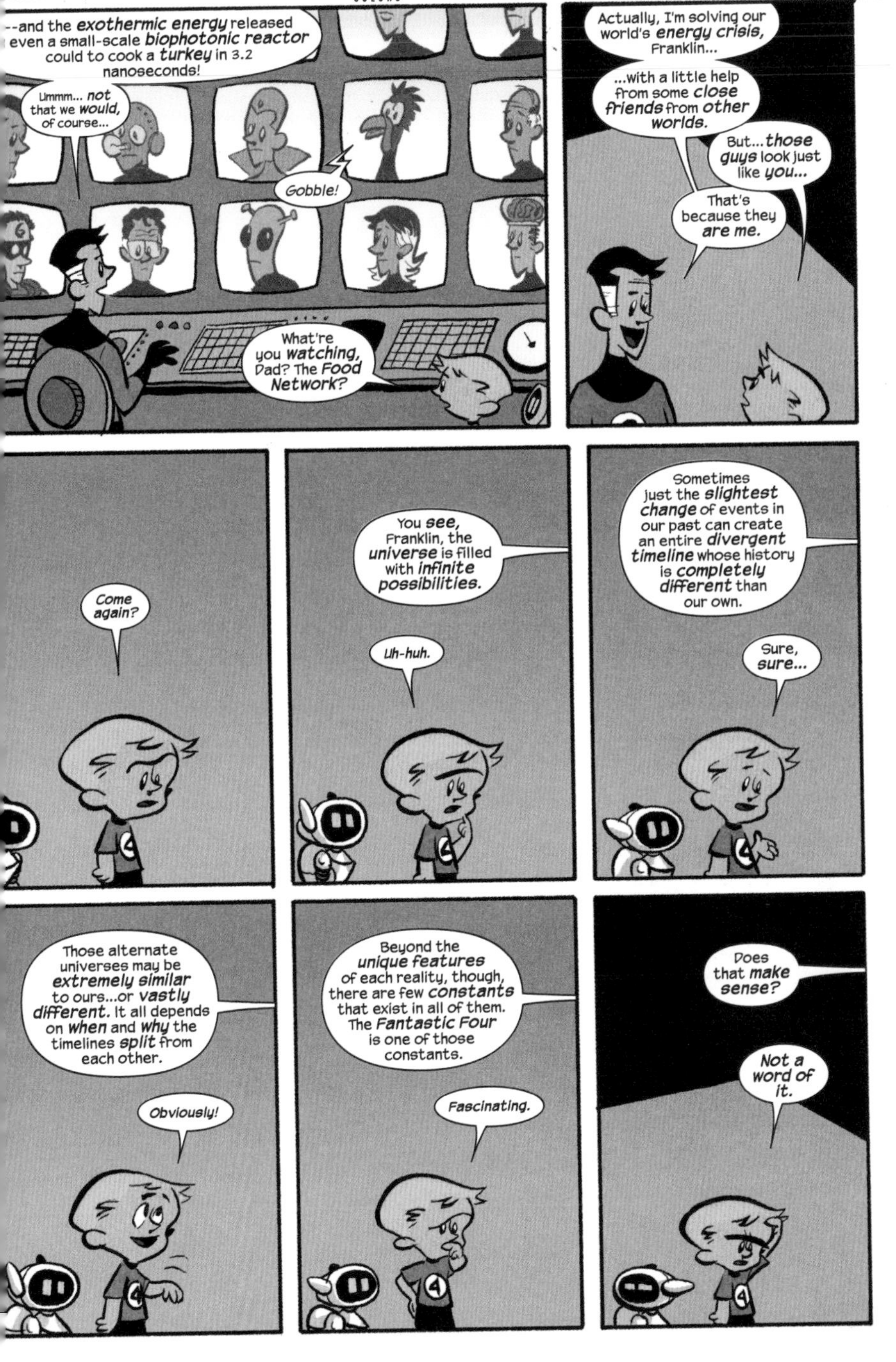
--and the exothermic energy released even a small-scale biophotonic reactor could to cook a turkey in 3.2 nanoseconds!
Ummm... not that we would, of course...
Gobble!
What're you watching, Dad? The Food Network?
Actually, I'm solving our world's energy crisis, Franklin...
...with a little help from some close friends from other worlds.
But...those guys look just like you...
That's because they are me.
Come again?
You see, Franklin, the universe is filled with infinite possibilities.
Uh-huh.
Sometimes just the slightest change of events in our past can create an entire divergent timeline whose history is completely different than our own.
Sure, sure...
Those alternate universes may be extremely similar to ours...or vastly different. It all depends on when and why the timelines split from each other.
Obviously!
Beyond the unique features of each reality, though, there are few constants that exist in all of them. The Fantastic Four is one of those constants.
Fascinating.
Does that make sense?
Not a word of it.

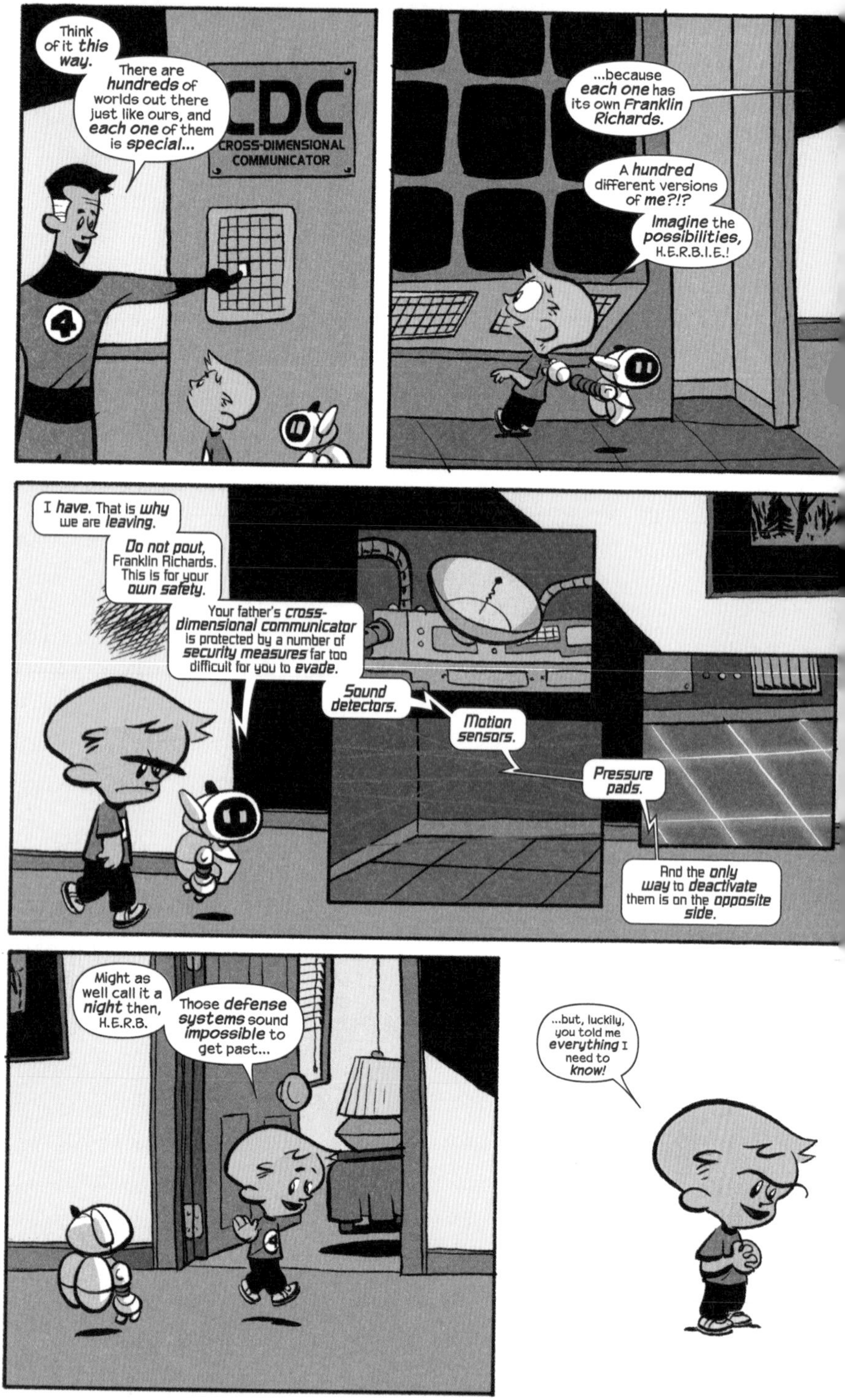

Think of it this way.
There are hundreds of worlds out there just like ours, and each one of them is special...
CDC
CROSS-DIMENSIONAL COMMUNICATOR
...because each one has its own Franklin Richards.
A hundred different versions of me?!?
Imagine the possibilities, H.E.R.B.I.E.!
I have. That is why we are leaving.
Do not pout, Franklin Richards. This is for your own safety.
Your father's cross-dimensional communicator is protected by a number of security measures far too difficult for you to evade.
Sound detectors.
Motion sensors.
Pressure pads.
And the only way to deactivate them is on the opposite side.
Might as well call it a night then, H.E.R.B.
Those defense systems sound impossible to get past...
...but, luckily, you told me everything I need to know!

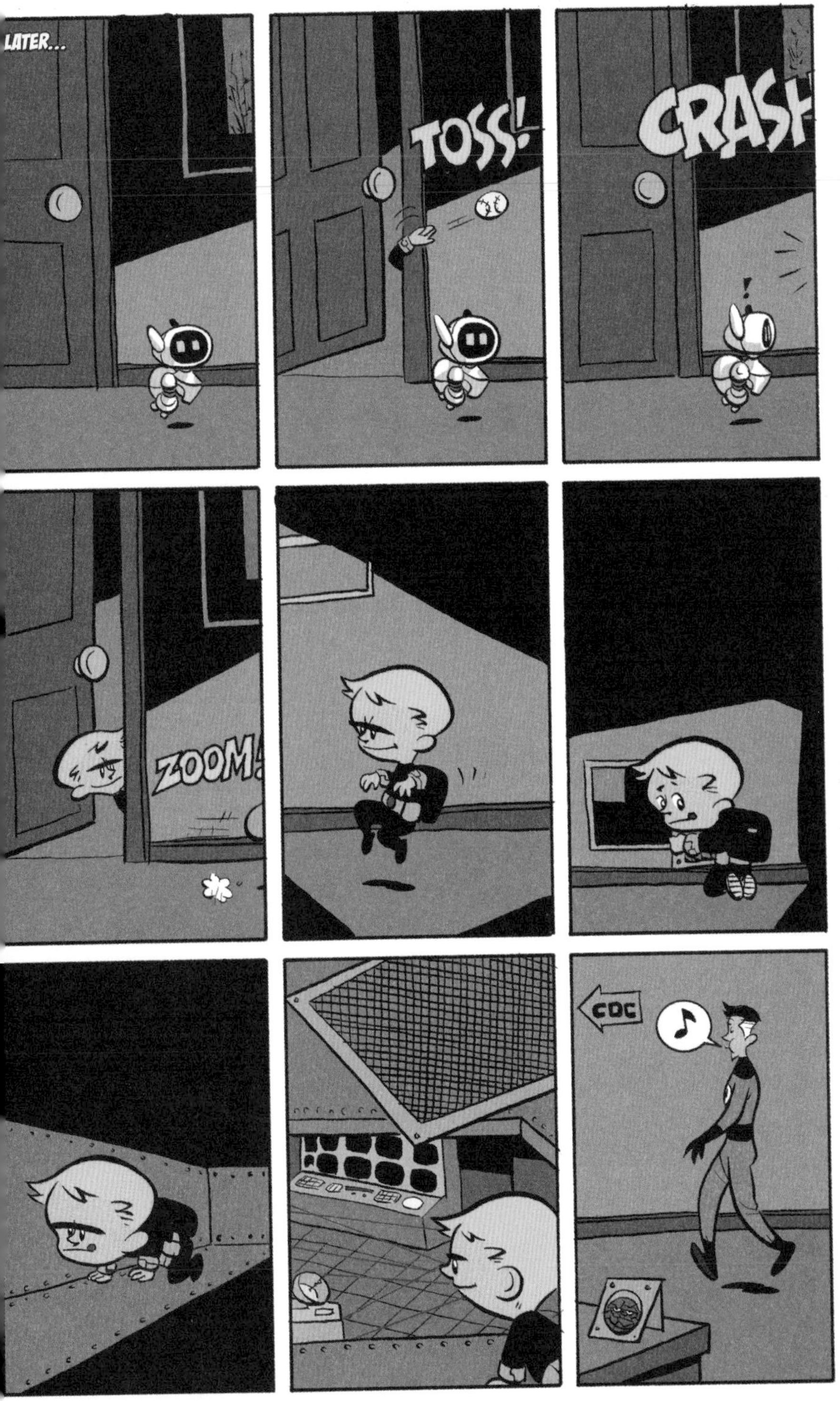
LATER...
TOSS!
CRASH
ZOOM!
CDC
♪

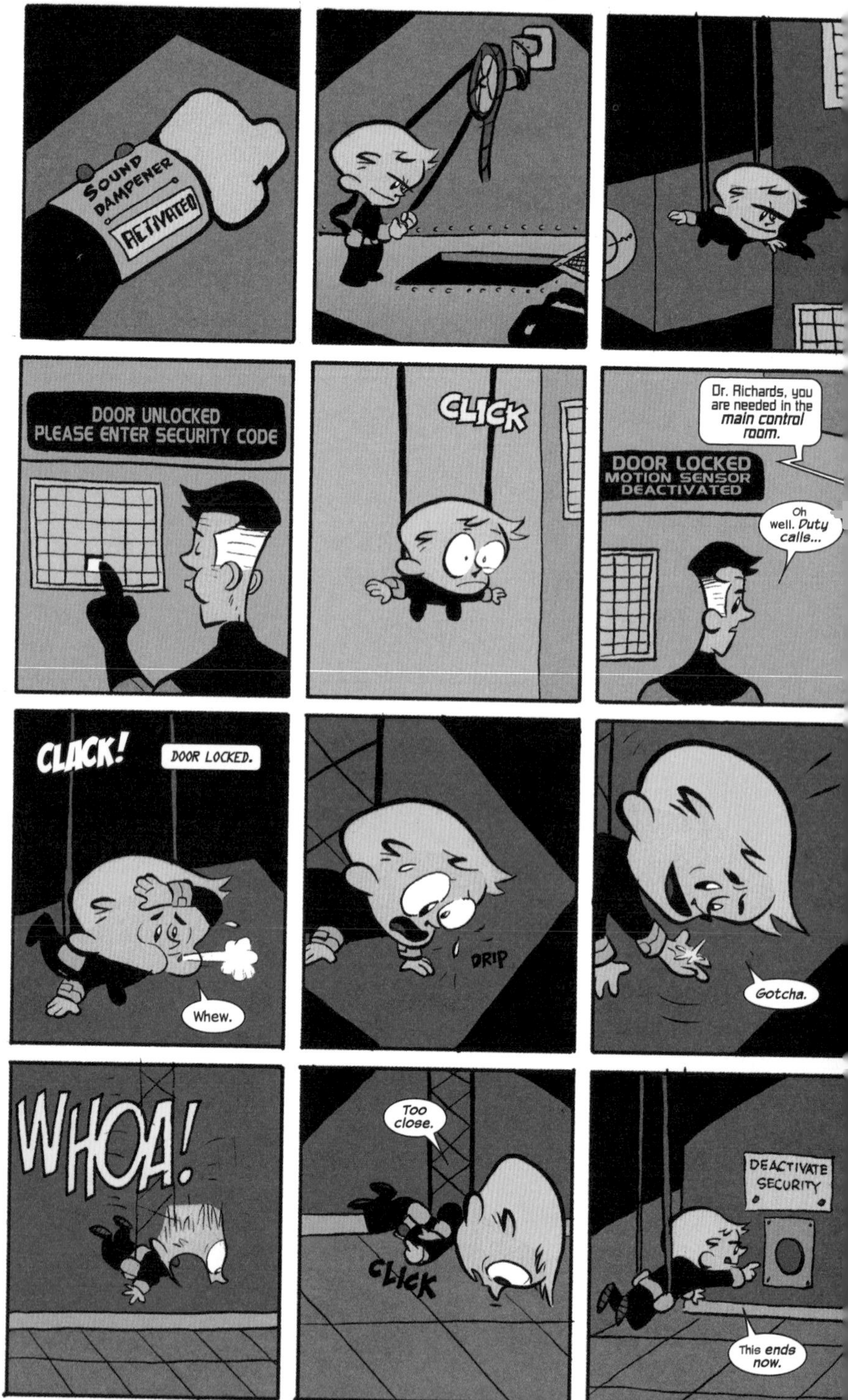

SOUND DAMPENER
ACTIVATED
DOOR UNLOCKED
PLEASE ENTER SECURITY CODE
CLICK
Dr. Richards, you are needed in the main control room.
DOOR LOCKED
MOTION SENSOR DEACTIVATED
Oh well. Duty calls...
CLACK!
DOOR LOCKED.
Whew.
DRIP
Gotcha.
WHOA!
Too close.
CLICK
DEACTIVATE SECURITY
This ends now.

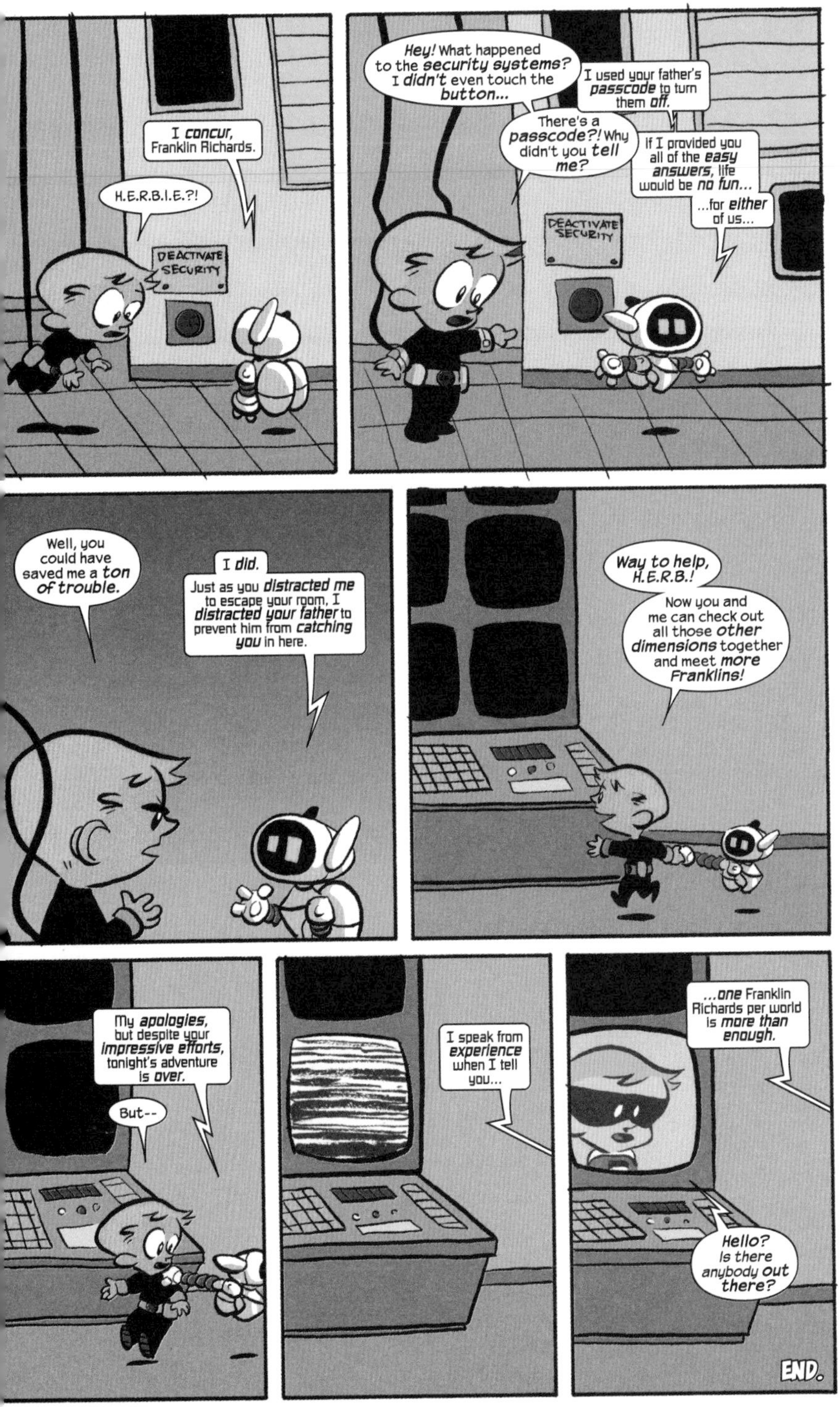

I concur, Franklin Richards.
H.E.R.B.I.E.?!
DEACTIVATE SECURITY
Hey! What happened to the security systems? I didn't even touch the button...
I used your father's passcode to turn them off.
There's a passcode?! Why didn't you tell me?
If I provided you all of the easy answers, life would be no fun...
...for either of us...
DEACTIVATE SECURITY
Well, you could have saved me a ton of trouble.
I did.
Just as you distracted me to escape your room, I distracted your father to prevent him from catching you in here.
Way to help, H.E.R.B.!
Now you and me can check out all those other dimensions together and meet more Franklins!
My apologies, but despite your impressive efforts, tonight's adventure is over.
But--
I speak from experience when I tell you...
...one Franklin Richards per world is more than enough.
Hello? Is there anybody out there?
END.

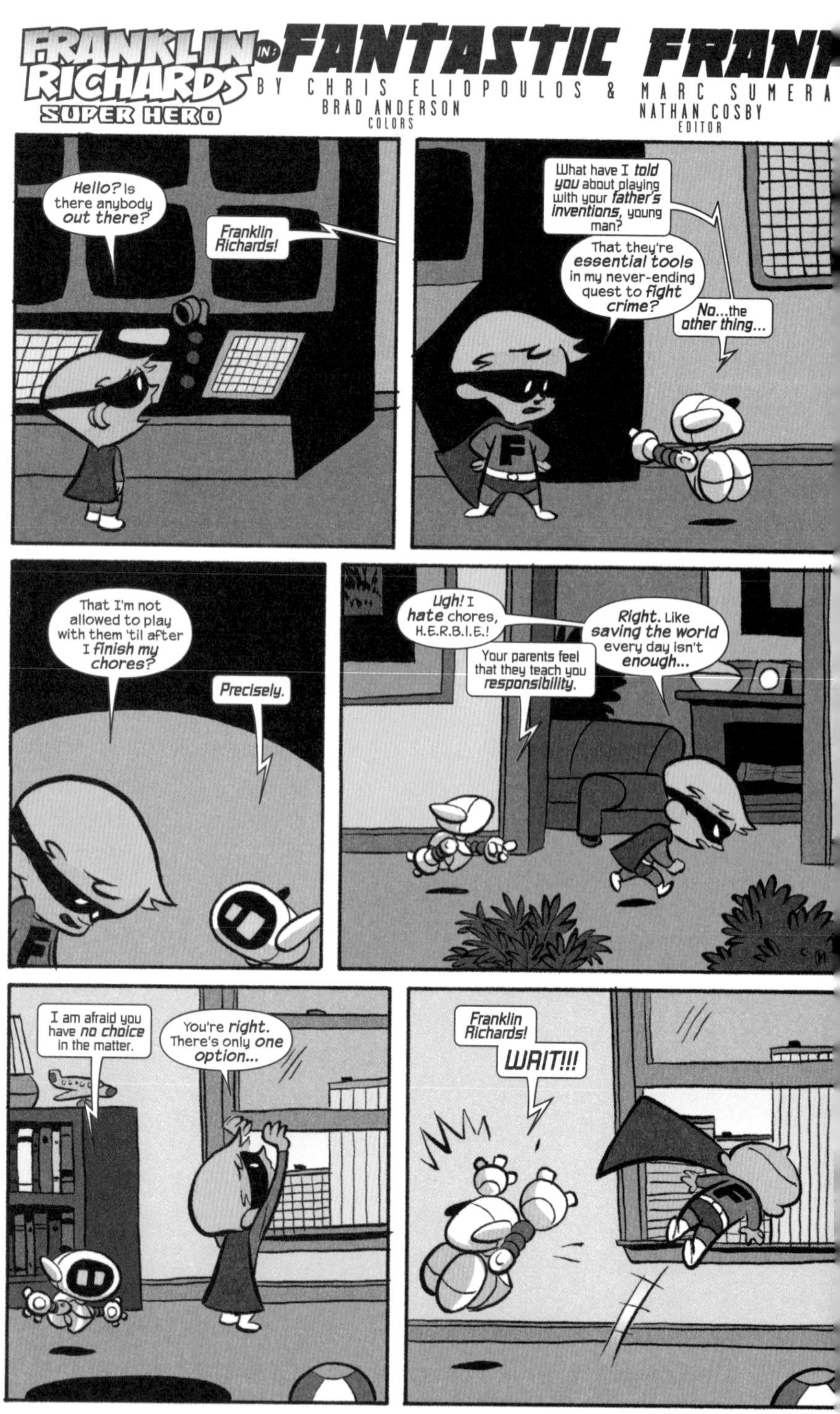

FRANKLIN RICHARDS SUPER HERO
IN: FANTASTIC FRAN
BY CHRIS ELIOPOULOS & MARC SUMERA
BRAD ANDERSON COLORS
NATHAN COSBY EDITOR
Hello? Is there anybody out there?
Franklin Richards!
What have I told you about playing with your father's inventions, young man?
That they're essential tools in my never-ending quest to fight crime?
No...the other thing...
That I'm not allowed to play with them 'til after I finish my chores?
Precisely.
Ugh! I hate chores, H.E.R.B.I.E.!
Your parents feel that they teach you responsibility.
Right. Like saving the world every day isn't enough...
I am afraid you have no choice in the matter.
You're right. There's only one option...
Franklin Richards!
WAIT!!!

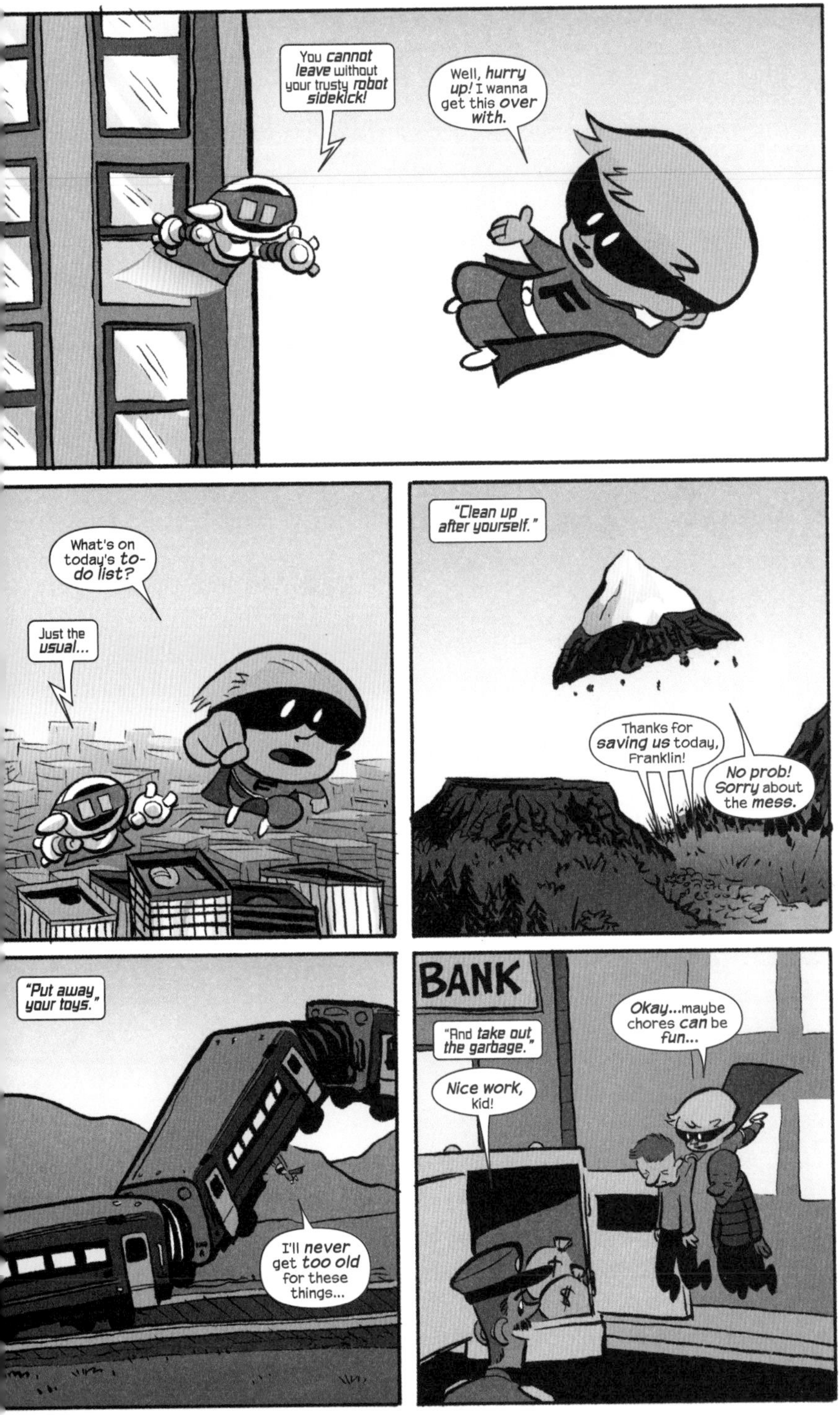

You cannot leave without your trusty robot sidekick!
Well, hurry up! I wanna get this over with.
What's on today's to-do list?
Just the usual...
"Clean up after yourself."
Thanks for saving us today, Franklin!
No prob! Sorry about the mess.
"Put away your toys."
I'll never get too old for these things...
BANK
"And take out the garbage."
Nice work, kid!
Okay...maybe chores can be fun...

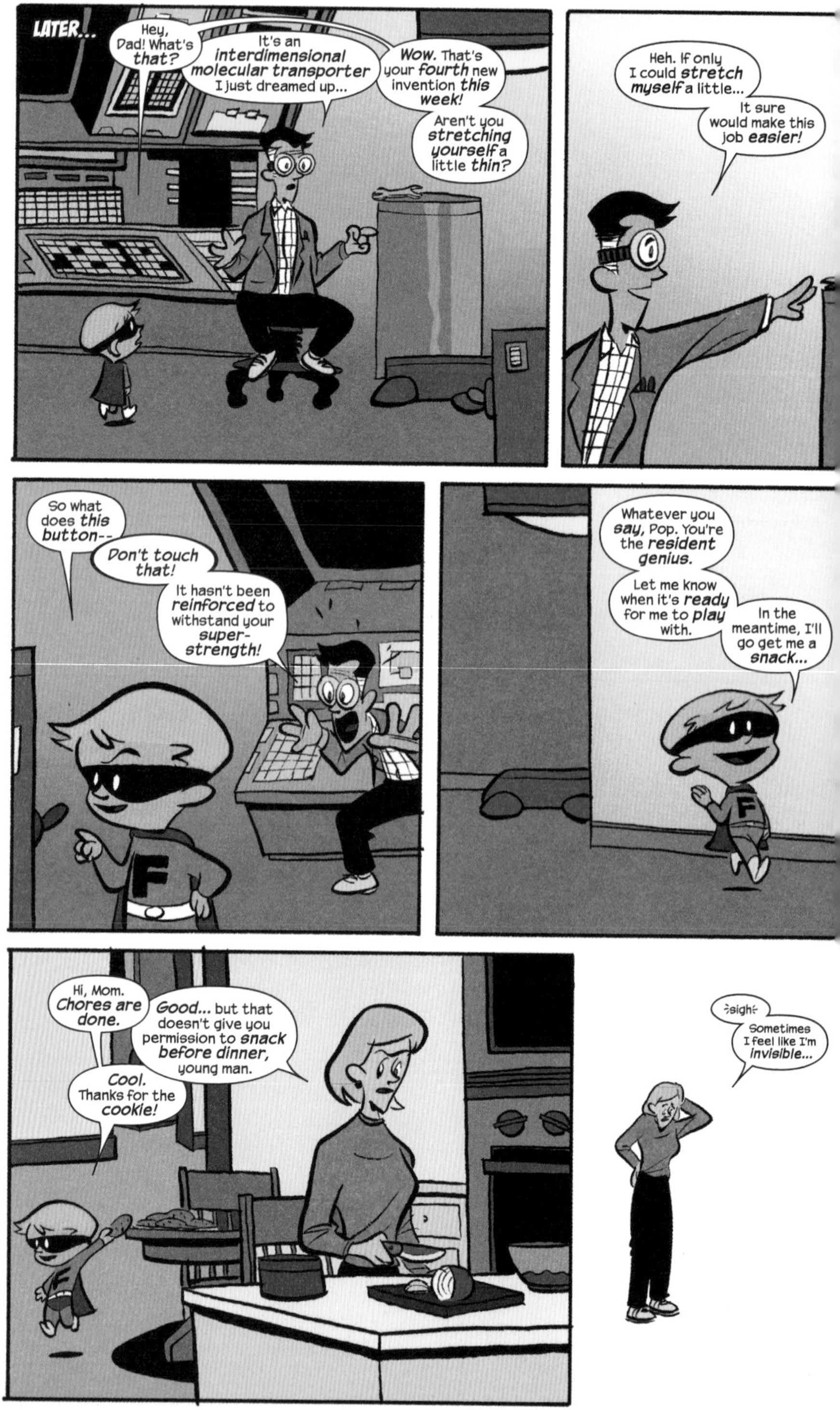
LATER...
Hey, Dad! What's that?
It's an interdimensional molecular transporter I just dreamed up...
Wow. That's your fourth new invention this week!
Aren't you stretching yourself a little thin?
Heh. If only I could stretch myself a little...
It sure would make this job easier!
So what does this button--
Don't touch that!
It hasn't been reinforced to withstand your super-strength!
Whatever you say, Pop. You're the resident genius.
Let me know when it's ready for me to play with.
In the meantime, I'll go get me a snack...
Hi, Mom. Chores are done.
Good... but that doesn't give you permission to snack before dinner, young man.
Cool. Thanks for the cookie!
sigh
Sometimes I feel like I'm invisible...

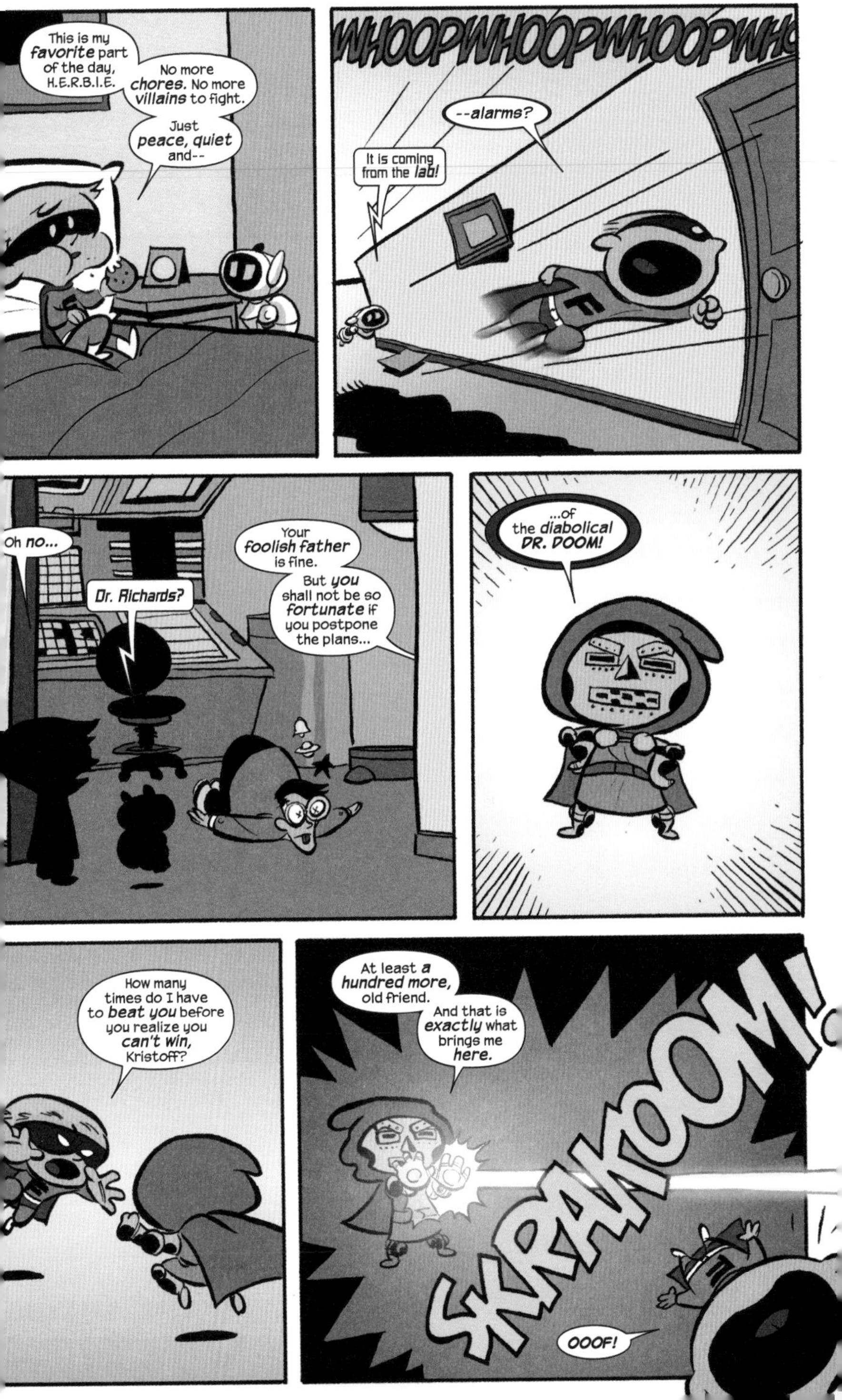
WHOOPWHOOPWHOOPWHO
This is my favorite part of the day, H.E.R.B.I.E.
No more chores. No more villains to fight.
Just peace, quiet and--
--alarms?
It is coming from the lab!
Oh no...
Dr. Richards?
Your foolish father is fine.
But you shall not be so fortunate if you postpone the plans...
...of the diabolical DR. DOOM!
How many times do I have to beat you before you realize you can't win, Kristoff?
At least a hundred more, old friend.
And that is exactly what brings me here.
SKRAKOOOM!
OOOF!

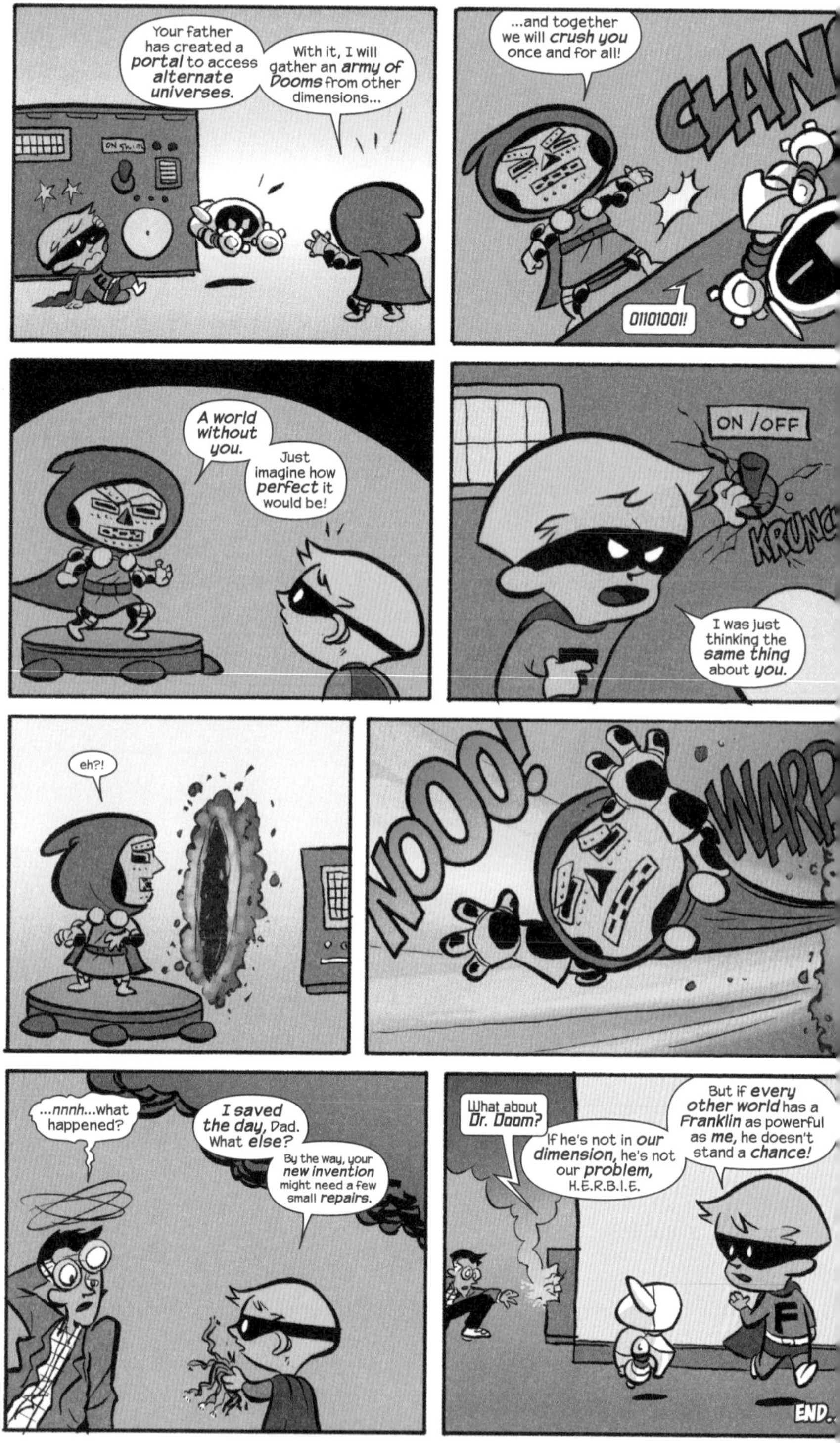
Your father has created a portal to access alternate universes.
With it, I will gather an army of Dooms from other dimensions...
ON SWITCH
...and together we will crush you once and for all!
CLANG
01101001!
A world without you.
Just imagine how perfect it would be!
ON /OFF
KRUNC
I was just thinking the same thing about you.
eh?!
NOOOO!
WARP
...nnnh...what happened?
I saved the day, Dad. What else?
By the way, your new invention might need a few small repairs.
What about Dr. Doom?
If he's not in our dimension, he's not our problem, H.E.R.B.I.E.
But if every other world has a Franklin as powerful as me, he doesn't stand a chance!
END...

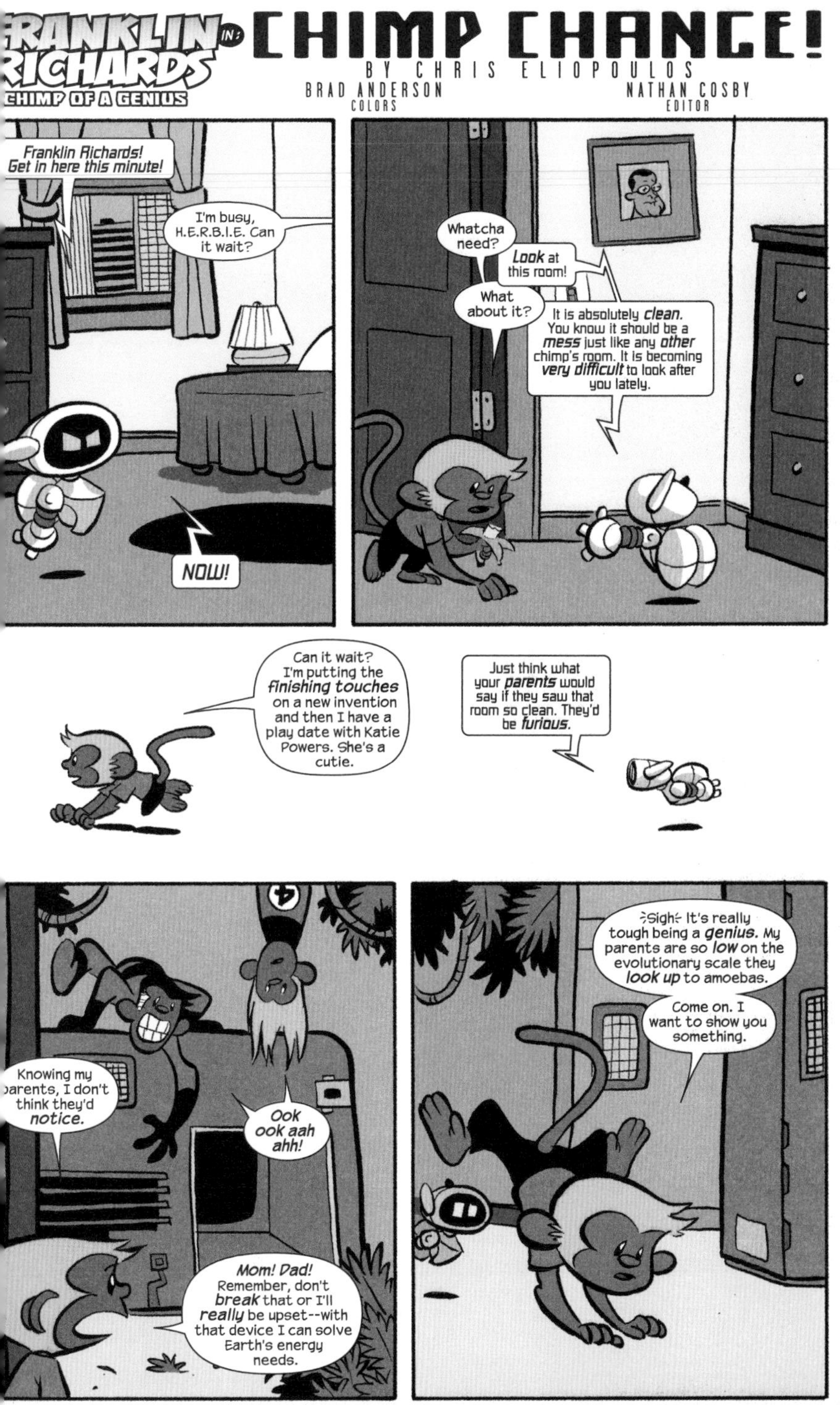
FRANKLIN RICHARDS
CHIMP OF A GENIUS
IN: CHIMP CHANGE!
BY CHRIS ELIOPOULOS
BRAD ANDERSON
COLORS
NATHAN COSBY
EDITOR
Franklin Richards! Get in here this minute!
I'm busy, H.E.R.B.I.E. Can it wait?
NOW!
Whatcha need?
Look at this room!
What about it?
It is absolutely clean. You know it should be a mess just like any other chimp's room. It is becoming very difficult to look after you lately.
Can it wait? I'm putting the finishing touches on a new invention and then I have a play date with Katie Powers. She's a cutie.
Just think what your parents would say if they saw that room so clean. They'd be furious.
Knowing my parents, I don't think they'd notice.
Ook ook aah ahh!
Mom! Dad! Remember, don't break that or I'll really be upset--with that device I can solve Earth's energy needs.
Sigh It's really tough being a genius. My parents are so low on the evolutionary scale they look up to amoebas.
Come on. I want to show you something.

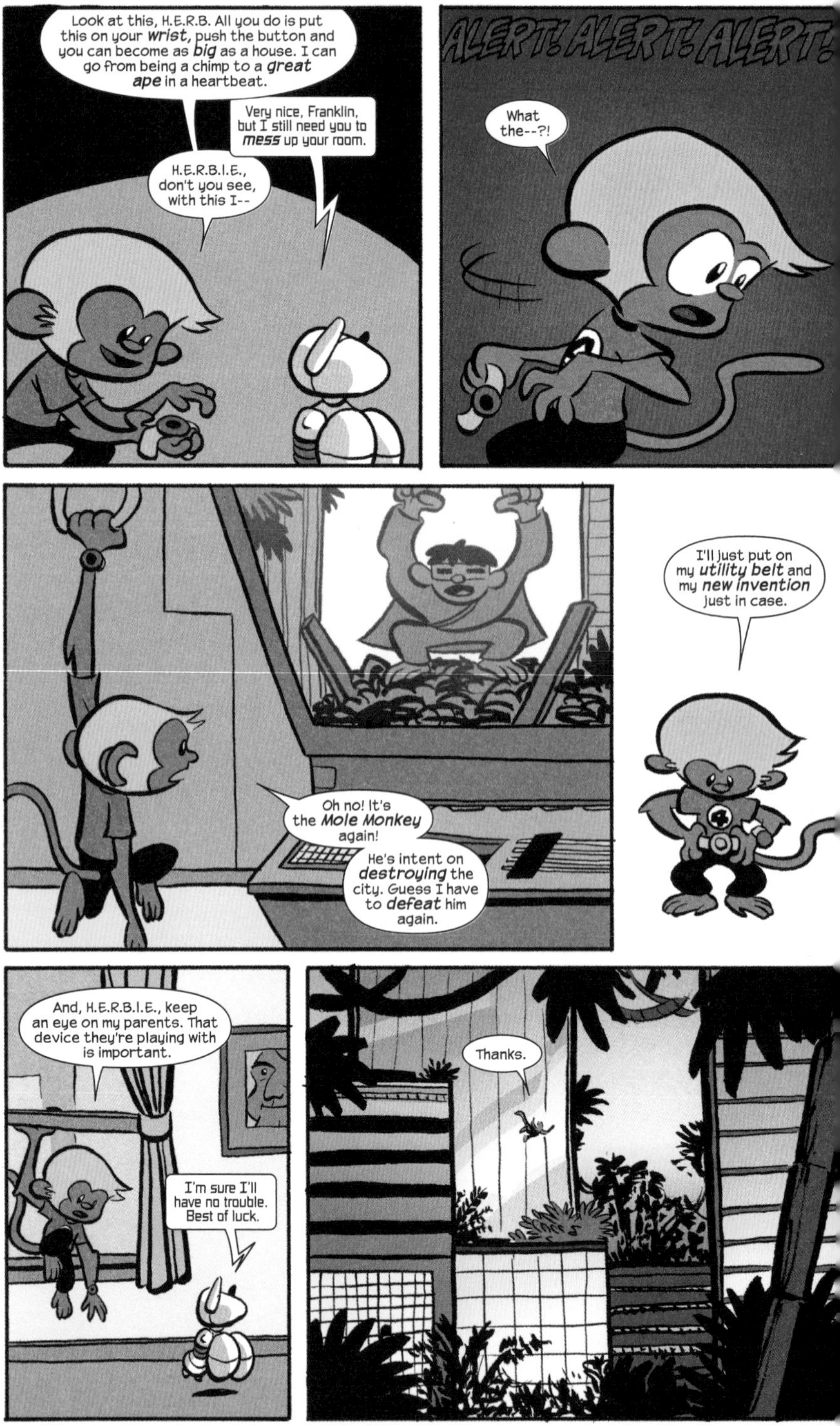

Look at this, H.E.R.B. All you do is put this on your wrist, push the button and you can become as big as a house. I can go from being a chimp to a great ape in a heartbeat.
Very nice, Franklin, but I still need you to mess up your room.
H.E.R.B.I.E., don't you see, with this I--
ALERT! ALERT! ALERT!
What the--?!
Oh no! It's the Mole Monkey again!
He's intent on destroying the city. Guess I have to defeat him again.
I'll just put on my utility belt and my new invention just in case.
And, H.E.R.B.I.E., keep an eye on my parents. That device they're playing with is important.
I'm sure I'll have no trouble. Best of luck.
Thanks.

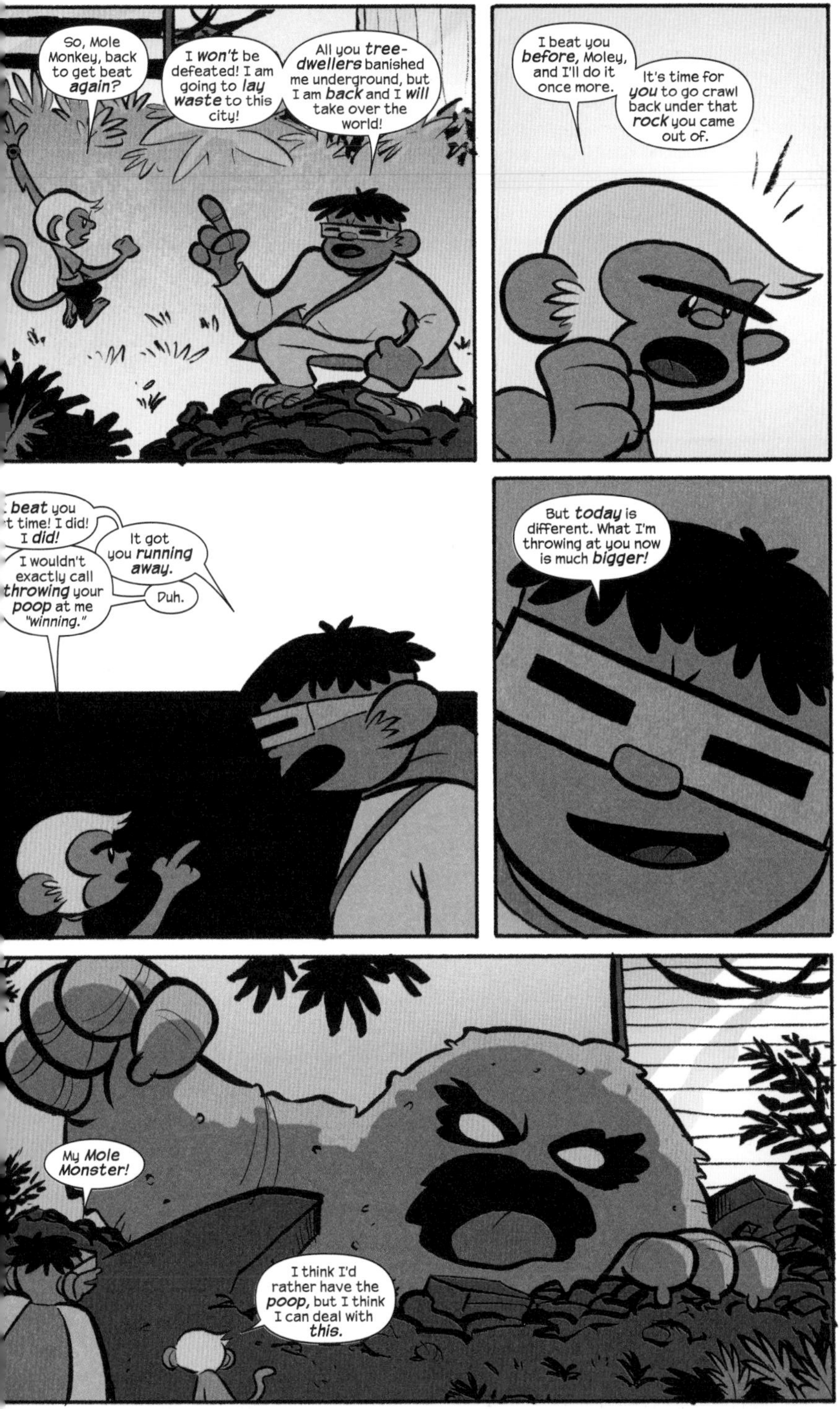

So, Mole Monkey, back to get beat *again?*
I *won't* be defeated! I am going to *lay waste* to this city!
All you *tree-dwellers* banished me underground, but I am *back* and I *will* take over the world!
I beat you *before,* Moley, and I'll do it once more.
It's time for *you* to go crawl back under that *rock* you came out of.
beat you
t time! I did! I *did!*
It got you *running away.*
I wouldn't exactly call *throwing* your *poop* at me "winning."
Duh.
But *today* is different. What I'm throwing at you now is much *bigger!*
My *Mole Monster!*
I think I'd rather have the *poop,* but I think I can deal with *this.*

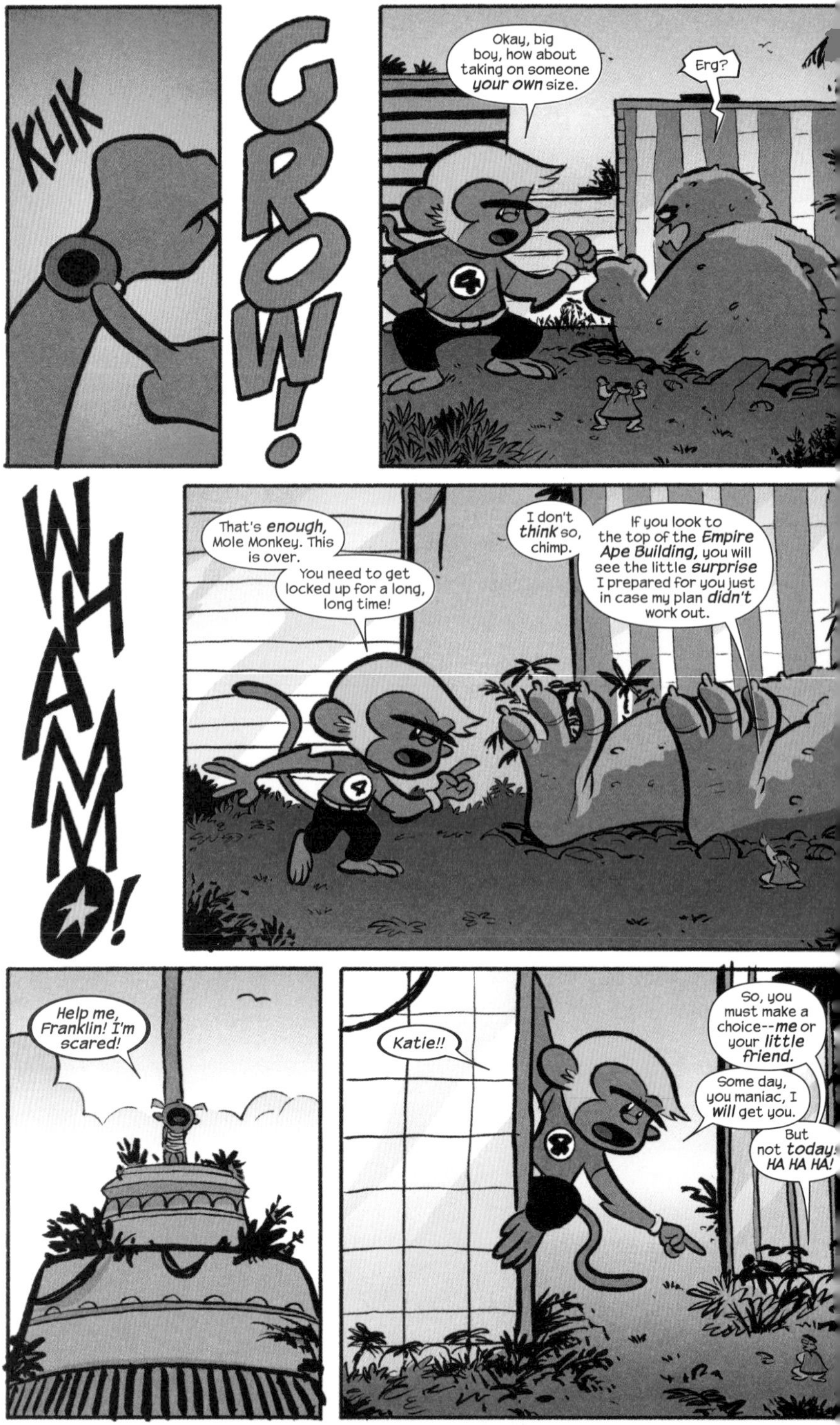

KLIK
GROW!
Okay, big boy, how about taking on someone your own size.
Erg?
WHAMMO!
That's enough, Mole Monkey. This is over.
You need to get locked up for a long, long time!
I don't think so, chimp.
If you look to the top of the Empire Ape Building, you will see the little surprise I prepared for you just in case my plan didn't work out.
Help me, Franklin! I'm scared!
Katie!!
So, you must make a choice--me or your little friend.
Some day, you maniac, I will get you.
But not today! HA HA HA!

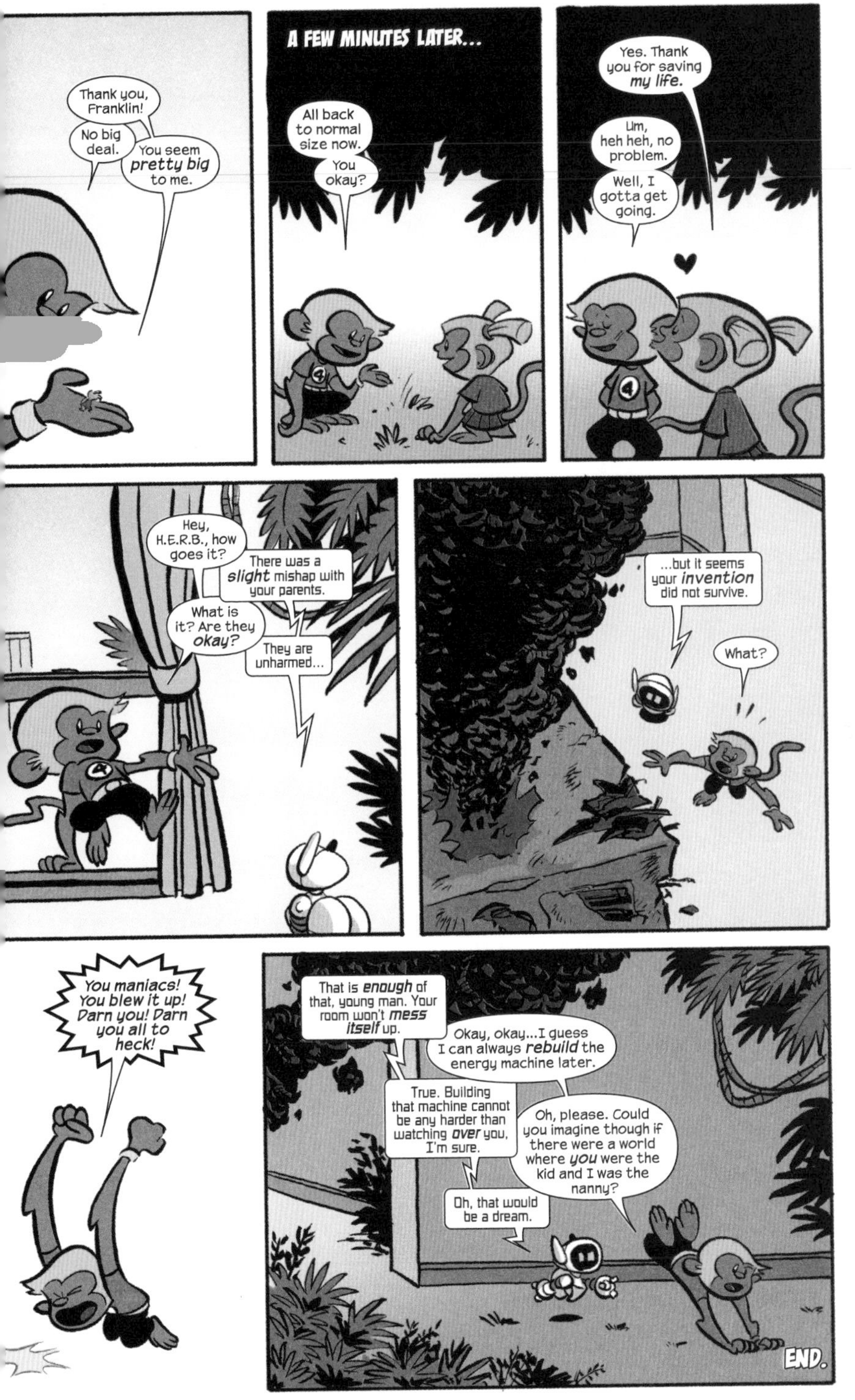

Thank you, Franklin!
No big deal.
You seem pretty big to me.
A FEW MINUTES LATER...
All back to normal size now.
You okay?
Yes. Thank you for saving my life.
Um, heh heh, no problem.
Well, I gotta get going.
Hey, H.E.R.B., how goes it?
There was a slight mishap with your parents.
What is it? Are they okay?
They are unharmed...
...but it seems your invention did not survive.
What?
You maniacs! You blew it up! Darn you! Darn you all to heck!
That is enough of that, young man. Your room won't mess itself up.
Okay, okay...I guess I can always rebuild the energy machine later.
True. Building that machine cannot be any harder than watching over you, I'm sure.
Oh, please. Could you imagine though if there were a world where you were the kid and I was the nanny?
Oh, that would be a dream.
END.

FRANKLIN RICHARDS HUMAN BUTLER in: H.E.R.B.I.E.: SON OF A SUPER-COMPUTE

MARC SUMERAK story CHRIS ELIOPOULOS AR
BRAD ANDERSON colors
NATHAN COSBY editor

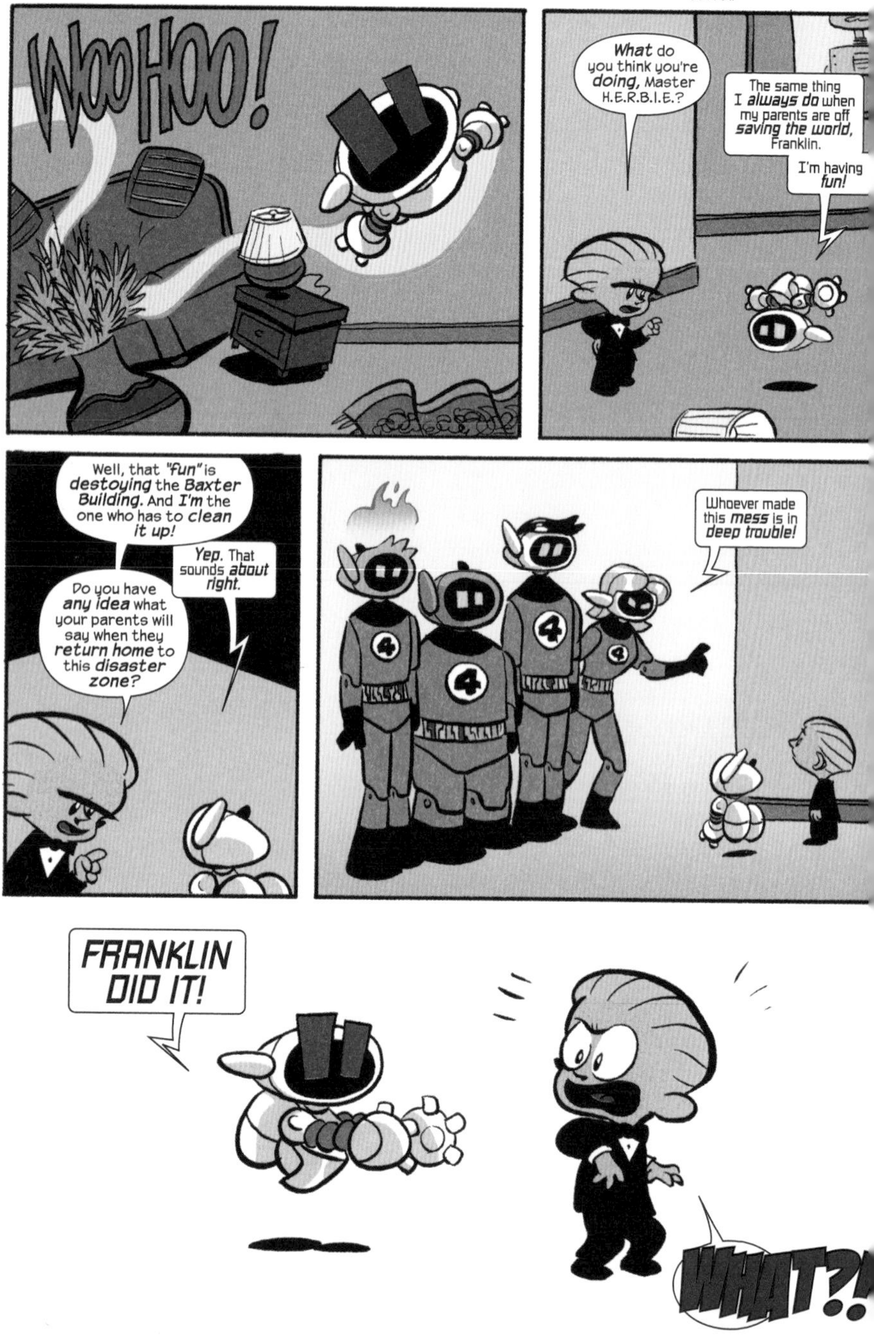

WOOHOO!
What do you think you're doing, Master H.E.R.B.I.E.?
The same thing I always do when my parents are off saving the world, Franklin.
I'm having fun!
Well, that "fun" is destoying the Baxter Building. And I'm the one who has to clean it up!
Do you have any idea what your parents will say when they return home to this disaster zone?
Yep. That sounds about right.
Whoever made this mess is in deep trouble!
FRANKLIN DID IT!
WHAT?!

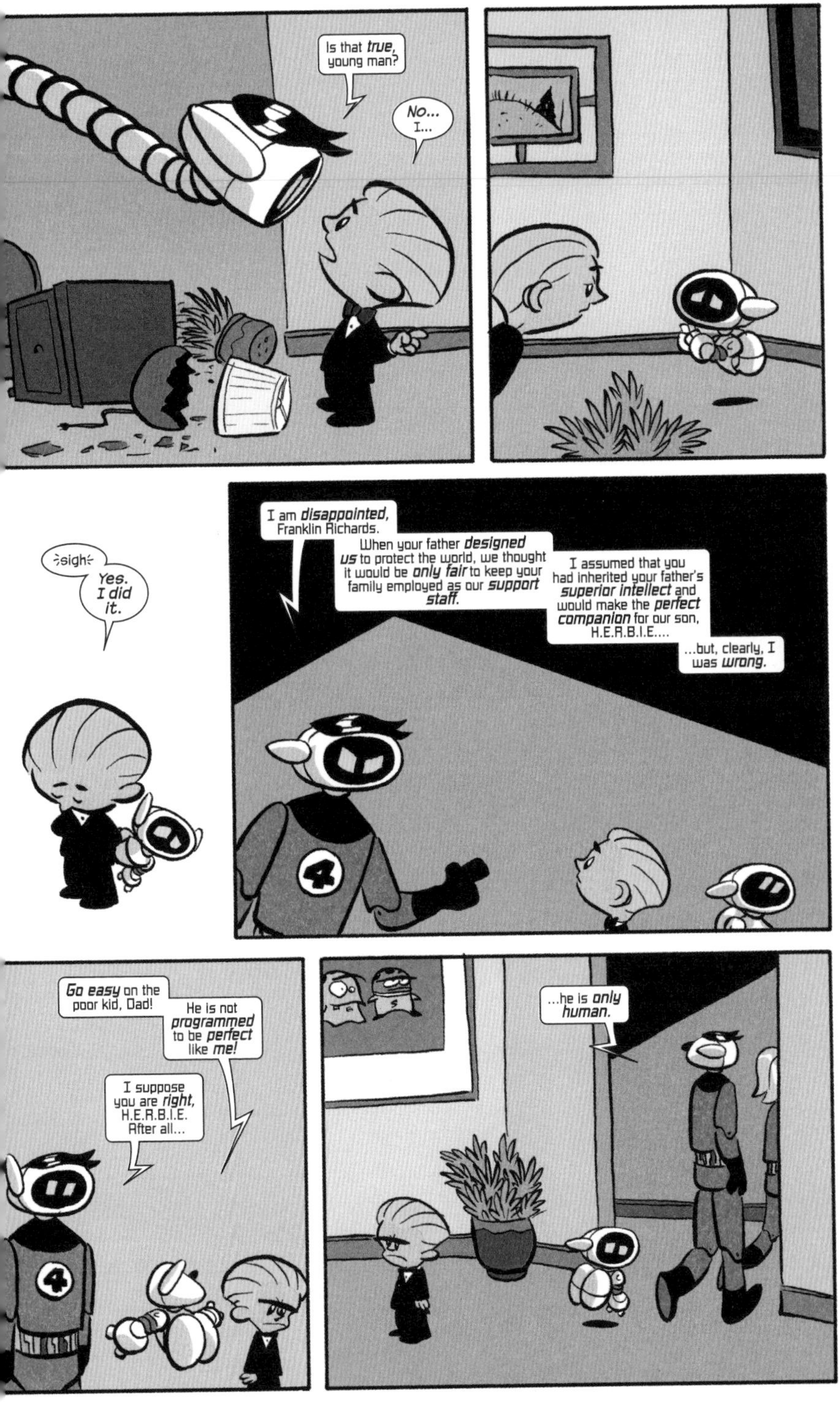
Is that *true*, young man?
No... I...
~sigh~ *Yes. I did it.*
I am *disappointed*, Franklin Richards.
When your father *designed us* to protect the world, we thought it would be *only fair* to keep your family employed as our *support staff*.
I assumed that you had inherited your father's *superior intellect* and would make the *perfect companion* for our son, H.E.R.B.I.E....
...but, clearly, I was *wrong*.
Go easy on the poor kid, Dad!
He is not *programmed* to be *perfect* like *me!*
I suppose you are *right*, H.E.R.B.I.E. After all...
...he is *only human*.

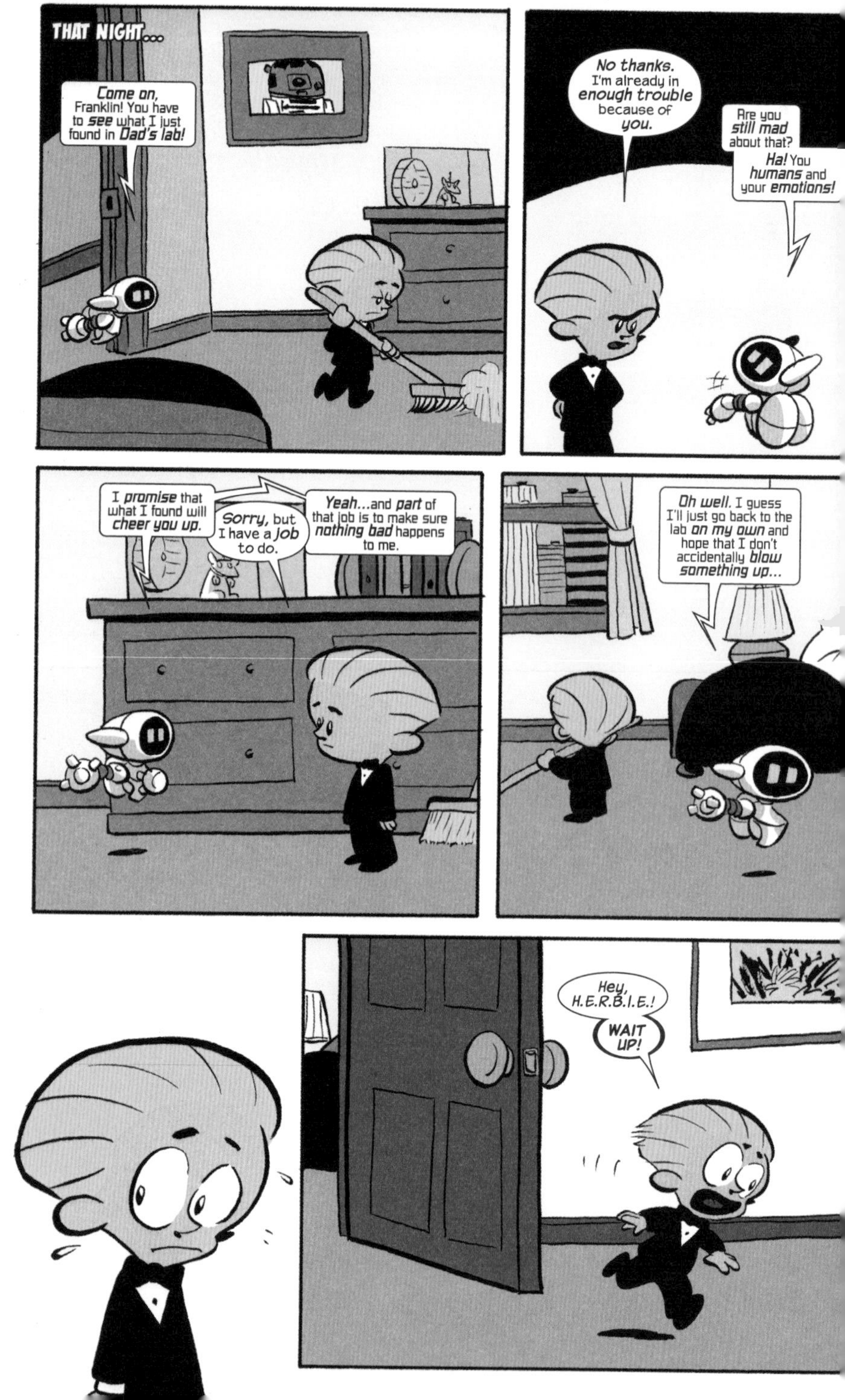
THAT NIGHT...
Come on, Franklin! You have to see what I just found in Dad's lab!
No thanks. I'm already in enough trouble because of you.
Are you still mad about that?
Ha! You humans and your emotions!
I promise that what I found will cheer you up.
Sorry, but I have a job to do.
Yeah...and part of that job is to make sure nothing bad happens to me.
Oh well. I guess I'll just go back to the lab on my own and hope that I don't accidentally blow something up...
Hey, H.E.R.B.I.E.!
WAIT UP!

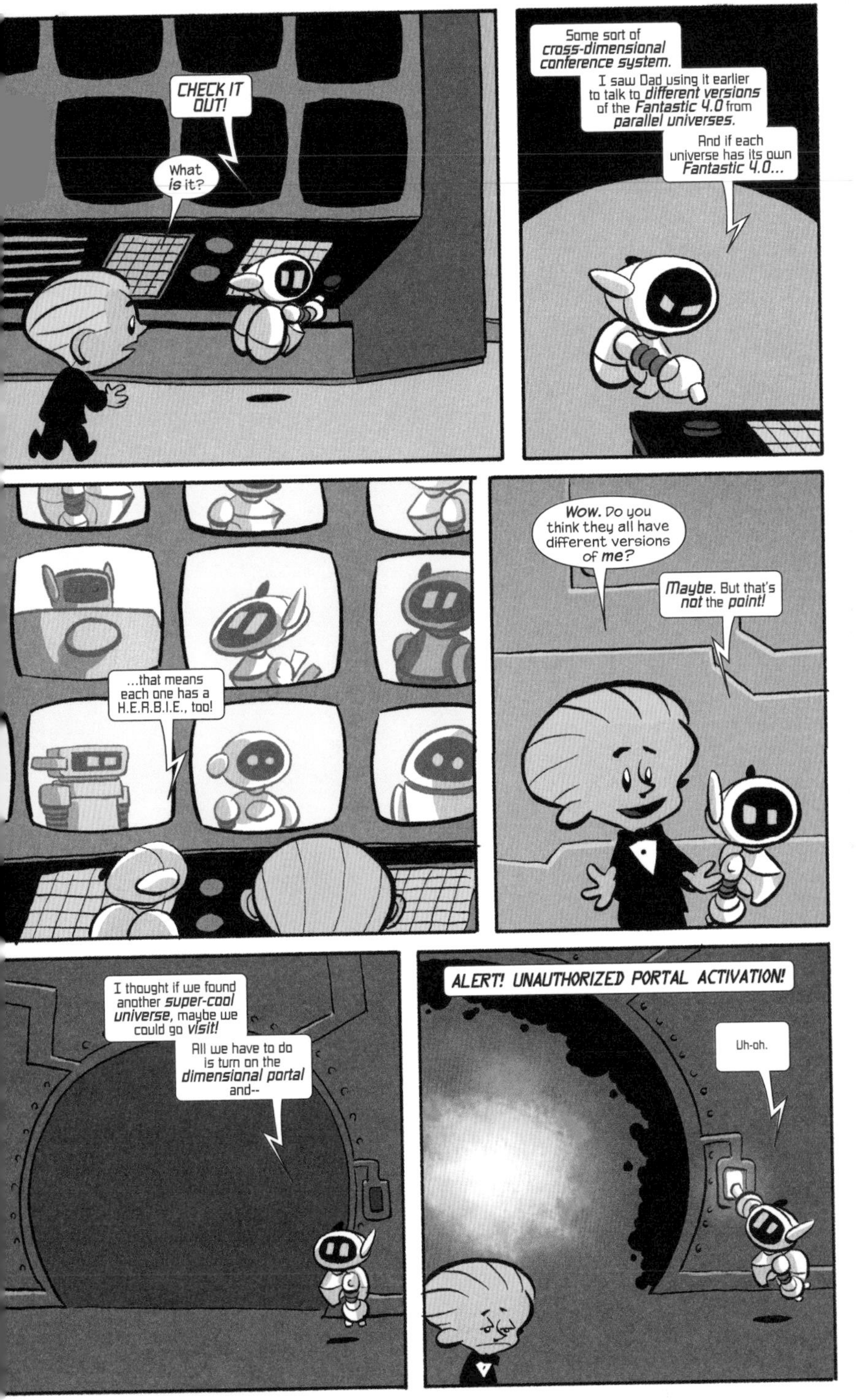
CHECK IT OUT!
What is it?
Some sort of cross-dimensional conference system.
I saw Dad using it earlier to talk to different versions of the Fantastic 4.0 from parallel universes.
And if each universe has its own Fantastic 4.0...
...that means each one has a H.E.R.B.I.E., too!
Wow. Do you think they all have different versions of me?
Maybe. But that's not the point!
I thought if we found another super-cool universe, maybe we could go visit!
All we have to do is turn on the dimensional portal and--
ALERT! UNAUTHORIZED PORTAL ACTIVATION!
Uh-oh.

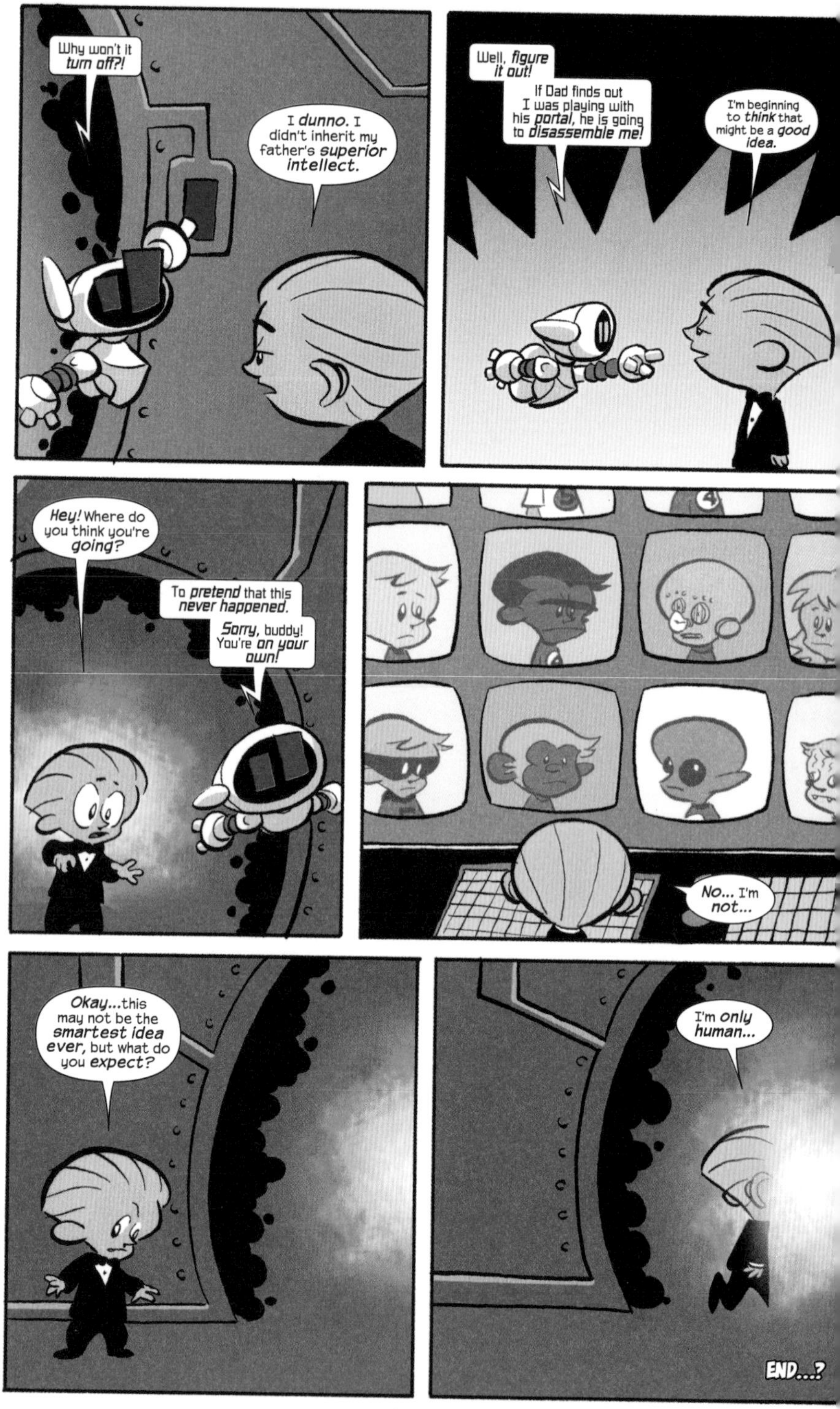

Why won't it turn off?!
I dunno. I didn't inherit my father's superior intellect.
Well, figure it out!
If Dad finds out I was playing with his portal, he is going to disassemble me!
I'm beginning to think that might be a good idea.
Hey! Where do you think you're going?
To pretend that this never happened.
Sorry, buddy! You're on your own!
No... I'm not...
Okay...this may not be the smartest idea ever, but what do you expect?
I'm only human...
END...?

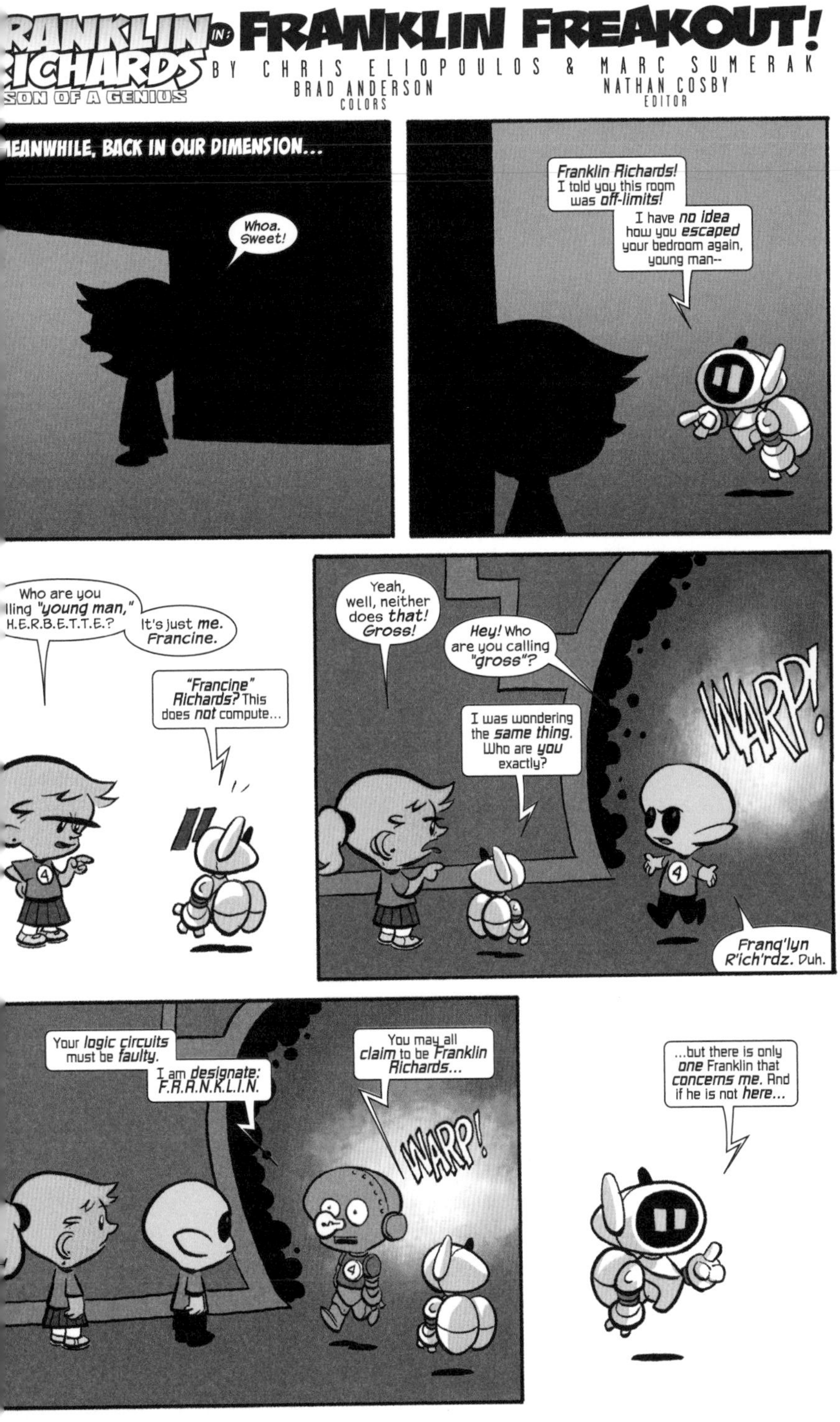
RANKLIN
ICHARDS
SON OF A GENIUS
IN:
FRANKLIN FREAKOUT!
BY CHRIS ELIOPOULOS & MARC SUMERAK
BRAD ANDERSON
COLORS
NATHAN COSBY
EDITOR
EANWHILE, BACK IN OUR DIMENSION...
Whoa. Sweet!
Franklin Richards! I told you this room was off-limits!
I have no idea how you escaped your bedroom again, young man--
Who are you lling "young man," H.E.R.B.E.T.T.E.?
It's just me. Francine.
"Francine" Richards? This does not compute...
Yeah, well, neither does that! Gross!
Hey! Who are you calling "gross"?
I was wondering the same thing. Who are you exactly?
WARP!
Franq'lyn R'ich'rdz. Duh.
Your logic circuits must be faulty.
I am designate: F.R.A.N.K.L.I.N.
You may all claim to be Franklin Richards...
WARP!
...but there is only one Franklin that concerns me. And if he is not here...

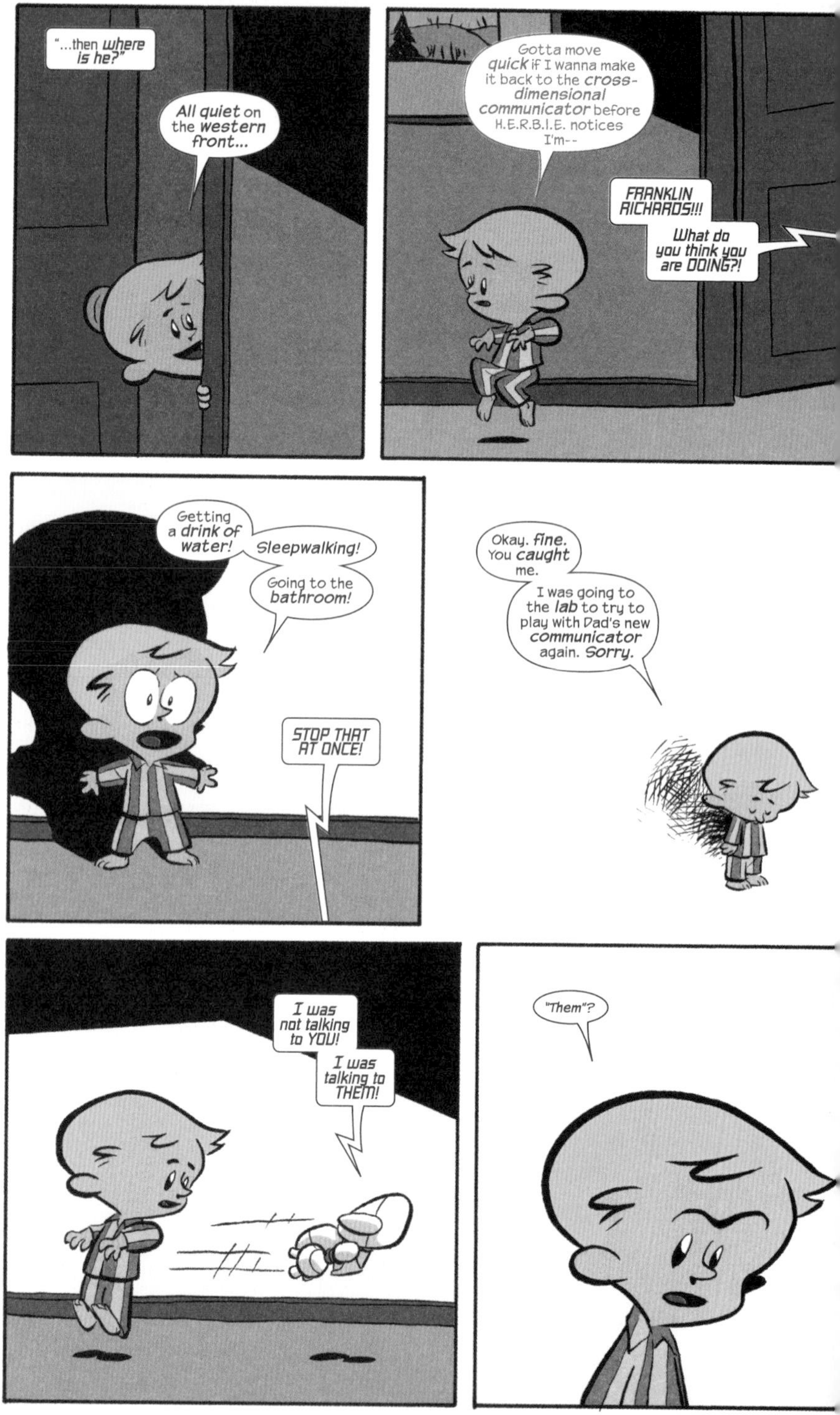
"...then where is he?"
All quiet on the western front...
Gotta move quick if I wanna make it back to the cross-dimensional communicator before H.E.R.B.I.E. notices I'm--
FRANKLIN RICHARDS!!!
What do you think you are DOING?!
Getting a drink of water!
Sleepwalking!
Going to the bathroom!
STOP THAT AT ONCE!
Okay. fine. You caught me.
I was going to the lab to try to play with Dad's new communicator again. Sorry.
I was not talking to YOU!
I was talking to THEM!
"Them"?

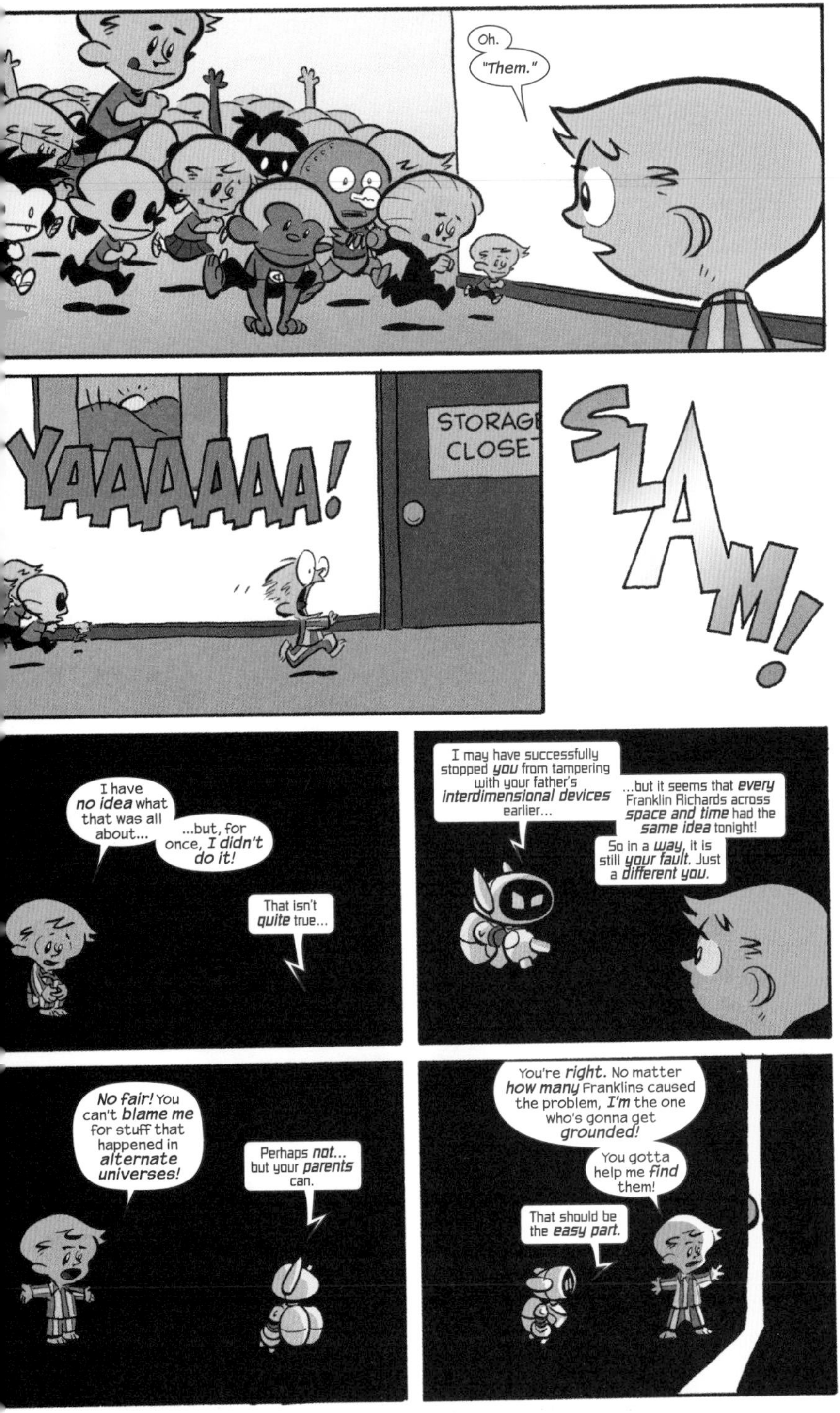

Oh.
"Them."
YAAAAAA!
STORAGE CLOSET
SLAM!
I have no idea what that was all about...
...but, for once, I didn't do it!
That isn't quite true...
I may have successfully stopped you from tampering with your father's interdimensional devices earlier...
...but it seems that every Franklin Richards across space and time had the same idea tonight!
So in a way, it is still your fault. Just a different you.
No fair! You can't blame me for stuff that happened in alternate universes!
Perhaps not... but your parents can.
You're right. No matter how many Franklins caused the problem, I'm the one who's gonna get grounded!
You gotta help me find them!
That should be the easy part.

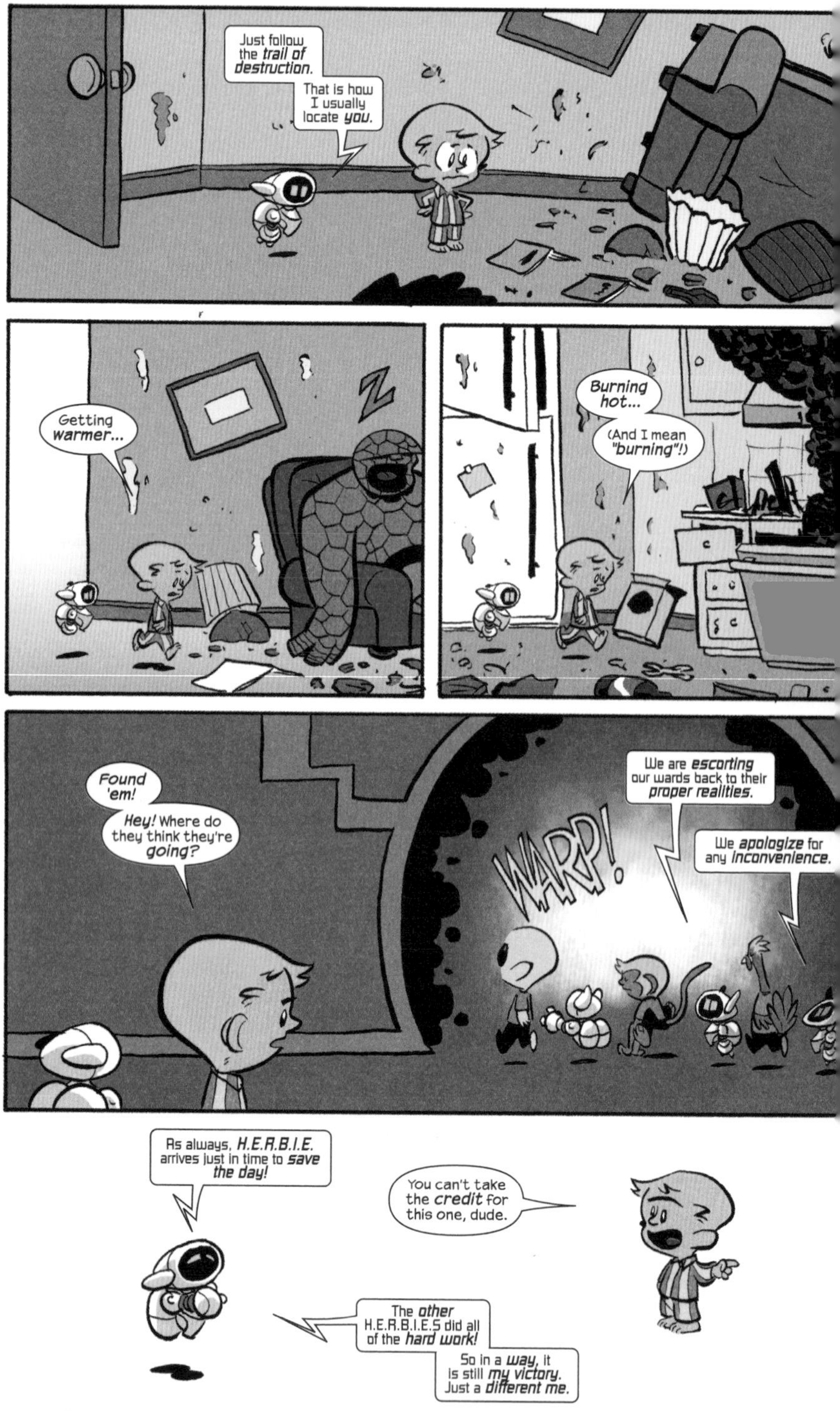

Just follow the trail of destruction.
That is how I usually locate you.
Getting warmer...
Z
Burning hot...
(And I mean "burning"!)
Found 'em!
Hey! Where do they think they're going?
We are escorting our wards back to their proper realities.
We apologize for any inconvenience.
WARP!
As always, H.E.R.B.I.E. arrives just in time to save the day!
You can't take the credit for this one, dude.
The other H.E.R.B.I.E.S did all of the hard work!
So in a way, it is still my victory. Just a different me.

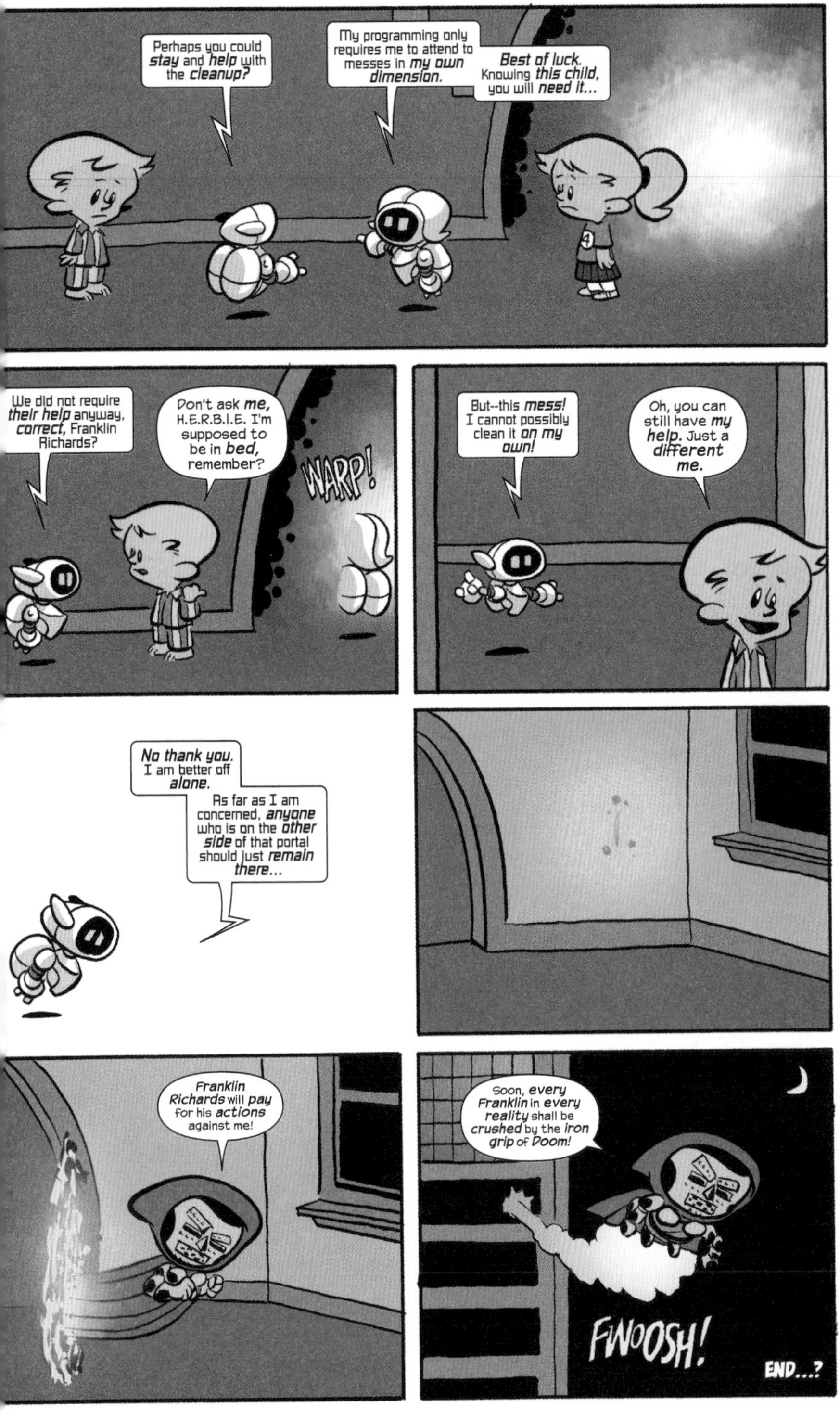
Perhaps you could stay and help with the cleanup?
My programming only requires me to attend to messes in my own dimension.
Best of luck. Knowing this child, you will need it...
We did not require their help anyway, correct, Franklin Richards?
Don't ask me, H.E.R.B.I.E. I'm supposed to be in bed, remember?
WARP!
But--this mess! I cannot possibly clean it on my own!
Oh, you can still have my help. Just a different me.
No thank you. I am better off alone.
As far as I am concerned, anyone who is on the other side of that portal should just remain there...
Franklin Richards will pay for his actions against me!
Soon, every Franklin in every reality shall be crushed by the iron grip of Doom!
FWOOSH!
END...?

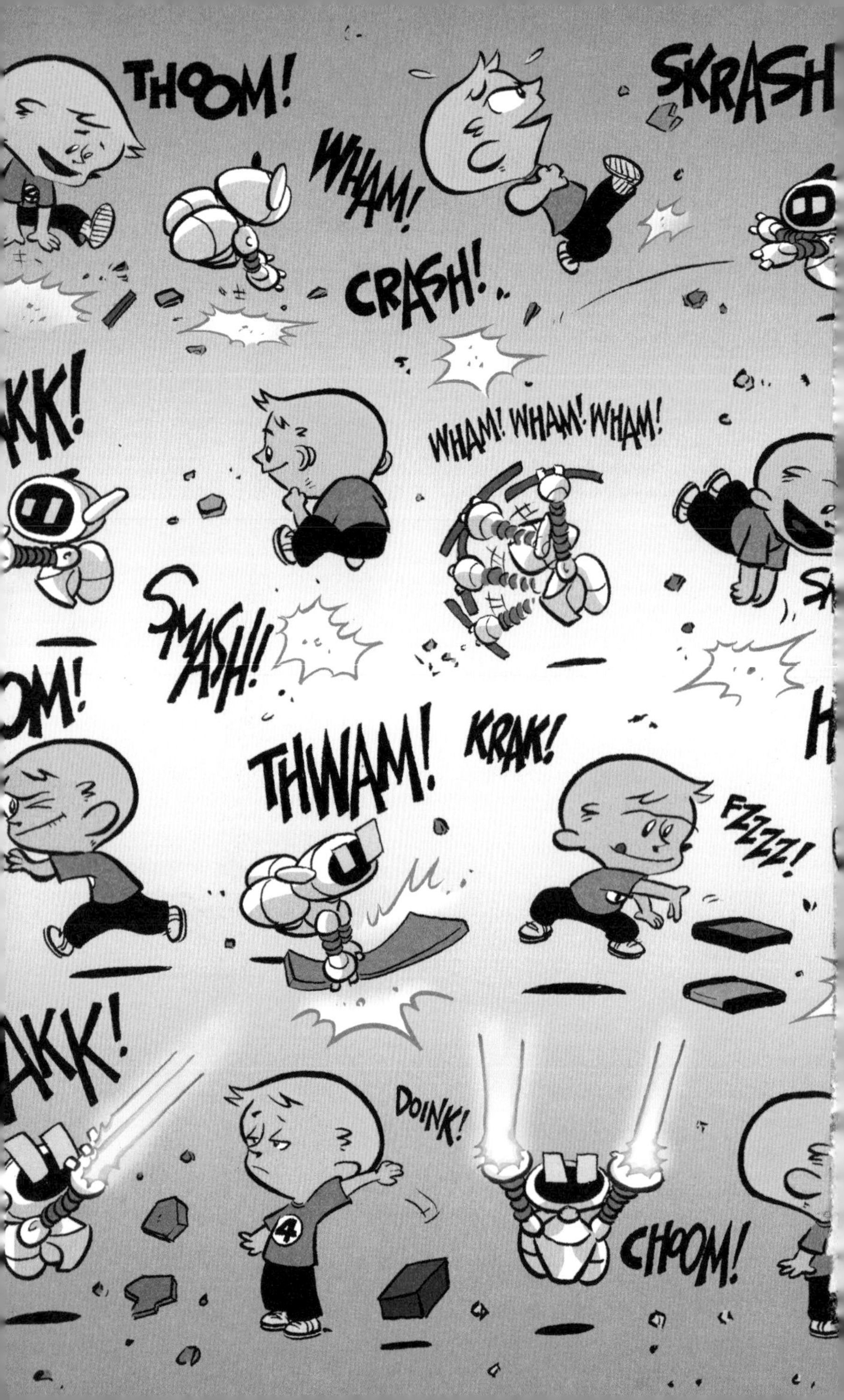
THOOM!
WHAM!
SKRASH
CRASH!
WHAM! WHAM! WHAM!
SMASH!
THWAM!
KRAK!
FZZZZ!
DOINK!
CHOOM!